*In Their Mother's Footsteps*

Born one of fifteen children to a middle-class mother and an East End barrow boy, Mary Wood's childhood was full of love but beset by poverty. Her formative years in a large family shaped her outlook on life, and Mary developed a natural empathy with those less fortunate and a lifelong fascination in social history. In 1989 Mary was inspired to pen her first novel and she is now a full-time novelist. *In Their Mother's Footsteps* is Mary's eighth novel.

Mary welcomes interaction with readers and invites you to subscribe to her website where you can contact her, receive regular newsletters and follow links to meet her on Facebook and Twitter: www.authormarywood.com

BY MARY WOOD

**The Breckton series**

*To Catch a Dream*
*An Unbreakable Bond*
*Tomorrow Brings Sorrow*
*Time Passes Time*

*Proud of You*

*All I Have to Give*
*In Their Mother's Footsteps*

**The Cotton Mill saga**

*Judge Me Not*

# *In Their Mother's Footsteps*

Mary Wood

PAN BOOKS

First published 2016 by Pan Books
an imprint of Pan Macmillan
20 New Wharf Road, London N1 9RR
Associated companies throughout the world
www.panmacmillan.com

ISBN 978-1-5098-8189-5



1 3 5 7 9 8 6 4 2

A CIP catalogue record for this book is available from the British Library.

Typeset by Palimpsest Book Production Ltd, Falkirk, Stirlingshire
Printed and bound by CPI Group (UK) Ltd, Croydon, CR0 4YY

*In loving memory of Maria Sobin*

Maria became my friend after reading my books. We met on Facebook, and our friendship developed and deepened to a mutual love when we met at book launch events that Maria attended.

I miss you very much, Maria, and will miss seeing the pictures you posted of you in the supermarket at midnight buying one of the first copies of each of my books. They were a source of great pride to me.

Rest in peace, dear friend. I hope heaven has a library.

# 1
# *Edith*

## London, June 1939 – The Past Gives No Peace

As Edith followed the dour-faced sergeant, a chill caused her to shiver. Even though it was summertime, a bitter cold permeated the draughty corridor of Bow Street Police Station. The peeling paint of the exposed-brick walls gave an appearance of dilapidation and added to the feeling of dread that assailed her every time she walked through the huge double doors of the station.

Although she worked part-time as a surgeon at Charing Cross Hospital, Edith also provided a free surgery for the poor of the East End of London. It was in this capacity that she was often called upon by the police, to medically assess someone who was being kept in custody.

'She's in cell number one. We can't make head nor tail of what she's saying – and nor will you, if you don't speak French.'

Edith's stomach turned a somersault at the mention of speaking French. Her legs wobbled beneath her. Swallowing hard, she quashed the emotions that had knocked her off-balance for a moment and made herself concentrate on the task ahead.

'We managed to get her name, and that's all. She's called Leah Bachelet. Otherwise she just keeps saying, "*Français, Français.*" I'd say she was trying to pull one over on us. Probably thinks she can get away with whatever she's been up to, if she pretends not to understand.'

'And what has she been up to?'

'By the way she's dressed, she's a prostitute, if ever I saw one. One of my bobbies found her scrounging in the waste-food container behind a cafe.'

Edith couldn't detect any compassion in his voice, but she thought the poor girl must have been starving even to consider delving into a rubbish bin for something to eat. When they reached the cell, the clinking of the sergeant's keys dismayed her.

'You locked her in! Was that really necessary? She must be scared out of her wits.'

He didn't answer her.

As the heavy door swung open, the stuffy atmosphere of the windowless cell and the stench of stale body odour and urine assaulted Edith. These smells always aroused pity in her for the inmate, no matter what he or she was accused of doing, but as she saw the tiny, almost childlike figure of Leah, she was overwhelmed with a feeling of compassion. Leah stared back at Edith from huge, terror-filled brown eyes that were sunk into darkened sockets. Edith was reminded of a frightened deer standing, unable to move, as the hunters on her family estate in Leicestershire levelled their guns at it.

The girl didn't move. She lay in a hunched-up position on a thin mattress that barely covered the brick-built bed. Edith had seen so many girls like her over the years, and all of them had affected her, but there was something heart-rending about this girl.

The sergeant spoke roughly to her, gesturing as he did so. 'Get up.'

Leah obeyed, cowering away from him.

Edith felt an anger rise in her as she saw how the girl's long, thick black hair clung to her head in a damp mass. Water still dripped from the ends of its matted strands. Her ample bosom was streaked with dirt, and was fighting against a wet, too-tight blouse. As Edith was about to protest to the sergeant, she noticed the girl's rounded tummy stretching her straight black skirt to its limits and realized that it was possible the girl could be pregnant. Incensed, Edith could hold back her rage no longer. 'This is barbaric. How could you leave her like this? She could go down with pneumonia.'

The sergeant snapped out his defence. 'She's only been in here for half an hour.'

Not sure if fear or cold was causing Leah's whole body to tremble, Edith ordered the sergeant to bring towels and blankets at once.

As he scurried away, she had to concede that she could see how he had reached his conclusion: Leah was dressed the way a prostitute would dress, even down to a slit in the right-hand side of her skirt, which reached her knee, giving a peek of a shapely leg.

But, to Edith, that was no excuse not to meet a person's basic needs. What if something had delayed her from getting here so quickly? It wasn't always the case that she could immediately answer a call from the many police stations in the area, to give a medical assessment of someone who had been detained in a cell.

Taking a deep breath, Edith put these concerns to the back of her mind as she tried to face what she knew was going to be an ordeal. French wasn't a language that posed any difficulty to her – at least not in her ability to communicate – but emotionally the cost of doing so was high, because painful memories would be evoked. Somehow she kept this inner turmoil from her voice and spoke gently to the girl. 'Please sit down, Leah. I'm a doctor. I'm here to help you – you don't need to be afraid.'

With a whispered '*Merci*', the girl sat down.

'When they bring a towel, we will get you dry and out of those wet things, and then I will examine you. Is that all right by you?'

Leah nodded her head.

'Do you think you might be pregnant?'

Again Leah nodded.

Before Edith could say any more, a female police officer entered the cell. Edith knew her from previous visits; her attitude was one of disdain and left no room for sympathy.

'So, you speak her language then?' The officer's tone was scathing. 'That'll be useful. Perhaps now we can get to the bottom of things. Not that we can't guess what her game is. You only have to look at her.' Throwing a blanket onto the bed, she shoved a towel at Edith. Her action revealed her repulsion at showing any compassion towards Leah.

Leah's fear was palpable as she cowered once more on the far corner of the bed. Edith offered her the towel and tried to soothe her. 'Take your wet clothes off, Leah, and dry yourself. Everything is all right, I promise you. Wrap yourself in this blanket to keep yourself warm.' Turning back to the policewoman, Edith asked, 'Has she had a drink or anything to eat?'

'You're the charity worker, not me.'

'That may be so, but you have human feelings, don't you?'

'I'm not called upon to do anything other than my duty.'

'Neither am I. So I will give you an order, as the doctor in attendance. This young lady is now my patient, and I am in charge of her until I hand her back to you. I am ordering that she is given a drink of hot milk with sugar in it – and a biscuit, if you have one.'

The woman huffed as she made her exit, making a play of getting her keys from her belt and pulling the door shut behind her.

Panic gripped Edith, for the action threatened to remind her of the past, which she'd managed to repress a few minutes earlier. She ran to look through the grille in the door. 'Please don't lock the door. It isn't necessary, and you have no right to lock me in a cell.' The officer's cruel eyes stared back at her. Edith almost started to beg, but kept her dignity, even though the feeling of being unable to escape, if the door was locked, was unbearable. This type of situation had long been in her nightmares.

The officer backed down and walked away. The fixed smile Edith forced onto her face as she turned to Leah helped her to regain control of her emotions. She'd had many years' practice at doing this. Somehow she managed to function normally and keep herself sane, but the smallest thing could prompt renewed agonizing over her long-lost illegitimate twin daughters. It might be tending to a young woman such as Leah, who she guessed was about the same age as Elka and Ania. Or speaking in French. Or a key turning in a lock. All these things had the power to send Edith reeling.

Elka and Ania would be twenty-two now. How she wished she could visualize them, but all she saw when she tried were the sleeping faces of two one-month-old babies – the age they were when she last saw them. But even that image was hazy, merging into a thousand other memories of babies for whom she'd cared over the years at Jimmy's Hope House.

Wherever she went, and whatever she was doing, she asked herself the same questions: What were *they* doing? What did they look like? What – if anything – did they know about her? Was the sun shining on them, or the rain raining on them? Over and over again, her thoughts and her heartache were ceaseless, and had been since that day she'd returned to Petra and Aleksi's farm in France, to pick up her children twenty-two years ago, and had found them gone. The only thing she didn't question was whether they were loved. She knew Petra had loved them.

*But why? Why did Petra take them, when she knew that I would return for them?*

Shaking these thoughts from her head, Edith returned her attention to Leah, who now sat looking lost in the huge blanket that swathed her. 'Leah, I have to go and telephone a friend of mine. She will send some clothes for you. I won't be long. If they bring you some milk while I've gone, sip it very slowly. And if there is a biscuit, dip it into the milk to soften it, then suck it before you swallow it. Your stomach can't take a lot all at once.' At a nod from Leah, Edith left her.

To the right of the cell, and past the other two cells adjacent to Leah's, stood a desk manned by the female police officer. She must be acting as custody officer today – a job she obviously relished, by the look of importance that emanated from her as Edith approached and asked for permission to use the telephone.

'She's not one of your fallen women. She'll be given a prisoner's garb soon enough. Your job is to get her well enough for questioning.'

'You don't yet know that she has done anything criminal. And even if she has, she deserves to be treated humanely. I will check her over, and I may need to take her to hospital or to Jimmy's Hope House, but first we need to give her some dignity. Once all that is done, I will help you to question her.'

The woman nodded towards the telephone on the wall. Taking the receiver off its cradle, Edith had to smile as she cranked the handle. The police station was a little behind the times with its telephone system.

While she waited for Ada to answer, a picture of her came to mind. Despite her fifty-four years, Ada's freckled skin looked almost as fresh as it had done when Edith first met her. Her figure had rounded, but was just as shapely as ever. She saw Ada as a bundle of love – lovely to look at, and with a generosity of spirit. A woman who took life's knocks in her stride.

*Unlike me.* Edith sighed. Her hand went to smooth down the occasional unruly grey hair that seemed to dance away from the rest of her dark mop and refused to stay in her bun. Although, she had to admit, she had kept her figure, too. She patted her flat stomach. *Not bad for a girl who has had her fiftieth birthday!* But it was in the way she coped with the past that she differed from Ada. She tended to dwell on things too much.

At last she heard Ada's voice answer the operator. 'Yes, put her through . . . Edith, is that you, love?'

'It is, Ada. We have a sad case on our hands.' She told Ada how she'd found Leah in such a poor state, and listed the clothing the girl would need. 'And on top of everything else, she is French and cannot speak much English.'

'Poor mite. I'll get onto it right away.'

'Thanks, Ada. Is Joe there?'

'Aye. I'm on the verge of divorcing him. He's as grumpy as owt. He'd planned on getting on with sommat he wanted to do in the grounds today, but the weather's beaten him. He's reet under me feet. I'll send him in the van with this lot. He'll be with you within the hour.'

'Thank you, Ada.' Trying not to laugh, Edith wanted to ask her to prepare a bed for Leah in the room with the other young, unmarried pregnant women they housed in their maternity wing, but was afraid of further annoying the eavesdropping policewoman. As it was, she was embarrassed to have to answer Ada's next question. 'Are you alreet, lass? You don't sound yourself.'

'I'm fine, Ada. It's just – well, you know.'

'Aye, I knaw. It's understandable. Didn't you say this one was French? Well, that'll have done it. Eeh, lass, I pray every day as sommat like a miracle will happen for you, and you will be reunited with your twins. But I know you'll get on with things as usual, just like you always do. By, it sounds as though this lass needs you to, an' all.'

'What would I do without you, Ada? We'll have a chat when I come back.'

As she replaced the receiver, Edith's smile widened. She thanked God for the friendship and comfort that Ada had brought into her life. It didn't matter how down she felt – Ada could always lift her spirits. Even if she didn't say anything funny, her northern tone and matter-of-fact way made Edith feel everything was all right in the world.

Needing a moment to herself, she peeped through the barred window of the cell that held Leah. Someone must have brought the hot milk she'd ordered, because a cup stood on the floor and Leah lay with her eyes closed.

Leaning against the wall outside the cell and out of sight of the female officer, Edith composed herself. Ada had been right. Speaking French – something she hadn't done often, since her world had been rocked all those years ago – had plunged her back into the painful past. Flashes of that past assailed her now. She made them go away by concentrating on the positive outcomes. Meeting her husband, Laurent, for one. Laurent had been an officer with the French Army. They had met during what Edith termed her 'wilderness period', the time when Albert – a cockney corporal with the British Army, to whom she'd felt a deep attraction – had gone off the rails and kidnapped her. *No, I won't think of that time, or of the ultimate outcome. I can't cope with it. Not now.* Instead, she thought of how she had come back from the war determined to find Ada.

Devastated when a young boy called Jimmy had been shot at dawn for cowardice, Edith had wanted to find his mother. Jimmy had told her about his mam whilst she tended his injury before the awful verdict was passed, and begged her to find her and tell her that he was innocent. He'd told her his mother's name was Ada O'Flynn. Edith had heard how Jimmy's brothers had been killed at the beginning of the war, and she'd felt a sense of duty to carry out Jimmy's last wish. Coincidence then brought Ada into her life. It turned out that Ada was one of the young women being helped by Edith's cousin, Lady Eloise, who ran a charity that assisted all those stricken by the events of war.

Edith and Ada had bonded immediately and had become unlikely friends. Even though they came from different classes, and different parts of the country, their friendship had grown as they helped each other come to terms with the horrors of war.

They became custodians of each other's secrets, and took comfort in sharing their heartache. Eventually they set up Jimmy's Hope House, to help women wronged as they themselves had been wronged, and later added the facility of Edith's free surgery. Funded by donations from Edith's friends who had been born rich, and from self-made businessmen who were her acquaintances, as well as from her own fortune and that of her family, the charity honoured Jimmy's bravery. But Edith knew that none of it could have been done – nor could she have got this far – without Ada by her side. Every day for the last twenty-odd years Edith had thanked God for Ada.

On examining Leah, Edith found that she was approximately five months pregnant, besides being malnourished and badly bruised.

Once Leah was comfortable, Edith told her about the suspicions the police had about her. Leah shook her head. '*Non, non*. It is not the truth.'

'Leah, you will have to talk to the police. I will help you. As soon as we have the clothes my friend is sending for you, we will tell the police that you will talk to them through me. Is that all right with you?'

Looking afraid once again, Leah agreed, but begged Edith

not to leave her, in pitying tones that wrenched Edith's heart.

They now sat in another soulless room: Leah and Edith on one side of a huge wooden table, and the sergeant and female police officer on the other side. Leah's voice shook as she related her story.

It appeared that she had graduated from university in Paris, where she had studied maths and history with the intention of becoming a teacher. But before she could start her teacher training, she and her parents and her younger brother, who was at home on holiday from his first year at university, had left France in the family's motor boat. Leah was very vague about the passing of time and couldn't remember exactly when this was. She only knew that it had happened not long after Christmas.

They were fleeing from northern France. Leah's father, a scientist with the French Navy, wanted to move his family to England. He had feared for a long time that Hitler would turn his attention to invading France, and the family lived on the border with Belgium, a most likely point of German entry into their country.

Her father's eventual destination for the family was America, but he hadn't been able to secure his release from his job and, therefore, the necessary papers to travel. He'd planned to sail to Britain overnight and use his wealth to pay their way, in whatever manner he could, including using false papers.

The boat had capsized and Leah believed that her family had perished. She had been picked up by another boat and brought to shore somewhere near the cliffs of Dover, where her rescuer had alerted the coastguard and then taken Leah to stay in his home. His wife had taken care of her while he brought their doctor to examine her. The doctor had left medication to help Leah sleep, but she hadn't taken it. When her rescuers thought she was asleep, she'd heard the man who had saved her speaking on the telephone. From the little English she knew, she deduced that he was calling the police. When the call ended, Leah was able to understand that the police would come to the house the next day.

Logic told Leah that this was bound to happen. She was a foreign national who had been involved in an accident that must be investigated. The police would want to know who she was, and why she and her family had been in British waters. Suspicion would be aroused as to whether they were trying to sneak into England and, if so, why. They would question whether she could legally remain. And if her family were found, they would need to know where they could contact her. Panic had set in when Leah realized the police would probably send her back to France.

The only relative she had there was her spinster aunt, who hadn't spoken to the family in years. Confused and choked by a painful grief, she'd waited until the couple were asleep. Then she'd stolen some money from the wife's handbag, which was hanging in the kitchen, leaving a note saying that she was sorry and would one day pay them back. She'd made her way to London, where she thought she would get a job – any menial job where the language wasn't a barrier; perhaps as a live-in chambermaid at one of the hotels.

Leah didn't go into details about her journey, but Edith suspected she must have slept out in the open, as it would have taken her several days. She marvelled that the girl had survived at all.

'I eventually got a train, but I had nothing left when I arrived in London. No money, no food. I was unwashed and I looked bedraggled. I sat on the steps of the station, trying to decide what to do. A man approached me. I couldn't understand him, but he made gestures as if he would feed me. I went with him. He took me to a house where I found myself to be one of many girls. There was another French girl there, and she could speak English. All the others were from foreign countries and had come to London by various means – some by arrangement with their families; or German girls whose families thought they were being taken to Ireland, to keep them safe. One girl told me that we had to let men do things to us or we would be beaten.' Leah's large, dark eyes filled with tears, which spilled over and made silvery lines down her cheeks.

'Oh, my dear. How long have you been in that place?' Edith knew she shouldn't have interrupted and was meant to leave the questioning to the police officers, but she hadn't been able to help herself.

'I don't know – months. I have been beaten many times. All of the women in there know about Jimmy's Hope House, where you say you are from. Some have been to you for medical help, and said that you and another lady who assists you were kind. The girls have a way of helping each other to get out; they told me to go to you, but said I shouldn't tell you anything, and that I should go back to them as soon as I can. If the man who runs the brothel finds that I am missing, he will take reprisals on one of them – maybe even kill one of them – and then he will find me. But I got lost . . . I've been gone for days. Those girls need help. Please help them.'

Edith was appalled. 'You are safe now. You are a very

brave girl. I will speak to the police sergeant. Hopefully he will let you come with me to Jimmy's Hope House, where we will take care of you.'

Leah nodded. Another tear plopped onto her cheek.

Edith wanted to take the girl in her arms and hold her tight. But she knew that was dangerous territory for her, and would result in undoing her resolve not to allow her past to weave its way into the present. Her priority now was Leah's welfare, and to get the police to take action to save the other poor girls, and bring to justice the evil man that she talked about.

Waiting for a decision from the sergeant, Edith willed herself to take Leah away from this wretched place. 'I will take on the responsibility for her, and make sure she is available to you whenever you need to question her, Sergeant. Can't you please release her into my care? I will sign anything you want me to.'

'Well, as I haven't any evidence of any crime to charge her with, I think that is the best option. But I'll pass on to CID the information she has given me, and they will want to speak to her – and with some urgency, if what she is saying is true. They'll contact the couple who rescued her, through the local police, who should have a record of the girl being found. If the couple want to press charges concerning the theft from them, we'll have to deal with that and she will have to go to court. In the meantime we need her to sign her statement. Then you can take her.'

Edith smiled as she released a deep sigh. The sergeant was human, after all.

She felt proud of the way she had held herself together and suppressed her own anguish. But then hadn't she been doing so for the last twenty-two years? Well, she would carry on doing so. Continuing to help young women like Leah would sustain her, as it always had done. As did having her beloved Laurent, and dear Ada, by her side. She was blessed in many ways.

But despite these positive thoughts, the desolate feeling deep within her wouldn't go away, and she knew she would never feel truly fulfilled until she was reunited with her children. Would that ever happen?

# 2

# *Elka*

### Krakow, Poland, July 1939 – Petra Reveals All

Though the sun was shining, Elka felt chilled to the bone as the men in black lowered her mother's coffin into the stony cavity and laid it on top of her father's.

Made of lead, her father's coffin was well preserved. Looking at it made Elka feel sad that she had no memories of her father, only recollections that others had given her. She and Ania, her twin sister, had been just fifteen months old when he had died in August 1918, a victim – like her maternal grandfather – of the flu pandemic that had broken out towards the end of the Great War.

The sound of a sob drew her attention away from these thoughts. Dear Ania would need her more than ever now. A mirror-image of herself, with her tall elegance and red-gold curly hair, Ania looked imploringly at Elka from beautiful hazel eyes that asked her to take her pain away.

Unable to speak, Elka enclosed Ania in her arms, but as she did so, she sensed movement on her other side and turned her head to look over her shoulder. Babcia Petra's usually strong countenance had crumbled. Elka let go of

Ania and caught hold of their grandmother's sobbing body just in time to save her from falling.

Babcia Petra's distress took Ania's attention away from her own unhappiness. She moved quickly to help Elka and, speaking softly, managed to soothe their grandmother. 'We are still here for you, darling Babcia Petra.' This helped their grandmother regain her composure and she stood bravely upright. Looking at her, and seeing her frailty, reinforced Elka's decision not to leave Poland.

Babcia feared that, as Jews, they faced untold horror if the Nazis invaded Poland. She had been urging Elka and Ania to leave the country, even though she would make no plans to leave herself. Her only reason was that she had left during the last war and had spent many years in a kind of exile in France. Once she'd returned home, she had vowed she would never leave again.

The tales of what was happening to Jews in Germany, and now in Austria, since Hitler's army had been getting stronger, frightened her. It was these tales that were prompting Babcia, and all of their community, to fear the future. They'd heard that Jews were not allowed to front their businesses and had to register their wealth and property. All Jews over fifteen had to carry an identity card, which must be shown to police on demand. Synagogues were being destroyed, and Jewish doctors were being prohibited from practising. Babcia Petra was right to be afraid. Elka and Ania were afraid, too. But how could they leave Babcia now? Or Dziadek Gos and Babcia Miriam, their father's parents, even though they had never acted as grandparents should towards them? They had treated Elka and Ania differently from their cousins, Jhona and Isaac, the sons of their father's younger brother. Their grandparents had played with the cousins and lavished gifts on them and, upon each of them reaching twenty-five, had made them directors in the family jewellery business.

Not that any of this affected her own and Ania's relationship with Jhona and Isaac. They all adored one another.

Lifting her eyes at this thought, Elka caught Jhona's glance. Neither of them looked away, both compelled to convey to each other something deeply felt within them, something forbidden – the kind of love that you shouldn't feel for a cousin. A love they didn't acknowledge, but that bound them together.

The first shovelful of earth hit the coffin, and the pain of realization struck Elka. After feeling nothing other than relief since her mother had sighed her last painful breath at noon yesterday, she now wanted to scream, as each mourner pitched more and more soil onto her coffin.

Tears she'd thought she would never shed tumbled from her eyes and ran down her cheeks in streams. The salty taste of them dried her mouth. The deluge weakened her body, so that when her turn came, she found it difficult to dig into the mound of earth and throw some onto her mother's coffin. But as this was a Jewish custom, she had to do so, to help her mother on her way. The thud made her feel as if her heart had shredded into little pieces and would never heal.

An arm came round her. 'Elka, my darling.' Dropping the shovel, she gave in to her need to be held by Jhona and sank into his body. Nothing would look amiss; this was one cousin comforting another, that was all. But they both knew it wasn't all, and that this moment of weakness had undone their unspoken resolve to deny their true feelings. A mixture of grief and happiness quivered through her. This was where she belonged.

'Come along, you two – we have to go.' Isaac's urgent plea alerted Elka to how long and how intensely she and Jhona had been holding each other. Coming out of his arms, she saw that Isaac and Ania were supporting Babcia Petra. Her sister gave her a look of pity and love. Had she guessed the truth?

Though they were identical twins, she and Ania were very different souls. Ania cared about everything, but in a quiet way: the welfare of the poor, and of animals; and for her work, teaching children in their Jewish Community School behind the synagogue.

Like Elka, Ania had gained certificates in languages, something that came naturally to them both. All of their lives Babcia and their mother had made them speak in French, Polish and Yiddish, and they had developed a love of the English language since their first lesson at school – an essential language to have, if they ever wanted to travel abroad. She and Ania had found English to be magical and intensely personal, as if it belonged to them, and often conversed in it. For some reason, although she spoke the language very well herself, Babcia would become upset with them if she heard them using it.

Ania had always wanted to work with children, but Elka was looking towards a career in medicine. She had no idea why, as her family on both sides were merchants and jewellers, and there was no one at all connected to the medical field. And yet the desire to become a doctor was very strong and she was waiting anxiously for the post each day, hoping it would contain a letter saying that her application to medical school had been successful.

In her heart, though, she doubted the letter would come, given the current situation in Poland.

Much had changed for her people, since the death of Poland's ruler, Józef Pilsudski, in 1935. His policies had been inclusive of all Polish people, regardless of their religious beliefs, but anti-Semitism had gathered pace soon after he died, with the growing influence of the Endecja party.

Elka's worry had increased on hearing about academic harassment, such as the introduction of ghetto benches last year, which forced Jewish students to sit in sections of lecture halls reserved exclusively for them; and the semi-official quotas of Jewish students who were allowed to take placements. Now the number of Jews in Polish universities was half what it had been a couple of years ago.

At the same time as the quotas were brought in last year, Catholic trade unions for Polish doctors and lawyers had restricted their membership to Christian Poles only. And then there were the anti-Semitism riots at universities, which terrified her because they were growing in size.

Settling back into the soft leather seats of the horse-driven carriage, Elka put these thoughts out of her mind. Ania sat on one side of her, with her head resting on her shoulder, and Babcia Petra sat on the other. Taking Babcia's hand in hers, Elka stroked it gently. The paper-thin skin revealed thick blue veins. Babcia's vulnerability was evident today, more than ever. Elka felt a new strength enter her as she decided to do all she could to protect Babcia and Ania. But how was she to do that, with Poland under threat of invasion and so many of her fellow countrymen turning against her people? Somehow she must find a way.

*

From the moment they had returned to their sumptuous top-floor home in their apartment block on Podgorska, opposite the beautiful River Vistula, a strange stillness had descended on them. It was as if any noise might shatter the lingering spirit of their mother. After a quiet dinner they had retired early.

Despite having slept soundly, Elka felt tired and heavy-eyed. The dark rings around Ania's eyes showed that she, too, was exhausted. Babcia Petra looked frail and drawn and yet, after they had breakfasted, she took a deep breath and stood up. Her demeanour was one of determination.

'Are you all right, Babcia dear?'

Babcia looked over at Elka and then at Ania. 'No, I am troubled. Come, let's withdraw to the sitting room. I have something to tell you.'

As Babcia Petra sat down in her usual high-backed, ruby-red velvet armchair, the strength seemed to leave her and she looked drained. Elka wondered if she was worried about her future. Their mother had left Elka and Ania all of her considerable fortune, as well as this apartment block, which she had bought after their father died. The other apartments were rented out to a discerning Jewish clientele, bringing in enough revenue to maintain the building and add to their income. Knowing that Ania would feel the same way, Elka had no qualms about reassuring Babcia Petra. 'You have no need to worry, Babcia Petra – we will take care of you forever.'

'I am afraid you may not feel the same, after you hear what I have to say. You see, I – I'm not thinking of my future, but yours. The time has come when I must tell you the truth about your birth . . . I – I hope you can forgive me.'

Elka opened her mouth to speak, but Ania's reaction forestalled her. Ania had shot out of her seat and stood glaring down at their grandmother. Her body shook. 'What do you mean by "your birth" and "the truth"? What is there to know?' Elka looked from their grandmother to Ania, feeling unsure and afraid. Was Babcia Petra about to confirm something that had niggled at her for a long time? Had Ania ever had the same thoughts, and wondered at times why they both looked so unlike any of their family? And at the cold indifference to which they had been subjected by their father's family? Or how, often, when speaking of their father, their mother had referred to 'my dear late husband' instead of '*your father*'? Had Ania wondered, too, if their mother had had an affair that resulted in their birth, or if they were even adopted?

But none of these thoughts prepared her for what their sobbing grandmother told them.

'My God! Babcia Petra, how could you have done such a thing – it is wicked. You stole us? You are not our *babcia*? Mama was not . . . I can't believe it!'

'I'm sorry, Elka. Please believe me when I say that I – I did it for the best. Your mother was a high-born English lady, your father a corporal in the British Army. He killed himself after he . . . well, he forced himself upon her. But he was not well in his mind. Your mother could not acknowledge you as her children, for she would have been outcast by her society, maybe banished to a convent. You would both have been taken from her and put into some orphanage, and then, if adopted, you might have been split up and never known that the other existed. Your mother's plan to have you taken care of, and for her to visit you, may have failed, but I loved you. I did not want anything bad to happen to you.'

'Is our mother still alive? Did she love our father?'

'I don't know if she is alive, Ania dear. But yes, she did love your father. It was an alliance that would not have been possible in her own society, because he was from a much lower class. But this was wartime, and they had been thrown together. Though their union was forced onto your mother, I think that in a strange way she wanted it, too. She couldn't help falling in love with him. And she loved you both very much. It broke her heart to leave you. That hurt me, and made it very hard to do what I did. But my daughter had no children of her own and couldn't have any, and I knew that you would have a good and loving future with her – and with me – and that might not have happened with your real mother.'

'Why are you telling us now?' Ania asked this in a cold, disrespectful manner that held hatred and anger.

'I – I want you to know that you are not born Jews. And to give you a reason to leave Poland. It is dangerous living in this country right now, for the Jewish community in particular. What we are experiencing at the moment is nothing compared to what I fear is to come. I thought that, if you knew the truth, you would leave.'

'But where to? How would we begin to find our *real* family?'

'I – I have an address, Elka, my dear. It is that of a woman in France whom your mother loved very much: an aunt of Edith's cousin, called Marianne.'

'Edith? Our mother's name is Edith? And all of this happened in France?'

'Yes, Ania. Your mother was a doctor. She was working

in the Somme area in the midst of the fighting, and your father forced her to leave with him. There were strong feelings between them. He was deserting – he'd done something very bad, though I don't know what. He kidnapped Edith, but he was mentally disturbed as a result of everything he had been through in the trenches, and ended up shooting himself. Your grandfather found Edith in a deserted farm about a mile from the farmstead we were running at the time. The poor girl was desperately ill. He brought her back to me and we took care of her, day and night, and nursed her through pneumonia. When eventually she was strong enough to re-join her unit and get in touch with her family, she discovered she was pregnant. She dared not contact anyone else, for fear of the repercussions – not just of her family abandoning her, but of being prevented from practising medicine ever again.'

'Poor Edith.'

'Ania, Edith is our mother – not some woman to whom this tragic tale happened. *Our mother.* And a very brave woman, whose heart must have broken to lose us.'

'Yes, I know. I just find it difficult to think of her like that. But, Elka, you are just like her. That is the reason you have an inclination to be a doctor! So what about me – how do I take after her?'

'You both look very like her, except that she had dark hair and was smallish, but your eyes and your features are hers. Your hair and your height, I think, must have been your father's, but I don't know for sure. My dear Aleksi would not talk about what your father's body looked like. You, Ania, have many of Edith's caring ways and even some of her mannerisms, which is strange, as you have never known her. And you, Elka, have her strength of character, as well as wanting to heal the sick, as she did.' Babcia sat up straight once more and faced them both. 'Now that you know your true roots, I hope you're convinced that you both have to leave Poland.'

Elka felt a disgust that was akin to loathing and couldn't keep the emotion from her voice. 'How did you get the address of this woman in France? Did our mother give it to you? Were you meant to contact her through this woman?'

'Yes, but I never did. I – I wanted to save you, I—'

'Save us! You stole us from the mother who loved us!'

'And now you have done so again: you have stolen from us the woman we thought was our mama. All the years of our loving her and thinking of her as our mama, we were living a lie! Oh, I can't bear it. I want Mama back.'

Hearing the anguish in Ania's voice compelled Elka to go to her side. Holding her sister, she said gently, 'Don't – don't torture yourself. Oh, Ania, don't cry . . .'

'But I don't know who is lying in Mama's grave now. I don't know what to call her. I – I thought she was our mama, but she wasn't. What about our cousins who are not our cousins? And Babcia? She is not our grandmother. And Dziadek Gos and Babcia Miriam aren't our grandparents, either . . . Oh, Elka, how are we to bear it?'

'I don't know, but we will, darling. Together, we will.' Elka turned to look at Petra. 'Do Dziadek Gos and Babcia Miriam know about us?'

'They do, Elka, but – like your mama – they thought Edith had died giving birth to you. They were happy for their son and welcomed you. But after your papa – their son – died, they lost interest. But I have loved you from birth and have looked upon you as my grandchildren ever since. And I love you as a *babcia* should, and I always will. I'm sorry.'

As Petra's body crumbled, Ania left Elka's arms and ran to her. Drawing Petra to her, she hugged her, but Elka could only sink back onto the sofa behind her sister and stare at them both. A coldness had entered her heart. This woman, whom she had loved and trusted, had betrayed them. She wasn't the loving grandmother she had portrayed herself to be. Elka didn't believe Petra had thought she was protecting them. Their real mother had loved them, she was sure of it, and she was rich; she would have been able to find a way of keeping them and taking care of them, without this 'society' that Babcia talked of ever knowing.

Confusion consumed Elka, but now she knew that Petra wasn't their grandmother, she would not give her the title of Babcia any longer. She had made them live a lie; had lied to their mama, who wasn't their mama any longer. If Petra loved them, how could she have done this to them all? *Dearest Mama, you were deceived, too. You thought our mother and father were both dead and that we would be rejected by our real family. Oh, Mama, Mama, how I wish you were here now . . .*

Once more, tears poured from her. Clinging onto the back of the sofa, Elka allowed the racking sobs to take hold of her – somehow they helped to release her pent-up confusion and anger that had risen in her and made her want to slap this woman, who had caused such pain.

'Come, Elka, come here. Please forgive me.'

Petra was back in her chair, one hand holding Ania's, the other stretched out towards Elka. Her expression betrayed her heartache. But Elka could not go to her, or forgive her. Taking her eyes from Petra – the woman she now hated – Elka looked up at Ania. It seemed as if her darling sister had shrunk, as her trembling body bent in a way that made it look too heavy for her to hold straight. Her mouth was slack and her eyes looked empty of all life. Ignoring Petra, Elka cried, 'Ania, Ania, it's going to be all right.'

With the new-found strength that the situation gave her, Elka managed to get to Ania before she fainted. She helped her sister to the sofa. Taking no notice of Petra's pleas, she rang the bell cord next to the fireplace to summon their maid to call for the doctor.

When the doctor had left, and with Ania now sleeping the slumber of the drugged, Elka sat by her bed and thought everything through. Logic would not confirm the scenario that Petra wanted them to believe. The only redeeming part of Petra's abhorrent act was her real motive – her deep sorrow at the knowledge that her daughter hadn't been able to have children. Petra hadn't been able to bear this, for their mama . . . Mama? Yes, Elka wouldn't question the status of the woman they had just buried. She had truly been – and would always be – their mama. She had done nothing wrong. Neither had Edith, their real mother. All the blame lay with Petra.

A feeling of shock pulsed through Elka as the hatred that had consumed her earlier intensified. She would never forgive Petra – never!

She and Ania would leave for France. They would find this Marianne and, through her, find their mother. *But what about Jhona?* The implications of this thought suddenly registered with her. Those she had thought of as family were no longer so. *Jhona and I aren't cousins! Our love isn't forbidden. Oh, Jhona, my love.*

A small part of her felt joy at this revelation, though she wondered if their path towards being together might still be strewn with difficulties. Dziadek Gos had refused to attend their house yesterday after the funeral. Now, as she remembered his words, with the new knowledge that she had of her status, it seemed that he meant to cut all ties with them: 'I see no reason for us to return to your home with you, Petra. Your daughter – our daughter-in-law – is now laid to rest. I think that should be an end to it.'

Suddenly, clarity concerning the real reason Petra had told them the truth came to Elka. Petra had known that the time had come when she *had* to tell the truth, or Gos would do so. Or at least the truth as he knew it: that she and Ania were not part of his family.

How little he knew. Now that her own and Jhona's love for each other was no longer illegal, Gos would never be rid of her! Nor she of him. But this last thought did not deter her. Checking that Ania was peaceful, she decided to go and find Jhona as soon as she could.

This decision made her clutch at her heart. Something good would come from all of this. No, not just good – something wonderful. Her life to date had been turned into a sham, on hearing the truth of her birth, but now she realized that she'd been given a gift so great that even her fears for the future faded, in light of the wonder at being able to declare her true love. And she knew that love was returned. Jhona's love for her showed in his every look, and yesterday in the way he had held her. Every cloud has a silver lining, they say. Hers had a lining of future happiness. But even as she thought this, she wondered how true it was. There was still the turmoil caused by the invasion of Poland's neighbouring countries, and the terrible threat hanging over her people and her beloved country.

Pulling herself up straight, Elka decided that – no matter what – she, Ania, Jhona and Isaac would escape. They *had* to.

# 3

# *Ada*

## London, July 1939 – Full Circle

Ada swallowed hard as she looked over at Brendan. He'd emerged from the door leading to the stairs, with his head bent forward to lower his height, looking immaculate in his army uniform.

'Eeh, lad, it's like me life's come full circle. I can't believe we're facing war all over again. I couldn't bear it, if owt happened to you.' 'I'll be fine. It won't be like last time, Aunty Ada. Don't worry. All this talk of, and preparations for, another war must be opening the wounds of your loss again, but this time soldiers will be much safer. They will have proper training and equipment, and there won't be trench warfare on the scale there was back then. Anyway, there's nothing certain about there even being a war. So stop worrying, eh?'

'I knaw, but I feel it in me bones that there will be. That Hitler fellow is causing so much unrest, it can only end in war.'

'Ha, those bones of yours are blamed for a lot these days: you not being so quick on your feet; the aches and pains you suffer; and now they'll be blamed if war breaks out.'

She laughed with him, loving his sense of humour, as always. She knew Brendan got that from Paddy, along with his handsome good looks, dark curly hair and deep-blue, twinkly eyes. But those were all he'd inherited from his da, for in nature Paddy could be likened to a hair shirt, whilst Brendan was more of a silk one: kind and caring, intelligent and hard-working – everything his da hadn't been.

After all these years, the affair of her late first husband, Paddy, and her sister Beryl still hurt, in a small place of her heart. Brushing the thought away, she asked, 'But why you, lad? I know they're only making preparations, but you work in the War Office – you should be exempt.'

'Very few are exempt, Aunt Ada. We'll all have a part to play. War Office personnel will have to be as ready as the next man. I expect women will do our jobs, if we have to go and fight, just like they did last time.'

'Aye, well, at least it's officer training you're going on. You should be safer as an officer. Eeh, lad, me and Joe are reet proud of you. You getting on so well, with a high-up position as an interpreter. It's a real feather in your cap. Eeh, life should be grand, but now it's shrouded in this cloud of uncertainty.'

'I've been lucky that I had you and Joe, and Aunt Edith and Laurent, and Lady Eloise. It is all of your efforts on my behalf that you should be proud of.'

'We've both been lucky to have them in our lives. And don't forget Aunt Rene and Aunt Annie. I had me troubles, but them troubles brought these wonderful people to me.'

'Where is Aunt Annie?'

She's resting. She'll be up and about soon. And Joe will be in shortly, an' all.'

'And what are you doing home so early?'

'I got an afternoon off, as I wasn't needed after surgery.'

'Good, you could do with a rest, but you foiled me. I wasn't expecting you to be in. I was just coming down to look in the mirror, as you get a better view in this one. I didn't mean you to find out like this. Seeing me in uniform must be a shock to you.'

'Aye, it is.'

They both fell silent. Ada's memories nudged her, making her heart thud against her ribs, but she wouldn't let them take hold of her.

'I had a letter from Rene. It's funny she ain't never married. She was a nurse when I met her, and still is one – well, a matron, but that's the same thing. Eeh, it were a good day and a bad day when I met her. She was the one who introduced me to Lady Eloise. It was—'

'When you were injured in the explosion of Low Moor Munitions Factory.'

'Eeh, sorry, lad – I've told you that story afore.'

'Many times, Aunt Ada. You're getting old. Ouch! That hurt.'

Ada had playfully thrown an apple from the fruit bowl, thinking Brendan would dodge it, but it hit his arm. 'By, I'm sorry, lad, but you should mind your cheek!'

As he turned to admire himself in the mirror, Ada rubbed her ribs on her left side. She'd long since come to know that emotional pain could hurt in a physical way. And now seeing her nephew excited and looking forward to 'doing his bit' caused her fresh hurt, as her fears for him churned up painful memories from the past that constantly ate away at her. But then, Brendan wasn't a stranger to emotional pain himself.

He'd suffered it in bucketloads, despite being surrounded by love. She looked around the cosy kitchen. It didn't look much different from when Annie had first brought her here to live with her. A fresh coat of paint every few years and new tablecloths and antimacassars – matching the colours of the pretty curtains, which had stood the test of time – couldn't change the heart of a place that beat with love and a warm welcome.

Annie, onetime maid of Rene, who had nursed Ada after she'd been injured in a devastating explosion at Low Moor Munitions Factory, had brought Ada down to London to live with her – 'Just till you're settled, luv,' she'd said in her cockney accent.

That was after it came to light that her son Jimmy had been shot for cowardice. Ada had known she needed to get away from the pointing fingers of the lasses of Low Moor, especially from those who had lost their sons fighting. They'd have forgotten that she'd already lost two older lads in the first battle of Flanders in '14, and would have wanted to hold her to account.

Ada shut the oven door on the pie that she'd peeped at, satisfied the crust was browning nicely. She'd have to wake Annie from her slumber, to give her time to rouse herself sufficiently to get ready for dinner. Ten years older than Ada, and riddled with arthritis, Annie needed help; and it felt good to give something back to her by taking care of her.

Her thoughts turned to her sister, Beryl. She had been the one to cause Brendan so much upset. He'd had to contend with having his mother in and out of mental institutions; trying to live with her, when she was allowed out, and then coming back to Ada when Beryl was sectioned again. But Brendan had shown his strength of character by never giving up on Beryl, visiting her whenever he could, and even more so when she'd been moved to Bethlem Royal Hospital in Bromley, which was close to them.

Brendan had coped better when he'd reached an age when he could understand – especially as Beryl had gradually taken to him, after her initial rejection of her son. She'd even come to love him, which was easy for Ada to do, but something Ada never thought would happen, where her sister was concerned.

The same couldn't be said for the feelings Beryl harboured towards her sister, for Ada knew they still held bitterness and blame. That was something Ada could do nothing about. Her own conscience was clear. Beryl's affair with her Paddy had caused her downfall. *Aye, and a whole lot more, if the truth be told.*

'That was a deep sigh, Aunt Ada. You're not afraid for me, are you? I'll be fine.'

'Aye, I've heard that enough times, lad. But this time I'm sure it's reet.' The words were easily said, but belied her true fears. 'Anyway, I don't think as you're telling me everything. I can understand them taking you from your job, if they were short of men, but they're not. Aye, they have to get ready in case, but your job's important and there's thousands of others that can go and become militiamen. That's what they're calling those conscripted, ain't it?'

As he nodded, Brendan's face took on a look of confusion, sparking a worry that made Ada's stomach churn.

'Yes, but that doesn't mean I will be deployed. All War

Office staff will be attached to the military. Look, Aunt Ada, you've been through one war – you know you shouldn't ask questions.'

Aye, she knew it alreet, but him saying that must mean that he was doing something secret. *Oh God, how am I to go through it all again? And why . . . why is so much asked of me?*

'It'll be alright, Aunt Ada, I promise. Now what's for tea? It smells good.'

'Steak-and-kidney pudding – Joe's favourite.'

'Oh, so it's not mine then? You didn't cook it for the best man in your life then?'

Laughing at him, Ada hit him playfully with the oven cloth, which she had been twisting around in her hands, and told him to go and get changed.

A cough made them both quieten and turn in the direction from which it came. Joe stood in the doorway of the back door. Behind him stood a young lady who looked familiar.

'You'll never guess who this is, our Ada. Come on in, lass, and let me introduce you. This is Ada, who you've come looking for, and this is . . . By, lad, what're you doing dressed like that?'

Surprised and inquisitive about the young lass Joe had with him, Ada stepped in. 'There's nowt for you to worry over, Joe. I'll tell you all about it later. Lass here looks familiar, and I've a mind she's linked to our past, but I can't think how. So come on, get on with your introductions.'

'Me name's Ginny, Missus. Me mam were Betsy Smithward, and me dad were Harold Smithward.'

'Eeh, Betsy's lass. But you said "were"? Has owt happened to them, love?'

'Aye, they've both passed on. Me mam died of cancer, and me dad took his own life. He couldn't live without her. He was having to cope with a lot from his injuries during the war, and he'd gone downhill more and more as the years passed. Mam devoted herself to him.'

'By, that's sad. Come on in, lass, and sit yourself down. I've a pot on the go. You'll be glad of some tea, I shouldn't wonder.'

'Ta, Missus.'

'Ada. I'm Ada, and this is me nephew, Brendan.'

Brendan greeted the newcomer warmly, but Ada could see that he was mystified. 'Betsy and our Jimmy were walking out afore Jimmy went to war,' Ada told him. 'Harold was the only one of the pals to come home. He and Betsy found love together, but I never knew that they had married or had children.' Ada turned back towards Ginny. 'Eeh, lass, it's nice to meet you. Though I'm sad to the heart of me to hear of your mam's and dad's passing. Joe said you'd come looking for me?'

'Aye, me ma still had the letter you sent her. She gave it to me and told me to come and find you, if ever I found meself on me own. I – I reckon she knew what me dad would do, after she were gone. Anyroad, she said she were sorry she didn't keep in touch with you, but she thought it best. She said she got snippets of news about you, while me da was working for Lady Eloise's charity, and was happy that you were fine and having a good life.'

'Oh, Betsy, love her heart. She should have kept in touch. Was she happy? Were they both happy?'

'Yes, they adored each other, they . . . I – I have sommat to tell you. It might come as a shock, though Ma said you might have guessed. She said she was sure you had noticed that she'd put weight on the last time you saw her, but you were so distraught she kept the truth from you. It's why she never wanted to bother you.'

'Oh, my God! No! I – I mean . . . Eeh, but please let what I'm thinking be so.'

'You're talking in riddles, the pair of you. What? What's going on?'

'Sommat absolutely wonderful, Joe, if I've guessed what Ginny came to say. Am I reet, lass? By, that red hair of yours – so like mine – tell me I am reet? Your dad were our Jimmy, weren't it? You're me granddaughter!'

'I am, Ada.'

'Oh, come here, me little lass, come here.' Ada enfolded Ginny's tiny body in her arms. Her heart beat loudly, sending joyous feelings sweeping through her. Jimmy's child – her own Jimmy's child!

Neither Brendan nor Joe spoke, and both stood looking aghast at her. Ada held Ginny away from her. 'Look at her. Joe, Brendan – look at her, she's so like me at her age. Her hair, her freckled face, her build . . . Oh, Ginny, this is a happy day for me. A happy, happy day. Sommat of me Jimmy lives on.'

Ginny's face lit up with joy, but tears glinted in her eyes. 'Me mam asked me to ask you to forgive her. She said that everyone accepted that I were me dad's – Harold's – child, because Jimmy had fallen out with her a couple of weeks before he left, and Harold had courted her a while then. But when they came on leave a few weeks later, Jimmy was sorry, and he and me mam promised themselves to each other. It was then that they went too far. Mam said that when she heard of Jimmy's death, she were distraught, but she couldn't get near you, as you were suffering so much. Then Harold was injured and came home, and he and his mam took care of her. He'd always loved Mam, you see.'

'Did he know?'

'Aye, she was truthful with him, and she told me he said, "Well, babby is growing in you, and I love you, so I'm bound to love babby. Besides, I loved Jimmy, so it'll be an honour to bring up his child." They never had any children of their own. But I was theirs – Harold was me dad in everything but name.'

'Of course he was. And you could have none better. Harold Smithward was a grand lad. A grand lad.'

Joe moved forward and put his arms out towards Ginny. 'You know, I were astounded when I spotted thee in the street. I thought I'd gone back years, to when me Ada were a young 'un, but I didn't guess your story. Not even when you told me Betsy was your mam. But it's grand to have you here, lass. How long can you stay?'

'I – I hoped you'd take me in for a while. I won't be any trouble, but me mam and dad's cottage was a Mill cottage. Me granny – I mean, Harold's mam – was allowed to keep it on, because her husband had been killed in an accident whilst working in the Mill. After she died, me dad was allowed to take on the rent, on account of him having been a Mill worker before the war, and returning wounded. But when he died, they contacted me and said they were sorry, but I had to find other accommodation. I needed a change. I needed to get away from folk who'd always pointed a finger at me and speculated about me, and were now condemning me dad for killing himself and leaving me alone. So I followed up on what Mam had told me about you being me real granny, and I came here.'

'Oh, lass, you're so welcome. None more so. Eeh, I can't take it all in. Me own granddaughter.' Ada hugged Ginny to her again. Inside, her emotions were churning – she had so much to take in, and all in such a short time, but the warming happiness welling up inside her enabled her to cope.

'By, Ada, the lass must be as starving as your husband is, woman. And there's a powerful, nice smell coming from that oven. Ginny can share Brendan's dinner here, 'cause no one gets a share of my piece of steak-and-kidney pud. I love it too much.'

'Joe! And less of the "woman" – show a bit of respect. Go and wash yourself, and it'll be on the table when you come back. Eeh, men!'

Ada didn't miss Brendan's wink at Ginny. 'And you needn't start with your cheek, lad!'

'Ha, I never said anything.'

Ginny giggled at this, further endearing herself to them all.

'I'm Brendan. I'm not good at sorting out who is who, in family relationships, but I think I am your half-uncle, because your biological dad was my half-brother. But it is a bit more complicated than that, as he was also my cousin; so we're cousins once removed, too – I think!'

'Aye, I know. Me mam told me . . . and it was still talked of. I – I mean—'

Ada had turned away and was busy at the stove, but hearing that the scandal of her late husband Paddy having an affair with her sister Beryl was still talked about sent a shiver through her. She had to handle this, and handle it now. 'I'm glad you know. But you're not to worry about it, or be embarrassed. It's all history. Me sister's not a well lass, as you've probably been told. And despite the circumstances under which Brendan came into the world, none of it were his fault. There's nowt that comes between our love for each other. He's like a son to me, and has brought me a lot of comfort. Ha! That's got him blushing.'

'Aunt Ada, you're naughty. Of course I'm blushing, but it's with pride at your words, as well as the embarrassment they caused me. Ginny, that's your granny right there: she says it as it is, no matter what. But you'll never find a kinder or nicer person.'

The door to the stairs opened and Annie walked in. 'My, I've nearly slept me life away. Weren't any of you going to call me? I'm gasping for a Rosie Lee.'

'Oh, you have the full set now, Ginny. This is Aunt Annie. Annie's an honorary aunt. I'll explain it all later. Aunt Annie, meet Ginny.'

'Crickey-o'-Riley. You 'ave ter be related to Ada – you're 'er spitting image.'

'She's our Jimmy's child, Annie love. Can you believe it?'

'Well, I go to sleep for an 'our, and yer leave me for three, then you present me with a grandchild of yours. Blimey, Ada, 'ow did that 'appen?'

'Sit down, love, and I'll explain everything. Come on, Joe, park yourself. Let's get supper out.'

Ginny couldn't believe how comfortable she felt among these people. They were a mixture of cockney, like Annie was; northern, like her granny and Joe were; and, well, she couldn't quite place Brendan. He spoke with a posh accent, but occasionally mimicked all of them. Something in her felt very drawn to Brendan, to the point where she wondered if there was anything in the law that prevented half-relations marrying each other. But then she shook off the thought. Of course there would be – especially in their case, as the man who was her real grandfather had been Brendan's dad!

Still reeling from grief for her parents, she nevertheless felt herself laugh properly for the first time since the matron of the hospital where she was nursing had sent for her and told her of her father hanging himself. At that point she'd thought she would never smile again.

It seemed these folk had encased her in love, and that – and the banter that existed between them – warmed her. But it was Brendan who caused her first tentative giggle, and it was Brendan who got her laughing. Having excused himself, he'd quickly changed out of the uniform he'd been wearing, into casual trousers and a shirt topped with a hand-knitted pullover, before they all sat down to dinner. Once they were all served, there had been an attempt to discuss his war plans, but he'd batted away most of the questions and had turned the conversation towards the antics of the three people he lived with, and who had brought him up. In a northern accent he'd said, 'Eeh, Ginny lass, you'll rue the day you knocked on that door. These three will split your sides with laughter, and won't even know they're being funny.'

Annie clipped his head, telling Brendan he wasn't too big for a thick ear; and her granny and Joe had both given him a telling-off. Ginny had found herself laughing out loud.

'What I'm wondering,' Annie said, 'is where's Ginny going to lay 'er 'ead?'

'She can have my bed. I can stay on the sofa until I have to go away next week,' Brendan offered.

A silence fell. Ginny broke it. 'Oh, naw, I couldn't do that. I can stay in a hotel till I find sommat. I have some money.'

'Naw, we'll manage. Now I've found you, Ginny, I'm not having you go anywhere else. Brendan's reet: you can take his room. You men can get that shake-me-down from the attic and we'll put it in front of the fire in the parlour. I'll set the kindling going, to air it through. Now, Ginny, tell us about yourself. We don't even know what type of work you do.'

'I'm a nurse. Me ma allus wanted to be a nurse, so she steered me in that direction. I'm hoping I'll find a position down here. I could have stayed up north, as they offered me a room in the nurses' hostel, but I felt disorientated, with all that I've told you about. Besides, knowing I had a granny down here, I were eager to find you. Especially given how me mam talked of you. She loved you very much, Granny, and missed you from the moment Jimmy died, as she said that was when she really lost you.'

'Aye, it were all too much for me. I tried to explain, when she and I met that last time, and I could see as she was taken with Harold, so I gave me blessing to her. I didn't want her riddled with guilt. Like you, lass, I had to get away. You've experienced the tongue-wagging and the finger-pointing of the folk up in Low Moor. They are salt-of-the-earth types and a good community, but a bit on the judgemental side, when it comes to sommat going on. I just wish your mam had answered me letter; but then I understand how she'd think it best to leave things alone. It sounds as though she had a lot on her plate.'

'Ta. You understanding that helps a lot.'

'Reet, first thing is that you're very welcome. You settle in for a few days and find your feet, and then I'll be able to help you find somewhere to work. Me friend is a doctor. Eeh, I've so much to tell you, lass. There's a lovely place that offers help to folk, and it's named after your real dad. To honour him. You see, me friend knows for certain that your dad weren't no coward, and she started this charity. Me and Joe work there, and it could do with a nurse.'

'Oh, that sounds grand. Ta ever so much, Granny.' The name slipped off Ginny's tongue as if she'd known this woman all her life. Well, all of them really, because that's what it felt like – as if she'd always been a part of them.

As the meal came to an end, Ginny insisted on helping Ada and Annie clear the pots, while Brendan and Joe climbed up to the attic. As she passed a plate to Ada at the sink, Ginny had a sudden urge to cradle her in her arms. This woman, her granny, had been through so much, and yet she stood strong. Ginny thought she would take Ada as her inspiration, and not allow the hurt of losing her parents – and of finding out she wasn't who she thought she was – to consume her. On a sudden impulse, she pulled her granny to her and held her close. Unable to stop the deluge of tears that came, she leaned heavily on Ada.

The gentle patting of her granny's hand on her back soothed her, as did the kind and loving tone of Ada's voice. 'Now, now, lass. We've found each other. Naw regrets. Everything that happened did so for a reason. We've lived our lives apart till now, but I don't blame your mam for that, nor your dad. They did what they thought was best. Betsy put it reet in the end, and that's all that matters.'

Ginny knew her granny was right. Her ma and da had

only ever thought of her, and what was right for her at the time. She lifted her head and dried her eyes on the pinny that her granny had wrapped around her. As she did so, she felt strength enter her. She would cope. She could go forward. She had a wonderful granny to help her do so.

# 4
# *Elka*

## July 1939 – Love Wins Through

Elka took a moment to compose herself as her carriage drew up outside the door of Jhona's house on the corner of Dietla and Starowisina. Looking up at the huge, imposing building, she felt nervous. Was she doing the right thing in coming here? 'That should be an end to it,' Gos had said. What if she was turned away?

The door opened to her driver's knock. A footman came down the steps, opened the carriage door and stood stiffly, waiting for Elka to alight. As she did so, her stomach muscles clenched. She glanced up towards the second-floor window. Jhona stood looking down at her from his apartment. He smiled, but didn't leave the window to come down and greet her. It felt as if somehow she had been expected, and the stage was set for the next scene to be played out.

When she was shown into the office of the man she'd thought of as her grandfather, she saw that Gos was standing, waiting to greet her. 'I thought you would come before now, Elka. I telephoned Petra and she said she had told you the truth two days ago. How is Ania?'

His tone had a warmth to it that she had never heard before. Stunned by this unexpected turn of events, she stammered her reply. 'Sh-she is in shock, Dziadek Gos . . . I mean – oh, I don't know what to call you.'

'You may call me "Dziadek Gos" for now, although I have never been like a grandfather to you – not in the way I have been to Jhona and Isaac. But that was not because I didn't love you both, but because I had difficulty in living a lie. Before he died, I told my son that I didn't believe the story that came with you. But he chose to believe it, so I went along with it. As you grew up, I became even fonder of you both; but to show that would mean I was colluding with Petra, and I couldn't do that. Tell me what Petra has told you, and if you believe it to be the truth.'

'Please may I sit down?'

'Of course.'

Elka crossed to the window seat, thinking that sinking into one of the elegant moss-green and gold, high-backed chairs would somehow diminish her. She had been shocked – and warmed – to learn that this man had loved her, and that his honesty had prevented him from showing it. Somehow it was as if she had found a friend and confidant.

'Before you begin, I am sorry for my part in this, and it is bigger than you know. I went along with it – yes, disapprovingly, but I did so. I did that because of my own and Babcia Miriam's great love for our son and for your mama, and because of our feelings for you children; but when you grew up, we asked that the truth be told. We did not want to deceive you and may have treated you in a way that seemed harsh and cold, because of how we felt. But we did not want the break from us to be as painful as I can see the break from Petra has been.'

'I don't want to break from you. But I cannot forgive Petra, and I feel nothing but a deep loathing towards her. Ania has been brought very low – the doctor has given her something for the shock. She has spent most of the last two days sleeping, but I didn't feel I could leave her side, and I didn't want to do this on the telephone. Petra didn't tell me that you had rung. I cannot believe that all I have ever known has been a lie. Has Petra told you that our real mother isn't dead?'

Gos listened to Elka in silence, as she related her mother's story. His face had a troubled look, and when he finally spoke it was in a voice that held shame. 'I have a confession. But please, when judging me, think of your mama – her love for you, her belief that your real mother was dead – and our great love for her. I know that, in shielding her, I did a great disservice to you and Ania, and that is partly what drove me to keep my distance from you. Guilt is a powerful thing.' Clearing his throat, he hung his head. 'I knew the part of the story Petra told about your real mother dying was untrue. Three men came here, when you were children. Investigators acting for your real mother, and trying to find you for her. I am sorry. Please forgive me, but in each case I denied knowing you.'

Elka found she couldn't swallow, such was her shock. She wanted to pound this man with her fists, and to scream and scream at him.

'Please try to understand. I couldn't hurt your mama.'

'I do understand.' And she knew that she did, as a picture of her mama came to her. How heartbroken she would have been to have Elka and Ania taken from her. She hadn't deserved that. But then neither had her real mother deserved all that she must have gone through. *Oh, it is all so confusing. I feel anger towards Gos, and yet I understand. If only none of this had happened.*

'I only want your happiness now, and will do anything in my power to help you and Ania follow whatever path you decide upon.'

'Thank you, Dziadek Gos. I am angry, but I can see why you took the action you did. A small part of me is glad that you did so. Mama's life was not ruined, and neither was our childhood. We are women now, and able to deal with it. Our real mother must have suffered so much, though. You do understand that all I want is to go to her?'

Without answering her, he rang the bell on his desk. 'Come and sit over here with me, Elka dear. I have ordered tea.'

Quivering with the effort it took not to break down, Elka did as he bade.

'I am shocked to hear the truth, and I find Petra's action in stealing you both detestable. I did know that your real mother was still alive and looking for you, but in not engaging those men in conversation and saying that I knew nothing of you, I preferred to think she had given you willingly to Petra, but had changed her mind and wanted you back. Thinking that appeased my conscience, as did knowing the heartache it would cause your mama to have you leave. But what you tell me is appalling – outrageous! How can one woman steal another's children? And Aleksi, I cannot believe he allowed it. He must have been duped by Petra, too. She deserves to be punished for her actions.'

'No! No, I couldn't bear that. Please don't call the police. Let's deal with it in our own way. Please.'

'Don't distress yourself. I will only do what you want me to, my dear.'

It was so strange to hear Dziadek Gos speak to her with such endearments, and to feel such warm feelings towards him. Elka felt as if she was being given a consolation prize, for she had always loved her grandfather and had wanted his love.

The door opened and gave her another surprise. Jhona walked in carrying a tea tray.

Her whole body wanted to surge forward and go into his arms the moment he put the tray down and looked up at her. But something in his expression stopped her. 'You knew?' she asked.

'Not until after your mama died, and I couldn't speak of it then. I respected Dziadek Gos and Babcia Miriam's wish to wait until Petra had told you the truth. I am shocked and very sorry for what you must be going through, although I must confess to feeling a selfish happiness that things are so. Forgive me, Dziadek Gos, but may I have some time alone with Elka?'

'Of course, my boy. And I am very happy about what you have told me, and hope all works out for you.'

The door had hardly closed on Dziadek Gos when Elka found herself in Jhona's arms. His embrace gave hope to what had seemed impossible. It made her feel extreme happiness, as she let this love that she could now acknowledge pour through her. Unexpectedly her joy turned to tears, as the tight knot into which she'd tied her emotions whilst she cared for Ania released itself.

Jhona held her sobbing body. His strength was unyielding, his words of comfort a balm to her sore heart. Wiping her face with his huge handkerchief, he told her, 'Let it all come out. I love you, Elka, and will always be here for you. Once you have come to terms with what you have learned, we can go forward, knowing we will not be sinning. I think we would have taken our feelings to another level, no matter what. But now we are able to be open and honest. I love you, Elka. You are the completion of me.'

Her happiness won. She smiled through her tears, and then knew the bliss of having his lips on hers. The kiss didn't last long; it couldn't, as her body wouldn't stop heaving with sobs, but while it lasted it sealed their love. Elka felt her heart beginning to open to feelings that held a promise of so much more to come.

When she came out of his embrace, it was to find that Jhona wanted to speak urgently about the future. 'We have plans, as a family. We're going to America. And very soon. I don't want to leave you behind, Elka. I cannot leave you behind.'

'But I must go to France. I have to find a woman that my mother looks upon as an aunt. Her name is Marianne, and I have an address. This woman knows where my real mother is. Oh, Jhona, I have so much to tell you.' They sat together while she revealed the full story. 'So, you see, I have no choice. I need to go to France. But I need Ania to be well, as I cannot go unless she does.'

'Ania has to decide for herself. Please don't say that your decision rests on hers. I couldn't bear to leave you, now that we have found each other properly. I will go to France with you, and I want us to be married.'

'Oh, Jhona, I want that more than anything in the world. When are your family planning on leaving?'

'Within the week. It has to be soon, as the borders will close and travelling will become very difficult. We can go with them, as they plan to go to England first and get a passage to America from there. We can go to France instead, then we can join them later, after you have found your mother.'

'Yes, that is an excellent plan. I will go home at once and prepare, and I will try to persuade Ania to come, too.'

Doubt shuddered through her. In her waking moments, Ania had talked of forgiving Petra, and wanted to stay with her and protect her. Elka's heart felt heavy as she accepted that she might have to leave her beloved sister behind. The hatred she felt for Petra compounded this thought. That selfish woman should make amends and leave Poland, too.

A small part of her understood the feeling Petra had expressed, about not wanting to leave her daughter and her husband behind. She felt the same, having just buried her mama, but her parents were dead now. They were at peace, but if they were alive they would understand. *Why can't Petra see the pull she has on Ania? Why can't she forget her own needs for once and ensure Ania's safety?*

As the carriage rocked from side to side and the gentle clip-clop of the horse's hooves lulled her, Elka tried to equate the part of her that felt a huge amount of happiness with the deep sense of loss for her mama, which was going to be even harder to bear if she was soon to be separated from her sister.

Looking out of the windows, she watched the familiar scenery of the wide streets of Krakow slowly pass by, with the beautiful architecture of its tall buildings. People were going about their business. Shops displayed their wares – a kaleidoscope of colour, enhanced by the hot summer sun beaming down on their windows. Poland was a country of contrasts. Summertime scorched it with long, hot hours of sunshine, and yet its winter months were freezing cold. Both seasons were beautiful, but what came to mind now was the fun to be had on the ski slopes.

Would they ever return to those days? Would she and Ania, and Isaac and Jhona, ever again make the trip to the alpine town of Zakopane, which nestled below the Tatra Mountains, and feel carefree and happy again?

A shudder shook her body, as if her blood had turned to ice. She couldn't think why this should be, but suddenly the stunning Tatra Mountains seemed to loom in her mind as a sinister place, a place of terror. Telling herself she was being silly, Elka let her attention be drawn to the sparkling diamond shapes that the sun was casting on the Vistula river.

'Driver, pull over, please. I'll walk from here.'

Alighting from the carriage, Elka walked over to the low wall that edged the river and sat down to gaze at the Vistula, letting the sound of the lapping water soothe her.

A couple walked by. She recognized them, as she had played with their children when she was a young girl. She went to greet them, but the man pulled his wife away and spat on the ground in front of her, before hurrying off. Elka watched them go, not letting herself react to the feelings of fear and humiliation that shrouded her. She wanted to shout out, 'I'm not a born Jew', but she would never betray her people in that way.

Whether born Jewish or not, she was a Jew. Determination entered her as she watched their retreating backs. She knew that her resolve was linked to the sinister feelings that had trembled through her a short while ago. Whatever it took, if she was given the chance, she would do all she could to defend her faith and protect her people.

Within that category, she counted all Polish people. They were a part of her – non-Jewish Poles and Jewish ones – and that is why the chasm opening up between the two groups hurt her so much.

One day it would all come right again, although something told her it wouldn't be soon, and she feared what it would take to make it right.

# 5

# *Edith*

## London, July 1939 – Life's Pattern Changes

As Edith walked towards the bottom of the garden a soft wind played with the tendrils of hair that had escaped her bun. Here, in the grounds of her home in Holland Park, in West London, she should be able to find peace, but always it eluded her.

The scent of the unfolding rosebuds wafted over to her. Breathing in deeply, she let the aroma calm her. Her late mother, Lady Muriel, had designed the garden and taken particular pride in the rose bushes, seeking them out in catalogues, having great planting ceremonies and even undertaking the pruning of them herself, not trusting her precious roses to the gardener.

*Oh, Mother, how I miss you. What a comfort you would be to me now.*

Seeking a distraction from the encroaching doldrums, Edith idly pulled a dead head off the bush of Mexican daisies that nestled in a bed next to the path, before turning and looking back at the house. Something in her hoped it would work its magic on her as it had done in her childhood, but it was no longer the sprawling three-storey dwelling that she had grown up in, as it had now been converted into two apartments.

Despite the passage of time, the legacy of the war hung heavily in the house. Edith's brother Christian, who lived in the downstairs apartment, and her husband Laurent both had to cope daily with the physical injuries they had sustained, whilst for her the memories of the events leading up to the birth of her children, and then having them torn from her, weighed heavily. Nevertheless, the three of them ploughed on, attempting to get on with their lives and find happiness as best they could.

The familiar sound of the wheels of Laurent's wheelchair rumbling over the paving stones surprised her, for she had thought he was still in the house. He must have been in his shed at the bottom and to the left of the garden; it was concealed by bushes on this side, but opened up a view towards Holland Park on the other. It was a place Laurent loved, and where he channelled his inventive talent into all sorts of wonderful innovations to help his own disabilities, and those of others. She turned towards him with a little trepidation in her heart.

The air between them had been tense this morning and he'd breakfasted alone in their bedroom. After all these years he couldn't get used to his *failing*, as he termed his impotence. Most of the time they jogged along happily, Laurent's attentions to her during their love-making bringing her fulfilment. She would always assure him that their intimate time together was enough for her, but sometimes he would hope they could go further. She dreaded these moments and, when they happened, prayed fervently that at last he would be able to enter her fully. He never had. The moment he tried, he lost the ability. Such an occasion had taken place this morning and had left him frustrated and angry.

Laurent's hand stretched out towards her. Edith smiled down at him, taking his hand in both of hers. His mouth opened as if to speak, but she shushed him. Their eyes held for a long moment.

'Are you all right, darling?'

'I am, Laurent, my love. I'm just gathering my thoughts before I go along to Jimmy's Hope House to do my morning surgery. I told you that I was on a late at the hospital afterwards, didn't I? I haven't any operations scheduled, unless anything comes in, so I should be back home for eleven.'

'Yes, you told me. Sit for a moment with me.'

She perched on the low wall and was now level with him. He hadn't put his prosthesis on, so didn't attempt to rise from his chair.

She looked into his beloved face. He was still handsome, despite the scar that twisted his cheek on one side, where plastic surgery had covered the hole that had left his jawbone exposed. His dark eyes glinted with love, but also with anguish. She hoped he wasn't going to talk about the intimate side of their marriage. They had never done so, away from the bedroom – and then only when triggered by incidents like this morning.

'I am getting increasingly concerned about world affairs, darling.'

She sighed inwardly with relief. This was safe territory. 'I know. Do you think that Hitler will go further? Poland even?'

'It's a possibility. But unlikely, as he knows Britain would intervene.'

Laurent was aware of Edith's worries; knew of her certainty that her girls were in Poland. And she knew that he didn't really believe what he was saying. Somehow she found a smile and patted his hand. Neither of them spoke. A peace settled around them. Laurent broke it. 'We don't know for certain that your girls are still in Poland, darling.'

'I know we don't, but the not knowing is worse.'

'I'm so sorry. I feel so much for you, losing your babies; and then I was never able to father—'

'Don't! Don't torture yourself. All I ever wanted was to be with you. Nothing else matters.'

'It does matter, Edith. I may not be able to perform, but I so want to make you mine.'

'I *am* yours. We have been together in a loving relationship for twenty years. That counts for a lot. Your way of loving me fulfils me in every way. Yes, I wish we could make love fully, but you have never left me wanting, or feeling selfish for needing your attention in that way. I'm so sorry it haunts you that you cannot go further, my darling.'

The conversation seemed to have turned away from war very quickly, but she suspected that underneath he'd wanted to air his feelings about their experience that morning.

'Edith, whilst we are talking about it, I have something I want to tell you. I have been making some enquiries. There is a therapist—'

'Oh? I – I . . . You mean, it may be psychological and not physical? I – we – have never given that a thought!' *A white lie*, she thought to herself, *but a charade I have had to keep up.*

'And you are a doctor! But, you know, I have always thought that my case was hopeless, otherwise you would have suggested help for me. In a way, you not suggesting it has prevented me from seeking help.'

'I – I don't know what to say.'

'No, don't say you are sorry. I shouldn't even be discussing it right now, after asking for your forgiveness. But I had to tell you sometime. I have been afraid that whatever I said would make it seem I was accusing you.'

'Well, you are. You are saying that me being a doctor has stopped you seeking help.'

'*Don't!* Don't do this. Edith, it has been so difficult for me. Twenty years of hell.'

She felt more hurt than she'd ever been by anything that had happened between them so far. She thought about the times Laurent had been so low that he'd not spoken to her for days, and the way he could cut her off and become cold towards her. Slowly she felt the tears she'd denied herself smart her eyes.

She had spent many years wondering whether Laurent's problems were a result of psychological damage. But how do you tell your beloved husband that you think he has a mental-health issue? That he needs counselling? Would he have believed that she truly thought everything he'd been through – his injuries from being blown up, losing his leg and half of his face, and what he'd witnessed in the bloody trenches of Verdun and Ypres – could have an effect on him, sexually? She doubted it. He was far more likely to think she blamed him, or wasn't satisfied with what he could achieve; or that she thought him inadequate. And that would have made things worse. She'd even been afraid to mention it to their doctor, a man who embodied old-fashioned ideas and abhorred female doctors.

She composed herself and squashed the desire to pummel

Laurent with her fists. 'What made you decide to seek out a therapist?'

'I finally plucked up the courage to speak to Dr Frieth. I told him everything. He said he had wondered the same thing, but, as I am married to a doctor, felt sure that if there had been a problem, you would have dealt with it. He said that some women were very cold and frigid, so they were quite happy not to be bothered by their husband. When I told him that wasn't you, he just said, "Selfish then." And that made me wonder . . . Edith? EDITH!'

Ignoring his shouts, she ran towards the house. Somehow she found her handbag, despite the blinding tears. Humiliation stung her. How dare Dr Frieth say such a thing! Even worse, Laurent thought there might be some truth in it. Storming out of the front door, she felt a small amount of satisfaction at slamming it behind her, and with such force that she heard something crash to the floor.

Wiping away the tears, she fumbled in her bag and found the key to her car, hoping against hope it would start and not need cranking with the starter handle, because that would mean she would need help. Straightening her clothes as she sank into the deep leather seat gave her a moment to compose herself. The engine responded to her first pull on the starter. *Thank God.*

Taking a deep breath, she steered the beautiful, dark-green Wolseley away from the kerb and allowed the feeling of pleasure that she always experienced when driving to soothe her frayed nerves.

'Morning, love.' Ada jolted Edith out of her thoughts, as she walked into the surgery in Jimmy's Hope House.

*Everything is as normal, then? My whole world isn't falling apart, even though it feels it is, with the accusations Laurent has made. Has he really thought all these years that I've been selfish?* She shook the thought away from her. 'Good morning, Ada. Another nice day?'

'Eeh, Edith love, what's to do? Has sommat happened? Come on, lass, the world hasn't ended yet. There's time for a pot of tea and a natter, afore it does.'

As always, Edith knew Ada was right; but a little of her world had died, with the cruelty of what had been simmering in Laurent's head, and she wondered if their relationship would ever again be as it had been previously.

She was brought out of her thoughts by the chink of tea being poured and the smell of freshly brewed tea leaves. Ada hadn't spoken while she'd set about making the tea, but now she demanded, 'Reet, lass, what's on your mind? A trouble shared is a trouble halved, thee knows.'

Hiding the real reason for her distress, Edith chose to put the focus on her usual troubles. 'Oh, you know: all this talk of war, thinking of our loved ones having to go through what we did and . . . well, it looks likely that Hitler will invade Poland.'

'By, that's the rub of it. I might have guessed. Elka and Ania, bless them. But you have to hold on to the hope that they're not in Poland. Remember you told me that they are Jews, so the family could have moved to America. Many Polish Jews have, according to the news. And you can't blame them, either.'

'Yes, Laurent said something similar, but I have this gut feeling. You see, Petra once talked at length about her own daughter. She said that her husband and his father refused to leave when trouble broke out at the beginning of the last war. They did go over the border to Russia, but that was as far as they would travel. They have a jewellery business and the father wouldn't leave that, and neither would the husband of Petra's daughter.'

'And yet, knowing what we do about the family, the various investigators you've employed have never found owt out about where the girls are and what they are doing. You'd think it would be easy just to go round all the jewellery firms in Poland.'

'I know, I used to think that, but without knowing a surname, it seems much more difficult. Oh, I don't know. I have asked myself many times: why haven't they been found?' She sighed. 'Anyway, enough of worrying about that. Is Leah all right? Has there been any news on what is happening at that house she was kept in?'

'No real news. That copper came round yesterday afternoon and said that plans were in place, but he didn't tell us much. He now believes everything Leah has told him, and the police are acting upon it, but we can't get that across to Leah – perhaps you could talk to her before surgery opens? Mind, my Ginny is helping, bless her. The girls mime a lot to each other, and I have even heard Leah giggling, so there's hope yet. Poor lass, she has a lot on her plate.'

'Yes, she has. I'll ring the sergeant and see what I can find out, then go and explain everything to Leah. You know, I'm still amazed at how Ginny turned up. I can't tell you how good it feels to have Jimmy's daughter here, in the house that honours him. And she's a lovely girl. A capable and talented nurse, and a godsend. She has a lot of your ways as well.'

'Eeh, she's another poor lass, then.'

'Go on with you, Ada. If I had an ounce of what you're

made of, I would be a million times better person than I am. But, as it is, I have you as my best friend and that keeps me sane.'

'Aw, that's a nice thing to say, but enough sloppiness. You run along to Leah while I get everything ready for your surgery – you're under me feet and holding me up.'

Edith didn't miss the catch in Ada's voice and smiled to herself.

With surgery completed, and hearing from Ada that Leah was now fast asleep and not so restless, Edith wrote a note in French and gave it to Ada to give to Leah. 'It explains that I will see her first thing in the morning, as I won't be able to come back later tonight. She still seems to want me to be with her every minute, but that is because when she's with me she can communicate.'

'I'll see she gets it afore I go. Now get yourself off, or you'll not have time to eat before you take over your shift at the hospital.'

'I know. Thank you. Dear Ada, what would I do without you? I thank God for our friendship.'

'You'll never know what you'd do without me, 'cause I'll allus be here for you.'

They smiled at each other and then, on an impulse, Edith took Ada into her arms.

'Eeh, Edith lass. What's got into you? You'll crush me pinny.'

They both laughed.

Edith's heart was heavy when she sat down at her desk in the office of the hospital ward and listened to the surgeon from whom she was taking over. He was updating her on the patients in their care, but not much was going in, because her mind was elsewhere. Leah's continued fear had stayed with her. As had her row with Laurent. But nothing compared or weighed her down like the fear for her daughters. She could do something about the first two, but knowing what had happened – or was happening – to her daughters seemed to be a lost cause.

Hope, she thought, was a good thing; but also a bad thing, as it kept pain alive. Would her pain ever diminish?

# 6

# *Elka*

## France, Early August 1939 – A Painful Decision Followed Through

The battle between them had raged for days, as Elka tried to persuade Ania to leave Poland with her. Turning from the sitting-room window, she decided to have another try. A heavy sigh escaped her as she looked at Ania sitting on the sofa, her attention consumed by a pile of school papers that she was wading through. *How can Ania carry on life as if nothing has changed?*

Walking over to her, Elka plonked herself heavily on the chair next to the sofa.

'Elka, you have that look about you again. Can't you accept that I want to stay? Look at all this work done by my pupils – they deserve that I stay. *They* can't leave. Oh, the rich ones amongst them have already gone, but the children who are left are the sons and daughters of those who don't have the means to pay bribes and obtain false papers. They need an education.'

'Ania, please, I beg of you! Please change your mind.'

'No. Apart from the children, Babcia is not well – she needs me. Why can't you wait until she is stronger?'

'She is nothing to me. How can you still respect her, let alone love her? She stole our lives from us.'

'But she replaced it with a good life. We *have* had a good life, Elka – you can't deny that – and a life full of love. I am still grieving for Mama, and Babcia is, too. How can we leave her?'

'She is asking us to do so. Every day she urges us to go. And we can see what frightens her, for the papers are full of what is happening to the Jews. You will be in grave danger if you stay.'

'I am not a born Jew. I will tell them. Besides, as I have said, not all Jews can get out, and how can we abandon them?'

'We must. We must do what we can to save ourselves, and then do what we can from outside Poland. If we are incarcerated or controlled, how can we change things? We will do more good from outside the country. We can bring influences to bear, or work with Resistance movements or maybe with groups that are helping Jews to escape from Austria. Can't you see that? Besides, if we find this Marianne, we should find our *real* mother. Don't you want to do that?'

'Of course I do. But I don't want to leave Poland at this time. I need to stay.'

'Oh, Ania, how can I leave without you? But I must. Jhona is leaving, and I must go with him. He is coming with me to France, and from there we will see what happens.'

'I am happy for you. Are you and Jhona to be married before you go?'

'There is no time. And there are difficulties. Legal papers relating to Jews are going astray. We dare not risk losing valuable identification papers in the system. Dziadek Gos is taking the rest of the family to America, so we will join them later and marry then. They will be devastated that you are not coming with me.'

Ania carried on marking her pupils' work. The rustle of the papers and the scratching of her pen nib as she worked grated on Elka's already-frayed nerves.

When finally Ania looked up, her expression held disdain. 'It is strange that, after treating us almost like lepers, Dziadek Gos and Babcia Miriam are now acting like loving grandparents. After all, we were formally adopted by their son, which means they were our adoptive grandparents.'

'You know why, Ania. You seem to put more store by Petra, who lied to us, than you do by Dziadek Gos and Babcia Miriam, who tried to be honourable and to avoid living a lie. They have told us that they didn't stop loving us. They were just afraid to show it.'

'Well, it is nice to have their love. Despite everything, I love them very much. You know, talking of leaving, it is possible that any conflict will be over very quickly. The Prime Minister of Great Britain is saying that if Germany invades us, Britain will wager war on Germany. And so, even if that doesn't deter Germany, the might of Britain may soon defeat them.'

'How can we be sure? Hitler has built up massive aggressive and defensive strategies. His army is vast, as are his navy and air force. I am afraid that unless the whole world fights side-by-side against him, he will defeat Great Britain. Jhona says that, to do so, Hitler will have to take France. And that is why there is even more urgency. We need to get to France to find this Marianne, before Hitler turns his attention to that country. Besides, France is the country of our birth.'

'I know, but I can't go. Anyway, when did you become such a political animal? I wasn't aware that you knew so much about what forces the Germans possess, or their aims.'

'I needed to know. I have been trying to get into medical school – and what has been happening here, and abroad, has had an effect on that. Besides, Jhona is very interested in it all. He and his family have been moving assets and have only registered half of their wealth on the compulsory register for Jews. He has had to keep abreast of all that is happening.'

The door opened and Petra shuffled into the room, supported by her stick and holding a wallet in her hand. The conversation stopped. Elka stood and turned towards the opposite door, as if to leave.

'Don't go, Elka, I have something important here for you.'

Stiffening, Elka did not reply, but looked over at Petra in disgust.

Petra lowered her eyes. 'I have papers showing your true nationality. Here.' She put out a hand containing the cloth wallet. 'Take them. I haven't said so before, as I hoped I wouldn't need to, but you may require these. I had to register you both as English citizens, as you had no country of origin. We registered you again here, and that is why you have Polish papers, but these papers were never rescinded. In here is proof of your dual nationality. You are entitled to be considered a British citizen – and Britain is where you should head for, as soon as you can. And, Ania, you *must* leave; you *must*!'

This both stunned and pleased Elka. As dual nationals, they could come and go in each of the countries in which they were registered. Getting into England would pose no problem if the borders were closed to Eastern European residents. She would apply for a British passport the moment she was settled in France. But any euphoria at this new twist was short-lived as she heard the determination in Ania's reply to Petra.

'I am *not* going, and that is an end to it. Apart from not leaving you, Babcia Petra, I have to stay to take care of the children in the school. And, well, neither of you know this, but I am in love. Oh, nothing has been said by either of us, but we know how we feel – and he isn't leaving. He thinks the invasion will happen and, if it does, then us teachers need to stay, to take care of and protect the children.'

'You mean Baruch Elburg? But he's a political activist, he will lead you into danger – oh, Ania.'

'Yes, Elka, he stands up for what he believes in: that Poland should be a free state, where all races and religions can live freely together. But I believe that is a good ideal and has brought Baruch great respect from many Catholic communities, and from those who are forced to live according to Communist ideals – and that is a rare feat for a Jew to have accomplished. He is forming a Resistance group, who will rise up and fight the Germans if they try to invade. Baruch believes that other nations will back them, and the result will be a free Poland at last!'

Defeated by the sheer conviction with which Ania spoke of her beliefs, and by the power that she knew love could nurture, Elka gave in. Opening her arms and moving towards her sister, she asked, 'Will you forgive me, if I go?

My heart wants never to leave your side, but I am compelled to go in a different direction from you.'

Coming into her arms, Ania held Elka tightly to her. 'There is nothing to forgive, my darling sister. I will miss you, as a part of me will be gone, but we have to take the paths that are beckoning us. I will be happy knowing that you are safe, and with Jhona. Be happy for me, too, as I will be with the man I love, and where I want to be.'

Tears flowed down Elka's face at the finality of this comment, and at the thought that she might never see her sister again. Their tears mingled as they clung on to each other.

'Are you ready, Elka darling?' Jhona came into the room. He had been waiting outside the apartment door, to give Elka one more chance to persuade Ania to leave. With the realization that the time had come, a physical pain shot through Elka, tearing at her resolve. Ania drew herself from her sister's arms. Her expression was one of shock. 'Are you going now? This minute? Oh, Elka, no!'

'I have to, my dear. You know that I have been packing for days. We must leave now, before the borders close. Jhona, Isaac and Dziadek Gos are all driving. We are heading for Kołobrzeg. There will be a boat waiting for us there to take us across to Sweden, and from there we will all fly to England in a private aircraft. In England we will go our separate ways. Jhona and I will travel to France, and the rest of the family will try to get a passage on a liner to America. Will you come to Dziadek Gos and Babcia Miriam's house, to say goodbye to everyone?'

'I can't. I'm sorry, but it will be too painful to me. I will write a letter to them all. Can you wait while I do that?'

When Ania left the room to write her letter, Elka felt uncomfortable in Petra's presence, so she gestured to Jhona to follow her. 'We'll wait outside, darling.'

Once the door had closed behind them, Elka froze as Petra's agonized cry reached her. 'No . . . no, please don't go. Not without forgiving me, Elka – please!'

Elka returned to the room. 'I will forgive you, if my real mother forgives you for taking us from her. I do feel better towards you, since hearing that it is because of her love for Baruch Elburg that Ania won't come with me, and not solely out of duty to you. Before that, I hated you for not leaving Poland to ensure that Ania did so. But I will bear no malice towards you. You brought me up, with Mama; you gave Mama to me and you have been an important part of my *pretend* life. Yes, you gave me love; but the love I gave you, you did not deserve. Ania and I may be twins, but we are very different, and always have been. She may be able to get over and see past what you have done, but I cannot. I hope you keep well. And I beg you to watch over and guide Ania. But that is all I can leave you with. Goodbye.'

Every limb trembled as Elka closed the door. Though she now loathed Petra, that loathing didn't exclude all the feelings she'd had for her in the past, and parting from her hurt more than she wished to admit.

Petra's sobs nearly undid her, but Elka could not force herself to return into the room, and Petra did not attempt to come after her. Better to have done with it all.

'Are you all right, darling?'

'No, Jhona, I am far from all right, and it will be a long time until I am. It will take until I am reunited with Ania for me to feel completely all right. We are two halves of a whole and we need to be together.'

'You're not thinking of *not* coming, are you?'

'No, my darling, because – despite what I have said – you are a bigger pull on my heart than my sister is. I can't live without being near you.'

His arms enclosed her. She could hear his heart beating. Each beat seemed to tick away life as she knew it, and she wondered how her new life would pan out. Would she ever achieve her dream of finding her real mother? And, if she did, what would her mother be like? Would she have another family – half-sisters and half-brothers to her and Ania? Would the time come when she herself would become a doctor, like her mother? Above all, would war come again, as it had done in her mother's day; and, if so, would they all survive it? *Oh, how I hope so. I want to marry Jhona and have his children – I want to live!*

The journey had been long and tiring. Elka and Jhona had spent a week in England. Parting from the rest of the family had been painful, but also full of hope, as they had at last felt safe and the future held more security for them all. Now here she was, three weeks after leaving Poland, outside the address she had for Marianne in Nice.

Looking up at the windows above her, Elka wondered if they were the same ones that her own mother would have looked out of, when she stayed here. And whether her mother still visited. Petra had said that her mother was about twenty-eight when she gave birth to her and Ania. That would make her about fifty now.

Jhona rang the doorbell. Its jangling played on Elka's nerves, bringing them to a fever pitch of excitement and fear. She heard footsteps coming down the stairs towards the door.

A woman of around sixty years of age opened it, then stepped back in shock, before recovering and saying in French, 'Oh, I – I'm sorry, I thought for a moment you were . . . No, that is silly of me – how can you be? How can I help you?'

'Did you think I was Edith Mellor?'

'What? How is it that you know of Edith?'

There was no easy answer. 'I am her daughter.'

'No. No, this is not possible.' Many emotions passed over Marianne's face. Elka started to explain, but before she could continue, Marianne gasped, 'So that's why Edith disappeared! Oh, my poor Edith. Look, come in. Come inside. We have to talk. I – I am confusing you.'

As they followed her up the stairs, Elka introduced Jhona and then asked the question she hardly dared to ask, as she dreaded the answer. Gos had said it had been a long time since the last investigator had come looking for them. 'Is my mother still alive?'

'Yes. Yes, of course. I – I mean, well, Edith Pevensy – Mellor – is still very much alive. Are you sure . . . I mean, does she know about you? Oh dear, I'm not making sense. If what you are saying is true, she will of course know about you. Oh, my poor darling Edith, this explains so much – so much.'

'Do you speak English?' asked Elka, when they entered the vestibule of the grand apartment. Marianne nodded.

Elka switched to speaking in English. 'I have so much to tell you, and you will have questions, but Jhona's French is not good. He speaks Russian, which I don't, or at least not well enough, and English, and I want him to be able to understand what we are saying.'

'That is fine. I have no Russian, so all in all English will be the best language. I am listening, my dear.'

Relating her story a few minutes later, whilst drinking the delicious wine that Marianne had offered them and nibbling at the little pastries she produced, Elka noticed tears streaming down Marianne's face. This woman must love Edith very much and it was hurting her, but Elka had to keep going – she had to tell it all.

Marianne didn't interrupt her with questions, but at the end she said, 'Oh, that wicked woman. And my poor darling Edith. How she must have suffered, and still is suffering, as she has never been the same girl she was before she disappeared. I understand it all now. Why didn't she come to me? I would have helped her. I would have made sure you were taken care of, without any scandal ever getting out. Edith could have been with you all this time. Oh, Edith. And what happened to you, my dear, and your sister, is terrible, just terrible.'

Marianne rose from the beautiful chair she had been sitting on. With its carved gold-leaf arms and legs, and its pale-blue upholstery decorated with a diamond pattern of little pink rosebuds, Elka thought it, and everything about this elegant apartment, suited this lovely lady.

As Marianne came towards her she resembled a gliding porcelain doll. And although she had her arms open, Elka thought better than to rise too, or the tiny Marianne would be dwarfed by her. Instead she held her own arms out and accepted the cuddle that Marianne gave her. With a gentle hand stroking the curls off her forehead and a lovely voice telling her about her mother, Elka knew she had done the right thing in coming, and wished Ania had come with her.

After telling Elka about her mother's background, Marianne said, 'Life hasn't been easy for Edith since the war ended. During the time that she was lost to us – the time when you were born – she met the love of her life.'

Elka listened as Marianne told her about her mother's husband, Laurent.

'Laurent was badly injured and disfigured during a particularly bloody campaign. It was a miracle that he survived, but Edith's love brought him through. They were married soon after the war, but have never had children. I'm not even sure that the marriage has been consummated.'

Elka's cheeks flushed. Marianne had said this so matter-of-factly, but she remembered hearing that the French were very open about what they discussed. Taking a sidelong look at Jhona, who hadn't spoken other than to greet Marianne, Elka saw a smile curl on his lips. She wasn't sure if it was because of her own embarrassment or because of what Marianne had said, but she smiled back.

Marianne didn't miss this. 'I see you have a ring on your finger, but not a wedding ring. Oh, it is so different for you young people. Travelling together without chaperones – that would never do in my day!'

This seemed so different from what Elka had been thinking about the French, and left her confused as to how to answer. But Jhona saved the day. 'Please don't worry about Elka's honour, for it is safe with me. I love and respect her too much to expect anything from her before we are married. And my religious beliefs about the sanctity of marriage prevent me from even thinking of taking advantage of our travelling alone together.'

'Of course. I wasn't passing judgement, just regretting that the lack of freedom shackled me. I have no wish to put those shackles on you. I see, by your clothes and hair, that you are a Jew. Jhona, I am afraid for your people. Anti-Semitism is rife. I am glad you are out of Poland, but what of Ania? Elka, were you and she bought up as Jews? Why didn't she come, too? Surely she will be in grave danger?'

After Elka had explained, Marianne nodded her understanding. 'It is how it is: love has its own shackles, I'm afraid. So, what now? I take it you want to contact your mother?'

'I do – more than anything in the world.'

'Well, it all has to be handled with care. You can stay with me for as long as it takes, but I have to warn you: I have a less-than-conventional life. I have a lover. We have been together many, many years, and although we have separate apartments, we often stay over together – more so since we got older. Her name is Georgette, but she likes to be known as George.' Pausing a moment, Marianne looked from one to the other. Elka tried not to look shocked. She had heard of such things, but had never openly discussed them. Looking at Jhona, she could see that he was perplexed. Elka said, 'Your private life is your own. We are not judging you, but maybe we will feel more comfortable in a nearby hotel.'

'Yes, I think that may be sensible. Now, as for contacting Edith, I think I should send a letter to her. There is no worry about anyone else opening it. Your grandparents are both dead. Otherwise I would be very worried, because your grandmother thought nothing of opening mail that wasn't for her. And Laurent is typically French and has no desire to rule his wife or curtail her freedom, which is just as well, because Edith is headstrong and would rebel against such restrictions; so he won't open her mail, either.'

'You take after her in that too, then, Elka.'

Even though it was true, Elka felt annoyed at Jhona for pointing this out.

Marianne laughed. 'Ha, you do – I can see that. That is exactly the kind of look to which Laurent is often subjected.'

This mollified Elka, as she rather liked the comparisons made between herself and her mother. But the thought of having to wait for a return letter made her impatient. What if her mother rejected her? No, she loved Elka, she wouldn't do that. But why not? A lot of time had passed. She might not have told her husband about her twin daughters. 'I think I would rather have my mother's address and travel to England to see her.'

'No! *Ma chérie*, no. You cannot. You must let me handle this, for it is very delicate.'

'Very well, but please, could you send a telegram?'

'No! That's impossible. The local post-office staff in England would know everything then. A letter is the only way I am willing to contact Edith. It is the kindest way, and the safest. She deserves our discretion, and deserves to be given the chance to handle you coming back into her life in the way she thinks best. In her society, this will cause a great scandal. I am sure Edith would rather put up with that than not see you, but she will want to consider her family.'

'Very well, but may I be permitted to write a letter, too?'

'Of course. As Edith didn't want ever to be parted from

you, she will be nothing but pleased to hear from you, I am sure. That's settled then. *Fait accompli!*'

*If only it was*, Elka thought. There were still so many questions hanging in the air. All held doubt and fear, but she had to hang on to the fact that her mother had loved her and Ania and hadn't wanted to give them away.

# 7

# *Edith*

## London, September 1939 – The Three Prongs of Happiness

'Britain is at war with Germany.' Goosebumps rose on Edith's arms. Neither she nor Laurent spoke. The arm of Laurent's wheelchair dug into her as he tightened his grip on her.

The silence between them gave some space for Edith's thoughts and fears. There was a jumble of them, and a jumble of faces. Faces dear to her: Jennifer and Mark, friends who were her colleagues in the tent hospital on the Somme; now a happy family unit with three boys, one of whom was old enough to be called up for war. *Dear God, why, oh why, do we have to go through this all again? Wasn't it enough that my generation fought for world peace? Why do our children have to do so, too?*

Connie and Nancy came into her mind – two lovely nurses from that time. Connie was still single, and still a nurse. Would she return to war? Nancy was married, with two girls. Like their mother before them, Edith was sure they would want to volunteer for war work. And what of Brendan, who was now an officer attached to the War

Office. Would he be called upon to do active service? *Dear God, how would we face that? How would Ada face it?* Something told Edith they might not have to, as it was becoming increasingly obvious that Brendan was doing important work in the War Office and wouldn't become a fighting soldier.

Then there was her brother, Douglas. Would his sons have to go? *Oh, I can't bear it! My nephews, Thomas and Henry!* But even as she thought this, she knew she would have to face it, just as her own parents had had to bear Douglas, Christian and herself going to the last war.

'You won't go, will you, darling?'

Laurent's voice roused her from her thoughts. 'No, I couldn't leave you, my dear. Besides, this war will be fought as much on home soil as abroad. The ability the Germans now have to fly bombers long-range means that they will be all over us. I think I will be needed here. But it is our nephews we should be worrying about; and Eloise's girls and all of our friends' children, and your pupils from the university and . . .' She couldn't say it. To give voice to her fears for her long-lost twins would be like admitting the dread that lay inside her. *Hitler has invaded Poland. My girls are in Poland – I'm sure of it! What if Petra has brought them up as Jews? Hitler's regime hates the Jews. There are reports of horrific reprisals!* 'Oh, Laurent, I have prayed and prayed.'

'I know, darling. I can only say what I have said many times: try to hang on to the hope that your girls are not in Poland.'

There was no point in doing anything other than nodding her head. She avoided everything that might cause conflict between them. They hadn't got back to an easy relationship since that day Laurent had told her about going for counselling. Even their love-making – or at least what they had, in place of full marital relations – had almost ceased. The one time she had approached Laurent he'd pretended that he was tired, something he'd never done in the past. He'd always responded to her need. Now she felt afraid to show him when she felt a yearning for his caresses. Instead she had taken to having a longer-than-usual bath at those times and to finding relief by herself. She was always left feeling guilty, as if she had done something sinful.

'Darling, don't reject me. I'm here for you. We're going to need each other.'

'Me – reject you! Laurent, sometimes you take the biscuit.'

'I'm doing my best, Edith. I'm sorry. I know I am not the same towards you. I don't want to be like that, but . . . Well, it is revisiting everything. Oh, I don't know.'

He sounded so dejected that her heart went out to him. 'Do you think the counselling is helping you? You seem to have withdrawn into yourself. You never talk to me. Tell me, Laurent – tell me how you feel, and what is going on inside your head.'

'Guilt, mainly. Guilt because of those who died while I lived. Guilt because I have never been a proper husband to you. Guilt because I didn't seek help, in the beginning. Though, as I said before, that was partly your fault . . . No. Don't go. Now we have begun to talk, please let us see it through.'

'I can't take all this blame, Laurent. I have told you why I never suggested that you seek help. My motives were not selfish as your doctor chooses to make you believe. They were because I didn't want to hurt you.'

'Isn't that shifting your responsibility?'

This was unbearable. They couldn't discuss it; it was impossible. That beast of a doctor had carried his loathing of women medics to the point of souring her beloved Laurent's mind against her. Feeling lost, all she could do was run, and get out of the space that held Laurent's accusations.

Once out of the room, she tore down the stairs. Reaching the bottom step gave her sight of a letter on the hall table, which stood outside the door leading to Christian's apartment. If only he was the Christian of old, she would have run to him and sought her brother's counsel. But that person was lost in a body that wouldn't move – a hell imposed on him by war, and now they faced it all happening again.

Picking up the letter, she recognized Marianne's writing. For a moment she wished she was with the uncomplicated Marianne. She was probably the only person in the world to whom Edith could pour out her heart.

Sighing, she walked towards the back of the hall, through the small sitting room that used to be her mother's and was now the only room open to her and Laurent on the ground floor. She went through the French doors into the garden.

The sun was scorching, and the birds that she loved to listen to carried on as if nothing had changed. Oh, how she longed to be as free as them. But did she really? Could she ever be apart from her darling Laurent? Because, despite the state of his mental health, she loved him with an all-consuming love.

Had she been selfish? Not intentionally, but maybe she had. It was just that he'd always been unpredictable and, where their love-life was concerned, she preferred to tread on eggshells, praising his efforts in making sure that she reached a climax, and reassuring him that it was enough for her. Telling Laurent that dealing with his problems might free him from his impotence could have tipped him over the edge.

What else could she have done? Despite the leaps and bounds made in the last twenty years to give women greater liberty, they were still thought not to have sexual longings. Oh, women could be passionate when being made love to, but if they approached a man for sex, they would be thought of as nothing but sluts. That was a man's domain, like so many other things.

There was still a long way to go. Would anyone ever be brave enough to fight for women's rights? Get them equal pay when they did the same job? Even now, after all this time, her male colleagues did not consider Edith to be as good as they were at their job. She'd even had a male patient refuse to let her operate on him.

But the spirit she had felt in her to fight all of this had gone. It had been drowned in everyday living, coping with her work at the hospital and at Jimmy's Hope House. And Laurent's ever-changing moods made everything more difficult. Thank God she had Ada. And Ginny too, now. What a surprise that had been, but a wonderful one; and Ginny was proving a godsend at Jimmy's Hope House. She'd taken to midwifery as if she'd been doing it all her life. Besides looking like Ada, Ginny had many of Ada's qualities; something that would stand the girl in good stead.

There was her cousin, Lady Eloise, too. She was a great

comfort. And although it was difficult to, because of his hearing problems, she loved to chat to Eloise's husband, Jay, and their girls were a delight – but none of them came anywhere near the relationship she had with Ada. Ada was her confidante: the keeper of all her secrets, her fears and her emotional distress, besides being the king pin of Jimmy's Hope House. *Oh, how I thank God every day for having Ada in my life!*

Climbing the step of the raised platform they had built, not long after they married, Edith sat down on the bench they had placed there. From here she could see over the wall and into the park, a favourite view of hers.

Though her mood would prevent her from enjoying the letter fully, she would read it and hope that it lifted her spirits. But nothing had prepared her for its contents:

*My dear Edith,*

*I am hesitant as I write this letter, because I do not know how you will receive the news. How I wish that I could bring it to you, but I am not such a good traveller now, and time is of the essence. None of us know what will happen in the near future – there is so much that is unsettled, and unsettling.*

*I have no way of skirting around this, so I will be direct.*

*A girl, called Elka . . .*

Edith drew in a breath that caught in her lungs, as if it would never release itself again. That name threw her into a turmoil of fresh emotions that she didn't know if she could cope with. Her hands shook as she lifted the letter and read on. By the end, her own cries were assaulting her ears. They came from deep within her; they were a release, and yet an accumulation of all the pain she'd kept knotted inside her. A voice – anxious and almost alien – cut through her anguish.

'Darling, darling, what is it? Come down, please come down. I'm sorry . . . Oh, my darling Edith, forgive me.'

Unable to move, or to stop the deluge of salty tears that streamed down her face, she stared down at Laurent. Locked in his wheelchair without his prosthesis, he couldn't get to her. But she didn't care. Not at this moment. This moment belonged to her. It was time for everything to pour out of her. In doing so, it scorched her very soul, and the thought came to her: *No more!* Somehow she shouted the words, 'N-NO MORE!'

It was over. She didn't care what everyone thought or said. She was going to be reunited with her babies. They wanted and needed her. *Oh, thank God!*

'Please, Edith, you will be ill. I – I didn't mean to cause this, I was angry.'

'*You* were angry!' The words rasped in her throat. 'I don't care. I just don't care.' Once more her words merged with her tears. The desolation that had been locked inside her had unfurled. The floodgates were open and she wondered if they would ever close again. 'Leave me alone, Laurent. Go – go away. I don't want to look at you. Just leave me alone.'

As she relaxed in the bath an hour later, Edith's body still heaved, but there were no more tears. They had been washed out of her. She hadn't seen Laurent since, and wondered if he'd done as she'd suggested and gone out. But she wasn't going to devote any of her emotions to him at this time. Her anguish had subsided, and now she was filled with joy.

She was going to see one of her children and she knew the meeting would go well. The letter from Elka that had been enclosed with Marianne's had been full of love, and told her how much Elka had been hurt, on discovering the truth. It also said how she had loved her other mother and was still grieving for her. This hadn't hurt; it had only shown what a wonderful young woman Elka was, as had the way she had spoken of her sister with caring and love.

Edith felt determined. She would leave for France as soon as she could arrange it. She wouldn't let the worry for her second child, deep as it was, spoil the elation she now felt. This was a beginning.

The door opened slowly and Laurent manoeuvred his wheelchair into the bathroom. Through the steamy haze she saw that he had a rose in his mouth. A smile she didn't think she would ever again give him touched her lips. 'What are you doing? Oh, Laurent!' He was completely naked. 'Laurent, what are you doing?'

'Hush. I'm getting into the bath with you.'

Giggles followed as he struggled with the hoist that he used to help himself into the bath. It was an ingenious device, like so many he had invented, and she had said he should patent and market it.

The splash his body made sent the soapy water in a wave, hitting her face and making her screw up her eyes and spit out the nasty-tasting suds from her mouth. 'Laurent!'

He had positioned himself behind her, in the huge bath they'd had specially made and installed in the centre of this room, which used to be a playroom, but was now divided into a luxury bathroom and dressing room. It was another alteration that made access easy for Laurent.

Once he was sitting with Edith between his leg and his stump, he pulled her towards him and whispered, 'I'm sorry. I was a beast to you. You didn't deserve it, my darling.'

As she leaned against him, a calmness came over Edith. 'I wasn't crying over you. Well, partly. I have had news.' Telling Laurent made the incredible contents of the letter real, and once more she cried, but these were tears of happiness. They were not mingled with anger at him, or at Petra, or at the sheer injustice of it all; they flowed because inside her she was beginning to feel that once more she could be whole again.

Laurent didn't interrupt her, or try to stem her tears. He just held her, stroking her hair, soothing her and letting her talk. She needed that. She needed to air her worries about Ania, without being reassured by words that couldn't know the truth.

Eventually he spoke. 'My darling, I am so happy for you. At last, news after all these years. But I don't think you should go to France, I think you should send a telegram to Marianne. Ask her to bring Elka and her young man here. There has been another announcement: France has declared war on Germany. This will mean that my country is in grave danger, because I believe Germany will invade France next. If they succeed, they will have easier access to these shores, but all of that will take time, and we can sort something out before then.'

Though this news made her heart lurch and a feeling of fear gripped her, she remained strong. 'Germany will never win; we have so many allies. They didn't beat us in the last war, and they won't this time.'

'We have to accept that Hitler is very powerful. He has prepared well – I have seen all along what his intention is. He wants to rule the world, bringing us all under German control. I am very afraid. He will wipe out the Jews and all such as me, who are maimed. We are of no use to him. He talks of a superior race. He is evil beyond words.'

'Laurent, Marianne tells me that my daughters have been brought up as Jews. Oh God, Ania is still in Poland – it will be impossible to bring her out. What if she is killed?'

'We have to think there will be a way. Remember last time? It was hope that supplied us with courage. We must latch onto that now, and continue to hold on to it. And we have to do our bit to help. I want to volunteer my services.'

'What? How? No!'

'I can't fight, but as you know, my scientific mind can be channelled into inventions, and I am good at it. With war being a possibility, these last few months, I have been concentrating my time and effort on what might be needed. I think this war will be fought on many fronts and in many ways. It will be fought in the air, on land and at sea, and I believe espionage will play a major role too. I am going to contact Winston Churchill. He is a forward-thinking man. A warrior at heart. Look at his record in the Second Boar War. He will understand. He has been advocating preparing for war against Hitler for a long time, but no one would listen to him. Now he has been appointed First Lord of the Admiralty again, and he will have a great deal of say in our country's weaponry and tactics. I will ring him. He and I got on very well, when we met at Eloise's party a few weeks ago.'

'Yes, I remember. You talked war all night, leaving me to my own devices.'

'Ha! You can talk; you and Mark talked medicine all evening, leaving poor Jennifer to amuse herself.'

'I know, but she was quite happy with Eloise. She is joining Eloise's charity, now that her children are all at boarding school. Oh, Laurent, to think that after all these years Eloise is still mopping up after the last war, providing help to the disabled and their families. I wonder what a lot of them would have done without her? And here we are, ready to go to war all over again.'

'Your own charity work continues as well, darling, and may have to expand. As you say, this war will be fought on all fronts – the home front being one of them. It is possible there will be much destruction and many orphaned children. Oh, it doesn't bear thinking about.'

'Let's not. We are getting too far ahead. Our memories are causing us to feel doom and gloom, when the Allies may crush Hitler a lot sooner than we think. I just want to snuggle into you and dream of seeing my daughter Elka, and hope for my Ania's safety.'

Laurent's arms tightened around her. Inside, a flame lit that had been ready to ignite from the moment he'd held her naked body to his, but because of what had been said earlier, she had felt unable to approach him.

It was a shock to her when, after a few moments of silence, Laurent's hands unclasped and found their way to her breasts. A moan escaped her. Sliding her body forward, she was able to turn sideways and lean her head back and offer her lips to his. His kiss, light at first, deepened into one of desire. For a moment she felt guilt rise within her, but then a miracle happened – something she never thought to know again, after the way their relationship had deteriorated. Laurent's desire showed in the hardness of him.

Afraid to do anything, she held her breath. Laurent's hoarse, whispering tone told her what she wanted to hear. 'Darling, oh, my darling, I want you. I need you. I don't know how or why, but I know that at last I can make you mine.'

Tears plopped onto his cheeks. She licked them away as she positioned herself over him and lowered herself onto her darling husband for the first time ever. Their joy didn't require any movement. Their bodies shuddered with pleasure the moment he entered her, a pleasure that had both of them crying out in sheer ecstasy as they reached the peak of an act they had so long wished for.

When they got out of the bath, she helped Laurent to dry. He made her smile as he asked, 'Is it still possible for us to make babies?'

Laughing, she said, 'Possible, but not probable. I am fifty, remember! But I'm still fertile, so you never know.'

'Would you mind very much?'

'No, I would be ecstatic! I don't feel fifty. Especially now – I feel like a young woman again; young and in love, and so very happy.'

Turning his chair towards the door, he said, 'Well then, let's go to our room, and I will show you how a Frenchman makes babies.'

'Oh, is it different from other men, then?'

'You will see.'

The flame she thought had been extinguished, with the single act of having him inside her, rekindled. Her mouth dried, the muscles in her groin tightened and it felt to her as if their life was just beginning. It was ironic that it should happen now. She had no idea why it had occurred, for the counselling had only served to sour Laurent's mood until now. Maybe it was the thought of being needed again, in a role that would fulfil him – of being useful in the fight against Hitler – that had broken him free of the restraints of impotency.

As a doctor, she knew it could take something as simple as feeling like a real man again to become one, but she hadn't known what to do to make that happen. As a woman, she felt almost grateful for the declaration of war, for no matter what it would mean in the future, for now it had given her back her husband. And she was ready; ready to get to know and accept the love-making of her darling Laurent.

Edith was startled by the shrill sound of the telephone ringing as she rested back on the pillow, every ounce of her drained by Laurent's second passionate loving of her.

'Leave it, darling.'

'I can't, I'm sorry. It might be Ada calling me. She would only do so if there was an emergency. I must answer it.'

Laurent rolled over. A contented sigh showed that he wasn't angry. As she sat up, his hand stroked her bare back, sending shivers through her. Life was, at last, on an even keel. They were a proper couple – truly man and wife, and no longer in name only. The thought thrilled her.

Ada's voice held excitement as it crackled down the phone. 'It's a girl. Leah has had a girl! By, lass, Leah were as good as gold. Did all she were told to do. She remembered all the words you'd taught her that she was likely to hear, and what they meant. I'm reet proud of her. And the babby is a grand little thing, weighing in at five pounds four ounces and with lungs on her that could shout that Hitler down!'

'Oh, that's wonderful news. Are you sure that Leah and the baby are all right? According to my calculations she had another four weeks to go!'

'Aye, Leah's a bit tearful, thinking of her mam and dad, but there's no need to worry over that, and though babby's a bit on the small side, she's fine. Not at all like a premature babby, so happen she's on her due time. I'll make sure to stay with her till Ginny gets here. I rang because I thought you'd want to know, and because Leah wants you to name the babby. It's that Sister Frances that attended the birth, and she's already called the priest to baptize babby. You know what these nuns are like – and Sister Frances is the holiest of them all. She heard the news about war beginning and thinks Hitler's on his way already, and that all babbies should be christened immediately, just in case.'

Edith joined in with Ada's laughter. 'Oh, Ada, you're a tonic. But I'm honoured to be asked to name our latest little one. Let me think. Oh, I know: *Felicia*. In France it is a name that means "great happiness". Felicia Marianne. Yes, I think that very appropriate, and it fits how I feel right at the moment, as well as honouring someone I love very much who is also French, as Leah is.'

'Grand. You sound happy. Different, somehow. Sommat tells me that I really shouldn't have disturbed you. Well, I'll not keep you. But I'll say this: whatever has lifted you from the sadness that's been lurking in your eyes of late, hang on to it, love, as Chamberlain's announcement is enough to dampen us all, if we let it.'

'Oh, we won't do that. No little man with a silly moustache stands a chance against the forces that drive us, Ada. I just wish Hitler wouldn't try. But you are right. I'm filled with great happiness. I won't go into details, but I've heard from Elka and—'

A scream of joy cut off her words. It brought home the reality, as only sharing the news with Ada could.

'Yes, yes, it's true. Oh, Ada. At last. At last . . .'

'I can't believe it. How? Eeh, the day of doom and gloom has turned into a grand day. But I have to go; tell me all about it tomorrow. By, lass, I'm reet happy for you.'

'Thank you, Ada. Sharing it with you has made it complete. You've been by my side throughout it all, and have been a source of strength and comfort to me. Give Leah my love, and little Felicia a hug from me. I'll see you tomorrow.'

Ada's goodbye was full of unspoken emotion. Edith stood for a moment after replacing the receiver. *Tomorrow: I wonder what that will bring. Every day brings something. Today has brought happiness, as well as trepidation about what the future holds for us all.*

But she wouldn't think of all the tomorrows, or of the war. She'd go back to bed and snuggle up to her darling Laurent, and bask in the three prongs of happiness that had assailed her: hearing about Elka and Ania; the arrival of Leah's baby; and feeling, at last, like a fulfilled and true wife to Laurent.

# 8

# *Ania*

### Poland, October 1939 – A City Under Siege

'You should have gone . . . you should have gone.'

'Hush, Babcia. We will be all right.' But even as she said this, Ania could feel the eyes of the Nazi soldiers, who were on guard along the Vistula embankment, following their progress.

'We're Jews. They hate us. Even though they have only been here for three weeks, the Nazis are turning Jews out of their homes and taking possession of them for themselves. They are bound to want our block, for it is one of the most beautiful and well kept. They will kill us.'

'No. I have heard they resettle Jews and take their businesses and homes, it's true. But that is all – they don't kill them. And yes, the stories about the conditions that Jews are forced to live under in other countries are horrendous, but this war won't last; the same won't happen here. The British and French won't let it happen. It will all be over soon. We just have to do all that we can to survive.' Ania's words were brave, but she didn't believe them. Stories of Jews being beaten with sticks and turfed out onto the streets were already circulating, and they terrified her.

'But we don't know what Britain is doing. No news is coming through, because it's all cut off. Oh, Ania, I will not survive, I know it. Leave me. Please, Ania. Flee the city before it is too late.'

'I can't. I have to stay. Baruch has already said there will be work for me to do. The Resistance will regroup. We will fight back.'

'But what of me?'

'Don't be afraid, Babcia. I won't abandon you. But I don't know how it will all work out. We still have to plan everything. Baruch is hoping that if I tell the Germans I was adopted and that I can speak many languages, they will consider me useful. Then I may get taken on in a job where I can have access to information that might be very valuable to the Resistance.'

'You have told Baruch who you really are?'

'Yes, but it seems many in the community had already expressed their opinions of me and Elka, saying that we do not look like Jews, with our golden-coloured hair; and that our features are those of Western Europeans. So Baruch had wondered for a long time if I was a true-born Polish Jewess. Come on, let's make our way home.'

'I didn't know that, but that's good. The Germans won't recognize you instantly as a Jew. But doing what you plan will put you in great danger! How can Baruch ask this of you?'

'It is not him asking, Babcia; it is Poland and her Jewish community. Much will be asked of us all. We have to fight back.'

Some of Ania's tenants, all Jews, were standing in the doorway of their apartment block as they turned into Starowisina. An assortment of bags and sacks was scattered around them. Behind them and across the street stood armed soldiers, their guns pointing at the group.

'What's happening? Is everyone all right?'

Frightened, hollow eyes turned her way. Some of the men nodded their heads. The women wept. The children, some of whom were her pupils, looked too afraid to cry, but the shaking of their bodies told her how they felt.

'Ruben? Joseph? What is going on?'

'We have been told to gather our things, as we are needed for labouring jobs.'

A truck rumbled along the street towards them.

'But what of the jobs you already have? And what of your shop, Ruben?'

A sharp pain jagged her side. A rough German voice told her to move along. Babcia's voice screeched in protest. Ania turned towards the soldier who had dug the butt of his gun into her side, and asked him in German why he thought he could treat the Polish people in this way.

'*Du sprichst Deutsch?*'

'*Ja.* I speak many languages.'

In German he ordered her to tell the women and children to go back inside. 'Tell them their men are going to work at Plaszow and will return in a week.'

'If that is so, why are they taking so many belongings with them? And what is the nature of the work?'

The soldier cocked his gun. '*Tu was dir gesagt wird.*'

Deciding that she would be wise to do as he said and obey his orders, Ania turned to the crowd that had now gathered.

'Inside, everyone. Your men will be home in a week's time. Come along. Everyone keep together and we will all be all right. Have you done the work on your English, children?'

'Ania!'

'Babcia, don't criticize me. We have to keep things normal for the children. If they see us breaking up, what do they have to cling to or look up to?' In a louder voice she said, 'I will expect you all in my apartment at six tonight. You older ones will have an hour working on your English papers, and you younger ones will have an hour of French conversation. Educated people will be needed, no matter what their race. Remember that.'

Her words worked. The women ushered their children inside, shouting goodbyes to their menfolk as they did so. Ania felt relief as the threatening atmosphere dispersed. But most heartening of all was seeing the children lose that look of despair, even if only temporarily. *Teacher doesn't think the men are leaving permanently, so that can't be what's happening* – that is what she had tried to impart. For five minutes of this appalling hour, when it looked as if all their fears were becoming a reality, it seemed that she had succeeded.

But as she looked back and saw the bullying tactics the soldiers employed, as they herded the men towards the truck, she knew that the five minutes were just that, and that the world as they had known it had truly ended.

She thought of Elka and thanked God, as she had done a million times, that she had escaped to safety. Already she had received a letter from her sister. It had spoken of the beautiful South of France, of what a wonderful woman Marianne was, and of her excitement at the possibility of meeting their birth mother; and about their mother's entire family, which was now their family, too. But none of that fitted with what Ania's eyes and ears had to contend with at this moment.

'Babcia, go upstairs. I will come up in a moment. I want to try and get more information about what is happening.'

'Be careful, my dear Ania, be careful.'

Looking out into the street, Ania saw that several trucks were now full of men of around forty years of age and under. The noise, as they gathered speed driving towards the river and then turning right, shook the old buildings in the street. Dust billowed around her. Silent, sullen folk milled about. To one, a Polish butcher she knew well, she called out, 'Do you know what is happening, Józef?'

'They are going to build some kind of barracks, or camp. No one is sure what its purpose is, but it is to be built in Plaszow.'

'So it is true: the men are only going to work?'

'Not in that way. They are not going willingly; it is forced labour.'

'Were they all Jewish?'

'No, there were many non-Jewish Poles, too. Those selected were the fittest.'

With lessons over, the children left. As she closed the door on the last of them, Ania savoured the smell of the stew their maid had placed on the table. She knew it would be mostly liquid. On their trip to the market that afternoon she and Babcia had found only one stall selling fish. The trader had just a few scraps left. They had bought these and a bag of fish heads. Together with the potatoes that one of their neighbour's sons had brought in on his bicycle, from a farm on the outskirts of the city, a meal of sorts had been put together. Ania didn't care how unpalatable it was; she was really hungry and would savour every mouthful.

As Babcia helped herself from the delicate bone-china tureen she said, 'Ania, when you were growing up, you were very shy. You always bowed down to Elka's demands. You preferred to play with your dolls, or to study, whilst she was the leader and played boy-type games. I looked on her as the strong one, the determined one, and on you as the gentle, kind-hearted one. But you are showing that you have the strength and courage that your mother had. I am proud of you.'

'Thank you, Babcia. Tell me all you know of my mother, as I fear I may never meet her.'

Babcia didn't deny this, but went on to tell Ania what she remembered of Edith. As Ania listened, she tried to picture her mother in her head. What she heard, she liked. She hadn't wanted to feel love for this woman who had given birth to her. It had been too painful, and it felt like a betrayal of the woman who had brought her up, nurtured and loved her. But then Babcia Petra spoke of Edith with love, so why shouldn't she allow herself to feel some emotion towards Edith, too?

'Did you love my mother, Babcia?'

'I did. And I hope that one day she will forgive me, because what I did, I did for the love of my own daughter, and because of my fear of what might happen to you both.'

'Let's leave it at that. I forgive you, and I think Elka will in time. Now, I have to go out. I have to meet up with Baruch.'

'No, I beg of you . . .'

'Babcia Petra, I must.'

These words quietened her grandmother and she made no further protest as Ania kissed her head. Taking her jacket from the hook behind the entrance door, Ania left the room.

On reaching the bottom of the stairs, she turned in the opposite direction to the front door and made her way towards the cellar door. Unlocking it, she slipped inside. Sliding the bolt across the moment she'd closed the door behind her, she descended the many steps into the dark, dank space below. Routes that would be less likely to be discovered by the Germans had been established by Baruch and his followers, in preparation for a possible occupation by the Nazis. Now that was a reality, and what they had done enabled movement without detection, and for meetings to take place. But not without fear – that was one factor none of them had thought of, as they'd gallantly made their plans.

A shudder went through Ania as she made her way along the wall, remembering where each trunk of essentials and oddments was stored, until she came to a cupboard. She felt for the handle, moving the two shelves that held a panel in place and then lifting it out. Behind lay a gap that led to the cellar next door, and then to a door leading through to their courtyard.

As she climbed through and replaced everything that would cover the escape route, she realized that one day she might need to do this in terrifying circumstances, and not just to see her darling Baruch. *Am I up to it? Will I cope?* Dismissing the negative thoughts that crowded in on her, she took a deep breath and told herself: *I am, and I will. If called upon to do vital but dangerous work, I will find the courage to do it, from somewhere.* They were brave words, but they didn't quell the fear that clutched at her chest.

As she slipped through the gate and into the alley behind, Baruch's waiting arms encircled her. The fear died as her heart quickened. This is where she belonged, where she could forget everything. But then his anxious voice grounded her once more, with the enormity of how their lives had changed. 'My darling, you are safe. I worried so much when I heard what was happening in your street earlier.'

'Yes, I am here. A soldier shoved the butt of his gun into my side and I am bruised, but that is all. It is worrying that they took the men, and made them take so much with them. They say they will be back after a week, but I don't believe it.'

'Neither do I. I think they are being forced to build a labour camp – a concentration camp. It is what has happened in Germany, and there is talk that some men have been taken to Germany to work, too.'

'Oh, Baruch. What will become of us? The Resistance didn't even get a chance to fight.'

'I know – it was hopeless. Once Mayor Klimecki surrendered, there was nothing to be done. Though I have never known a braver man: riding out to meet the Germans and asking them to stop shooting, as Krakow was defenceless, and offering himself as a hostage, took a great deal of courage. We had to lay down our arms, but many of our number were shot, and some were hanged in the square, in full public view. Only a few of us were able to sneak back into society without being detected.'

'Oh, my darling. What will you do?'

'We are going to find a hiding place in the Tatra Mountains, around Zakopane.'

'But when will I see you again?'

'I don't know, but we will establish a link along the way, so that I can send messages to you and you can contact me. We are in touch with a man who will help us, Major Jan Wlodarkiewicz. He has formed a secret army in Warsaw. We are going to be attached to his unit eventually. He is in the process of organizing everything at the moment. We had a message from him that told us we will be a much-needed force; that all past hurts must be put aside, and that we Jews are not looked on as different from the rest any longer. We are all Polish – Jews and Gentiles – and we must fight together.'

'That is a good thing for him to say, and it puts my heart at rest. We can only fight our enemy if we stand as one. What will happen now?'

'The major will send someone to instruct us. I told his messenger about you. He sent a reply saying that all of those who are fighting for freedom would be in your debt and greatly helped by having someone with the language skills you possess. He asked if you would be willing to try and get work in the government offices the Germans have set up, or at Gestapo headquarters. He says to do so, you will need to denounce your Jewish faith.'

'I have already thought of that, but . . .'

'It may be the only way you can help our people.'

Leaning heavily against the wall, Ania felt her world collapsing. 'What of Babcia Petra?'

'She will have to be sacrificed. She does not deserve your love and loyalty. She is the reason you are here, and not with your real mother in England, away from the danger and the persecution that our people suffer. You are English.'

'Don't ever say that, Baruch. That persecutes me. You are separating me from all I have ever known. From yourself even. I am a Jew, and I am Polish. And I will remain of that faith, and that nationality, for the rest of my life.'

'I am sorry. I just want you to be safe, but I also want you to see that you can help our people far more by denying your Jewish faith.'

She could see that, but how was she going to do such a thing as deny her own grandmother? Whatever Baruch and Elka thought, to her Petra would always be her beloved Babcia: her grandmother. 'I – I will think about it. I will discuss it with our rabbi. Whatever he decides I should do, I will do.'

'Ania, my darling, it hurts me to ask this of you, when all I want to do is protect you, but we have been forced into this situation. I love you, Ania.' He stepped towards her once more and took her in his arms. 'I have something planned. I know I should not ask it of you at such a time, but will you marry me?'

'Oh, Baruch, yes. Yes. But when? How?'

'Right now. The rabbi is waiting for us. He and my family agree that the marriage must be conducted in words only. There can be no entry in the register, or any papers that tie us together.'

She felt like crying out at the injustice of the world. A world that was making her deny her faith and the man she loved. But Baruch's grip tightened on her and helped to steady her. Locked as she was in his arms, everything seemed possible. Everything would be all right.

'Come, my darling, we have to go to Stara Synagogue.

I will have a message sent to Petra to tell her that you are safe with me and are staying with my family tonight.'

It all seemed so incredible. Here she was: recognized as Baruch's wife, having gone through the rituals that made her so, without any records being made. She'd had the shortest and simplest ceremony possible. Only Baruch's mother, father and sister – and her husband – had attended.

After the ceremony they had laughed at silly jokes whilst enjoying the little feast the rabbi had managed to get together, as if nothing was amiss and the world was as it should be.

And now the marriage bed awaited them. Baruch's sister, Ruta, and her husband, Chavivi, had prepared their own bed and had left their home to spend the night with Baruch's parents.

Alone with Baruch after such a happy evening, Ania felt the nerves in her stomach twitch. This was the moment she had longed for, and yet she felt such fear. She didn't know what was expected of her. What she did know of the act that was to take place seemed a very strange thing for a man and a woman to do, and yet she longed to do it with Baruch.

'Are you all right, my Ania – my wife?'

'Yes, just a little nervous.'

'Don't be. I am not experienced, but I know that we will help each other. Come here.'

Meeting at the bottom of the bed, they held each other. It was a moment that turned into a deep kiss. Never had Baruch kissed her like this before. Such passion and longing came from him and lit a response in her, so that she did not object as he began to peel her clothes from her. His fingers were not practised at this task and so, laughing at his attempts to undo her buttoned frock, she moved away from him and undid as many buttons as were necessary for it to fall to her feet and for her to step out of it.

Baruch gazed at her for a moment and then, tugging at her silk slip, whispered, 'Everything. I want to see you without clothes.' Her giggles died, and her earlier feelings intensified as she complied with his wishes and saw that he, too, was undressing.

They stood naked now. Their breath came in short gasps. Their eyes held each other's. There was a tension between them, as if an invisible wire held them entwined. Both moved towards the other at the same time.

Their union just happened, and it was as if they had been lovers forever. Neither had any expectation of the other – they just were as they were meant to be. They cried tears of joy, whilst clinging and calling out to each other. There was no final relief from Baruch on entering her, and neither was there much pain; Ania had expected more, from the tales she'd heard. Instead, as Baruch pulled out of her after quickly reaching his climax, Ania had a sense of something that she had missed out on – something she still sought.

This feeling grew as she returned Baruch's kisses with a fervour she hadn't known herself capable of. With her shyness now gone, she sought to hold him in her hand for the first time. Finding that he did not reject her touch, but responded to it, she tentatively slid her hand along the length of him. His moans of pleasure gave her permission. Her movements increased and Baruch pulled her close, his free hands finding and stroking the heart of her womanhood.

Now she knew for sure there was something more for

her. Building inside her was an urgency. A need. Something she almost fought against, as she was afraid it would draw her into it. When, finally, they joined together again, a crescendo of intense feelings swathed her. Wave after wave of deep, indescribable pleasure made her claw at Baruch and holler her joy, as she savoured the last surge of the beautiful, all-consuming sensations.

As a calmness stilled her, she knew she had nothing else to give. Lying under Baruch, she took his urgent thrusts, unable even to muster the strength to hold him, until his voice rasped with joy and he slumped down on her.

They clung together for a long time, both sobbing, without knowing why.

But then they had a lot to cry about. Not least the terror that the future held, and the deep sadness of not knowing when, after tonight, they would ever see each other again.

# 9

# *Ginny*

## London, October 1939 – Finding Recognition

'Oh, she's a bonny little thing.'

'Bonny? What is this "bonny"?'

'Ha, it's a good thing, so don't be worrying yourself. It means she is a pretty girl – *belle fille* – I think. Is that reet?'

'Ah, *oui*, Felicia is good pretty.'

'Oh, Leah lass, I wonder if we'll ever get to talk to each other properly, but we must keep trying. You should say: "very pretty", not "good pretty". "Very."'

'Felicia is very pretty.'

Ginny clapped her hands. 'Well done.'

Conversation *was* getting easier between them, as Leah was making rapid progress with her English. But Ginny was also proud of the few words she'd learned in French. Her imagination had been fired by the romantic sound of it, and by her desire to converse properly with Leah. *And if I'm honest*, she thought, *I have to admit that learning French is bringing me closer to Brendan*. She'd been surprised to learn that Brendan spoke French. She'd been discussing with him her desire to be able to communicate with Leah when he'd told her that he would be able to help. He'd explained to her how Edith and Lady Eloise had paid for a private education for him, and how he'd been taught languages and had a natural aptitude. He'd said that French was his favourite. By, she loved the conversations she had with Brendan, and learning a new French phrase from him every day.

Ginny knew she was treading dangerous water. But something compelled her to flirt with Brendan. He occupied her every waking hour – and a good bit of her sleeping ones. She had wished a million times that they weren't related.

Her job here, in Jimmy's Hope House, helped. It was a busy place and she was always needed somewhere.

'Reet, let's shift you over and rub your buttocks, Leah. We don't want you getting bedsores or owt. You've still another four days in bed. Then after I've made you comfortable, I'll give you Felicia and you can put her to your breast. It's three hours since she last suckled, the lazy madam.' Ginny accompanied what she said with miming actions.

Leah understood, but now she looked indignant. '*Madame*? Felicia? *Non*, she is *mademoiselle*!'

Ginny laughed out loud. 'It's just sommat we say, when . . . Ha, never mind. Oh, Dr Edith, am I glad to see you come through the door.'

'Is there something wrong?'

'Naw. I'm just about to make Leah comfortable, which she understands, as it's our routine every day, even if she doesn't understand the actual words. But I've blundered by referring to Felicia as a "little madam". I said it because she isn't waking up for her feeds. Leah is all confused.'

'Ah! Don't worry, I'll explain.' Dr Edith laughed as she told Leah what Ginny had meant. But after Edith left, the smile on Leah's face changed to a twisted sob.

'Eeh, Leah, what's to do, lass, what's to do?'

'*Ma mère et mon père . . .*'

This Ginny did understand, and doing so cut her in two. She knew the words stood for 'mam' and 'dad', and the sobs – well, the loss of parents was something they both had in common. Swallowing a huge lump, she sat down on the side of the bed and thanked God that she'd talked to Brendan about this possibility happening, and what she could say to show she understood. His reply had been, '*Je comprends. Ma mère et mon père sont morts récemment*' – 'I understand, as my own mam and dad have recently died.' She'd practised and practised it, and now it came out as a sob that she'd never intended.

Leah's tiny hands took hold of hers.

They sat like that for a moment, each in a pit of misery. Ginny couldn't comprehend how bad this girl must be feeling. She was three years younger than herself and in a foreign country, where she'd been treated so badly. Now she'd given birth, and all whilst coping with the death of her parents.

More tears sprang from Ginny at these thoughts. Lying beside Leah, she held the girl to her and together they sobbed out their grief.

It was a few days later, when Leah was up and about and helping Ginny, that Leah asked, 'Have you a man?'

Whilst Leah felt she was mostly following Ginny around, Ginny didn't mind, as they had somehow found comfort in each other's company.

'Naw, I've been too busy training for me job to bother with men.' She was getting quite good at miming as she spoke. Leah understood straight away.

'But Brendan, no? You like him?'

A burning sensation crept from Ginny's neck and spread over her face. 'Eeh, naw – he's me relative!' Seeing a blank look on Leah's face, Ginny just laughed.

'Oh? But you very pretty, you should have a man.'

Ginny sighed. It was as if everyone thought a woman couldn't function without a man by her side. It shocked and surprised her that Leah should think like this. If young women didn't stand up for equality, who would? 'Have you a man, Leah?'

'*Non*. I detest men!'

Ginny laughed at this. 'Every lass who's just given birth hates men. You wait, love. Six weeks down the line, you'll be back to normal. I – I mean . . .' For once Ginny hoped Leah hadn't understood, as that seemed a callous thing to say. And in Leah's case, she probably would hate men for a lot longer than was usual.

There was still a jumpiness about Leah, as if fear was her constant companion. 'Look, you're alreet here, you've nowt to worry over. Come on, help me change all the babbies' bottoms. That'll take your mind off everything. We only have to do this in the afternoon while the new mums are resting, thank goodness. The smell's worse than the gas works. I just don't know how something as lovely and fresh as a newborn babby can produce such stinky poos.'

Whether or not Leah got the gist of what she'd said, Ginny wasn't sure. But she laughed and screwed up her nose, asking, 'Stinky poos? What is this?'

'Follow me, I'll show you.'

They had six babies in the nursery, all under eight weeks old, which Ada had told her was a bit unusual. The nannies were finding it difficult to cope, so Ginny had taken on a couple of their duties, changing nappies and helping to bottle-feed the two babies whose mothers refused to take to them to their breasts.

Ginny loved this new job and was more taken with midwifery and nursery duties than she thought she would be, but something was missing. '*Eeh, lass*,' she told herself, '*it's the hospital you miss.*' And she knew she missed caring for the sick and the dying, the comforting of them and doing what she could for them – the wonderful feeling when they recovered, and the peace inside her when she'd helped someone in their last moments; plus the drama . . . well, all of it.

With a shudder she realized that this step she'd taken, in the midst of her anguish, probably wasn't the one she should have taken. But how could she ever leave this place now? Being here, at Jimmy's Hope House, felt as though she was honouring the memory of her dad. How could she turn round – after all the kindness shown to her, and the happiness brought to her granny through having her here – and say it wasn't for her. Shrugging her shoulders, Ginny pulled herself up. *By, snap out of it – give it a chance. Best foot forward, Mam would say. Oh Mam, Mam . . .*

Looking over at Leah, Ginny watched her cradle little Felicia to her and wondered how Leah would feel, or act, when the time came to make her decision. All unmarried mothers' homes had a ruling that the baby was taken from the mother after the first few weeks, no matter what, and put up for adoption. But here the mothers could make their own decision. If they chose to keep their child, they were supported for a while until they could get back on their feet – they were housed and were helped to train for a job, if necessary. If they chose adoption, then they were helped in that too, because families taking babbies from here had to agree to let the mother stay in contact, if she wanted to. It was a wonderful system that worked, and all without the word 'shame' – or anything of that nature – being uttered.

Suddenly the scene in front of her changed, and a stab of fear pierced Ginny. Leah shook Felicia as she cried out in anguish, '*Mon bébé, mon* bébé*!*'

Ginny rushed towards her. 'Leah! Leah, what—' Her words were drowned out by a howl of pain-filled terror, a sound like none she'd ever heard. With it, despair filled Ginny.

Near enough now to see Felicia, her heart dropped at the blueness of her skin. Grabbing the baby from Leah, she lay her down. Frantically she searched her memory for something she and a few nurses had giggled over – a book containing ancient methods of medicine. In it they had read many funny things, but one had held their interest: a discovery in the eighteenth century by the Chinese of how to save a drowning person. Among the strange suggestions, such as blowing tobacco smoke into the rectum using a pipe, had been blowing air into the lungs by placing your own mouth over the patient's. *It has to be worth a try. Owt's better than nowt. Oh God, help me – help me.*

'Leah, stop screaming and fetch Dr Edith. GO . . . Dr Edith, NOW!'

As Leah ran out of the nursery, her howl became one long scream of Edith's name. The nursery throbbed with the sound of terrified babies, taking over Ginny's thought processes and leaving her confused. Pulling herself together, she lowered the sides of the cot and placed her mouth over Felicia's. Concentrating fully now, she decided that as the lungs in this case were so tiny, she'd better go carefully. A gentle puff, then remove her mouth. The baby's chest expanded, but didn't go back down. Ginny pressed lightly on the little chest and felt air brush her cheek. Blowing a second time and then pressing gently, she saw a little of the blueness fade. Encouraged now, she continued. '*Come on – breathe, Felicia, breathe.*'

On her fourth attempt, hope rippled through her as she pressed the air out and little Felicia gasped another lungful of her own accord. Tears of joy and anguish flowed down Ginny's cheeks. 'Oh, thank you, God, thank you. Keep going, little one, keep going.'

The door of the nursery opened and Edith, Ada and Leah dashed in. 'What's happening, Nurse Ginny?'

'She stopped breathing, Doctor, but she's breathing again now. I – I blew into her mouth.' As Edith examined the child, Ginny explained about the Chinese method and how she came to know about it.

'Good work. I think it might be the same book that I and my colleagues laughed over, but all of us have since used various methods from it.'

They stood in silence as they watched Edith working. Granny Ada stood on one side of the trembling Leah, and Ginny on the other. Reaching her arm around Leah's tiny shoulders, Ginny felt her granny's arm already there. They looked over at each other. Concern was etched on Ada's face.

Irritated by a noise that Ginny had ceased to hear or

take any notice of, Edith asked, 'Please see what you can all do to quieten the babies. I can't hear through my stethoscope.'

Leah didn't move, but Ginny and Ada raced around the cots on a hopeless mission, until Ada said, 'In that cupboard over there, Ginny, there's a bowl full of rubber pacifiers. Fetch them as fast as you can and stick one in each of their mouths.'

It worked. The only noise now was that of sucking, and the occasional sob from the little ones who had been really distressed. Those who had just been venting their frustration now lay content. 'Eeh, thank God,' Ada said as they returned to Felicia's cot.

Leah had quietened now, though her body trembled and her face was a pitiful mix of love and fear. There was nothing Ginny could say; she could only hold Leah to her and try to give her some of her own strength.

Edith straightened her back. She took a deep intake of breath. The expression on her face was one Ginny had seen hundreds of times on the faces of other doctors.

'We need to get Felicia to hospital.' Looking at Leah, Edith repeated this and added something in French. Leah let out a moan of anguish. Holding her tighter, Ginny asked, 'What's wrong with babby, Doctor?'

Edith shook her head. 'I'm not sure. I need to have her looked at by a heart specialist. I think she may have a heart defect. I'll take her myself. Leah can come with me. She needs to, but she can also carry Felicia. It will be the best comfort for both her and the little one.'

'I'll stay here as long as I'm needed. Is there anything outstanding?'

'Aye, and me,' Ada chipped in. 'I won't leave Ginny.'

'Thanks, both of you. Ginny, it was a wonderful thing that you did. Without it, Felicia would have died before I got to her.'

Ginny said nothing. To her, it was her job – what she existed to do.

As she walked towards the door Edith said, 'Would you check on Maisie Brown for me? I was on my way to her. She's due any time. And there's a child in the sick bay: Reggie Garrop. I had left him till last as I think, by the reporting of his symptoms, that he may have measles. If he has, isolate him and set things in motion to check the other children when they come back from school. Thanks, Ginny. Oh, here.' Edith paused at the door and dug her keys from her white coat pocket. 'The small one is for the medicine cupboard – there's a list in there of the regular doses for those in the sick bay. But little Reggie may need something for the fever, and, if things move on, Maisie will need an enema. I'll leave it all in your capable hands.'

The door swung closed behind her, leaving Ginny with a mixture of feelings. Fear for little Felicia was the biggest of these, but a sense of pride nudged it. Edith trusted her. She had recognized her skills and felt comfortable with giving her the responsibility that she knew Ginny was capable of.

Not that she had felt belittled in any way, but so far it had felt as if Edith thought she was making all the medical decisions herself. Now, at last, Ginny felt a proper part of Jimmy's Hope House, and a settled feeling entered her, though it didn't give her the peace it normally would have done, as her heart feared for little Felicia and for Leah.

*

Not two hours later, her fears were founded as Edith returned to the home with Leah.

As they entered the office where Ginny sat, she knew that the worst had happened.

There was a stillness about Leah. As if she'd closed down her inner self. Her pale face seemed smaller and more pinched, and her mouth was set in a hard line and looked as though it would never stretch into a smile again.

Edith, too, had a look about her that told of despair.

Standing on legs that would hardly hold her upright, Ginny asked, 'Felicia?' At Edith's despairing shake of her head, Ginny's body swayed, but she got a grip on herself. Leah would need her now. 'Oh, Leah, I am so sorry. *Je suis désolé.*'

A tear seeped out of the corner of Leah's eyes as she stared at Ginny.

'Sit down. Come on, take a seat here, lass.'

This time Edith translated, but Leah had understood what Ginny said, as she was already making for the chair that stood in the corner of the office.

'What can I do for you, dear Leah? What can I do?'

'Nothing. *Rien, rien.*'

'I – I . . .'

'All we can do is be here for her, Ginny. It seems an inadequate thing, but nothing can ease the pain of Leah's loss. Can you get a sleeping draught and prepare it for her? I'll pop along and get her a hot drink of cocoa. She likes that.'

As Edith left, a sound came from Leah that echoed around the room.

'Oh, Leah. Leah, me poor lass. Eeh, I can almost touch your pain. Tell me what happened?'

'She die. *Elle est morte* . . . Oh, *mon Dieu, aidez-moi* – help me!'

Ginny dropped to her knees beside Leah and held the girl's shivering body.

'I held her . . . in my arms. She die.'

Still Ginny held Leah close to her. There was nothing she could say. Nothing that would help.

'Her eyes. They look at me. Then they close – Felicia gone, gone; *disparue, disparue.* No, noooo!'

The door opened and Edith came back in. 'Oh dear, poor Leah.' She crouched in front of Leah and spoke to her in French in a soothing tone. Ginny struggled to understand. But her words did have a calming effect on Leah. Turning her head towards Ginny, Edith asked, 'Will you bring the sleeping draught along to her bed, Ginny?'

'Yes, but – well, I was planning on sleeping over, as Maisie is progressing now and I thought they might call me during the night. But what if we instruct them to call the district midwife and I make up the other bed in the overnight room? Leah could sleep in there with me, and I can take care of her.'

'Yes, that would be a good idea. Thank you, Ginny. Does Ada know you're staying over?'

'Yes, I sent her home. She were dead on her feet, bless her.'

'Um, I know how that feels, and you must be tired, too. Thank you for everything, Ginny. I feel as though I have a right-hand woman on the medical side now, and it has taken a lot of pressure off me.'

This warmed Ginny's aching heart a little and she managed a smile. Edith smiled back, and Ginny felt that she had found a friend in Edith. Not just acceptance because she was Ada's grandchild, but real acceptance for herself and her skills.

With Leah asleep, Ginny lay awake thinking over what Edith had told her: when they'd reached the hospital, the heart specialist – a friend of Edith's – was waiting for them. Whilst he was examining Felicia she stopped breathing again. They tried to resuscitate her, but she didn't respond. The specialist suspected a congenital heart condition, but his post-mortem would reveal what type it had been. In the meantime, gentle questioning of Leah had revealed that she had been exposed to rubella, as it had been rife amongst the girls in the house where she had been held captive for weeks. By the time she came to Edith, she had been clear of the infection and had been afraid to tell Edith of it, in case she couldn't take her in.

But it made no difference now. Nor would it have done. As Leah was clear of rubella when she arrived at Jimmy's Hope House, Edith would have taken her in whether or not she'd known. Yes, she would have monitored Felicia closely, but such defects often didn't show until the child had begun to develop and wasn't doing so as quickly as other children, or had sweating bouts and feeding difficulties. Felicia had shown the last symptom already, as it hadn't been easy to get her to take, or keep down, her feed. *Poor little mite, she must have had a severe defect, for it to have taken her so quickly.*

Ginny curled up in a ball. Her heart felt heavy and her chest clogged with tears, but she didn't give way to them. She had to stay strong for Leah. And she would. Whatever it took, she would help Leah through this.

# 10
# *Elka*

## France, late October 1939 – A Reunion is Planned

'Oh, Jhona, why didn't we force Ania to come with us? Kidnap her, or something. I can't bear this parting from her, and not knowing if she is all right.'

Jhona switched off the wireless. 'Tell me: what were the details of the news broadcast? What has intensified your fears, darling? My French still isn't good enough to translate it all.'

They were standing by the wireless in the small breakfast room just off the main kitchen of Marianne's apartment. Sparsely furnished, it contained only a small round table with four chairs and a sideboard on which the wireless stood – though there was nothing sparse about the design of the furniture because, like everything in the apartment, it was elaborately carved and the table had a solid, mottled-green marble top.

With her voice reflecting her anguish, Elka related the news broadcast. 'The last of the Polish Army has surrendered to the Germans. And now Russia is moving forward into our territory, too. Poland is completely occupied. Warsaw is all but flattened. The Germans have set up their government office in Krakow and are reported to be killing, or deporting, Jews. Oh God, why, oh why?'

'What is it, my dear? Why are you so distressed?' On Marianne's entry into the room, Elka jumped back from the embrace Jhona had been giving her. Marianne protested at this. 'Oh, you mustn't leave Jhona's arms on account of me, Elka. It's where you should be. You Polish are as cold as the British, when it comes to love. I can't imagine why you two aren't sleeping together, as you are obviously in love.'

'But not married and—'

Marianne cut Jhona short. 'Oh, for goodness' sake, get married then! What is marriage, other than the issuing of someone's permission to allow what God has intended to be joined! Why do you need it? Follow your hearts. With the news full of doom and gloom, who knows what little time the world has left.'

Elka smiled at the adorable Marianne. 'We know you are right, but we can't come to terms with your ways.'

'Well, see a rabbi – or whatever it takes. Rid yourselves of your frustrations. But first, I have two letters for you, one from each of the people I know you are worrying about.'

'Oh, thank God. Jhona, will you tell Marianne the news we have heard about Poland? I need to read my letters.'

Hurrying away from them both, Elka went to the room that Marianne had always said was Edith's favourite. She sat on the window seat where she knew her mama had often sat for hours when visiting.

She tore open the letter from Ania. Her heart sank at the contents. Though happy for Ania that she was married to her love, Baruch, Elka couldn't help feeling a pang of regret. They had always said they would have a double wedding. Besides, she didn't like Baruch – he was trouble with a capital T.

Reading on gave her further concerns:

> *I don't know how much information you are getting about what is happening, but as I write this letter, we are completely under the rule of the German Reich here in Krakow. It is difficult to get letters out. I used a courier for this one, bribing him with a high price, and pray you receive it.*

At this point Ania switched from Polish to Yiddish and spoke of her marriage and of the work being asked of her.

'Oh no! Don't let this happen, please.'

Elka hadn't realized this had come out so loudly, but the door opened and Jhona and Marianne stood there, looking very concerned and asking what was wrong. Neither of them reacted the way she thought they would to her news.

'But surely it is good that she has her man by her side? And the young have to fight back. Who will do so, if they don't?'

'Marianne is right, darling. And Baruch is not a bad fellow. His heart is good. Yes, he is a political animal, but we Jews need people like him to stand up for us. Ania could do a lot worse.'

'But she is thinking of working for this Resistance group, and as a spy! My God, if she is caught . . .'

'It hasn't happened yet. Her ideals are sound, and she is in the very best position to do such work. I think she would easily secure a job interpreting, and this will lead her to discover valuable information. She will be safe as long as she denounces her Jewish faith. God, and the Jews, will forgive her for that.'

'But what if they don't believe her, Jhona?'

'Her story is convincing. She has just found out that the woman she thought of as her grandmother stole her at birth. Now she hates her, and all Jews. It is perfect. And she has proof!'

'I'm so afraid for her. I can't bear it.'

'War gives things to us all that we cannot bear. But take heart,' Marianne told them. 'The French and the British are amassing on the Belgium border. They will defeat the Germans. And soon the Germans will have to take their troops out of Poland and Czechoslovakia to fight, and both countries will be liberated.'

'And if that doesn't happen, I intend to fight. I—'

'No, Jhona!' This had come out fiercely, but as it hung in the air between them, Elka knew she was wrong to have said it, and now changed her mind. 'No, you are right. Ania is right. You all are. I will fight, too.'

'Then will you marry me? I think Marianne is right about that, too. We should not waste a moment of our love for each other.'

'Oh, Jhona, I will.'

Marianne clapped her hands in joy. Elka was whisked from her seat and twirled round by Jhona. Their laughter filled the room. Somehow it felt right to rejoice, despite all that was happening in the world around them.

'We should have champagne!'

'Ha-ha, let me read the rest of my letters first. I will join you in a moment.'

*How surreal is that! One minute I am experiencing deep anxiety, and the next I am being proposed to, and dancing around the room.*

Reality hit hard as Elka continued reading Ania's letter. Petra was deteriorating. Food was hard to come by, as the supply chains had dried up and Jews were only allowed to shop in certain shops; and many of the menfolk from the apartment block had been taken to work in a labour camp. The Germans were turning people out of their homes and onto the street, taking their homes for themselves. They hadn't yet taken her own and Ania's apartment block, but it was crammed to the rafters with displaced Jews.

Ania told of her sadness at not seeing Baruch, and of her love for him making her life feel complete, now that they were married. Sitting quietly for a moment, Elka absorbed this and all the other news the letter held. Sadness and fear enfolded her. Why was all of this really happening?

After a moment she thought about Ania's marriage and how they had giggled as growing girls each time they found out something more about the intimate side of being married. *Well, Ania knows now what it was all about; and I will too, very soon.* At this thought she tried to kindle some joy, but all she could feel was a deep sadness.

As the letter came to an end, Elka sat quietly for a moment to compose herself, before beginning to read Edith's letter. Referring to her birth mother by her Christian name didn't really sit easy with Elka, but for the moment she was unable to think of her as her mama. The pain of her loss was still very raw, and she didn't feel like replacing the woman she'd thought of all of her life as

Mama. Not yet, not ever. Marcelina, Petra's daughter, would always be her mama.

Edith's letter was all she had hoped it would be. It spoke of her love for the man who was Elka's real father, and told his story. And how painful it was for him to carry on, as his mind gave him a distorted view of life. It said that he was a very brave man and that he had been mentioned in dispatches, though his name had since been erased, due to his actions. Elka pondered this for a moment. There were no details about how her father had died. It was strange – Petra had told her that her father had committed suicide. *Maybe it was too painful for Edith to say the words.* Going back to the letter, she read about Edith's friend Ada, and how it was her son's execution that had tipped Elka's father over the edge. Then the letter told of the family she had yet to meet. Marianne hadn't mentioned any of this, but then she must have wanted to wait for Edith's acceptance of Elka. She read about her Uncle Douglas and his family, and about her Uncle Christian's plight. She felt a sadness at reading this, but also joy, because Edith's descriptions of them made her feel that she would like her uncles and cousins. And she knew that she would like her mother's cousin, Lady Eloise. Then came Edith's loving description of her husband, which ended with her saying that Laurent had some very important work to do at the moment and it was because of this work that Edith couldn't travel to see her, but she asked Elka and Jhona to visit her in London. *Oh, that would be wonderful. My mother wants to see me. She truly does love me!*

The tears Elka had fought against brimmed over as she continued to read Edith's words:

*My darling daughter,*

*I cannot express what it meant to hear from you. My heart bled with joy and yet suffered agonies over the injustice done to us all by Petra. But we have each other now, and I can smother you with the love that is bursting to be released and given to you. I have kept it safe and never lost it.*

*My dearest wish is that my darling Ania was with you. Oh, how my world would have been complete then. But I respect her wishes and know we will meet one day. I have enclosed a letter for her. Would you post it on for me, and pray with me that it reaches her? We will pray every day together for her safety. That gives me great joy, as until now I have prayed alone for you both.*

*Please come very, very soon.*

*I am your devoted mother.*

*xxxx*

*

'We will marry in England!'

'Oh?' Jhona sounded disappointed. She had barged in on them. He and Marianne were already drinking champagne.

'Edith needs us to go to her! We will go soon, in a few days. Please come too, Marianne, and bring your friend, George – it will be a wonderful wedding. Please . . .'

'Of course I will. I didn't think I would ever make that trip again, but you two have breathed new life into me, and having you as companions on the journey will help. I will telephone to make arrangements immediately, but I know that George won't come. I'm sorry, but she is working on a painting she is passionate about. However, it would be nice if you would stay for dinner. She is coming over and is intrigued by my tales of you and would like to meet you.'

'That would be lovely. I am sorry we were a bit off about it all at first. We have never been used to anything like that. But now we have got to know you and your lifestyle, we understand and feel more accepting of the situation.'

'She means since she has started to read the books you write! I can't get a word out of her, once she picks up the one she is reading now,' Jhona said.

'That is true. You make your reader understand how every emotion feels, Marianne. I want to feel those emotions.'

'Don't you already, darling?' Jhona's voice held mock-indignation.

'Yes, some of them. Now be quiet, Jhona, you are embarrassing me.'

'Never lose that. It is sweet. We French are far too open – we have no mystery. I have learned from you too, my dear. I think it right to retain something of who you are. I wish I had done.'

Jhona changed the subject. 'I would like to go back to the hotel before dinner, if we have time, Marianne? I would like to freshen up and write to my parents and my brother and grandparents. I have the address of where they are staying in England. I would like to try and delay their departure, now that we are going there. And as it has been decided that we are getting married there, I want them to be at the ceremony.'

'That would be wonderful. Oh, can't we send a telegram to make sure they wait? What if they have a passage booked to America already?'

'Yes, that's a good idea. I will draft it and get it sent in the morning.'

As they left, despite the bad news from Ania, Elka felt happy and more light-hearted than she had done since her mama died. Linking arms with Jhona, she loved the feel of the wind on her face and the sound of the waves splashing on the shore as they walked.

The shop windows glittered with delicate pieces of jewellery and displayed clothes that were simply wonderful, adding to the magical feeling that was gripping her.

'Let's buy our rings. Our engagement and wedding rings.'

As Jhona said this, it all felt real to her. They were going to be married – really married. No war could spoil that for them, could it?

He pulled her closer to him. 'Everything will be all right. We will be all right. But, Elka, I don't want to wait. I love you so much. Please will you come with me to my room when we get to the hotel? I – I will respect your wishes if you say no, but I have to ask.'

For a moment she was stunned, for she hadn't expected this. But then she knew it was right that they should do so. Nothing could prevent their love. Waiting for a ceremony wouldn't make any difference. Yes, it would make their love public, but what they wanted to share was their own – a sealing of their feelings for each other. 'Yes, I will, my darling; yes, I will.'

# 11

# *Ania*

## Krakow, November 1939 –
## The Horror of Occupation

No one challenged her as she walked the streets of Krakow. From the beginning of the occupation, some six weeks ago, Ania hadn't obeyed the order that all Jews must wear the Star of David. The Star marked you out as a Jew and meant that those wearing it were prohibited from walking on the same side of the street as others, and from entering cafes and shops. They could only use Jewish-owned shops, but the Germans dictated when these shops could open, and often that was only one day a week.

Those Jews who knew Ania well also knew why she had to reject her faith and her community. Those Jews who didn't, but knew her to be of their faith, spat at her, making her feel sad and fearful that one of them would betray her to the Germans. The Germans, and those Polish who didn't know her, accepted her as an Aryan. Something in her hated the deceit, but she knew it was the only way she could help her people and her country.

Many notices had started appearing on walls, shop windows and lamp posts, warning of severe penalties if people were caught fraternizing with, hiding or helping Jews in any way. Fear paved the streets, which now teemed with German soldiers. Jews were disorientated, their shops forced to close on certain dates, their businesses ransacked or taken from them. They milled around in groups. Soldiers kicked out at them and knocked them to the ground at regular intervals. It was as if they weren't human. And yet among them were doctors, surgeons, lawyers, businessmen and highly skilled workers. Even Ania's fellow teachers were confused and afraid. But they still tried to acknowledge her in some way, and she knew she had their support.

Cringing against the cruelty of what was happening to her friends, she found it difficult to walk past them and, as she did so, she went against the wishes of her heart. As she passed one group, a young man, with whom she had been on greeting terms, stared at her. His mouth opened, and she looked away. In Yiddish he said, 'Traitor!' Others looked up at her and one of them spat in her direction.

*Oh God, if only they knew.* Remembering that the young man was a highly skilled engineer, she wondered why he hadn't joined the free army. Was he a coward? Maybe his name-calling covered for his own cowardice.

When she came to the end of her street she felt more at ease, because those she met now were familiar to her, her friends and neighbours. They did not glance at her and she felt safe with them.

As she arrived at the door of her apartment house, a German soldier barred her way. Speaking in German, she asked that he let her pass.

He surprised her by asking in English, 'Vhy do you vant to go into this block? It is a residence of the Jews. Have you not seen the notices?'

Answering him in English, she asked, 'Why are you speaking in English?'

'Aah, so it is true. You do speak in many languages. But you haven't told me vhy you live here?'

Without faltering, she had her answer ready. 'I own this block. I was left it by my grandfather and I have to collect the rents. I also have an apartment here, as it is cheaper for me to live in my own property. I have seen the notices, and I am going to make arrangements for the rents to be paid to an agent, so that I do not break the new rules. I am also arranging to move out of the building.'

'*Kommen Sie mit mir!*'

Hesitating, she didn't know whether to go with him, as he had ordered, or protest, but decided it would be better to obey him.

The eyes of many Jews watched her as she got into the car parked a few yards away from her door. As they drove past the young man who had called her a traitor, he stood watching, a wry smile twisting his face. *Has he told the soldier the truth about me?* She knew the man to be an acquaintance of Baruch. Did he know what Baruch was doing and where he was? If he had betrayed her, would he betray Baruch, too?

As they neared Gestapo headquarters, her heart somersaulted, making her feel sick. Swallowing hard, she held her head high and followed the soldier inside.

'Vait here!'

English must be his second language, she thought, as he hadn't attempted to speak to her in Polish.

The door he'd gone through, and then closed behind him, opened once more. A stout man stood there and motioned with his head that she should follow him into the room.

In German he said, 'You are a mystery to us. We have been told that you are a Jew. You live in a Jewish house. You taught at the Jewish school. You were very close to a man whose whereabouts no one knows. You own Jewish property. And yet you do not wear the Star symbol, nor do you look Jewish. Many papers were destroyed in the bombing, and all we know of you has been told to us by other people. Tell me: who are you and what are you up to?'

Thinking the truth might be a better story than any she could make up, Ania decided to tell it as it really was, though she had to begin with a lie. 'I hate the Jews! They are deceitful, and they steal.'

'We know you were one of them, so don't lie: TELL ME WHO YOU ARE!'

His scream made her jump and sent a tremble through her. 'I am a Polish citizen who was bought up by a Jew.' He listened to her story without interrupting. She finished by saying, 'So, you see, a Jew stole me from my real family, brought me up as a Jew, but the moment my sister and I found out, my sister left to try and find our real mother. I chose to stay. Poland is my country.'

He was quiet for a long time, his thick bottom lip rolled over his top one. His small black eyes peered from their fleshy sockets, travelling from her feet to her head. A podgy hand flicked a pen, making it leap around in his palm.

Sweat formed beads on her forehead and dampened her body.

At last he spoke. 'You could be useful to us. First, you will surrender the deeds to your property. Then you will move out of there and into an apartment near here. There is one being prepared for staff close by.'

'I will not collaborate. And I do not have the deeds. My sister took everything with her. I don't even have access to our money. I have been living on the income from the apartments since she left.'

'Very astute. We know you live with a Jew. Who is she?'

'She is the woman who stole me.'

'So, as you hate her, you will not mind us killing her?'

'No! No, please . . . Please!'

'Ah, so you do not hate her – you lied.'

Regaining her composure, she told him, 'I did not lie, but I cannot bear for her – or any human being – to be killed.'

'She is a Jew.'

This was said in the same tone that he might have said, 'She is a snake!' His next question shocked her. 'Do you know where Baruch Elburg is?'

*God! Whoever betrayed me has betrayed Baruch, too.*

One of the beads of sweat broke free and made a cold trail down the side of her face. 'No. He told me he was getting out of the country. I did not agree that he should go. We argued. I haven't seen him since, so I assume he has fled. Many Jews did – they have gone to America.'

Again silence and an intense scrutiny. When he spoke again, it was slowly and calculatingly. 'You worry me . . . As I see it, I have two choices. No, three. I can make you wear the Star of David. I can take you at face-value, and you do seem to be a truthful person. Or I can be done with you, and have you shot.'

If she had a choice, she would take the Star and wear it proudly. She would stand side-by-side with her people and gladly suffer what they did.

'You say you will not collaborate . . .'

'I have changed my mind. I don't want to die. Nor do I want to wear the Star of David.'

'Very well, but you will be closely watched, so don't try anything. If I suspect anything, the woman you have lived with will be shot, and you will be made to watch. And if my suspicions prove to be true, you will be shot, too!'

'I – I understand.'

'You will be our interpreter. We are struggling to get things done, because of the language barrier. Only some of us can converse in other languages, and mostly that is English. You, I understand, speak German, French, English, Polish and Yiddish – am I correct?'

'Yes, that is so.'

'Then the first thing you will do is inform all of your tenants that they will pay their rent into this bank, from now on.'

She felt like spitting at him, but instead took the paper he handed to her. She nodded her head. 'And what am I to live on then?'

'You will be paid a salary and will receive a food allowance.'

Speaking to the soldier who had bought her here, he said, 'Take her back to the apartment house.' And to Ania, 'Fetch just what you need – personal items. There is furniture in the apartment you are going to.'

As she left the building, she knew she should be rejoicing. This was exactly how Baruch had planned things. He would be so pleased with her. *But how am I going to get information to him, or stand a chance of seeing him, if I am under twenty-four-hour guard?*

*

On arrival at her apartment, she gave the order to Ruben's wife, Rebecca, regarding the new rent payment. Her eyes held shock, then pity. 'What is happening: have they taken the building from you?'

Knowing that the soldier was watching her, Ania spoke to Rebecca in a tone she'd never previously used to her. It gave the impression that she held her in disdain and was putting her in her place. 'I have to go to Gestapo HQ to work. Look after Petra.' She finished by telling her to move out of her way.

She knew Rebecca had understood, even though she cringed away from her. A tear plopped onto Ania's cheek, following the trail that the bead of sweat had taken. Another followed it. The soldier couldn't see her face. Before he did, she wiped the tears away and swallowed hard.

The young man who had called her a traitor came round the corner. His head moved in quick jerks, as if checking that he wasn't being watched. Then he nodded his head at her and raised his eyebrows, as if asking her something. Suddenly she knew it was him who had told the Gestapo about her. But, if it was, then it must all be part of a plan. As she nodded at him, another tear spilled over. He made a gesture as if to say it would be all right, nodding his head and looking optimistic. The soldier turned at that moment and lifted his gun. The young man raised his arms and spoke to the soldier, asking if he wasn't even allowed to appreciate a pretty woman now?

The soldier looked from Ania to the young man, then back at her. She translated what had been said. Relief flooded through her as the soldier dropped his gun and scowled. '*Abschaum!*'

Looking directly at the soldier, Ania said, 'Just so that

he understands – and for your future use – the Polish word for scum is *Szwołocz*!'

The soldier clipped his heels and turned away from them. Again the young man winked, before turning and walking away. How she wished she could speak to him. He must be part of the Resistance; in fact, she felt certain he was.

The incident had lifted her. She no longer felt as alone as she had. She searched her memory for his name, but couldn't remember ever hearing it. She felt sure he was trying to convey that he was on her side, and that he knew what had occurred in the Gestapo office.

She'd cycled past him many a time when leaving work. But what she knew of him had come from Baruch. They had passed him once together and Baruch had greeted him. To her enquiry, Baruch had told her that he was an engineer and they had been at university together. But Baruch had never mentioned him being one of the Resistance. Perhaps she had better be careful.

Petra cowered in her armchair as the soldier entered, and a look of horror crossed her face as Ania walked in behind him. 'What? Ania, my—'

Speaking in Yiddish, but again using a tone that belied what she said, Ania snapped, 'Don't worry! Stay calm. I have to speak to you like this, as I am being made to work for them. I have to make it sound as though we are not friends.'

Babcia answered in Yiddish. 'No, you must not. No! Ania, please, it is too dangerous.'

Petra's body shot back in the chair with the brutal kick that the German gave her.

'*Nein, Tuen Sie ihr nicht weh.*'

At this protest from Ania, he turned on her. His hand rose. She tried to dodge it, but his blow caught her shoulder and made her reel backwards.

Her back caught on the edge of the sideboard, drawing the breath from her lungs. Looking up at the soldier, she felt the dread in her turn to terror. His look held hatred and something she dared not define. Cocking his gun, he pointed it at her head. She could only whimper her apology and beg for mercy.

The moment froze. All sound and movement ceased. His stare took in the whole of her body. In her fall, her skirt had lifted, showing her thigh.

His tongue swiped his top lip. What she did not want to recognize before was now clear to see. Drawing up her knees, she covered them with her skirt. In a sudden movement he turned from her and realigned his gun. Her scream of '*Nein, nein!*' went into the blast that blocked her ears and filled her nostrils with the stench of sulphur. Petra slumped forward. 'B-Babcia, Babcia, no . . . No!'

Blood seeped from Babcia's beloved body. It soaked her skirt and dripped onto the floor. Her moan, deep and agonizing, told of her pain. One long, drawn-out groan released her last breath.

Gasping in shock and grief, Ania looked up at the soldier, 'Why? Oh God, why?' Her mouth went slack and spittle ran down her chin. Sucking in a deep breath, she felt the room sway.

A bruising grasp on her arm brought her back from the sinking feeling that had cast a veil over her reasoning. As it lifted, reality hit her and terror engulfed her. The carpet burned her and Petra's blood, which was sticky and warm, clung to every part of her as the soldier dragged her into the middle of the room.

Turning her over, he pointed the gun at her head once more. This time she did not beg. She looked over at Petra, seeing the shocked look in her dead eyes, and a fleeting thought came to her: *What does it matter if I die now? We're all going to die. They will kill us all.*

'Take off your pants.'

'What! No, no, not that – no, please. Please!'

'Do it.'

The gun came nearer her face. She didn't want to die. Only minutes ago she had lost the will to live, but now – facing death – she knew she wanted to live. With her heart bleeding, she slipped off her boots and then her stockings, before pulling off her knickers.

At this, he got on his knees beside her.

Using all her strength, she rolled away whilst kicking out at him and catching him on his buttocks, which sent him toppling. As she got up, she made a grab for the gun, but he was too quick for her. Taking hold of the barrel of the gun, he swung out with it. The long wooden butt caught her shin, doubling her over with the sharp pain that zinged right up to her knee.

His hands grabbed her, pushing her to the ground. His body rolled on top of hers. Crushing one of her legs under him, he forced the other one away from it and got between them. As he held her with one hand, she could feel him fiddling with his buttons. The weight of him pushed all the air from her. Powerless now, all she could do was concentrate on her struggle to breathe.

He felt wet and hard as he brushed her thigh. He repulsed her, but she could not beg, or move. Desperate for air, Ania pushed at him. As she did so, he moved inside her. Though now she was able to fill her lungs, her world crashed around her: her love for Baruch was negated; she was violated.

Tears salted her tongue. His sweat mingled with hers. His thrusts went on and on, each one painful. He was treating her as if she were an animal.

As she cried out in agony and despair, a picture of her beautiful Baruch came to her. His gentle, passionate love was all she'd ever wanted her body to experience; not this vile, bruising intrusion.

Drawing in a hot, painful breath, she expelled it with a scream, which only made the soldier thrust more deeply. In her anguish, Ania called out to God, her tone one of despair. But her cries were drowned by his holler of extreme pleasure, as his body stiffened and he held himself rigid.

Frantic to get him out of her and stop him pumping his seed into her, she pushed at his chest and moved her body sideways. But all she achieved was to increase his ecstasy and to feel him pulsating inside her. After a moment he rolled off her sobbing body. She turned away from him and vomited. Though she was frantic for air, her body heaved and heaved, dispelling vile-tasting bile.

'Ugh! You're disgusting . . . Disgusting!'

If she could have spoken, she would have told the soldier that it was *he* who was disgusting, but she couldn't. The retching of her insides prevented her from doing so.

Kicking her in the back, he said, 'Get dressed, I'll wait outside.'

When at last she'd stopped retching, Ania rose. Going to the bathroom on legs that would hardly hold her, she somehow managed to wash herself, before going to her room and dressing in clean clothes. It felt to her as if she would never stop crying. Through her weakening tears and the pain in her back, she made an extreme effort and got down her suitcase, to put inside it as much as she could.

Picking up a photo, framed in silver, she looked into the lovely faces of her mama, her beautiful sister Elka, and Babcia Petra, taken just a year ago. *Oh God, why? Why?*

After everything was in her suitcase, she pulled the sheet off her bed, rolled it up and draped it over her case, before dragging it through to the living room. With her body still shaking from shock and the relentless sobs, she bent and gently kissed Petra's hair, then covered her with the sheet. 'Goodbye, my *babcia*. In some ways I am glad your end came quickly. We are all going to die at the hands of these Nazis – better that you have gone now. Rest in Peace.'

She felt a stillness after saying this. But though the outward signs of her distress remained, inside a calm feeling had settled on her. Or maybe acceptance was the word? Yes, she accepted that she was no longer an individual, but a dirty piece of meat that could be used by their conquerors – as, when and how they wanted. But worse was the feeling that came with this: she was no longer solely Baruch's. Not only was she sullied, but she would have to do things that were abhorrent to her, in order to serve her country and her people. She hoped God would forgive her. She hoped Baruch would.

*Oh, Baruch, Baruch, I don't feel up to what is being asked of me, but I will do all I can. I make that promise to you, my darling. Together we will strive for freedom for Poland and, above all, for the Jews.*

## 12

## *Edith*

### Leicestershire and London, November 1939 – Secrets Revealed

Edith's body shook as she stood in the room that she most loved in Hastleford Hall. It was the one that she had asked to be incorporated into her apartment within the Hall.

When they visited, she and Laurent brought their own staff, so as to cause no disruption to Douglas and his family. The rooms she had taken for their use were on the west corner and comprised this room – a beautiful square room, furnished in soft greys, with deep royal-blue cushions and curtains – a kitchen at the back of the house, a library-cum-study, a dining room, three upstairs bedrooms and two bathrooms. Small, but adequate for their needs, for the length of time they would spend here in the country.

Looking around the room, at her family gathered there, made her feel more nervous, but she drew in a deep breath. 'I have asked you all to get together because there is something I have to tell you.'

'Oh, dear old girl, you look as if whatever it is will be dreadful. You're not going to war again, for God's sake, are you?'

'No, Douglas. Though I have someone very, very dear to me who is already at war and I have no way of finding out if she is safe.'

'You're talking in riddles now, Edith – will you just get on with it.'

Getting on with it, as Douglas requested, wasn't that easy. Her family was going to be shocked and disgusted, and maybe even angry, that she was prepared to bring a potential scandal down on their heads. But she hoped they would forgive her, and accept her daughter. It was only days now till Elka would arrive.

'Would you like me to tell them, darling?'

'N-no, I must do it, Laurent. Thank you, darling, but I must.'

'Edith, what is it? You seem afraid. I can't imagine you have done anything to be ashamed of.'

'I have, Eloise. I mean, I'm not ashamed now – I have accepted it, and I want . . . Look, you all remember when I went missing . . .'

No one spoke for a few seconds as she came to the end of her story, then Andria, Eloise's eldest, who reminded Edith so much of Andrina – her dear late cousin, and Eloise's much-missed twin sister – broke the silence in a way that made Edith want to laugh. 'Aunt Edith, that's simply spiffing. I love that you have a past! What do the twins look like – have you a picture of them?'

'Andria! This is serious.' Eloise's voice didn't hold anger, only concern. 'Edith, my dear, you have been through a terrible ordeal. Why didn't you confide in us?'

'I . . .'

'I can imagine why. Good God, Edith, I don't know what to say.'

'Are you angry, Douglas?'

'Not with you, my darling.' Getting up, he said, 'Come here, my poor darling.'

The feel of his rough tweed jacket as her brother held her didn't detract from the relief and comfort Edith felt at his gesture. Over his shoulder she saw the disapproving look on the face of her sister-in-law, Janine. Her heart sank. As Douglas released her he said, 'That bastard Albert! What a cad he turned out to be.'

'Douglas! Mind your language in front of the ladies and the girls – they're not your farming crowd! I am very upset by it all. The boys will be ridiculed! Why do you have to bring the girls to England, Edith? Why can't they stay with Marianne in France, and you can visit them there?'

This told Edith more about Janine than she'd ever realized. 'I'm . . . No, actually, I am not going to be sorry any more. I didn't ask to be taken away from you all and, although I did have feelings for Albert, I didn't go willingly to him. I mean . . . Oh, I don't know, it is so difficult for me. But I am not going to be ashamed any longer. I have suffered more than you can ever know. That is at an end. My girls are coming back into my life. This is a wonderful time for me, as I have missed them so much. It felt as if half of my heart had been torn from me. Whether them coming into your lives gives you problems or not, nothing will really change – except that, if you don't accept them, you will lose me.'

Several people muttered 'No', and then spoke at once, saying they were fine with it. Douglas's youngest son, Thomas, said, 'Mother, Aunt Edith's girls are our cousins. Their coming into our lives will not affect us at all, will it, Henry?'

Henry, Douglas's eldest, answered in his usual joking manner. 'Well, only in a good way – we'll be seen as interesting, for once. Nothing much happens in a farming community, other than cows calving and sheep lambing: too bloody boring for words. Thank you, Aunt Edith. This will blow the wigs off our lot. And I, for one, can't wait to meet cousin Elka and cousin Ania.'

Eloise was suddenly standing by her side, without Edith knowing she had moved there. Her hand clasping Edith's did as much for her as Douglas's hug had. Eloise's words settled everything.

'I, for one, know how Edith must have suffered, and it breaks my heart that she felt she had to hide such a massive thing from us all. That in itself speaks volumes about us, and the stuffy way we view ourselves in the context of society. We suffered when Edith was missing, not knowing if she was alive or dead; and yet it was fear of us and what we would do or say, and of how society would outcast her, that kept her away and made her have to endure this terrible ordeal. Edith has helped many a young society girl keep in contact with the child she had out of wedlock; and yet she has, all this time, been separated from her own.' Wiping away a tear, Eloise continued. 'It is us that should be sorry. Not Edith. And now it is up to us to make this time as simple for her as we can. Tell us how you want to manage this, Edith darling, and we will help you achieve that.'

'Thank you, Eloise. Thank you so much, my darling.'

As she came out of the gentle hug Eloise gave her, Edith swallowed hard and gave herself a moment to compose herself. Her hesitation stemmed from the fact that she still hadn't revealed to anyone, except Laurent, that Albert had taken his own life. And so, after being open and honest with them, she now had to lie. It hadn't been her intention to do so, but revealing the truth, she now realized, could take away the little respect they still had for her. She had gone against the ethics of her profession and had not reported a death. Her lie, if revealed, could be a fatal blow to her career – to her life, as she knew it.

Laurent had agreed, and Elka and Marianne were in accord with what she was about to say, as they had already discussed it by letter.

'We want the girls to be seen as belonging to me and Laurent.' As Edith said this, Laurent, who had been by her side the whole time, took hold of her other hand. The gesture helped her to continue: 'You see, it is known that Laurent and I met during the time I was missing, so the age of the twins fits with that. We also think it best to perpetuate the lie that I lost my memory, as I have always maintained that when I met Laurent and fell in love I didn't know who I was. This was to cover up the real reason why I did not come home, or ask Laurent to help me to return to England. Now I will say that Laurent and I lost touch, but then found each other again, but by that time our children had been taken; and that this has been just as painful for Laurent as it has been for me. Which it has as, knowing the whole story from the beginning, he has suffered along with me.'

'Well, that is a relief to me, I must say. I couldn't bear the thought of having to tell people that you went with a common—'

'Janine! Edith didn't *go* with that scoundrel – not willingly anyway. Have you any concept of what that means? Even to her, it is too painful to admit that Albert is the father of her children. For heaven's sake, show some compassion.'

There was silence after this outburst from Douglas, during which Edith felt again the acute shame she had experienced in the days of her pregnancy. She wanted to reveal the truth, no matter what they thought. No, she hadn't wanted to allow Albert to take her as he did, not at first; but once he had, she gave herself as willingly as she did now to Laurent. But she accepted that this had to be a private shame – like her lie about Albert's true fate – which she would have to carry with her to her death.

Janine, though, was not in the mood to let them off the hook. 'Why didn't you report her as a missing person, Laurent?'

'I didn't know that she was. Janine, this is all very painful for me and Edith. The finer details of what really happened are not important, though I am sure you must realize that someone who is hiding from her family, and life as she has known it, is not going to tell anyone she meets who she really is.'

'Oh, I was just wondering. The main thing is that we have a good cover story. Though what will we say, if we are asked why none of us have ever said anything about the twins in the past?'

'We will just say that Edith and Laurent kept it to themselves. There was nothing they could do to find their children. Where would they look? And so, to save us all suffering, they dealt with it in their own way. Now that we do know, we are very happy to welcome the girls.'

'I just cannot understand how you can simply accept it all, Douglas. Edith hits you with this awful scandal and you help to find excuses, without any recrimination whatsoever.'

'Janine, please – it is you who is not behaving as you should. Have you no feeling for what Edith has been through? Or what her other daughter, our niece, may be going through in Poland at this very minute?'

'That isn't the point.'

'Janine, it is as I said,' Edith broke in. 'You either accept things as they are and treat my daughters as part of the family, or the whole family will break down, as I won't tolerate any disdain towards my children. None of this is their fault – it's mine. I won't have my happiness marred by petty conventions that you imagine have been violated. I am quite sure my own and Laurent's friends will accept everything; and that society, though surprised at first, will come to accept the situation, too.'

'It will be in all the papers, you know.'

'Yes, I do know, thank you, Janine. But it is best that we show a united front – even supply a picture of us all together, and make an announcement that we are ecstatic about it – than give even a hint that we are divided, or ashamed of it all.'

'Very well. Yes, I can see that. Let that be an end to it. When is Elka coming?'

'Next week. Then she and Jhona will be married as soon as everything can be arranged – the papers and that sort of thing. Our solicitor is looking into all of that for us.'

'Well, in that case, I will throw a party for them; just a family party, but it will be nice for us to all get to know them, before everybody else.'

'That is very magnanimous of you, Janine, thank you.'

Douglas put his arm around his wife and told her, 'I

knew you would come round, darling. It is a big relief to me. Thank you.'

Janine looked suitably smug, but Edith wasn't convinced. However, it was enough for now, and it warmed her heart that her family was prepared to stand by her and her girls. Her happiness would be complete, if only she could hear that Ania was safe.

The train belched smoke and steam, blocking Edith's view of those who were alighting. Was this really happening? In just a few moments would she be holding her beloved child?

She had come alone. Laurent had agreed that it was best Elka met her mother first and was introduced to him later on. Her glimpse of herself, as she'd passed the many windows of St Pancras Chambers on her way into the station, had told her that she looked chic, in her long mink coat and matching bowler-type hat, which sported a long feather to give it a feminine touch.

Inside herself, she felt like the young girl who had given birth to the twins, but the image in the mirror had shown signs of age: the deep smile-lines around her lips, and the crow's feet that now adorned her eyes. Although those eyes, she knew, shone with the renewed life she felt, from Laurent's recent love-making. Sometimes she thought he wanted to make up for all the lost time, as he loved her most nights when they went to their bed – and even sometimes in the afternoon, if she was home. Not that she was complaining; it was all so wonderful and at last she felt fulfilled as a woman.

Why these thoughts should visit her now, she had no idea. But they soon vanished as she caught sight of

Marianne, looking quite sprightly, considering that she had cried off visiting for a long time, blaming her frailty. And then she saw them. The couple stood, looking hesitant, but smiling so that Edith had a chance to greet Marianne, before they came forward.

She could no longer blame her marred view on the smoke and steam, and knew it was tears that distorted her vision. This moment held a surge of love, a gripping fear and an uncertainty, which made her vacillate between running and standing still.

Elka felt no such compunction. She dropped her valise and rushed at Edith. 'Mama, Mama!'

Feathers from her scarf tickled Edith's nose, and the sweet scent of her daughter and the feel of her soft skin gave Edith the comfort of knowing this was really happening; it wasn't a dream. Their tears mingled and their arms held on to each other as if they would never let go, but Edith still couldn't speak. Her throat had tightened and would not let her do so.

The hug went on and on. Emotion drained from them both. At last Edith was able to release herself a little and hold her sobbing Elka. 'It's all right. It's over. And now it is a beginning. My darling, my baby.'

Something told her Elka's rasping sobs were twofold: they were joyful and yet full of sadness, too. Edith understood. It wasn't just sadness for the lost time, but sadness for her sister, and for the woman Elka had thought of as her mama for so long. Edith had prepared herself for this.

'I have something for you. It is a thank-you to your mama, for bringing you up and loving you and caring for you.' From her purse she took out the locket. 'There. It is empty, but I am hoping that you have some photos of your papa and mama that we can have made to fit. Look, there is an inscription on the back.'

Turning it over, she waited while Elka read, 'In memory and with thanks. Marcelina and Feodor.'

Through her tears, Elka said, 'Oh, Mama, you understand?'

'I do, my darling. I don't want to replace your mama and papa – may God rest their souls – and I don't want you to feel that you have to stop loving them, or forget them. They are very special to you. And we two finding each other must not alter that. Let me look at you. Yes, you are like me. You have your father's hair and complexion, but you are like me, as Marianne has said.'

'Yes, I can see that I am. I want you to know that I love you, Mama, and I understand that none of what happened was your fault. I want to hear about my father one day. But I am also longing to meet Laurent, who I will call – and think of as – Papa.'

'My darling girl, thank you for that. But there is just one thing. And this is for you to hear, too, Marianne. I can't answer your questions now – I will explain it all in full later on – but I must just tell you, because it could have consequences for me: I have told no one except Laurent about the death of Albert, your father. As far as everyone else is concerned, I don't know where he is or what happened to him. Is it possible that you can all keep the secret of his death for me?'

All of them nodded. Her request had subdued them and Edith was sorry about this, but her admission was driven by fear of anyone finding out the truth. She knew Elka had been told what had really happened by Petra, and would have related it to Jhona and Marianne. And although it seemed so inappropriate to mention Albert's death now, she'd had to.

With an effort to lighten the moment, she put on her widest smile. 'Now come on. Forget all that for a moment, and introduce me to your lovely young man.'

Elka's expression lifted from one of wary confusion to happiness. 'This is Jhona, my fiancé.' Simply that, but the tone in which it was said held such love that it warmed Edith and gave her the feeling that everything was going to be all right with her daughter.

The fire blazed up the chimney, giving them a warm welcome, when they reached Edith's home in Holland Park. On the way they had talked and talked, but now they relaxed and, to Edith's delight, Jhona and Laurent chatted away as if they had known each other forever. Yes, their conversation was about war, which was disconcerting, but any common ground at a first meeting was good.

She, Marianne and Elka found plenty to talk about as they sipped their pre-dinner sherry; and, but for her worry about Ania, Edith felt that she had never been happier.

As if Elka had picked up on this thought, she said, 'Mama, I have had a letter from Ania. It arrived just before we left. She is working for the Germans and that is why she was able to get a letter out. She slipped it in with their post. It isn't good news.'

'Oh, my dear, I had hoped you would say anything but that. But in my heart, I knew it could be no other.'

'I know, and that is why I haven't wanted to show you the letter. It is written in Polish, so I will translate it for you.'

Shocked and upset more than she thought she would

be to hear of Petra's passing, Edith took a moment to compose herself after hearing the contents of the letter. At least Ania was all right. Though God knew for how long. The Resistance work she was doing was so dangerous. *Oh, how can I bear it?* But then she knew she must, and just minutes later she knew she would have much more to bear, as Elka told her, 'Jhona and I have decided to be active, one way or another, to help in the war effort. We don't know how yet, as it is difficult to know where we will be needed.'

Swallowing hard, Edith said, 'I would expect no less from my daughter. I am proud of you both. Afraid and upset, but very proud.'

'You do know that I want to be a doctor, like you, Mama? But this war will of course interrupt that. Tell me about your war, Mama, in the hospital tent and . . . and why my father's death must remain a secret.'

Talking about her lie concerning Albert's death wasn't a comfortable feeling, but they all understood. Edith was reluctant to talk about the part she'd played in her war, but she knew she must. Her war was the beginning of this beautiful young woman's life; it was important to Elka, and she needed to know. *But how I wish I did not have such memories to impart. And I wish with all my heart that the Germans are defeated quickly, and that Ania will be freed, and Elka and Jhona do not have to be involved.*

# 13

# *Elka*

## London, January 1940 – The Honeymoon is Over

It was the day after their wedding. The car chugged along, slowly manoeuvring in the snow-logged country lanes. All the waving goodbye was over, and Elka and Jhona were on their way to London. It was going to be heaven to have a few days there on their own, leaving her mother, Laurent and Marianne and her uncle and aunt and cousins, and all those members of their Polish family who hadn't yet left for America and had attended the wedding, back in Leicestershire.

'Oh, Jhona darling, the wedding was wonderful, wasn't it? Despite everything, it was wonderful.'

'It was, my darling. And I am proud of how you coped with the sadness that is always in you, where Ania is concerned.'

'I did make a concerted effort not to let my fears – and the pain of not being with Ania on my special day – mar things. There was a moment though, with Edith. We walked in the garden together and were admiring how beautiful it all looked, with its coating of snow. It reminded me of

Poland and brought Ania starkly to my mind, as if she was standing with us. Mama and I both cried.'

'Yes, I could see when you came back that you were a little down. But then the band struck up Bach's Polonaise, my mama was whisked onto the dance floor by Dziadek Gos, and Babcia Miriam and my father lined up behind them. And then you and I . . .'

'Yes, and it was so funny. Isaac stopped the music and organized all the guests into couples, taking Edith's hand, and we all led them in the Polonaise dance.'

'It was the most ungainly rendition of our beautiful, graceful dance that I have ever seen!'

They both collapsed in a fit of giggles at the memory.

'Did you see the way Isaac looked at Ginny? He couldn't take his eyes off her all evening, and when her step-grandfather led her onto the floor, it wasn't long before Isaac excused them and whirled Ginny around in a waltz.'

'I did. And do you know what that cheeky brother of mine did? He only asked me if I could think of a reason why he might leave with us. When I questioned this, he said he wanted to get back to London, to spend some time with Ginny, as she and her grandparents had left by train straight after the wedding. They had to get back to Jimmy's Hope House.'

'Oh dear – Isaac has got it bad. I hope he doesn't change his mind about going to America. I want him safe.'

Their mood became solemn again. Jhona broke the silence. 'Are you all right, darling? Have I tired you?'

'Oh no. And I have missed lying with you so much. Last night was the bringing together of all my dreams. It has been such a long time to have to control ourselves.'

'I know. But never again . . .'

His words trailed off into silence. 'There *will* be an "again", won't there, Jhona?'

'Yes, it is possible. Elka, we have to be realistic. The war . . .'

'But nothing is happening. All the papers are calling it the "Phoney War", so we may yet escape it all.'

'Elka, won't you change your mind about us leaving for America with our family next week?'

'Absolutely not! I have made my mind up to enter medical school. I am going to talk to mother about it. As her daughter, I will have automatic entry into Charing Cross teaching hospital and will only have to qualify for a place at London University – and that should be easy to do.'

'Oh? I'm glad you are so confident. And just when did you think you would discuss this with your husband?'

'Right now. You have only been my husband for twenty-four hours – I couldn't possibly do so before.'

'Ha! You little minx. But I am not objecting, I think it is a wonderful idea, darling. I know you will be safe, and doing just what you want to do.'

'And . . . ?'

'And what?'

'Just when are you going to discuss with your wife the plans *you* have?'

'I cannot get used to that term. Wife – my wife. Ha! It is wonderful.'

'What are you doing? No, don't stop the car, or we will get stuck in the snow, Jhona . . . Oh, Jhona.'

He had stopped the car, got out and was now on her side and opening the door. Lifting her out of her seat, he held her to him. 'My wife . . . my wife – MY WIFE!'

The white world of trees and fields spun around her as Jhona twirled her round in his arms. All the joy she had ever felt in her life surged through her, and her heart felt as though it would burst with the love she had for him. Playfully she shouted at him, 'Stop it, put me down. Jhona, put me down!' But before he could, he slipped.

The soft mound of snow cushioned their fall. Their screams turned to laughter that echoed around them. Elka wanted to capture the moment and keep it near her forever.

Jhona's lips enclosed her shivering ones. The warmth of them took away the cold and encased her in a glow that reached the very heart of her. She trembled from the yearning she felt to be one with him.

He lifted her up once more, but this time he held her close to him and walked away from the car, his steps unsteady as his feet sank into the deep snow. 'Where are you taking me? You're mad, Jhona. We have to make the main road before dark . . . Jhona!'

But her protests fell on deaf ears. Close by was a barn. Realizing his intentions increased the anticipation within her and tensed the muscles in her groin. She snuggled her head into his neck and kissed and sucked in his skin.

Jhona's breathing deepened. His voice was gravelly as he spoke her name between kisses. Reaching the barn, he kicked open the door and took her into the semi-darkness. Here they were sheltered from the bitterly cold wind. Expectation helped to warm her through.

The bales of hay smelt musty, as if they were rotting inside, but they also gave off a heat that encased her body as Jhona placed her down on them. 'I'm sorry to use you, my precious Elka, but I am driven by my love for you.'

'Don't be sorry. I need you as much as you need me. These are the times that we will treasure when—'

His kiss stopped her putting into words what they both knew: that soon they might be parted from each other. His gentle caresses turned to a passionate exploration of her body, arousing feelings that made her cry out with joy and beg him to enter her.

Clothes were removed somehow, during the frenzy that followed, and she felt it was an exquisite moment when Jhona filled her with himself and made her part of him.

Everything else now forgotten, she gave herself to the moment. She responded with an abandonment that took her to a place she never wanted to come down from, as a crescendo of sensations swept through her, leaving her limp with exhaustion and her face awash with tears of ecstasy.

Reaching his own climax soon afterwards, Jhona joined his cries to hers. Together they rode the path of love, then clung to each other as if they would never let go. Their tears of joy mingled as their bodies heaved and let go of all the pain inside them.

They cried for the plight of Ania and because they missed her so much; and for the family they were soon to say goodbye to: Jhona's grandparents and parents and brother – whom she had looked upon as relations all her life – already had a passage to America. They cried for Marcelina, Elka's beautiful adoptive mama and Jhona's aunt; and for Petra, as they came to forgive her. And they cried for their beloved Poland: a sometimes harsh country, with a history of strife and depression, but with hard-working and good people who were accepting of all, until others divided them. But then, deep at the heart of their sorrow, lay concern over the fate of their own people. The Jews were being oppressed once again, and no one was coming to their aid. Their plight was not being made into a major issue, for only the odd incident was being reported, but they knew from Ania's letter that terrible suffering was being imposed on the Jews.

Drained of emotion and shivering with cold, they helped each other to dress. Elka felt cleansed of the knotted pain that she had held inside her, and lightened by sharing it. 'My darling, what just happened didn't mar the joy of what went before – it only enhanced it, as we share so much and understand each other. We are now bound together and can face whatever may come, as we know that each of us has courage, and that our courage gives us strength.'

Jhona looked deep into Elka's eyes, penetrating her very soul. 'Our love will bring us through,' he said. 'And we will not be parted. I had been thinking that I would join the British forces, as they are taking refugees, but now I will try to do war work that doesn't take me from your side.'

'Oh, Jhona, that is wonderful news. You have skills in design and working with precious metals, and you have language skills, too. All of these will transfer to any work you choose and will help the war effort, just as much as if you were brandishing a gun in combat.'

They reached Edith's and Laurent's home the next day, after spending a night in Buckinghamshire. They were surprised to be met by Brendan getting out of his car. His full officer's uniform gave him an official air, and he looked as though he had been waiting for some time. Looking at him, Elka was struck by the reality of the wartime state they were now in. Brendan's attire as well as his demeanour were a stark reminder of it. There was a stiffness about him, and he was far removed from his usual relaxed, funny and likeable self.

Seeing him in uniform hadn't been their first reminder that Britain was at war. All along their route they had witnessed the banks of sandbags that people were stacking around their homes. And they had seen others busy painting over road signs. They had listened to a dozen conversations about what was happening, when they had taken breaks for lunch or refreshments at inns along the way, but all that was done in an enthusiastic way, as if it wasn't really happening. But all at once Elka sensed danger, and felt that Brendan was going to bring the reality of war to their doorstep.

After greeting and congratulating them, he apologized for not being at their wedding. 'I did try to get leave, but there is so much going on at the moment, and I am part of a team. All of its members were needed over the last few days. Look, I haven't just come to pass on my good wishes and excuses – I could have done that any time, rather than disturb your honeymoon. There is something I need to discuss with you. It is urgent and very, very secret.'

'Oh? That sounds serious, Brendan. Look, come in. It's good to see you, and don't worry about disturbing us. The times are what they are, and we all have to make sacrifices.'

As Jhona said this, Elka knew that the lightness he'd injected into his voice belied the way he was feeling. She sensed that he was just as concerned about the situation as she was.

Once inside, Elka asked the maid to show the men into

the sitting room and bring tea. 'You two make yourselves comfortable in there: warm yourself by the fire that I'm sure is blazing up the chimney. I'll just pop upstairs for a moment.'

'Is Uncle Christian here?'

Elka hadn't yet got used to this man, especially someone in his position, the nephew of a friend of her mother, calling her relatives by the same titles as she did. It was a funny custom of the British – as if it was polite to use terms given to relatives rather than a given name. Poles would always address a non-relative adult by the title of *Pani* or *Pan* – Mrs or Mr.

'No, he was well enough to come down for the wedding and, I think, had a marvellous time – his expression was one of happiness the whole time. Mama thought it would be nice for him to stay in Leicestershire for a while.'

'Oh, that's good. My God, what he has to go through is unbearable, and all brought on by the last war. It beggars belief that our country, and his generation, have to face that all over again.'

'Yes, it does. I won't be a minute.'

Running up the stairs, she escaped and had a moment to herself, sitting on what was now to be her own and Jhona's bed. Looking around the room calmed her nerves. Edith had given Elka full rein over furnishing and decorating what had in the past been used as a guest suite. The work had started within a week of them getting here, and it had all been completed whilst they were away. The maid had been given instructions as to where Elka wanted everything placed.

The creams, reds and golds blended and gave the room a sumptuous, yet warm and welcoming feel. And the oak furniture, though heavy and from a different era, sat well in their new surroundings. In this room she had kept the red touches to the cushions and tie-backs on the curtains, complemented by a beautiful reproduction of the poppy-field painting by Monet, which hung above their bed.

She changed out of her travelling clothes into a comfortable pair of loose navy-coloured slacks and a white pleated, chiffon blouse with ties, which she knotted into a huge bow at her neck. Then she walked through into their sitting room and smiled at how lovely it all looked. It was just as she'd pictured it. She had achieved the lived-in look that she'd wanted, by commandeering an old comfy sofa and chairs that had been long abandoned in the attic. Having the sofa covered in a deep-red velvet enhanced the idea that many a family had sat on it and enjoyed a fireside chat. How she wished she and Jhona could do just that, as they had planned, and enjoy toasted crumpets with their afternoon tea while they chatted over all that had happened at their wedding. But it was out of the question to bring Brendan up here, because the feeling she'd had earlier now revisited her. She did not want this room tainted with whatever he had to say.

After her visit to their mostly cream bathroom, livened by red-spotted towels folded in neat piles on the shelves and set into a recess that had once been a chimneybreast, she rejoined the men, refreshed and ready to hear all that Brendan had to tell them.

Had she thought she was ready? After hearing Brendan talk, she knew she wasn't. It was all too much to take in! Spies? Special agents? Clandestine operations!

'I can see you are shocked, but Section D is very well

prepared and organized. I put you both forward as candidates for this job because I could see, when we first met, that you both have the determination and courage to carry through what you feel is right. You have shown that in the way you took on the journey to France, which can't have been easy, even though your family had money to pay the way. And, since then, in the way you have adapted to life here and how you handle the dreadful situation that your sister and your people are in. And, of course, most importantly, because of your language abilities and your knowledge.'

'What exactly are you asking of us? Where do we fit in?'

'We need propaganda delivered to the Polish people, Jhona. They are cut off from the outside world. They must think they are abandoned and that they fight alone. They do not realize how much Churchill admires them and knows how they are fighting back in a courageous way. We want to get this information to them, and encourage them to continue their efforts. We want to find out what the Polish people need in order to help them in their fight, and to inform them that we will help all we can. Plans are afoot to supply them with agents to help to organize the different Resistance groups into a force to be reckoned with. And we want to assure them that eventually we will liberate them, and that we entered into a state of war to defend them – and we will. If you agree to this, have you any contacts that you think would help you?'

'Yes, my brother-in-law, Baruch Elburg. He and his men are in hiding. They are in the Tatra Mountains, between Slovakia and Poland. I have a good idea where, as we all went on skiing holidays there, to Zakopane. His family and ours are well known there and we have many friends in the area. They will be hiding Baruch and taking care of him. They will also be helping him all they can, I am sure of this. It won't be difficult for us to make contact.'

'That is excellent. So you both ski? Are you good at it?'

'Elka is better than me – she won competitions – but I am also very competent. Why do you ask?'

'Because that skill will be needed, and we were planning on teaching it as part of your training. We see the only route into Poland as being via those very mountains, and the method of transport will be to ski over them. Look, you will hear all the details of that later, but tell me about this Baruch?'

Elka was astonished. The mountains were treacherous, and skiing over them took tremendous skill. But she didn't object; instead she answered his question. 'Baruch leads a faction of the Jewish Resistance. He began to gather followers before the invasion. Being politically minded, he could see what was going to happen. None of us took much notice, and we thought of him as an agitator. We have since come to admire him and wished we had listened to him.'

'This just gets better. He sounds exactly the man to coordinate operations in Poland. And you are both the right material to make good agents. What do you think? There will be a very difficult training course to master, but I'm sure you're up to that.'

Elka felt elated at being able to do something for her people, but her elation was mixed with a fear of the danger involved, and a feeling of not having any choice. This task was being asked of her. She would rather it wasn't, but how could she refuse?

'Elka?'

Jhona had been looking at her – waiting and wanting, she knew, for her to be the first to accept. Holding his gaze, she nodded. 'This is ours to do, no matter what the consequences. We *have* to do it.'

'I agree, my darling. And at least we will be together.'

'For the most part, yes. But you will be required to carry out separate missions, too.'

Neither of them commented on this, although it made Elka feel a little more afraid. But she was determined not to show it. Ania sprang to her mind, as did the need to get her sister out of Poland. She told Brendan all she knew about what Ania was doing and the risks she was taking. 'Will there be a chance of getting her out? That will be my bargaining point. I will do all that is asked of me, as long as the powers-that-be work on a way of rescuing my sister.'

'I will put it to them. I understand that Ania is identical to you?'

'She is. We are mirror-images . . . Wait a minute – she could be me! What if I go in, and she comes out? It would work, I know it would.'

'But, darling . . .'

'No, Jhona, I don't mean that I should stay there. What if she meets us in the mountains and then, using my papers, she is air-lifted out with you? I could hide until you can return to collect me with my papers. It's perfect – it is a wonderful solution.'

'It's not a bad idea and it could work, although there is the matter of training. You will see, as you progress through it, that you will need some very exacting skills. Ania won't have those, and she will need them, if she is caught. Combat skills – how to kill an attacker with a knife;

the use of some of the excellent equipment being devised by scientists and inventors like Laurent—'

'Laurent! Laurent is inventing things already? I knew he had been talking to Mr Churchill, but since we have been here, he has just seemed to be a teacher.'

'He is, but in his spare time he comes up with some astonishing gadgets that will help in espionage – pens that become a knife or a radio, that kind of thing. A lot of them are simply ideas at the moment, and not all have been taken up yet, but if this war goes on and Hitler does manage to hold us back, Churchill is thinking we may very well need such gadgets to help agents support the Resistance groups that will form everywhere.'

'That won't happen, will it? I mean, surely the Allied forces will beat Hitler back and liberate Austria, Poland and Czechoslovakia?'

'It is hoped so, but Churchill is not underestimating Hitler's might and influence. We have to be ready. It is the fools around Churchill who are frustrating his efforts. But he is working away at topics like the espionage tools we will need, and is trying to increase the arms budget. He is very worried about what will happen if Hitler throws his full might against us in Belgium. The Nazis could well take France.'

'Oh no!'

'I'm afraid so. That is why Laurent wanted his mother to come here with you, but she refused. And it is why people like you are so important to our war effort. Initially as a means of reaching those who feel they are in the wilderness and encouraging them to hold on, but later, who knows? Anyway, can I go back and tell Command that I have the perfect couple for the job?'

'Yes,' they both said, in unison.

Jhona reached out to Elka and squeezed her hand. 'We can do this, darling. I know we can. We know the area; we know the people – our people. It is the least we can do.'

'We can, darling. I will be sorry to put back my medical training, but that is a small sacrifice to pay, compared with what we may be able to achieve. When do we begin training, Brendan?'

'Is tomorrow too soon? I know it is a lot to ask, but there is great urgency. We have to reach out to these people, and we have to do so quickly. The training will take about six weeks, depending on how you both adapt. We would want to have you on your first mission within the next two months.'

'That soon?'

'Sorry.'

'Just tell us where to report and we will be there,' said Jhona. And Elka nodded.

'We have no specific training station. It will take place at a number of locations – with the RAF for parachuting, the Army for weaponry, and the Secret Service for clandestine operational training. You will be instructed very soon about your itinerary. And thank you. Thank you so much. I had faith in you, and you haven't let me down.'

As the talk turned to more general matters, Brendan revealed his fears and concerns to them. 'There are things being talked of that sometimes make my skin crawl with fear. This war will be a different kind of war from the last one. Hitler is ruthless. It is thought that if we don't beat him quickly, the fight will be brought to this country. Maybe by invasion, but certainly by air raids. It is terrifying.'

'It is already happening in our country.'

'I know. I'm really very sorry, Jhona.'

The silence that fell encompassed all of their fears for the future.

'I wonder how many of us will survive it all?'

'It doesn't bear thinking about, Elka. No one will be safe – at home or fighting abroad. But come on, you two. This is your honeymoon. It will be cut short, but I mustn't encroach any further on what time you have together. I'll go now. I'm driving over to see my mother.'

'We were sorry to hear she isn't well. Poor lady. Illnesses of the mind are very difficult to understand. Far easier if someone has a broken leg or something,' Elka said.

'I know. I do my best, but it's difficult. I sometimes wonder what it would be like to have parents. I do get a short glimpse of it now and again, if Mother is thought well enough to come out for a while, but it is fraught with anguish on her part, as well as mine. I don't know what I would do without my Aunt Ada, and Aunt Annie, and your mother and Laurent and another of my Aunt Ada's friends, Aunt Rene. Aunt Ada is very close to your mother, and I have always looked on your mother as my aunt. She has done so much for me.'

'I know, Brendan, and I am proud of her. She is very loyal and loving and shows none of this nonsense about people of different classes not mixing. Her work for the poor and setting up Jimmy's Hope House reveals the kind of woman my mother is, and I hope I can emulate her. I will begin by telling you that I will look on you as a brother, if that is all right with you?'

'Oh, it is, Elka. And it means so much to me to hear you say that. I have been afraid of how you would view me, because in a way I have had from your mother the affection you should have been having all these years.'

Spontaneously they hugged. Coming out of Brendan's arms, Elka picked up on something he had said, which had made her think he knew the truth. 'You said, "Your mother and Laurent" and not "Your mother and your father"?'

'Yes, I know the truth. Only Aunt Ada and I know, outside your own family; everyone else is to think that Laurent is your father. Aunt Ada told me a long time ago about Albert and how he tried to save her son, my step-brother Jimmy. And she slipped up by telling me how he had taken your mother and held her hostage. When you contacted her, Aunt Edith also told me the story, and that she hoped to pass off Laurent as your father. I wasn't sure if she had told you that I knew, or not. It makes you wonder what happened to this Albert, though. You must be curious.'

'No. I – I mean, a little. I am just happy with how things are. And I am glad you know the truth about my parentage. It is easier not having any secrets, but you must be careful to refer to Laurent as my father.' *No secrets! The secret I hold about my father's real plight is already weighing heavily on me. But, for my mother's sake, I mustn't let it out.*

Not wanting to discuss it any further, Elka took a deep breath and steered the conversation in a different direction. 'Anyway, it means that I have a British soldier's blood in me, which makes me all the better as a candidate for the work you are asking of me. Now, off you go, we have a marriage to get under way!'

After Brendan had left, Elka leaned back in her chair and for the first time since meeting him gave thought to how life must have been for Brendan. He had grown up knowing her mother, in the way that Edith should have known her. He was a man who had suffered a life of contrasts: of knowing her mother's world, and the deep love of his aunt, and of coping with a mentally ill mother, and on top of all that, he was having to cope with Ginny turning up and her being the daughter of his half-brother. Elka felt Brendan showed great strength and courage in the way he faced up to it all. She would latch onto his courage and take heart from it. She would be inspired by it and would carry out what he had asked of her in a way to make him proud, because already she wasn't looking on Brendan just as a friend, but was coming to love him like a brother.

The beautiful grounds of Bethlem Royal Hospital gave no hint of the misery encased within its walls. Parking the car, Brendan took a moment to take in its beauty, imagining himself to be in the grounds of a country mansion. However, this didn't last long.

Pulling his shoulders back, he went inside the hospital. The usual smells of carbolic and bleach hit him, and he heard cries of anguish and saw some patients shuffling around as if lost in their own world, their mouths slack, saliva running down their chins. These were the harmless ones. Sometimes his mother was one of them, allowed to roam the corridors at will, but at other times when he visited he would find that she'd had a violent episode and was being kept in a locked ward.

Brendan hated this place. Yet he admired the work being done and the goals that the staff and doctors hoped to achieve for each of their patients.

'Brendan!'

The sound of his mother's voice cheered him. It told him that she was able to come and go within the confines of the building and therefore must have kept well, since he last saw her a month ago. Yes, he did ring and enquire in between his visits, but he knew from experience that he wasn't always told the truth about her condition.

'Hello, Mother, how are you?'

'Come this way, Brendan. I have things to tell you, and I don't want this lot knowing them. Nosy cow!'

This last bit was aimed at a passing woman who had eyed them quizzically. 'Don't call her that, Mother – she doesn't know what she's doing.'

As the woman went on her way, cowering against the wall, Brendan felt angry at his mother. He had visited sometimes and found her in the same state as the woman they had just passed, so he knew the pity of it. But today she looked as though there was nothing wrong with her, so her remark seemed very callous.

'Oh, don't think about her – she's mad. Come on, I know a quiet corner.'

'I have to register my presence first, Mother. I'll go and sign in, and then I'll come and find you.'

'No! I don't want them to know you're here. That way you'll be able to get me out without them knowing where I've gone, or who with.'

'That isn't going to happen, Mother. I'll talk to the reception and see if I can have a word with Matron. If she thinks you may be well enough to come out, then I'll make arrangements: find us a flat, and sort everything properly for you.'

'I've things I have to do. Why can't you get a place of your own now? Why do you stay with that bitch Ada?

You're a man now, not a boy. She'll be giving you all sorts of ideas, now there's a war on.'

Used to the way she spoke about his Aunt Ada, Brendan took no notice of the insult to her, but instead asked, 'I have moved out, because someone has taken my room. Wait here, Mother, I'll be back.'

Returning after registering his visit, Brendan found that his mother had moved further along the corridor and was outside the common room. 'Come on in, then. There's no one in here, we can have a chat.'

Brendan told her about Ginny. She listened and chatted with him about it, remembering folk from up north that she hardly ever referred to. To Brendan, it was a pleasant five minutes and he felt elated that he'd found his mother so well. Wanting to tell her what he could of his work, he asked, 'You know about the war then, Mother?'

'Yes, we've been told, and the radio's always on. Look, Brendan, I have a plan . . .' And then, as if she'd really seen him for the first time, she blinked and stared in horror at him.

'What is it, Mother, what's wrong?'

'She's done it! I'm too late. She's got you into the forces! Eeh, no, lad. No. I'll bloody swing for that bitch!'

'Mother, Aunt Ada didn't get me into the forces. All young men have to join. Anyway, I can't tell you what I do, but I won't be joining the fighting men. My work is here in England. I might be called upon to go abroad, but I'm not in danger. Now, what's this plan that you have? Mother? Mother, are you all right?'

His mother's face had turned purple. Part of him thought it was with rage, but another part of him glimpsed something evil beyond words, as she suddenly spat out her vile hatred of Ada, blaming her for everything. He knew there was no reasoning with her, so he allowed the tirade to go on unchecked. Arguing might only make her worse, as she would then think Aunt Ada had corrupted him against her. When at last she ran out of steam, her body sagged.

'You're tired, Mother, let me help you to your room.'

She went without protest, holding his hand as if she were the child, and he the parent. Once inside the ward, the Sister came up to them.

'Mother's very tired, I thought I would bring her for a lie-down.'

'Come on, Beryl, let's help you, love. You'll be as right as anything, when you've had a kip.'

'Thanks, Sister.'

Brendan hugged his mother and then left, feeling at peace with himself, knowing that his now-calm mother was in such caring hands.

He never left her side without feeling troubled, and so the peace didn't last long, because all she'd said came back to him as he walked to his car. *Oh, Mother. Mother, how I wish you could be well.*

# 14
# *Ada*

## London, February 1940 – Revenge is Mine

Folding the last of the clean linen, Ada looked up as the door opened. Ginny entered with Leah, and Ada felt so proud of how her granddaughter had been such a help to Leah.

They were oblivious to her presence as they chatted away in a mixture of French and English.

Ginny had come along so well with her command of the French language, and it seemed to Ada that Ginny could speak it almost as well as Brendan now. *Eeh, it does me heart good, to hear her and Brendan bantering and laughing together over their French.* But Ada felt a slight trepidation; she had to admit that she did worry for Ginny. It was obvious the girl was in love with Brendan. Not that he encouraged it; his attitude to Ginny was always the same, as if they were brother and sister.

It was getting to the point where Ada felt she might have to speak to Ginny about it. This was a forbidden love, for they were too closely related. Besides, she couldn't bear the thought of Ginny getting hurt. And that would happen, when Brendan fell in love with someone else.

Keeping quiet, Ada thought what a blessing it was, when Leah had arrived here. It had been the saving of the girl. And though she'd faced a lot since then, with the loss of her babby, she was among folk who loved her.

Edith and Laurent had found out that Leah's parents' bodies had been washed up a few weeks after Leah's rescue. And last week the poor lass had to go the morgue in Devon to identify them. It turned out that she could only do so by her father's watch and her mother's earrings, which were still attached to the corpses. There had been no trace of her brother's body, though – and that, Ginny had said, was playing on Leah's mind. Poor Leah. Ada didn't know how she coped.

After the visit to the morgue, Edith had taken Leah to see the couple who'd rescued her. Thank goodness they were a lovely, understanding pair. They accepted Leah's apology without condition, and were devastated to hear what had happened to her after she'd left their house. They promised they would keep in touch with her and had already written to her.

Leah was saving up some money out of what Edith was paying her, and she intended to send postal orders to the couple, when she had a few bob to spare. She was determined to pay off what she'd stolen from them. It shouldn't take her long, because now she worked long hours doing lots of jobs around the place and was a real help to Ginny. She'd moved permanently into the overnight room and had made it nice and cosy. It was a pleasure for Ginny to stay over, when she might be on call.

The sound of the girls giggling was good to hear. But Ada had to make herself known, or it would look as if she was spying on them.

'Have you girls got nowt to do then?'

'Eeh, Granny, you gave me a fright. What're you doing in here? That's the job of the mothers. You have enough to do!'

'I'd caught up and thought I'd give a helping hand. I came in for some supplies to fill the shelves of the surgery and saw a load of sheets dumped in a pile, so I thought the lasses must be busy.'

'They are at the moment. We've two lassies in labour, so we thought we would leave a couple of the mothers with them to reassure them, while we make sure we have everything to hand. I was just about to go and have a word with Dr Edith. But I think I'll send Leah along to fetch her, as Dr Edith will want to examine the girls before she leaves for home. There's one of them that I'm a bit concerned over.'

'Well then, it's lucky I happened to come in here, as it's all shipshape now and one more thing you don't have to worry about, lass.'

'Ta, Granny. Eeh, if that means you've all finished, why don't you get off home and put your feet up.'

'Happen I will, lass. But it looks as though you'll not make it home tonight. Look, I'll go now, and then, when I've had a rest and seen to your granddad's and Annie's tea, I'll pop back to see if I can be of use anywhere.'

'You're a good 'un, Granny – hold on a mo.' Ginny spoke to Leah. As she left the room, Leah said, '*Oui*, I bring Dr Edith. *Il n'ya aucun problème – j'y vais tout de suite*.'

'Eeh, it's grand how you can talk to her and understand her, but I'm reet lost when the pair of you speak in French. What did Leah say just now?'

'Oh, she just said that it wasn't a problem – she would go for Dr Edith immediately. Not those exact words, as French doesn't translate word-for-word. You have to get the idea of it – it's all backwards to us. Sometimes I think I'm making progress, then at other times I'm just baffled.'

'By, lass, I'd never understand it in a month of Sundays, but at least I can understand Leah when she speaks English now.'

Ginny smiled and turned her attention back to collecting items from the cabinet she'd unlocked.

'Ginny, lass. I – I, well, I'm a bit worried about you. I . . . Oh, don't mind me, I'm being silly. You're busy, we'll talk later.'

Ginny turned; she had a puzzled look on her face. 'You mustn't worry about me, Granny. I'm fighting fit. I have a job I enjoy. Life's good. Of course I still grieve for Mam and Dad, and if I look tired it's because that grief visits me at night mostly and keeps me awake. On top of that, I have the strain of keeping Leah going, too.'

'You're doing a grand job. Leah is coming out of her shell. And she's looking a lot better. I reckon she's putting on a bit of weight an' all. God knows, she could do with it.'

'Aye, she's getting there, though it put her back a bit, going down to Devon. But I reckon that's normal, and it's good we have each other. We understand how the other's feeling without allus having to use words.'

'That's good. But you know I'm allus here for you, lass. I know how it is for you.'

'I know. But I'm coping. Honestly, I am. Eeh, come here – I've not had a hug today, and I could do with one.'

Ada accepted her granddaughter into her arms and they

clung to each other. 'Eeh, me little lass. I'm glad – so glad – you came into me life. You've brought sommat special to me that I didn't even know I were missing. I love you, me Ginny. I love you all the world, as your dad used to say when he were a young 'un.'

'Oh, Granny. I feel safe when you cuddle me.'

'Then I'll do it every day. Even if we're apart, you'll allus feel me arms around you, lass. Now come on. You've to get on, and I'm to get on me way.' With this, they kissed and then hugged each other more tightly, before letting go. For some reason they both had tears in their eyes as they looked at each other. Then both of them giggled at the same time. 'Eeh, we're a pair of soppy ha'p'orths. Give over!'

Their laughter made them feel even closer and rang out as Ada left the room, giving her a good feeling inside her. But as she walked the corridors, a sadness that she couldn't put a name to tainted it, and she had the feeling she was leaving something behind. Brushing that thought aside, she sought out Joe, to tell him she was off home and would see him later.

As she reached the office, Edith was just coming out. 'Are you off now, Ada?'

'Aye, but I'm returning later. Eeh, lass, I'm worried about Ginny; but now, seeing you, I'm more worried for you. What's to do? You look done in.'

'I'm just shocked and concerned for Elka and Jhona, and I can't get Ania off my mind.'

'Eeh, love, I'm sorry about Elka and Jhona. I feel bad, as it were Brendan that recruited them. Oh, aye, he told me that much. He feels reet guilty about it. But he said their skills are so needed, to help their country.'

'I know, I can't blame him, though I am angry – angry at how the world is, so soon after we sacrificed our all to bring peace.'

'I know, and yet nowt seems to be happening. Not here, anyroad. On the night they declared war, the forecast was all doom and gloom, and I were ready to get into me Anderson shelter and stay there. But nowt's happened – it doesn't feel like there's a war on.'

'It feels like the calm before the storm. I find it unsettling.'

Ada shuddered.

'Are you all right, Ada?'

'By, lass, I don't rightly know. I've got a weird feeling in me. I reckon as someone has walked over me grave.'

'Don't say that. Ada, well, I – I have always wanted to tell you that I love you. Oh, you'll be thinking I'm – how do you put it? – a daft 'a'porth!'

Although Edith giggled, Ada didn't join in. There had been a sincerity in what Edith had said, and her giggle was just a nervous reaction at baring her soul. Ada stood for a moment, unsure how to react. For the second time in their friendship she found herself in Edith's arms. It felt good, and she found she couldn't let go. Edith's hug was comforting, and yet it deepened the feeling of trepidation that cloaked her and wouldn't leave her.

'Eeh, lass, I love you, an' all. It were a good day when you came into me life. It were as if our Jimmy sent you.'

'You must think me a big softie, but, Ada, our friendship means so much to me. You are the only one I can open up to. You're my shoulder to lean on and cry on and, yes, to laugh on, too. I'm so lucky to have you in my life.'

'I feel the same, lass. We've come through a lot together.

And it all started with my Jimmy. Well, I can't delay you any longer. Ginny needs you. But, Edith, you're the best friend a girl could have.'

Edith held Ada and then released her. Ada could see that she was close to tears. For a moment she wished with all her heart that Brendan had not taken Elka from Edith. But then he had his job to do. Just as she and Edith had had, in the last war. They hadn't faltered and she shouldn't expect Brendan to, or Elka and Jhona, either. Despite the heartache this war could bring down on all the womenfolk of England, she knew that they too would find the courage they'd need to stand firm and take care of the home front, just as her lot had done. At least that is what she told herself when she wasn't thinking: *Why? Why should they have to? Why is it happening again, and so soon? Didn't we give enough?*

Ada was surprised and pleased to find Brendan sitting in the kitchen when she arrived home, even though he looked despondent. 'Hello, lad, what's to do?'

Getting up, he held his arms out to her. She went into the warmth of them. 'Oh, something and nothing. I'm feeling guilty about Elka and Jhona. I so want to talk to someone, but I can't.'

Remembering Edith's anguish didn't stop Ada supporting him. 'Look, lad. Whatever you have them doing, they're adults. You didn't force them. Yes, you put a proposition to them, and I get the feeling that it is something risky you need them to do. But they had a choice. I'm proud of them – really proud of how they took up the challenge. But now that they have, we have to be here for your Aunt Edith. It's tearing her apart, having just got her daughter home and then Elka going off so soon afterwards. Have you spoken to Edith lately?'

'No. I don't seem able to. It's difficult, as everything has to be top secret. If she has questions, I can't answer them. I think she knows that and so she is avoiding me.'

'Aye, happen. By, war can make cracks appear in the best of relationships. But don't let it. Don't let there be a barrier between you and your Aunt Edith. You're going to need her more than you can realize.'

'Why do you say that, Aunt Ada?'

The shudder that had shaken her body earlier trembled through Ada again. 'I don't know. Eeh, look at the time. Your Uncle Joe'll be here any minute. He'd almost finished his day's work when I left. I'll just get that cottage pie I made this morning and pop it in the oven, then we'll have a pot of tea, eh? You'll stay for dinner, won't you?'

'Yes, I'd like that. I could do with some company. Though I'd like to change out of this uniform. I left some clothes in the wardrobe upstairs. I'll go and have a rummage.'

The gas oven jumped into life as Ada held a lighted match to it. 'Reet, lad. I'll have tea brewed for when you come down. Have you seen Aunt Annie?'

'Yes – and heard her. She's in the parlour snoring like a good 'un.'

They both laughed. Ada crossed to the pantry and retrieved the cottage pie from the cold slab. It just needed to heat through and cook the pastry that lined the bottom of the dish, and brown the mashed tatties on the top. It would be good with a few neeps.

She put her fears down to the stress of everything that had happened recently with Ginny, and little Leah. It was enough to put anyone in the dumps. Getting up from the oven wasn't an easy task these days, as her knees gave her gyp. *Eeh, I'm about ready for the knacker's yard!* Glad she could catch hold of the back of one of the chairs tucked under the table, she pulled it out and sat down.

The kettle hissed in the background, but a weariness prevented her from getting up and preparing the teapot. She just wished she could shift this feeling. It was as if all the bad things in her life wanted to knock on the door and visit her. Jimmy came to her mind. *By, it were wonderful to find out that me Jimmy had fathered a child.* But then another thought clouded her happiness, as the scene she'd imagined a million times – her beloved Jimmy standing in front of a firing squad – flashed into her mind, bringing with it a pain that sank her heart as if a lead weight had been tied to it.

She heard the clicking sound of the latch to the door that led to the stairs, and Brendan stepping back into the room. It soothed her, and his voice, with its light-hearted sense of banter, once more put her world to rights.

'Mmm, it smells good. I can taste it already. You're the best cook in the land, Aunt Ada. And, despite rationing, you always have a good meal ready for us all.'

Her spirits lifted instantly. 'Ha, you've a flattering tongue on you, lad. But talking of rationing, I have to do me share of queuing, I can tell you. Though I've allus kept me pantry stocked, so I'm not running short of flour and stuff yet.'

'You be careful you're not done for hoarding – they come and inspect, you know.'

'Get away with you, our Brendan. You'll have me thinking I'll be locked up. Hoarding indeed, ha! I bet a few have a bit put by. But it's what we've allus done: a jar of jam for today, and another at the back of the cupboard for a rainy day.'

'Not allowed, now. We all have to make sacrifices. They'll come, you know – they'll take you off and confiscate your jam . . .' His laughter died as the back door opened. Joe stood there, but it was the person who stood behind him that quietened Brendan. Ada's mouth gaped open.

'I met her walking along the road. I thought it best to bring her around the back.' Joe's voice held concern, but before Ada could reply or gather herself, the nasty tone of her sister Beryl cut in.

'By, you didn't expect me, did you?' Then, with a sound of triumph, she scoffed. 'Taken you by surprise, haven't I, our Ada? Well, I've come to make sure you don't send me lad off to war, like you did your boys. Lovely, they were, you know, Brendan. They were all handsome lads. I loved them, but she killed them off, she did. Then she got him here to kill your dad!'

'Beryl—'

Brendan cut Joe off from whatever he was going to say. 'Mother! Don't say that – it's not true. I told you: no one forced me to join up; only the government. We all have to join the military. Everyone at the War Office is in uniform.'

As Ada looked on, unable to speak, she saw Beryl glare at Brendan in a way no mother should look at her son. Beryl's hair stuck out like a lot of rusty springs. *When did it get so wiry?* Ada couldn't think, but the sight of it was nothing compared to Beryl's eyes. Red-rimmed, they were shot with veins. As young lasses, she and Beryl had resembled each other, with their striking curly, auburn hair and their stunning looks. But now Beryl looked twice Ada's age; she was thin and scrawny and constantly had sores around her mouth. Looking from Beryl's face to her clothes, Ada's heart sank even further, as she took in that her sister was wearing pyjama bottoms, topped with a blouse and cardigan. Holding herself steady, she kept her voice calm.

'What're you doing here, our Beryl? No one said owt about you coming to visit us.'

'I walked out. I've had enough. They are experimenting – using some sort of shock treatment. They said I was next. I'm having none of it. But then you'd know about such treatment, our Ada, with you helping at that place they named after your poor Jimmy.'

'I've never heard of such treatments, Beryl, and if you don't want it—'

Beryl carried on talking about Jimmy as if Ada hadn't spoken. 'Having a place named after him doesn't make up for him losing his young life, and never will. He'd still be here now, if you'd have stopped him going. She could have, you know, Brendan. She had a letter from the King himself, saying as they wouldn't ask her to sacrifice another son. But that didn't stop you. You're evil, our Ada, evil through and through!'

Ada felt at a loss. She was cut in half by the hurt this was causing. It was useless arguing against Beryl's incessant accusations, and she didn't want to further upset Brendan. Instead she tried to soothe her sister, ignoring her tirade about Jimmy. 'Come on in and have a cup of tea, lass.'

'Ha! Don't come Miss Goodie Two-Shoes with me. It's all an act, Brendan – and you fall for it. She'd like to see the back of me for good. It suits you, our Ada, to keep me locked up in that hole. Well, I'm out now and I ain't going back.'

'Mother, don't. None of us wants you in that place, but you're ill, and they can protect you and make you better.'

'Protect me! From *her*, you mean? Naw, lad, no one can do that. She stole you from me. Oh, she thinks she'll get me in the end. She can't bear the thought that your dad loved me, and not *her*! He told me so many a time. And we were going to go off, but *she* found out and stopped him. Then she schemed to get rid of him because, if *she* couldn't have him, then no one could.'

Joe had moved into the room, leaving Beryl standing in the doorway. He tried to intervene. 'Now, now, Beryl, I'm not standing for that. Poorly or not, you know what you're saying, and you know it ain't reet 'an all. Now let's get you something to eat and drink and you can have a rest, then I'll take you back to—'

'Naw!' In one swift movement Beryl pulled something from her handbag. The sun, shining through the doorway, glinted on the blade of a blood-stained knife. Spittle ran down Beryl's chin as she spat out, 'Touch me, and I'll run this through you!'

'Mother, no!'

'Get back, Brendan, you traitor! Take *her* side against your own ma, would you? Well, you're naw son of mine, and I'd stick this through you just as gladly as I would the rest of them.'

A shocked Brendan stepped back as the knife jabbed towards him.

Fear clenched at Ada. How did Beryl get the knife, and why was it bloodied? Her mind frantic with worry, she sought to find an approach that might work. Perhaps if she admitted all the accusations, instead of denying them? Softening her voice even more than she had done before,

Ada uttered a lie in an attempt to placate her sister. 'Beryl, lass, I'm sorry. I've wronged you. I know that. Can't we start again?'

For a minute Ada thought this had worked, as Beryl put the knife down on top of the gas stove next to her and opened her bag. But as Ada went to step forward, she grabbed the knife again. 'Stay there. I'm not taken in by you, you whore!'

'Beryl, please. Please think about what you're doing. We're your family. We're not your enemy. It's the sickness in your mind that gives you bad thoughts about us. If you were to accept that, and work with those who are trying to make you better, everything would come reet for you.'

'Shut up! Shut the mouth of you, our Ada! You're trying to wheedle your way out of what you've done. Well, you'll never do that with me. Never!'

Once more she placed the knife on the stove and delved into her handbag. This time she brought out a box of matches.

'Aye, that's reet, have a fag, love. It will calm you.'

'These ain't for no fag. I told you: I've had enough of you. All of you. I'll never get free while I have you all plotting against me.'

'Beryl, what . . . What're you doing? Be – Beryl!'

Beryl's hand had curled around the stove. A hissing sound and the stinking smell of escaping gas wafted over towards Ada. Beryl had turned on the gas ring that wasn't yet lit. Ada looked in horror from Joe to Brendan. Both stood like statues. In a flash, Beryl pulled a bottle from her bag and smashed it on the stove. The sound of the splintering glass made them all draw back from her.

Ada stared at the blood dripping from her sister's fingers. Then her eyes registered the purple-coloured liquid in the well of the stove, running towards the flame under the kettle, as more of it traced a path down the cooker onto the floor.

Joe realized Beryl's intentions at exactly the same time as Ada. The two of them moved forward together, both screaming, 'Noooo. Beryl, NO!'

The sound of the match striking and the flash of fire were simultaneous. As if breathed out by a demented dragon, the flames shot in all directions. Some ignited Beryl's sleeve.

'Oh God, Joe, she's on fire. Help her!'

Crying out in agony, Beryl stepped back, shutting the door behind her. The sound of the key turning made Ada open her mouth to scream once more at her sister, but a choking, acrid smoke rasped her throat and smarted her eyes, leaving her unable to utter a word.

Flames licked around the cooker and along the floor, catching the rag rug and then the table – everywhere that the liquid had splashed. Smoke curled up to and along the ceiling. Through rasping coughs, Joe gasped, 'Oh God, the gas pipe's melting. If the bottle ignites! Get out, Brendan – get out! Leave Ada to me.'

Ada, rigid with fear, stared at the blistering skin on her arms, and yet she couldn't feel any pain. Confused, she looked towards where Joe and Brendan stood, but smoke blocked her vision and she couldn't speak to let them know where she was.

Joe's calming voice came to her, bidding her to move towards him. Edging towards where she thought he was, she banged into something. She tried to grab hold of it as her body became unbalanced, but it crashed to the ground, taking her with it.

Flames from the burning rug licked around her legs and caught her skirt. Joe's shouts, and his coughing and spluttering, penetrated the fog of smoke that wouldn't let her breathe. She tried to call him, to tell him to get out, but couldn't.

Pain ground into her – a searing, agonizing pain – but then it stopped. All feeling had gone, but still she gasped for air. *Joe, where's Joe? My Joe, help me . . . !* Smoke filled her mouth, and a black tunnel – blacker than anything she'd ever seen – sucked her into it. And she felt a peace descend over her. A beautiful peace.

The blackness turned to light and there in front of her stood her lads: Jimmy, her darling Jimmy, grinning; and Bobby and Jack, just as handsome and looking exactly as they always had. They were smiling at her, too. She floated towards them. Unsure if she was ready to go, Ada looked back. On the kitchen floor she saw her own body. Flames from the burning rug danced around it, and the skin melted and blistered. But somehow it didn't matter. Nothing mattered. She had a new body and it was filled with happiness. She just wanted to go to her boys.

Brendan made it to the hall, praying that Ada and Joe weren't far behind him. Seeing the door to the parlour, he remembered Aunt Annie. In desperation he tried to open the door, but couldn't. Then he remembered that the sofa was pushed across it. Oh God, why had he agreed to Aunt Ada and Aunt Annie wanting to block off one of the doors that led to the parlour? They'd said it limited the space in the room, to have two doors leading from it, and he'd manoeuvred the sofa across the hall door for them.

'Annie, Aunt Annie . . .' Looking back towards the door that led from the hall to the kitchen, he prayed Joe and Ada would come through it, but they didn't. As he'd left the kitchen he had heard them talking – Joe coaxing, Ada mumbling – but after the crashing sound of a chair falling, he'd heard no more. Smoke was now creeping towards him from beneath the kitchen door. Getting down on all fours, he crawled towards it. Opening the door caused a ball of flame to rush above him, as if from a flame-thrower. Horror gripped him. 'Aunt Ada, Joe, Aunt Annie! Oh God, no. No!'

Getting up, he covered his face with his arm and rushed at the boiling inferno, but the heat drove him back. Flames licked the hall ceiling above him. Burning hot pieces of plaster dropped onto him. He had to get out. *Oh, Aunt Ada . . . Aunt Ada.*

Outside, he took in a lungful of air. A bout of coughing had him vomiting; huge retches that emptied his stomach.

Voices, bells, people running – all of it went on around him. *Someone must have called the fire brigade.*

''Ere, mate, let's give you an 'and there.'

'Help them. Help them!' His voice rasped his scorched throat. Then a thought shot into his mind. *Mother, oh God!* 'And . . . my mother, sh-she's round the back!'

'All right, mate. We'll see to 'er. 'Ow many in the 'ouse? Were you and your mum the only ones?'

Staring from smarting eyes at the big fellow who'd asked this, Brendan found he could not say the words. His mouth went slack and wouldn't work.

'Come on now, young man. You 'ave to 'elp us save anyone still in there.'

'My Aunt Ada and her husband, Joe . . . And my mother!'

'You said your mother was round the back, mate. Come on, try to think straight.'

'Annie. Aunt Annie! She was asleep in the parlour. Help me – help me.'

Through his shocked, blinding horror, Brendan heard the big fellow shout, 'John, Fred, get ladders. There's folk in there, and possibly one around the back.'

Brendan's body folded. He slumped to the ground.

'No one could survive this lot, Boss. It's burning from floor to roof. We'd never get in.'

As if confirming this statement, a massive explosion blew debris high into the sky, taking the guts out of the house and leaving a gaping hole. Using all his reserves, Brendan crawled away. Bricks and debris hit his back. When it stopped, he let his body go slack and, lying prostrate, allowed the sobs to rack his sore limbs.

A hand stroked his back. Turning his head, he looked into the face of a female ambulance driver. She didn't speak, but her hand came into his. He gripped onto it as if it would stop him from drowning in the grief that enveloped him. 'Th-they're gone. M-my fam-family. All gone.'

Her hand patted his and, in a lovely Irish lilt, she asked, 'Is it that you can stand, or shall I have them bring the stretcher?'

'I – I can stand.' But as he went to, Brendan's legs buckled underneath him.

'Bert, would you be bringing the stretcher over quickly. There's a young man in powerful need of it.'

*

A week later Brendan held on to Ginny's hand as he looked over at his Aunt Eloise, who stood with Rene, her friend. Tears streamed silently down both ladies' cheeks. Tears for Annie, who'd been nanny to Rene as a child, and maid to her when she was a young woman; and who had been a lifelong friend to them both. They were crying too for his Aunt Ada, their dear friend. The thought crossed his mind that they were crying heartfelt grief, but with dignity.

His Aunt Edith was the same. Standing on his other side, holding herself stiffly, she looked so tiny. He wanted to put his arms around them all, but ladies of their class would be embarrassed by such a gesture. As for himself, he didn't know which class he stood in. He'd been brought up with both the upper class and the lower, and loved both, and had been loved and accepted by both. His education had been almost that of an upper-class man, and he'd played with Aunt Edith's nephews on their huge estate in Leicestershire, and with Lady Eloise's girls on their estate nearby. None of them were his relatives, of course, but his Aunt Ada had told him it was always good manners to call close friends of hers 'Aunt', if they allowed it, rather than stumbling over their title, as if they were strangers. *Oh, Aunt Ada. Aunt Ada.*

'Ashes to ashes, dust to dust . . .'

The sound of the dirt hitting Joe's coffin bored into Brendan's pain and elicited a sob from Ginny. He let go of her hand and cradled her to him. Her hair tickled his cheek. It smelled clean and fresh.

Soon they would lower Ada's coffin on top of Joe's. *No! No, I can't stand it, I can't.* 'No!'

A hand steadied him, making him realize he'd spoken out loud. Turning, he looked down on Edith. Her expression told him to hold on. *Hold on to what? There is nothing*. But another sob reminded him that there was something. There was Ginny – and she needed him.

A few feet away from them, another coffin stood by a gaping hole. Inside were the remains of lovely Aunt Annie. She was another woman who had been in Brendan's life throughout his growing up – a nanny figure. He couldn't imagine how difficult this must be for Aunt Rene.

The handful of earth he'd taken felt cold, damp and rough. Leaning forward, he looked down at the casket. It was smaller than the one underneath it, as Aunt Ada wasn't very tall. On it there was a gold plate stating, 'Ada Grinsdale'. Just that: Ada Grinsdale.

Suddenly he needed to say something. He should have said it at the service, but he hadn't been able to. Now he knew he could. Taking no heed of protocol, he stood straight. Letting his arm drop from Ginny, he took her hand again. His voice soared, as if rising up towards the sky: 'Ada Grinsdale, a woman who gave so much for her country: three sons. Three sons killed in the Great War. She was a woman who took in her sister's child – me – and cared for me, loved me. A woman who was kind and never did any wrong to anyone. Who gathered friends from all walks of life, and who stood by those she loved, no matter what they did. And who, despite what she's done, would forgive her sister for taking her life and the lives of her much-loved husband, Joe, and her dear friend, Annie. I forgive my mother, too. Not to do so would go against all that my Aunt Ada instilled in me. Rest in peace, Aunt Ada. Rest with your Joe and your boys. I will never forget you. I will strive to make you proud.'

There was a muffled clapping of gloved hands and he

looked over at Edith. Tears tumbled down her face. He couldn't imagine how she would cope without his aunt. Others began to join in her clapping, and soon all the mourners and attenders were doing so. They drowned the sound of his handful of earth hitting Aunt Ada's coffin, but he saw the earth spread out around her name and, at that moment, he saw her smile – her lovely, giggly smile. He smiled back and turned and walked away.

Sitting down on a bench nearby, Brendan buried his head in his hands. He knew Ginny was sitting near him, but he couldn't acknowledge her. Already this morning he had attended his mother's funeral. Beryl had been judged to have murdered four people and had died as a result of her own actions. It appeared that, beside his dear loved ones who were being buried today and whose death Beryl had deliberately caused by the fire, she had stabbed a female kitchen worker to death at the hospital, who had come across her stealing the knife.

Even though Beryl was mentally ill, there was no condition attached to the murders that stated she was not of sound mind, or that she was unbalanced and didn't know what she was doing, because it was obvious that she had cunningly planned it all. That was made clear by stealing the knife and a bottle of methylated spirits from a hardware store on her way to their house.

Along with Ginny and Aunt Edith, there had been one other person at his mother's funeral. A stranger who had come up to Brendan and introduced himself as his mother's ex-husband. He'd seemed a decent chap, not at all as Brendan had imagined him, from the things he'd heard. The man's voice had held kindness as he'd said, 'I'd like to offer you me condolences, lad. You're not of me flesh, and you coming into the world changed me life, but I hold nothing against thee. I hope you don't mind me being here. I wanted to show me respects to Beryl. We had happy times, until I found out about Paddy . . . I take it you know about your father?'

Brendan had told the stranger that he did know, and added, 'Mother told me. She was very bitter about it all, but Aunt Ada never spoke ill of any of them. Nor of you.'

'No, she wouldn't. She was a nice lass, Ada. I wished I could tell her how sorry I am. Sorry for everything. But it's too late now.'

Brendan didn't ask what the 'everything' was. It was all too late now, as the man had said. His mother had always accused Ada of messing with her Bill, but Brendan hadn't believed it. Aunt Ada had never even mentioned him. So whatever the man was sorry for, he felt certain it wasn't any of Aunt Ada's doing.

'Brendan?'

He looked up now at the sound of his name on Aunt Edith's lips. He wished he could take the sorrow from her lovely face.

'They are ready to intern Annie's body, my dear. I think your Aunt Rene and Aunt Eloise will need you.'

She took his hand. Her soft kid glove felt warm and comforting and her words were said in a hushed tone. 'My dear, I wish I could lessen your pain. This is a terrible tragedy. Our dear Ada – I loved her very much. And you were right to say that her friendship crossed all class divides. She was a lovely person.'

'Thank you, Aunt Edith. I will understand if you want to . . . well, leave it at that.'

'Leave it at what? No, Brendan, no – I could not live

without you in my life. I want us to carry on as normal. I want you to come and stay in Leicestershire with us next week. The boys are very busy on the farm, as is Douglas, so they were unable to be here today. But they all send their love and feel deeply for you. They want you to go down and be with them as soon as you can.'

This warmed him. He hadn't imagined them dropping him from their lives, now that Aunt Ada was gone, but had felt he had to give them the chance to do so.

As he reached the graveside, still holding Aunt Edith's hand, and with the silent Ginny clinging to his other arm, Lady Eloise put out a hand to Brendan and guided him between herself and Aunt Rene. Edith took charge of Ginny. It was strange, but if his real mother hadn't suffered a breakdown after having him, he'd probably have been brought up in the North of England, where she and Ada came from. But here he was, surrounded by gentry and with all of them showing him love and kindness. That was down to his Aunt Ada. It was the measure of her. The measure of Ada Grinsdale – loved by all. *Rest in Peace, Aunt Ada. Rest in Peace.*

# 15

# *Brendan*

## London, Late February 1940 –
## Duty Comes Above All

'Come in, Officer O'Flynn. At ease, man. Take a seat.'

Brendan did as Colonel Wright told him to. He was a little curious as to why the colonel had summoned him to his office, and had to admit that he felt more than a little unnerved. A summons to the colonel usually meant a change of orders. Brendan's remit so far had been to work with a team preparing for clandestine operations, in readiness for the time when the need arose, and to recruit and train a force of specialized agents. It wasn't an easy job, because no one knew exactly what they were preparing for or what they would need, at this stage of the war.

'I need to talk to you about a change of plan concerning Agent PMm.'

Brendan was shocked. A change of plan concerning Jhona, known as PMm – 'Polish Mission male' – could mean that Jhona was going to be given a different assignment or taken off the programme altogether. Where would this leave Elka?

'Sir, may I ask why? Are there any problems?'

'No. It's just that we have other plans for him.'

'But, sir—'

The colonel raised his hand to stem any objections. 'You are to take his place, Officer O'Flynn. You won't complete the full journey with PMf, but for the part of the mission in which you will be involved, you will need training. You are to leave for that immediately.'

His words caused Brendan's heart to sink. He was due to go and stay in Leicestershire for a few days and take Ginny with him. God knows, they needed a break – especially Ginny, as she felt cooped up in Jimmy's Hope House and was finding it difficult, with no proper home to escape to. Plus there was her grief for her newly found granny, on top of what she was already suffering, with the loss of her parents. It was weighing her down, and Brendan feared she would become ill. Everything was arranged: Lady Eloise had agreed to come up to London to help with Jimmy's Hope House and be a comfort to Aunt Edith.

An inward sigh acknowledged the gulf that had opened up between himself and Aunt Edith. He found that they were avoiding each other, more often than not. This wouldn't help the situation at all. It was bad enough when Aunt Edith knew Elka would soon be deployed, but there had been some comfort in the knowledge that Jhona would be with her. Now Brendan was worried about how she would take this news and, even more so, how Elka and Jhona would cope with being separated.

'Sir, may I speak?' Brendan asked.

'Of course, as long as you aren't going to refuse. By the way, are you Irish, O'Flynn?'

'No, sir, I was fathered by an Irish man, but I never knew him. I'm British, sir.'

'Hmm, I meant to ask you before. I knew an O'Flynn in the last lot – a young boy. Sad business. Still, never mind that now. What did you want to say?'

Brendan was thrown for a moment, on hearing the colonel refer out of the blue to someone he was sure was Jimmy. He judged the colonel to be around fifty-five, so he would have been in his early thirties during the last war and a young officer. *Was he there when Jimmy was convicted?*

Shaking this thought from him and knowing he couldn't pursue it, he told the colonel of his misgivings about separating Elka and Jhona, remembering to refer to them by their code-names.

'Sorry, old chap. You know as well as I do that duty comes first. They will show their mettle – or lack of it – by the way they accept this, because it has to happen. Tell me: you have been involved in the planning of the Polish mission – what are your views on it succeeding? Oh, I know the official upbeat angle that is being taken, but what do *you* really think?'

'It is dangerous. Even more so for me, as I'm not much of a skier, and that's the only way in. The temperatures are going to be the killer.'

'I don't think that is a problem; at least the skiing isn't, as you are only to escort Elka to the border. Your main job is to give her cover and lend credence to her story. Once she reaches Poland, she will go alone.'

'And what about PMf's trade-off plan?'

'Getting her sister out, you mean? Well, that's not going to happen. I'm sorry, but it is impossible. You're not to tell her that, otherwise she may lose her motivation. It is going to be difficult enough anyway, when she is told her husband isn't going. So we have to keep up the myth that the plan involving her sister's rescue is still in place.'

Brendan's stomach churned violently, making him swallow hard as bile rose in his throat. *Good Lord! What an impossible thing to ask of me. How can I keep this secret from Elka?* But he knew he must, and he could see the sense in the action; he just wished they would give Elka a chance. He felt sure she would go anyway. To keep this secret from her would be an agony and would feel like a betrayal of her.

'When will you tell them that I am replacing agent PMm, sir?'

'They are probably being told this very minute. It isn't my job to do so; it is the job of the officer in charge of their training. I have no need to come into contact with them. You are different: you are a member of my team and a serving officer under me. I have a duty towards you.'

Brendan's thanks were not heartfelt. To him, it all seemed so callous, but then he had made the mistake of thinking that being emotionally involved with two of his agents wouldn't matter. Now he found that it did, as decisions like this one had to be seen through. He had to hang on to the fact that the aim of the mission was a good one, and that there was no one better equipped for the job than Elka.

The moment he was off-duty Brendan headed to Jimmy's Hope House. He hoped above all that his Aunt Edith was there. He needed to talk to her. He couldn't tell her anything about the mission, but he must inform her and Ginny that he wouldn't be able to go to Leicestershire after all. Maybe he could suggest dinner. He somehow needed to lessen the strain between himself and Edith, which had been created initially by his recruitment of Elka and Jhona and had been compounded by their shared loss, which had cut them both so deeply that it had almost severed their relationship with its intensity. They had been unable to reach out to each other. He supposed that was because neither of them could deal with the other's pain.

Oh, how he missed his Aunt Ada. Of all of those he'd lost on that awful day, he missed her most. He could have gone and talked to her and cried with her, and she would have understood and made him feel better.

As he walked through the gates of Jimmy's Hope House, he caught sight of a young girl standing with her back to the wall. She had a coat pulled up around her neck and it swamped her, leaving only her face peering towards him. Everything about her expressed fear. He was reminded of the rabbits on the estate of Hastleford Hall; they stood in much the same way, if you came upon them – as if they were suddenly turned to stone.

'Hello, there. Are you all right?'

'*Oui, je suis* . . . I – I mean, yes, thank you.'

She didn't look or sound it. 'You're French? You must be Leah – Ginny talks about you.' At this moment, more than ever before, he felt grateful for the private education that Edith and Laurent had paid for. His knowledge of languages, and especially of French, had helped build his relationship with Ginny as she sought to communicate with Leah; and now, he hoped, it would cement his own and Leah's friendship. In French he asked, 'Aren't you cold, standing out here?' She gave a shrug in response. Still sensing her fear, he told her who he was, which seemed to give her confidence. 'It's nice to meet you. Do you know if Dr Edith is here?'

'No, she has left, but Ginny is, although she may be busy. I can enquire. If you come in, I can make you a hot drink.'

There was something about her that compelled him to accept. Once in the light of the building and when she had taken off her coat, he could see that she was of slight, almost boyish build, with a beautiful elfin-like face. Her dark eyes were huge with a gentle slant to them, and her glossy-black hair hung to her waist. There was a vulnerability about her that made his heart lurch. And a feeling took him that made him want be with her, and her alone; he didn't want her to fetch Ginny.

Shame made him tingle at such thoughts. This poor girl didn't need the complications of his attentions. She had enough grief of her own to contend with. He turned away, deliberately sitting at the centre table with his back to her. *What on earth is the matter with me?* 'Look, if Ginny's busy, I won't stay. Thank you for the offer.'

'No. No, don't go. I make tea. I . . .'

Her protest hung in the air. In his haste to remove himself from her presence, he knocked over the chair from which he'd risen. The clatter trembled through him, giving his memory a painful jerk.

Outside, the cold air stung Brendan's face. He had to get a move-on, before blackout; it was already getting dusky. He looked at his watch: three o'clock. A small panic gripped him. Hurrying to his car, he steered it in the direction of the churchyard. He knew he should go back to HQ, but the thought of being alone in his room, in the house where many other officers were billeted, left him feeling very alone. He wished he could go to his Aunt Edith's house.

After the fire Edith had offered him a home, but he'd declined, not wanting to intrude on them. He had hoped he could sort a place out for himself and Ginny.

He'd found out that Annie had left her house to him in her will – or what remained of it, after the fire. It appeared that she'd always been advised by Aunt Rene in her financial matters, leaving all her legal papers and bank books with her. Among the papers had been insurance-policy documents that she'd kept up to date, and apart from the house, she had also left a good sum of money to Brendan in her will.

His heart had been gladdened by her thoughtfulness, and humbled by the love he knew she'd felt for him. The payout on the insurance was enough to repair and rebuild the house, a project that he hoped would begin soon. Not that he would ever live there again, but selling it would set up his future in the way Annie had intended. He would put the proceeds of the sale towards buying a flat for Ginny. The rest he would save, with the money Annie had left him; and then, after the war, he could sort out what he wanted to do. An involuntary thought popped into his head, and it involved Leah and his future. It shocked him: he had no right to think of Leah like that. He'd only just met her! He mustn't dwell on the impact she had had on him. He had to accept that he wasn't thinking straight. He'd been thrown into a quandary with the new orders, and all the change they had brought about; not to mention all that he'd been through. It had left him uncertain and grasping at straws.

He'd reached the gates of the churchyard. Hesitating, he wondered if this was really the place he should be. A voice stopped him from turning round and getting back into his car.

'Brendan! Hello. Fancy us coming here at the same time. How are you?'

Entering his Aunt Edith's hug, he felt for a moment that he would cry as she held him to her.

'What is it, darling? Is there something wrong?'

He couldn't answer. Suddenly he felt like the little boy he'd once been, dependent on Edith and his Aunt Ada, and Annie and Rene, for all his needs. Tears pricked his eyes. He blinked them away.

'Look, go and show your respects and do whatever you need to do. I'll sit in the car and wait for you. You can follow me home, and we'll talk.'

'Thank you, Aunt Edith, I'd like that. I – I wonder if I might stay over? You see, I won't get back to my room before the blackout.' Suddenly he wanted this more than anything and hoped it would help them re-establish the easy rapport they had been used to. An impromptu overnight stay posed no problems; he had his own room at Edith's house and a supply of toiletries, as well as a few changes of clothing that he'd always kept there.

'No problem, darling – we'd love to have you. We have so much to catch up on. I haven't seen anything of you for two weeks. I'm hungry for news, as Elka's letters don't really tell me anything.'

'You're a lifesaver, Aunt Edith. I was dreading being on my own tonight, or being cajoled into joining in the gung-ho bravado of the other officers. But I warn you: I won't be able to tell you much about Elka and Jhona, I'm afraid. Only that they are fine and should be home in a few days from now.'

'Hmm. That can only mean they are near deployment. Oh dear, my heart sinks at the prospect, but my head tells me they are doing something important and I have to be patient and supportive. Will it be for long?'

'Aunt Edith, you know I can't tell you. Now, let me go and talk to Aunt Ada. And, as you say, we'll have a chat when we get to your house. I so need one. You get off – I'll come along when I'm ready. I promise.'

She stood for a moment, gazing at him.

The easy manner she'd had with him had made Brendan feel happier, but now he wondered if he could see some form of accusation in her expression? He felt so guilty at being instrumental in getting Elka and Jhona into the work they were doing. Edith had every right to be hurt and cross about it. No, he was wrong. She smiled her lovely smile and tapped him on the shoulder, in a gesture that said everything would be all right, then left him with a wave.

Would everything be all right? Something had changed – he could admit that now. Something had happened to him when he'd looked at Leah. Something that had left her imprinted on his soul. He daren't think what his Aunt Edith would make of that. Leah was in her charge, and she was in a very delicate and vulnerable state. She had been through terrible experiences. He must never admit his feelings. He'd have to avoid going to Jimmy's Hope House.

His resolve weighed heavily on him. He knelt by his Aunt Ada and Uncle Joe's grave. 'Oh, Aunt Ada. What am I to do?'

He knew what she would have said: 'Take the path of truth, as long as it won't cause suffering. If it will, then bite on your courage, lad, and take the path you laid out for yourself and give your best to it.'

A feeling of loneliness came over him. So much had happened today to knock him off-balance, and yet he couldn't talk to anyone about it. Aunt Ada wouldn't have understood; she'd have demanded that he told her what was troubling him. His mind gave him her words as if she'd spoken them aloud: 'The world won't collapse, if I have an ear to what's going on. I'm not a spy, nor does anyone want to know owt as I know.' This last bit wasn't true. Ada just hadn't known how important she was, to all those who knew her and loved her. He still wouldn't have told her any official secrets, but he could have talked to her about the turmoil into which he'd been thrown.

Blowing a kiss to the mound of earth that was getting less pronounced as it settled, he turned away. In a few months they'd be able to have a stone erected, and on it he would put: 'Here lie a loving couple, who gave to others and took little for themselves.'

As soon as Brendan arrived at her home, Edith steered him towards the elaborately carved high-backed sofa with barley-twist legs and deeply padded yellow upholstery that stood in a little inglenook of the hall.

'Can't you talk about anything that is troubling you, Brendan dear? Your Aunt Ada used to say, "A trouble shared is a trouble halved." She was right, too. It is surprising how another point of view can lessen the weight of your troubles.'

'I know. I do have worries, and pain. For one, I – I did the wrong thing in recruiting Elka and Jhona. I should have realized the emotional pull on you, and what I would be putting myself through. And now . . . well, you will find out anyway. They are to do separate work. I think they will hate me. And I know you will come to feel that, too.'

'I can never think less of you. I was angry with you when you recruited Elka and Jhona, but I didn't stop loving you. My anger was selfish. Having just been reunited with my daughter, whom I thought was lost to me forever, I found you taking her away from me. But Laurent made me see that wasn't so. This bloody war was always going to separate us. Elka and Jhona had already told me they intended to do their bit. I would expect no less of them. It just hurts to see them go so soon. But if they are not to be together – oh dear, how will they cope?'

'I'm sorry. They really are ideal for what we need. There was no one else. But how I wish there had been.'

'I understand, more than anyone. I have been through it all, as has Laurent. We had difficult choices to make and we didn't falter. I'm proud that my children, and you – whom I look upon as I would a son – are doing your bit, now that you are called on to do so. You didn't ask for a war to begin, but you are trying to protect us all. Nothing more can be asked of you. You don't have my condemnation; you have my deep admiration. My initial reaction has passed. But is there no way my mind can be put at rest, concerning what will be asked of them?'

'No. I can't tell you. All I *can* say is that it will concern a communication line.'

'In France?'

Brendan didn't answer this. Not wanting to tell a direct lie, he hoped that staying silent would seem to her to be a 'yes'. He would hate her to suspect the real truth.

Her scrutinizing look made him glance away.

'Thank you. I feel a little relieved, at least. Now come through to the sitting room. Laurent is waiting for us.'

Brendan followed her, feeling even more wretched than he thought possible.

'There you are. You took a long time coming through,' Laurent said as they appeared.

'Sorry, darling. I thought I might get Brendan to talk about what is troubling him, but as usual he is having to be careful of what he says.'

'Nice to see you, Brendan. It has been too long. And, you know, Edith is very worried about you. Is there something we can do to help you?'

'Unless you can unwind the last few weeks and let us all start again, then no, Uncle Laurent.'

'Sadly, none of us can do that. But it is not good to let moroseness take hold of you. Your Aunt Ada could have done that, after all she had to contend with, but she didn't. She soldiered on.'

Laurent's words seemed like those of a father giving his son a lecture, but Brendan knew that he was right.

'Why don't you visit more? And talk to us?' Aunt Edith asked. 'No, don't answer that – I know why. The hurt has been so deep for us all that it has caused a small chasm between us. We have become guarded with each other, like fragile creatures afraid of reality; we prefer to dance around the issues, when we should be supporting each other. That must change now.'

'It will. I'm sorry – I've felt so guilty. Not just about Elka and Jhona, but, well . . . I left the kitchen; my mother had threatened me with a knife and I stepped back.' The words were tumbling from him, and he couldn't stop them.

He needed for them to know. 'Joe had moved forward, and so had Aunt Ada. That left me nearest the door to the front hall. When my mother smashed the methylated-spirits bottle, none of us moved.'

Everything that he'd lived that day – and relived a million times since – came pouring out. Then, when he'd said it all, and knowing that his face was wet with tears, he told them about the final minutes.

'I could hear Joe talking, coaxing, then a crash, then nothing. But it all happened so quickly, in a flash really. Oh God, why didn't I grab them both . . . Why?'

His body trembled when he'd finished telling it all. A silence hung in the air that gave him no clues as to how they felt. He'd dragged up the painful incident of the fire and had brought to life all the details they hadn't known. In doing so, he'd cleansed something within himself, as if releasing a burden. For them, though, he could see that it had been too much. 'I'm sorry . . . I shouldn't have told you this.'

'No. It is right that you should, and that you did. We should share our feelings, and what transpires when something so traumatic has happened to us. I was guilty of holding so many of my war experiences inside me that it stunted me from moving forward. I did that for years, and it caused a lot of strain to my darling Edith,' Laurent said.

Brendan noticed the look that passed between them and wondered about the nature of it. His aunt looked hurt for a second, but then Laurent reached for her hand, before continuing.

'The answer to why I held on to these emotions for so long lies in what you have just said. Brendan, you had no reason to believe that Joe and Ada weren't just behind you. It is understandable – the fire would spread rapidly. You say that your mother turned on the gas and that one ring was already lit under the kettle. This must have ignited the meths. Your mother lighting a match drew flames to her; she'd probably splashed some of the meths onto her sleeve. It only takes seconds for a large amount of gas to enter the air. And so with one gas ring already lit, and almost a never-ending supply of escaping gas, and with methylated spirits having been splashed everywhere, all the elements for an instant inferno were in place. Not to mention copious amounts of deadly smoke. The only outcome of trying to help them would have been your death as well.'

Brendan knew what Laurent said was true. Aunt Edith's gentle voice came to him. 'Maybe you should give yourself time. It has only been a few weeks since it all happened. Perhaps taking some time away would be good. You have your trip down to Leicestershire soon – that will help.'

'I'm not able to go. I need to contact Douglas, and to tell Ginny, too. As it happens, I do have to go away – but not for pleasure, though I can't say any more. Sorry. Thank you for understanding and helping me.'

'We are always here for you. You are family.'

Hearing Laurent use the word 'family' warmed him. And with a lovely kind smile on his aunt's face again, the strained feeling that had lain between them these last few weeks dissolved. He was back where he belonged, in the heart of his family.

'Eeh, lad, come here and let me give you a cuddle.'

'Ha, Aunt Edith! You sounded just like her. I'm one for using a bit of the northern accent meself, lass.'

They burst out laughing. But when Laurent thought he would have a go at mimicking Aunt Ada, it turned to real belly laughs, which made them double over and brought tears streaming down their faces.

'By, it's grand to see you both happy. It cheers me no end!' he said. His accent was more French than northern, but it topped his own and Aunt Edith's efforts, in how comical it was. It felt good to laugh. It broke the tension and made Brendan feel there was some purpose to life after Ada. They would find a way to carry on. They would miss her till their hearts broke in two, but they would also live with her memory – a precious gift that she left behind for them.

# 16

# *Ania*

## Krakow, Late February 1940 – The Horrific Reality of German Rule

As offices go, this one in the headquarters of the Gestapo in Krakow was like any other. Ten typists sat in rows, clicking away in a soothing kind of rhythm, but there was nothing soothing about the atmosphere. A tangible fear hung in the air. The typists were Polish girls, forced to work there under the threat of what would befall their families if they refused.

Ania tried to convey this threat to Baruch in her messages to him. She had begged him to make his men, and the Polish people, understand and stop treating these girls as if they were collaborators. She wanted them to stop carrying out reprisals. But the reprisals still went on, Ania realized, as her eyes rested on a girl in the corner. The girl's hair had been cut very short, but the style didn't hide the fact that a lot of it was missing. Angry red patches showed where it had been pulled out at the roots. *Surely Baruch will listen to me? Is he getting my messages?* She didn't doubt that he received the messages concerning secrets that would help the cause, but she wasn't so sure if he received her personal messages, and the thought that he might not both worried her and broke her heart.

She sent messages to Baruch through the young man who had taunted her the day she had been recruited. She always thought of it as the day she got the job in Gestapo HQ, rather than letting her mind dwell on the other things that had happened that day.

The young man's name was Stefan Baranski. He had been instrumental in bringing her to the attention of the Germans, for the sole purpose of helping her get this position. Unable to speak German at the time, he had told the Germans in English – despite having little command of English, either – that she lived as a Jew and yet didn't wear the Star, didn't look like a Jew, and that she spoke many languages. This had led them to seek her out.

Stefan had used knowledge of his German descent to further his own position. He had also denounced his Jewish faith and was now given special privileges.

One of the recent documents that had come to her concerned lists of people such as Stefan. They were typing-pool copy documents written in German, which were then sent for approval and finally came to her for translation. These lists were called the *Deutsche Volksliste* – the German People's List – and classified *willing* Polish citizens into four groups:

Group 1 comprised ethnic Germans living in Poland who had taken an active part in the struggle for the Germanization of Poland.

Group 2 included ethnic Germans who hadn't taken an active part, but had 'preserved' their German characteristics.

Group 3 were those individuals of alleged German stock who had become 'Polonized', but whom it was believed could be won back to Germany. This group included persons of non-German descent who were married to Germans or were members of non-Polish groups, as they were considered desirable, for their political attitude and racial characteristics.

Group 4 consisted of those of German heritage who had become politically merged with the Poles.

These groups were considered worthy of being – or easily manipulated into becoming – German citizens again and were even given German passports.

Stefan fell into Group 3 and had been taken off the hard-labour duties imposed on the Jews and been attending a school set up by the Germans. There he was learning the German language and was taking to it surprisingly quickly, besides being indoctrinated with the Nazi regime's principles. He was reviled by all Poles and Jews. Even Ania disliked him, as his methods towards those who went too far in their intended reprisals of him were often cruel, and he betrayed those helping the Jews. He insisted that he did all this to ingratiate himself with the Germans, and to give him more and more freedom of movement and greater credibility. He tried to convince her that his actions were for the greater good, but she wasn't entirely won over, and worried about him and whether he was truly to be trusted.

The latest work handed to her had instructed that all Poles were to wear a purple badge with the letter 'P' on it, to distinguish them. They were not allowed to travel on the trams and had to avoid certain shops and cafes. They even had to walk on the other side of the street if they saw a German approaching – something that brought the Poles ever closer to their Jewish neighbours, as they shared some of their suffering.

Within days of this order, many Poles were hauled from their homes – men and young boys alike – to be dispatched to Germany. They were to work in hard-labour camps. Ania shuddered at the thought of what they would go through. It was a pitiful sight to see them leave, crushed into railway carriages as if they were animals.

As this went on, weeping women and broken elderly, afraid and lost, lined the streets. Many were hit with the butt of a rifle if they tried to cling onto their men.

Such a raid was in progress as Ania left the office at lunchtime. Unable to shop in her usual store, because of the purple badge that had been imposed on her, she had to walk several streets out of her way to get to the little shop she was allowed to use. Bitter cold bit her cheeks, as the icy wind carried wails of distress and protest in its wake. But it was the screams of a woman not far from her that turned her blood to ice in her veins.

The woman was heavily pregnant, and a German officer was trying to pull a small boy from her arms. From what he was shouting, Ania knew he would kill the woman if she did not let go. She silently prayed she would do so, as maybe then both of them would stand a chance of living. But the woman clung on. Unable to hold his footing in the deep snow, the German officer let go and stood back. Once steadied, he swung his rifle, hitting the woman across her head. Falling backwards, she let go of the boy and stumbled on the kerb edge, landing on her back. Another soldier threw the boy onto the waiting truck. Ania controlled the gasp she'd drawn in, as she saw the officer lift his foot and brutally drive his boot into the mound of the woman's stomach, before spitting in her face.

Clutching the rough wall of the building that she was

near to, Ania stifled a scream. Despite the cold, sweat broke out over her body. Vomit rose to her throat, but she swallowed it down, leaving her throat stinging with the coarseness of the vile-tasting acid. Her fists clenched. She wanted to run after the officer and hit him, but knew she must stay out of sight.

When the soldiers had moved on further up the road and were intent on carrying out their mission, Ania ran to the woman. 'Let me help you – here, take my hand.'

The woman looked up at her. Between gasps of pain and through gritted teeth, she said, 'Don't touch me, Collaborator!'

To Ania, the woman might just as well have stuck a knife into her, for she couldn't have hurt her more. 'I'm not what you think. I tried to refuse to help them and I was raped and beaten. I have no choice; none of us girls working for them have a choice. Just as you had none, just then. Please let me help you.'

The woman stared through her tears, the hatred in her face dissipating. Reaching her hand towards Ania, she gasped in despair, 'My boy, my boy! Oh, Kakper, Kakper. Don't let them take him – please help me!'

Ania didn't reply, for her tightened throat wouldn't let her utter any words. Trying to get a grip and stop herself sliding, she helped the woman to her feet. With the movement, blood flooded from between the woman's legs, contrasting with the white of the snow on the pavement.

'Oh no! Oh God, no! My baby, my baby, my *baby*!' The scream caught the attention of the retreating officer. He turned round, lifted his gun to his shoulder and fired. Blood splattered Ania. She looked down into what had once been the woman's face, but was now a gaping hole.

Her grasp loosened. The woman's body slithered back onto the pavement. Shock held Ania rigid and unable to cry out. The gun was now pointed straight at her. Fear stilled her. Her sandpaper tongue wouldn't let her form the words to beg for her life. Then, slowly, the gun lowered.

'*Kenne Ich Sie?*'

Relief helped her to find her voice. 'Y-yes, you do know me. I – I work in Gestapo HQ as a translator. I was just passing. She needed help. I couldn't pass by.'

The officer's steely eyes took in her body, from her face to her feet, giving Ania the feeling of being stripped of her clothes. A smile curled his lips. 'I will see you later.'

Her body trembled violently. The meaning behind those words was clear. Her mind screamed as she looked down at the body of the woman through stinging eyes. *Why, why, why . . . ?*

A child's voice penetrated her anguish. '*Matka, Matka!*'

Horror seeped into Ania at the sight of the boy the woman had held, running towards her and his mother's dead body. The fear in her deepened to terror. 'No! No, child, go back, go back. Go back!' Her words were drowned in a blast of gunfire. The boy's body danced hideously, as bullets peppered him from the machine gun mounted on another vehicle.

Falling to her knees, Ania vomited. Unable to stop the spasm this time, she choked on the vile-tasting liquid that her stomach had rejected. Spitting the last of it out, she made an attempt to crawl away from the scene on her hands and knees. A bullet whizzed by her head, stopping her in her tracks.

'You!' In German he commanded her to get on her way.

She could not obey. Her legs were like jelly and prevented

her from standing. Her head spun with the pain of what she'd witnessed.

A hand came under her arm and lifted her roughly. A low Polish-speaking voice that she recognized as Stefan's grated in her ear. 'Do as he says and, in future, walk on by. Don't get involved.' He pushed her roughly forward and shouted, in surprisingly good German, 'An order is an order, woman. Do not disobey your superiors.'

Somehow, by clinging onto the walls of the houses, Ania managed to walk away. As she did so, something happened inside her. A kind of acceptance of how life was, and would continue to be. Stefan was right: she had to walk on by. She had to behave differently from the way her heart dictated, if she was to survive. Sometimes she didn't want to live and cried out for death to take her, but she knew she couldn't give up. If she did, who would get to the Resistance the valuable information to which she had access? For she wasn't only able to tell them about the badges and the daily horrors that she knew were to be imposed on the Jewish people, and now on the Poles, too. She also had access to other confidential material that she was able to take a look at discreetly. Names on lists that stated who was in a privileged position, and lists of the people of whom the Germans should be wary. Then there were documents and maps that related what military strategies were to take place in the area. And, most importantly, a target list of those to be captured and disposed of. She'd seen Baruch's name on one of these.

When she reached the store, the female manager who'd witnessed everything helped her to a chair and rubbed her frozen hands. 'What you just did will help you in the neighbourhood. Life will be easier for you. Now, let me get you a drink of water and clean you up.'

Grateful, but unable to say so, Ania just stared ahead. The few bottles, tins and jars on the shelves danced before her. The stench of the near-rotting vegetables on sale only increased her nausea. Closing her eyes and shaking her head steadied her.

Ania didn't know how she got through the rest of the day. Back in her apartment, she stripped and went through the ritual of scrubbing her body roughly with a flannel dipped in hot water. The store hadn't had any soap, so she used the last of the huge bar of hard green soap that she normally used to wash her clothes. When dry, she patted herself with talcum powder.

Suddenly the fear she harboured in her every waking hour escalated, as a knock on her door, followed immediately by a kick, sent it swinging into the wall with a crash. Instinctively she grabbed her towel.

'You won't need that.' The towel stung her as it was wrenched from her. 'Nice, and just what I imagined. Are you a virgin?'

Steely blue eyes stared into hers, then travelled down her body, just as they had done in her earlier encounter with this same man, though now he wasn't wielding a gun and she was naked. As he stared, his eyes glazed over, his lids half-shielded. Everything about the appearance of this German officer suggested the perfect Aryan specimen: tall, lean, with blond hair and square, handsome features.

Exposed as she was under his gaze, Ania cowered away from him, in her vulnerable position. He followed her, moving forward as she stepped back, but keeping close to her.

She lifted her head in defiance. 'No, I am not a virgin. I have been raped by one of your men.' She dare not tell him she was married.

He stepped back, relieving her of his close presence. 'What! Who was it? Give me a name!' Anger reddened his face from the neck upwards. His eyes had lost their lust.

Hope trickled into her. Maybe, just maybe, he was no longer interested, now that he knew she wasn't a virgin?

'I – I only know that when he took me to SA-Standartenführer Koertig, I heard the receptionist call him "Friedrich".'

'*Schweinehund!*'

Ania thought she would call Friedrich something stronger than a pig or a dog, but at this moment she felt almost grateful to him, as the officer turned on his heel and made for the door. As he reached it, he stopped.

Her heart thudded in despair when he turned round. 'It is of no matter. You will lie with me. I must have you.'

'No. Please. I – I . . . No!'

The space between them lessened before she could move. As he neared, she tried to dodge him and make for the door. His hand lashed out and the blow sent her reeling. Then a tight pain assailed her forehead as he grabbed her hair, clutching it and forcing her back towards him. His other hand locked in an agonizing grip on her arm, twisting it behind her back. Propelled forward, she could do nothing to stop their progress towards the bedroom. Once inside, he threw her onto the bed.

'You will do as I ask.' His hands unbuckled his belt. As he slapped the strap across the palm of his other hand, his voice became gravelly and she knew his thoughts were heightening his lust. 'Everything I want, you will give to me. I will punish Friedrich out of your body!' His spittle sprayed on her as he gritted his teeth. 'Everything, everything – I will beat you . . . beat you!'

The sting of the belt on her buttocks caused her to take in a deep, rasping breath. Drawing her knees up, she hunched herself into a ball at the top of the bed and huddled into the wall, pulling the pillow in front of her, but he snatched it from her.

Once more the belt rose like a snake high above her, ready to strike. A moan came from her. When it landed on her thigh she screamed out, 'No, no . . . no more, no more.' But something in his expression told of his extreme pleasure and she knew he wasn't going to stop. The next lash cut her back. An indescribable pain seared through her. Her scream pierced her own ears as it ripped from her in a holler that reduced her to nothing more than an animal. Then, unable to scream any more or even to speak, she grovelled through her tears and snot, gasping for breath, flaying her arms and legs, kicking him and clawing at him.

'That is good. Fight me, whore!'

After a few moments weakness seized her and her body crumbled in a heap. There was nothing she could do to stop him.

He removed his trousers, then positioned her without her protest. She took his thrusts and the hideous pain of him entering her with a moan that sounded to herself like a pitiful creature who was nothing – not a human being, just a thing worthy only of violation.

Unaware of it coming to an end, she lay still. Throbbing,

stinging pain swathed her whole body. Her bed beneath her was a bath of blood.

Conscious of a tap running for a few moments and then of a door slamming, Ania didn't move. Her mind emptied. She ceased to cry. A deathly silence enclosed her.

She didn't know how long she lay like that. All light had faded when finally, she made her way to her sink and filled a bowl with water, each step dragged out as if her body had turned to lead.

She didn't care that the water was cold. Not having the energy to heat it, she swabbed herself down, stopping to change the water when it turned red. The cold shivered through her body, bringing life back into her. Unable to bear the icy dousing for long, she wrapped herself in a towel and made it to her bed. Tearing the soiled top cover from it, she pulled back the rest of the blankets and climbed in.

Cold, humiliated and still in unbearable pain, Ania allowed her body to cry. In her anguish she called out for her beloved Baruch and for her dear sister, Elka. For her lost mama, for the mama she'd never known, and for her *babcia*. None of them came to her. How could they?

Exhausted, she dropped into a fitful sleep, where men were monsters grabbing at her, taking pieces of her flesh and laughing as they threw them in the air, until she stood – just a skeleton with a face. A face that she thought would never smile again.

# 17

# *Elka*

## London, Early March 1940 – A Mountain to Climb Alone

Holland Park, the peaceful haven in West London, lay just behind Edith's London home. The sounds drifting up from there – birds singing, trees rustling in the wind and children playing – were almost a rude intrusion to the sadness that clothed Elka and Jhona's sitting room on the top floor of the house. They had spent so little time here. Everything was still unused and had a new feel to it. Beautiful, but untouched by their personalities: that was how Elka saw it now.

Her heart ached as she sat close to Jhona on the sofa. The minutes ticked away the precious little time they had together. She'd tried being angry with Brendan, but in the end she knew it hadn't been his fault. But to have to part with Jhona was almost undoing her resolution to carry this mission through. Only the possibility of saving Ania kept her resolve strong.

Jhona clung to her.

'I will be safe with Brendan. You're not to worry, my darling.'

'But he won't be going all of the way with you. How will he be able to protect you?'

'I don't know. They haven't told me all the plans – as we have found is their way. I am worried they have something they need you to do, and that is the real reason we are being separated. I fear we will be parted for much longer that we expect.'

'I have feared that myself, but I didn't want to say anything. Our instructors seemed very interested in me being able to speak Russian. And now I have been summoned to the War Office tomorrow at eleven.'

'No! Surely they wouldn't send you to Russia? Why should they? I know Russia is occupying the eastern section of our country, but aren't the Russians still allies of Great Britain? Isn't it that they moved to protect part of Poland and will fight the Germans?'

'Yes, but maybe the British don't trust the Russians and need someone in Russia to find out what is going on. My thinking is that all they will need me for is as an interpreter. So please don't worry. It is I who will fear every minute of the time you are away.'

Elka agreed: using Jhona as an interpreter seemed the most likely plan. Or at least this was what she told herself. It wasn't really what she was thinking, but she didn't want to consider the type of mission Jhona might be asked to do. It was far better that they part with Jhona thinking she wouldn't be too worried about him. She would be worried, of course. She wouldn't put anything past those who had trained them, and who were now in charge of them. All of them had been focused on the job that needed to be done, and gave the impression that although agents were vital to the success of a mission, they were also pawns in a game.

Brendan's voice made them both freeze for a split second. He was calling up the stairs that they had to go. As they clung onto each other, Elka thought Jhona would never let her go. When he did, she had the strangest feeling that it would be the last time she would see him. Grabbing him and kissing him hard on the lips, she took a moment to scrutinize his beloved face.

'Go, my darling. Go!' Jhona's voice shook with emotion. 'And may God protect you and bring you back to me.'

Elka ran from the room.

Saying goodbye to her mother and Laurent proved almost as difficult. Edith remained brave and stood on the steps of the beautiful house in Holland Park, waving until they had disappeared. Her slight figure belied the courage that she held within her tiny frame.

Knowing now all that her mother had gone through during the last war gave Elka the courage she needed to face whatever she had to in this war.

The training had indeed been gruelling, and at times Elka had thought she would fail to come up to the required standard. But eventually both she and Jhona had mastered all that had been asked of them. Now the time had come, and all the techniques they had learned to keep each other safe now had to be applied to Brendan, who had different skills.

The noise of the engine of the civil plane that she and Brendan were on whirred in Elka's ears. She felt warm and uncomfortable in the stuffy atmosphere. There were few passengers.

They were flying to Budapest posing as journalists. Sitting together, the two of them were unable to show any of the sibling affection that had built up between them over the last few months since her arrival in England. This enforced restraint meant that for the most part they sat in silence. Elka reflected on the training she and Jhona had endured. As it was specific to their mission, they had rarely been joined by other trainees. They had both found the exercises to be more difficult mentally than physically. This was particularly so when they were put through the mocked-up circumstances of being caught, tortured and facing being shot. The enactment had been so realistic that she had actually wet herself when the gun had been held at her head.

They had had to take on board techniques to help them in all kinds of situations, and these had helped to give Elka confidence. The worst experience had been when she'd been taught how to kill a man. Despite this, she had to admit that she'd enjoyed learning some of the disciplines taught to her: how to use equipment disguised as ordinary items that anyone would have in their pockets, case or handbag. Examples of this were the lipstick that became a knife when a small button was moved to the correct position, and the pen that held poison, which could be administered by releasing the clip in the side of it, causing instantaneous death.

These things had fascinated her and yet frightened her. But it was the sinister cyanide pill that terrified her the most. *Would I be able to kill myself*? She didn't know. And she hoped she would never be faced with the decision of whether or not to bite on that pill.

Turning her mind to what lay ahead, she went over what

Brendan had told her as they had been driven to the airport. It appeared that there was a lot of German activity taking place in Zakopane, and at this very moment a conference between Russia and Germany was taking place there. The mission was now considered highly dangerous.

His words had struck fear in her, but she'd found that it was a different fear from that she'd experienced previously in her life. This fear gave her an edge and made her absorb what she was being told, with a kind of professional detachment she never thought she would possess. With this feeling came the knowledge that she was well equipped to cope.

Brendan had told her that a school had been set up close to the Slovak border in Zakopane by the commander-in-chief of the Security Police, SS-Brigadeführer Bruno Streckenbach. The school's purpose was to train selected candidates from collaborators among the Ukrainians, the Polish police and other Secret Police personnel, including intelligence-gathering sympathizers.

This meant that many high-ranking Gestapo and SS officers were based in or visiting the area, especially as Zakopane town had been turned into an entertainment centre for senior officers of the SS and Werhmacht, and the Gestapo had taken over the Palace Hotel as their headquarters.

The intelligence had also informed them that all Jews were to be removed from the district, and that some had already disappeared.

This hurt Elka deeply, and she wondered at the plight of her people. The good news was that it had been a member of Baruch's group who had supplied this information. He'd managed to get to Budapest and contact the

British Minister there. The map he'd left, showing where Baruch could be found, would be invaluable to her.

The banks of cloud below her looked like mounds and mounds of cotton wool. She was sure that the snowy Hungarian terrain lay beneath them. At this thought, her heart lurched. Hungary was a neutral country, but was not to be trusted. It had recently accepted Slovakian territory that was offered to them by the Nazis. Elka had been warned that the Hungarians were more likely to cooperate with the Germans than with the Allies.

To make things even more difficult, Sir Owen St Clair O'Malley, the British Minister in Budapest who held the information they needed, wouldn't be all that favourably inclined towards them, as he took a dim view of Section D's cloak-and-dagger work and refused to have anything to do with it.

Cold air stung Elka as she stepped off the plane. Pulling her fur coat around her helped to combat it a little, but also helped to steady her nerves, as she could hug herself under the pretence of holding the coat around her.

'Umm, more than a little colder than England, Miss Carter, don't you think? Lucky you, having a fur to keep you warm.'

It was strange hearing Brendan say this to her, though it pleased her that he was assuming his role and hadn't tried to whisper some encouragement to her. And especially that he had remembered her cover name.

'Call me Ella.' It was a name she had chosen as it wasn't dissimilar to her own and was therefore easy to remember.

'In that case you may call me Joseph and, if we really become friends, I might let you call me Joe.'

She laughed at this, and for a moment the feeling gave her confidence. But she would stick to Joseph. She knew Brendan had chosen the name after his Aunt Ada's husband. From what she'd heard about his life, the poor man hadn't had a good time of it. She wouldn't want to jinx Brendan.

As they entered the small hut-like building they both remained quiet while negotiating border control. Elka breathed a sigh of relief at not being challenged; she waited, holding her breath once more, as she watched Brendan's papers being scrutinized.

Just behind him, an incident happened. A young woman was pulled aside for questioning. The only reason Elka could imagine for this was the woman's obvious Jewish look. Brendan and Elka didn't linger to see the outcome, but Elka prayed the girl was let free and thanked God that Jhona wasn't with them. He too might have been recognized as a Jew.

Once safely through this first obstacle, they were met by Hubert Makinson. He handled Section D's Polish contacts, whilst posing as a Balkan correspondent for the *News Chronicle*, the paper for which they were supposed to be war correspondents. With him was Gerick Radinski, a former Polish intelligence agent, now living in a safe house in Budapest. Both were to help them with the next leg of the assignment.

After greeting them, Gerick told them, 'I have rented two apartments for you in the Alkotmány Ulitsa. They are in the same block, so they will give you the opportunity to talk to each other without raising suspicion, and for me to communicate easily with you.'

This warmed Elka more than her fur coat could have

done and brought a smile to her lips. 'Thank you, Gerick, you don't know how much that will mean to us.'

'But you must take extreme care. I have eyes and ears in every quarter of the city, so I will know if any rumours start, regarding your relationship to each other. Being affectionate like siblings may seem natural to you, but it could look like something different when it concerns someone who is supposed to be a work colleague, and it could lead to gossip. It could also lead to you slipping out of your cover story. If I see anything like that happening, I will report you and have you lifted out.'

This shocked Elka. She was reminded of why she was here. 'Of course. We will be very discreet, I promise you.' It didn't seem appropriate to tell him that they hadn't known each other that long and weren't affectionate with each other in an overt way.

As they drove towards Budapest, Elka saw many similarities to her beloved Poland in the buildings and the wide streets. Most buildings were of a grey stone construction and had four or five storeys. They were large and square, yet elegant. Some surprises lay in store in the cobbled back streets, though. Here there were rows of cottages, obviously poor dwellings, but nonetheless clean and pretty. Passing one of these, they heard music. On the steps of a corner building sat two gypsy boys in felt hats playing violins. The sound was magical and lifted Elka into another world. A world she dared not visit for long, as the memories would suffocate her and make her yearn to be back in the happy times she had known.

Crossing over the beautiful River Danube from Buda into Pest – once two different places, divided by the river snaking through what was now the united city of Budapest – Elka could see the striking parliament building, with its domes and towers paying homage to the sky.

The driver took them round and into a street that held its own beauty. Alkotmány, or Constitution Street, lay before her. Wide but cobbled, it bustled with life, with its many cafes and shops, their colourful blinds blowing in the breeze and seemingly doing a roaring trade. One would never guess that this tree-lined, prosperous-looking street was in a country separated only by a border from Austria, a country that knew the pain of occupation.

But these thoughts did not detract from her immediate love of the area where she was to stay. Here the buildings were majestic. Four-storeyed, they had church-like domed windows, many of them with ornate balconies in a variety of colours. Some were of the grey stone she had already seen, while others were painted – one pink, one yellow – and all made a picture that framed the wonderful parliament house at the end of the street. It was a view fit for a picture postcard.

Two days had passed since their arrival. They had snatched only an hour alone together. The urgency of their mission meant that preparations had begun immediately, and despite warnings of temperatures of minus twenty degrees in parts of the mountain terrain, they had set out on their first trip over the Tatra Mountains.

A horse-drawn wheeled carriage had picked them up from the point to which they had parachuted, at the base of the mountains on the Slovak border. Now they trundled through worsening weather conditions as they swapped that mode of transport for a sledge board, which was loaded with skis and the other equipment needed.

Beauty surrounded them in the white world of the snow-covered landscape, but none of it impacted upon Elka. Inside, she had closed herself to feelings of any kind, as she refused to let in the terror that constantly sought to invade her.

'Soon Joseph and I will leave you, Ella. You will enter Poland, guided by Jan Marusarz.'

Elka was surprised and thrilled to hear this from Gerick. 'The Olympic champion skier?'

'Yes, the very same.'

'Well, I *am* honoured. What does Jan do these days?'

'He works for the Polish Consulate.'

Feeling much safer on hearing this information, Elka began to believe that, with Jan guiding her, she would make it. She was further comforted by the thought that a man with Jan's capabilities and knowledge of the area wouldn't attempt to make the crossing if he thought it too dangerous.

This thought was soon banished when they met Jan, because he immediately voiced his concerns. 'This is foolhardy. A trip such as this is ridiculous in these conditions.'

'It has to be done, Jan. Time is of the essence, and if anyone can make it through, you can.'

A heated discussion followed between Gerick and Jan, with Gerick winning.

Obviously in a mood fit to kill anyone who crossed him, Jan pulled on his balaclava, covering his thick black hair and handsome face. Though it was six years now since he'd been a champion skier, he still had the lithe body of one and this showed, as he impatiently drove himself off the ridge and flew through the air, landing on the slope beneath them. Pulling to a halt, he turned back towards them and waited.

'Right – good luck, Ella.'

Brendan stepped forward. 'Good luck. I wish I could come with you, but I will be monitoring your progress and sending your messages on. Gerick, may I have a moment alone with Ella?'

Something about his voice and expression sent a cold shiver down Elka's spine.

Gerick nodded and moved away.

Using her given name, Brendan spoke in a low voice. 'Elka, I'm sorry. It won't be possible to get Ania out on this trip, and you mustn't try. There is nothing in place for you to do so. I was forbidden to tell you until now. It may be possible that you will see your sister, but the network that you hoped would be set up to enable her escape hasn't been.'

'Why – why? Oh, Brendan, they knew that was a condition of me going. What kind of bastards do you work for? Well, I'm not coming back without her, and that's that!'

'You must. Think of Jhona—'

'What! You don't mean . . . ? Brendan, are you saying Jhona is in danger?'

'I don't know. I have only been told to tell you that, when making decisions to obey or disobey, you should think of what consequences there might be. Remember that Section D is a ruthless organization. They have to be, to get the work done. But remember, too, that they are fighting to win a war. Tough decisions have to be made. They want you to set up communications with Baruch's men. Here, you will need this. There are instructions for the wireless code, and so on. They see Ania as a vital link in that chain of communication. They know, from what you have told them, that she is already *in situ* in the Gestapo office. She has access to so much more than many other people – vital information that may change the course of events.'

Elka wanted to hit Brendan. How could he keep this from her? But once again she had a lesson to learn. None of this was a game. It was for real. She was a member of a secret organization. She knew what was expected of her, just as Brendan knew what was expected of him. She must do her duty, just as he was doing – to the letter and without question – or she might jeopardize operations. In truth, this trip wasn't just about getting information to the Polish people. It was about setting up a line of communication with the Resistance. Her sister was going to be a part of that, and so was she. She would do her duty.

Smiling up at Brendan, she nodded. 'I understand. I don't like it. I'm breaking my heart doing it, but I will do so.' Turning, she took up the pose needed to begin the descent onto the slope. Just before she pushed herself off, Gerick stepped forward. 'Ella, just follow Jan's instructions. He will be fine, once he has skied for a couple of miles – his moods never last long. He has a list of shelters; all are with folk he has stayed with along the way. Baruch has been contacted and will be waiting for you. Everything you will need has been set up for you. I will see you when you get back.'

'Right-o.' Turning to Brendan again, Elka looked at his haggard face. 'Don't worry, my brother. We have to do what we have to do.' With these words floating away from her, she jumped and skied up to Jan.

'Impressive. You can ski then?'

She didn't respond to his sarcastic remark. She didn't blame him for being angry. It was madness – complete madness – to tackle this journey in this weather. Jan gave her a curt nod and set off again.

The bitter wind found its way through her balaclava and burned her face. Tears misted her view, brought on by the cutting air, and stung her cheeks as they turned to ice. But nothing would stop her keeping up with Jan.

Baruch stood outside a rundown lodge where, as carefree young people, he, Ania and Elka herself, with crowds of other young people, had once had such a good and happy time on a skiing holiday – their first without their parents. His awkward stance suggested something wasn't quite right, and his expression confirmed this, as Elka skied up to him. Jan had left her, once she was on familiar territory, and had prepared to make his trip back into Hungary.

'Good to see you, Elka.' Baruch hesitated, obviously unsure.

Elka could do nothing to reassure him that all was well between them. The old animosities had gone, but she was too cold to tell him so, or to show him by any gesture.

'Come inside and get warm. We have some brandy and tea.'

She didn't ask anything. Her frozen face wouldn't move to allow her to speak, but in any case her heart was afraid of the answers, so she undid the heavy wooden skis and stretched out her legs. Baruch steadied her. His hand held her at first, and then his arm came round her and held her to him.

Tingling pain took hold of her fingers and toes. Stamping, she tried to get her blood to circulate faster.

'Get blankets, and warm towels – hurry!' Baruch shouted orders and a woman hastily obeyed him. Stripping Elka's outer trousers and jacket from her, Baruch began to rub her limbs with the warm towels. 'You look so different. I knew you, of course, but your hair and . . . well, I don't know what it is that makes you look so different?'

As life came back into her, Baruch offered her brandy. Spluttering and coughing, Elka gradually came back to normality. 'They bleached my hair and my eyebrows. Otherwise, it is only the cold that has swollen my face. Is Ania . . . ?'

'She has not arrived. She was meant to come yesterday. I haven't had any word from my contact, Ste—'

'No names. It is safer. Unless it is a code-name?'

'No. We have no code-names.'

'You must set up that system then, as soon as you can. I know that you all know each other, but if anyone new comes into your organization, they are not to know any of your real names. Do it before you introduce me to anyone. My name is Ella Carter. That is who I must be to you. My cover is that I am a war correspondent attached to the Budapest *News Chronicle*. Now, memorize that, and never call me Elka again when we are in company or introduce me to any of your group as Elka. They must all know and accept me as Ella Carter.'

Baruch nodded. Something about him made Elka think he hadn't really taken in what she'd told him. It was as if something was distracting him. With a feeling of trepidation, she asked, 'So, what of Ania – where is she?'

'I don't know. That is what I was going to say. It was arranged that she would come yesterday; my contact and courier was to bring her. He told me that he could get her out for a couple of days, to see you.'

'He knows I am Ania's sister?'

'Yes. It isn't anything I have informed him of. You don't know him, but he knew of both of you before the war. Ania more, as he is a long-standing acquaintance of mine and knew Ania by sight, and he knew she had a twin.'

'No matter how much you trust him or anyone, Baruch, you shouldn't have revealed to him that I am coming. I have been taught – no, shown – that the most trusted may be the enemy.'

Baruch hung his head.

'Look, don't take what I say as criticism. You are doing a wonderful job, and all without the benefit of the training I have had. So much so that London wants to involve you more and will be supporting you.'

'What kind of involvement?'

'I'll tell you everything later. I'm hungry and tired. And there are too many ears. I need to eat. But I must know: do you know if Ania is safe?'

'I have no recent news of her. I am distraught. We have been apart since our wedding night. Usually I hear when my contact brings information, but with him not arriving on schedule, and at such a time when all my hopes were to see my Ania, I don't know what to think.'

'Don't give up hope. From what I know from Ania's letter, she isn't under suspicion and can come and go. She will find a way of contacting you. Especially if she knew I was coming. Did she know I was on my way?'

'I don't think so. I told my contact not to tell her. Just to say that I wanted to see her. I didn't want Ania to be disappointed or upset if you didn't make it through.'

'That is good, and it's how you have to school yourself to behave, Baruch. Don't give out any information that may be useful to our enemies. Always be careful of that. That is the number-one rule. What someone doesn't know, they cannot repeat.'

Baruch looked worried. Elka realized that he'd set up his operation without knowing any of the tactics and strategies that she had been trained in. And he had done well. Intelligence had informed them that he and his men had caused disruption and had held back the progress of the Germans on more than one occasion. It had also informed them that Baruch was a high risk, in that he was on the Gestapo's 'most wanted' list. From what she'd read of the papers given to her by Brendan as they parted, it was up to her to help Baruch obtain the skills that would equip him with the expertise that would safeguard him.

They had eaten and she had rested a while, before they sat down together to talk. All other members in the camp had been dispatched to another room of the lodge.

Elka began by telling Baruch that she had material that needed to be copied into thousands of leaflets and distributed. This didn't pose a problem, and Baruch immediately summoned a man whom he introduced as Paul. 'Don't worry, that is his code-name, Ella. You can see he is already getting used to it. He answered my call to him. We sorted out names for ourselves whilst you were resting.' Baruch told Paul what was needed.

'It will be with you in the morning – it's no problem to me.'

'Paul's family owns a printing press. He has been allowed

to continue running the family business because he is useful to the Germans. They have all the posters that need to be posted around the cities printed at his works, although the bastards pay very little for his services.'

'That's great. But no: there must be some other way. What if the Germans come whilst he is printing our material?'

'I have a small Adana press. My father bought it for me when I was a young student, to pique my interest. I printed everything for my school. It is a wonderful machine and will cope with this job. It's in my shed at home. I will soon get it going for you, Ella.'

'Thank you. I have to start distributing them very soon.' Elka felt particularly pleased; though she didn't admit it, she knew who Paul really was and of his family's business. Her grandfather, Gos, had used the family business and always spoke highly of them. She knew, too, that they had printed Jewish papers in the past.

The talk between herself and Baruch took the form of instructing him what the team in London required of him. She showed him wireless codes and how they would work, and what support London would give to him. 'Do you have a radio, Baruch?'

'We do. I use it to contact other groups like ours, to coordinate our operations.'

'I'll try it tomorrow, to make sure we have the range we need. But, Baruch, I would strongly advise you to find somewhere else to hide out in. I know this place is remote and little-known, but the Germans have a strong presence in Zakopane and many of their countrymen used this lodge in the past. They have you on a list of "most wanted" people.

They are bound to deduce that you are in the mountains. What if someone among them remembers this place?'

Baruch looked forlorn once more.

'Baruch, please believe what I said before. None of what I teach you, or tell you, is a criticism of what you have achieved so far. It is just that things are moving on. You have to be ahead of the game. You have to learn not to trust anyone. Not even me. Not even Ania. And especially not this contact you have. Cover your own and your men's tracks at all times. Find a new hideout. And, when you meet your contact, don't let it be in your hideout.'

'But—'

'Listen to me, Baruch. I know that you trust your contact, and that he is extremely brave to do what he does, but do you know how long he would hold out, if he was betrayed and captured? Would he break under torture? He might not. But if he does, then it is better that he does not have any vital information that he could give away.'

'Yes, I can see that. I have to protect the core of the organization against individuals who may be more at risk of discovery, capture and torture.'

'Exactly. Now, I have to go to bed. You have a lot to think about. And, Baruch, I know we didn't see eye-to-eye in the past, but I have a lot of respect for you, and we should all have listened to you instead of thinking of you as a political agitator and a troublemaker. I am glad that you are married to my sister.'

Getting up, she put her arms around him and hugged him. As she looked into his face, she saw a tear glistening in his eye. Something in her stirred a trickle of worry. Was there something he wasn't telling her? No, there couldn't be. He'd had plenty of time to tell her if there was something wrong. Maybe she'd been a little hard on him, picking holes in something he was so proud of – and he had every right to be so. 'It will all come right, Baruch. We have to believe that. People like you will make it come right. You will.'

# 18

# *Jhona*

## London, Late March 1940 – A Dangerous Assignment

'We have to know where they are getting their intelligence from.'

'I understand, but how do I go about such a task?' Jhona was feeling increasingly concerned as he listened to the colonel. Coming into the War Office in Whitehall had been nerve-racking enough, but as he sat the other side of the colonel's large mahogany desk, his fear of what he was about to hear intensified.

Just after Elka left, three weeks ago, he'd been interviewed and told that he would need further training. This had taken the form of more extreme methods of clandestine operations – to the point where Jhona felt he could become an excellent burglar or even a hit-man, as he could now open a locked door in seconds, as well as locked drawers, and even blow a safe! More killing techniques had been shown to him, so that if a conversation caused him any concern, he could strike so quickly that his victim wouldn't stand a chance, nor would he see it coming. It had been an intense time and an unnerving one.

Jhona allowed these thoughts to drift in and out of his head while he kept his gaze steady, looking the colonel in the eye, as he had been taught an honest man would. It was how he should look, if he was ever questioned. He found it a technique that gave him confidence and commanded respect. It also helped him to challenge the colonel. 'Yes, I speak Russian, and like a native. I spent most of my early years living in Russia. My grandfather took us there during the Great War. I was four at the time; I was ten before they decided to move fully back to Poland. In the meantime I was attending a Russian school. I have often visited old friends, right up until this war was imminent, and have stayed for holidays in Moscow and St Petersburg. But is that enough for what you are asking?'

'Yes, it is. We happen to know that one of your old friends, Vladislav Mihaylov, works for the Russian intelligence agency.'

'What! Vlady? Well, I never knew that.'

'That is the nature of the Secret Service. Even friends are unaware – and rightly so. How could it operate otherwise? It is essential that you maintain the outward appearance of your friendship, and that you keep the same easy manner there has always been between the two of you. But inside, you must always think of him as your enemy, who wouldn't hesitate to kill you!'

Shocked, Jhona wondered if he could ever think of Vlady in that way, or ever want to, but he didn't interrupt.

'We are sending you to Tehran, initially. We have a training school there, dedicated to polishing our chosen Russian-speaking agents. After that, we want you to contact Mihaylov and ask him to give you a home for a few months. Tell him you are going through a traumatic time and need to get away. You have made it to England and have been working as an interpreter in the Foreign Office. Say that you are on a sabbatical for health reasons, and that you wanted to go back to Russia, where you feel you can recuperate.'

'I can make Vlady believe that. He knows that I would choose to go there, as I have often expressed my love of the country, when with him. There is something about Russia that always relaxes me. It is like the next best thing to home, to me. Also, he and my other Russian friends know nothing about my marriage as of yet.'

'That is excellent. But I hope you feeling at home there hasn't given you a feeling of allegiance to the Russians?'

'No, of course not. It is just the place itself and the people, not the politics. Politically the Russians have often been at odds with, and aggressive towards, Poland. I hate it that they have invaded my country once again. But Vlady will know that even though this will have hurt me, I would still want to go to Russia. He knows that Poland is my first and real home. He often says I am a lost soul, but he knows where my allegiance lies. He will be glad that I got out, and will understand why. But how will I explain that I am able to work in Britain, and in such a high position?'

'War makes for strange buddies. We have a pact with your country that is so strong that we have entered a war because of it. Therefore we're going to welcome refugees and make use of them, if we can. You have language skills that we need. Besides, just as you are shocked at him being a secret agent, he would not be able to think of you as one. He is more likely to think of you as naive in going to his country at such a time, despite your love of it, and he will possibly try and manipulate you into becoming an agent for them. He will play on your vulnerability. You will say that the reason you are unwell is that you had a nervous breakdown, brought on by all that is happening. You will tell him of your marriage, but that your wife went back to her family in Poland, and that your family has already left for America. You won't name her as Elka, and he won't guess, as he still believes she is your cousin.'

Once more Jhona was shocked. *How does the colonel know about my own and Elka's background?* Choosing not to pursue this, he sought to change the subject. 'What do I tell my family?'

'Just that you have been deployed. What do they know about what you are doing?'

'Nothing. As you have just said, my own family has left for America. My wife's parents are both war veterans and think I am in training for a job at the Foreign Office and that my wife – their daughter – has gone to France to set up communication facilities, after her training in that field.'

'Yes. We know all about your in-laws. You should be proud to be associated with the Pevensys. They will pose us no problems; they know the way of it. Your father-in-law is an exceptional inventor. His work is much talked about at the moment, and some items are already in use. Well, Jhona, have you any problems with everything we have discussed?'

'Yes, a great many problems, but you already know about them. If I do go ahead, what about my identity? If I am to go to my friend as myself, it may be difficult. The Jews are having a hard time in Russia.'

'You will be given a new cover and everything you need, as you would expect. Once you are fully trained and equipped, you will send a letter from here to Vlady before you leave. In it you will tell him that you have to travel under a different guise, as you are afraid to be exposed as a Jew. And that you have paid for false papers.'

'I'm still not sure. Vlady can be very astute, and may hoodwink me and all his friends. He will suspect something, if I go from working in the Foreign office in Britain to wanting to spend time with a Russian agent. It smacks of coincidence and is highly suspect.'

The colonel stood up and turned his back to Jhona to look out of the window of his office. His view, Jhona knew, would take in the magnificent buildings of Whitehall, which dominated the corner of Whitehall Place. The area fascinated Jhona. In the lonely days since Elka had left, he'd explored it alone. Within a very short distance of the War Office he'd found Big Ben and London Bridge, Westminster Abbey and, above all, Buckingham Palace.

As he'd stood at the railings gazing at the magnificent palace, a car had driven from the back through an archway. The King and Queen and the two princesses had been sitting inside it. Princess Elizabeth, quite the young lady, had looked directly at him as the car had passed by. She'd smiled. Well, it was more of a grin really, and he'd felt proud that he, a foreign national, was serving her family. It was a strange feeling, but the moment had suddenly given a purpose to what he was doing. Yes, the ultimate goal was freedom for his own country, but to do that in allegiance with that young princess's country had become very special to him at that moment.

'You're right. We need a convincing angle to make sure Vladislav is taken in.'

'What will be my ultimate goal? I know you need information, but what exactly?'

'We believe there are double agents here. We also believe that young men are being recruited to become Russian agents and yet work in our country – British men in our universities, those with communist and socialist leanings. We want to know who they are. We also need to learn Russia's real military intentions.'

'And you think I can get this information?' Jhona had never seen himself as a spy. He couldn't imagine how he could be of use. How did one go about obtaining secrets? He was a jeweller – a Jewish jeweller. He made and designed jewellery, for heaven's sake! Nothing more, nothing less.

'Your new identity will be the key. You will tell Vladislav that it cost you an arm and a leg to set it up, but that there are people in Britain from many countries, and some of them are making their money by forging documents and precipitating the movement of displaced persons. You will tell him that you are doing this because you want to hide the fact that you are a Jew. You will tell him you have a new name and a passport that makes you a citizen of the Ukraine.'

'I don't understand. Why the Ukraine?'

'Because it will give you better access to Russia. Many Ukrainians are seeking to help Russia. You will tell your friend that it is the reason you chose that country, when seeking a new identity. This work will ultimately help us to save your country. Russia is a force to be reckoned with. We need the Russians on our side, not out there alone, grabbing what they can for themselves. It will take the world to stand together to beat Hitler. Yes, Hitler has made a pact with Stalin, but Hitler is not to be trusted. When Stalin comes to realize that, we want him on our side. In the meantime we need to know what he is up to.'

A trickle of apprehension ran along the length of Jhona's spine. At the mention of such powerful names as Hitler and Stalin, the reality of what was expected of him hit home. This wasn't a trip to visit a friend to see what intelligence he could pick up on the off-chance; this was part of something much bigger. 'You want me to become a double agent, don't you? That is what this is all about. I – I'm not up to it. Not brave enough. I'm sorry.'

'No man knows what he is capable of achieving until he is tested. The recent training you completed with your wife assessed you on many things that you didn't realize you were being assessed on. You were tested much more extensively than your wife. Once we knew your Russian connections, we went into overdrive to check if you were of the right calibre. You are. Make no mistake about it, Jhona – you are what we are looking for and what we need. We can teach you everything you need to know in our training camp in Tehran, though there are very few gaps in your knowledge now. You are perfect for the position: a Polish Jew who has chosen to take on a citizenship that is still acceptable to the Russians. Who is going to suspect that you are a British agent? You aren't even a British citizen.'

'And my wife? What will I tell her?'

'Nothing. You will be gone before she returns. We will tell her you have gone on a mission. To all intents and purposes, that mission is a long and secret one. She will be kept busy on missions herself. From now, until the end of the war, you will have no contact with your wife or any of your family. Not even when you are in this country.'

Jhona knew that his mouth had opened to speak words of protest, but none came. His heart had dropped as if it was a concrete block. His mind wouldn't comprehend what he'd just been told. He couldn't see Elka? Or talk to her, or write to her. *No!* 'No!' The word was out before he could stop it. But now that it was, he knew it to be a truth. 'I can't agree to that. I won't do any of this unless there is a way that Elka and I can receive news of each other. It is barbaric to expect anything less of a husband and wife. As it is, it is cutting me in two being apart from her. I won't do it.'

The silence wasn't comfortable and lasted for a few minutes. The colonel sat down again and clasped his hands together, leaving his two index fingers standing, as if making a church and steeple in the way children do. Leaning his chin on them, he stared intently at Jhona, increasing the uncomfortable feeling running down Jhona's spine.

'Very well. There are two schools of thought concerning how our agents conduct their private lives. One is that they should carry on a normal life, on the face of things. But they are usually the ones who remain in this country and work in a government office, passing secrets that they are specifically tasked to pass on. When an agent leaves these shores, it is very complicated. He has to be seen to be leaving his old life behind. No ties. Families can be in extreme danger, if an agent falls out of favour. Their torture can be a bargaining tool used against the agent, to make him talk and tell real secrets and to expose other agents.'

Jhona hadn't thought of that. He could cut the ties with his own family, as long as they were informed that he was doing war work and would be out of contact; but not with Elka. Never with her. On the other hand, would he want her to be in danger? He knew he wouldn't. The colonel stood again, and this time his action was dismissive rather than contemplative.

'I think I need to consult on this one. In the meantime you will be prepared for your mission. Instructions will come about where to attend. Information will be given to you for you to include in the letter to your friend, Vladislav. Something will be sorted out so that you are able to cope emotionally. This is essential, because we need you. We have none better. No one has your connections and your command of the language, let alone first-hand knowledge of Russia. Absorb what you have been told and come to some conclusions yourself, for time is of the essence.'

Jhona stood, clipped his heels and saluted. The colonel did the same. The gesture touched Jhona. It cemented the fact that he really was important to the British Army, and to Britain itself, and in being so, he knew he could achieve his ultimate goal – to be useful to his own people.

There was little change in the colonel's directive when it was given to Jhona a couple of days later. He must write a letter before he left, which would be given to Elka. He wasn't allowed to include any details about the job to which he'd been assigned – only that he was going on a mission that might take him away for a long period of time. The colonel added a note saying that he was sorry:

*Regarding our chat: I cannot break the rules, because Elka's safety is paramount.*

*If the mission Elka is undertaking is a success, she will be called upon to make many more. And so, like thousands of other couples, you will be apart, whatever you choose to do. War brings its own sacrifices.*

*The only thing that I can promise you, Jhona, is that I will let Elka know that you are all right. As I will let you know about her. And I will inform each of you if the other falls into mishap.*

*I am sure that Elka will understand, as she herself is restricted and cannot write to you. If it is at all within the realms of possibility – if there is an occasion when you're both back in Britain – then I will try to accommodate you meeting each other. But I cannot guarantee that.*

*Therefore if you decide to take on this assignment, you have to decide whether you can do so knowing that you will have little or no contact with your wife or your family, and whether this is a sacrifice you can make.*

*You will be making that sacrifice for your country, Poland, and for Britain, which is trying to support your country; and, most of all, for your wife's safety. Bear in mind that it is likely you will be called upon to make this sacrifice for the duration of the war.*

*Please inform me of your decision by tomorrow.*

*Sincerely,*

*Colonel Wright*

The last paragraph really pulled on Jhona's conscience. Part of him wished that he and Elka had never come to Britain. If they hadn't, then they wouldn't have been involved in the war in this way, but would more than likely have joined a Resistance movement and worked together.

Looking out of the window of the sitting room in which he and Elka had spent so little time, he gazed over Holland Park. The day was a pleasant one. A crisp late-winter sun shone down, giving a pleasantly warm feel, but remnants of frost still clung to the foliage.

Jhona's sigh held resignation. He could do nothing but accept the assignment. *Oh, Elka, my Elka. When will we be together again?*

But with this thought came another. He couldn't leave her without hope. He sat down to write the official letter. Placing that in an envelope, he then penned another. This one he placed inside the pocket of her favourite coat.

# 19

# *Elka*

## Zakopane, Tatra Mountains, Late March 1940 – Revelations Cause Pain

On her third day in Zakopane, Elka rose, intent on making sure the group moved today. Much was in place already. Everyone had learned their new code-names, and had taken on board what they must do to become an elite unit worthy of receiving instructions from London and passing back vital information to the intelligence core there. In turn, they would receive help in the way of equipment and ammunition.

When Elka entered the living room of the chalet, Baruch was waiting for her. The look on his face told her something was wrong. 'Elka, I have much to tell you that is horrific.'

Her stiff, cold limbs prevented Elka from answering Baruch. His tone worried her. Somehow she'd known there was more for her to learn. *Please God, don't let it be about Ania.*

She rubbed her limbs vigorously, before straightening and zipping up her thick, padded ski suit and moving nearer to the fire. Baruch handed her a mug of cocoa. The steam warmed her nose as she lifted it to her lips. The cocoa and the sweet smell of the pine logs sending sparks up the chimney reminded her of her childhood. Through the window next to the fireplace she could see that a fresh layer of snow had fallen during the night.

'What is it, Baruch? Not Ania? Have you had a message?'

'Yes, it is about Ania. But no, I haven't had a message. It is knowledge I already have, but I couldn't give to you straight away. You had so much information for me. But now that you are settled in and rested, and all that is left for us to do is move camp, I have to tell you.'

'You said she was all right. You said—'

'I know. I'm sorry. As far as we know, she isn't under suspicion, but . . . She – she's been treated badly by all.'

'What do you mean? Tell me.'

'She was raped.'

'No! No . . . Oh, Ania.'

Elka moved away from the fire. Her sagging body made it to the table and sank into a chair. Baruch sat down on the other side of the table and buried his head in his arms. The brown-gold curls of his long hair cascaded over his hands.

'When did this happen? Is she okay?'

'It happened at the very beginning.'

Elka sat listening to how Ania was brutally raped, as Petra lay dying from gunshot wounds.

'But she didn't say anything in her letter!'

'She doesn't know that I know. My contact overheard a German soldier boasting about it in a bar.'

'Couldn't you have got her out, Baruch? You got out – how could you have left her there?'

'It was a perfect plan. When Petra told you of your real birth and provided you both with papers, you were ideal for the job of infiltrating the Nazi regime's operation here. Your knowledge of languages was particularly useful. You chose to leave. Ania didn't – she wanted to do this. She has courage, and we had no choice but to use that courage. If our Freedom Army is to have any chance of succeeding, it needs intelligence. Do you think I would use my wife in this way – the woman I love beyond anything – if there was any other way?'

His outburst threw Elka. It made her sound like a coward. Shame prickled her conscience.

'Baruch, we made choices. You are right – in choosing her path Ania showed great strength. You have shown that same courage and strength. But I am back. There are few who could accomplish what I have taken on. I did not flinch from the task and have brought information for you from the outside world – information that will help your army and enthuse and lift the Polish people. Jhona, too, is preparing for clandestine work. I don't know the nature of it, but there is already an indication that he will be used in the near future.'

'I know. Forgive me. I'm sorry, Elka. I'm just so very worried about Ania.'

'I wanted to get her out. They stopped me.'

'I know, you told me. And your plan was a good one. I wanted that for my Ania. The news that has filtered out about her health is not good. It is gnawing away at me and breaking my heart.'

Elka didn't know where she found the strength, but she crossed the room and put her arm around Baruch. 'Ania will survive this, and then we will help her to forget. You must get another contact back into Krakow, and you need one in Warsaw, too. We have to make sure the leaflets that

Paul is preparing for us are distributed. Our people need news of the outside world.'

Elka wasn't sure how she was able to focus on their mission and comfort Baruch, after receiving such awful news. She only knew that she had to. And that nothing was ever going to be the same again. But they had to work towards a time of peace. This war had to be won; Hitler had to be stopped.

The chain of contacts was soon mobilized and information began to flow both ways, but still no one had any further news of Ania.

A week had passed. A new hideout had been constructed further up in the mountains. From there a signal could be sent as far as Hungary. Contact had been made with Brendan. He had set up various channels – a network that would ensure messages were relayed to London.

In two days' time Elka would need to start her journey back to Hungary, in readiness for flying back to England. Part of her wanted to leave so badly; to be held by her Jhona. But a huge part of her wanted to have some news of Ania before she left.

As the days passed, Elka's heart hurt more and more, as none of the communications from within Krakow gave any news of her sister.

Then a message came in. Ania had been in hospital! A lad who had been delivering bread to the Gestapo headquarters kitchen had come across a commotion outside the apartments where Ania lived and had asked the ambulance driver – an uncle of his – what was happening. The uncle had told the boy that one of the collaborators had been attacked and badly beaten.

The news shattered Elka, as did hearing of Ania being called a collaborator. Her heart filled with despair for the suffering of her darling sister. She wondered how Ania was coping; she'd always been the more fragile of the two of them. It was unbearable.

'Baruch, what are we going to do? I must go to her. Please don't tell me the people think of her as a collaborator! Oh God, not that!'

'They do, but it is the perfect cover for Ania.'

'Cover! She will be vilified, spat at. And this attack, would it have been by our own people? How can you do this to the woman you love – to my darling sister? How, Baruch?'

'We don't know who attacked her. Don't you think it breaks my heart to know of her plight? It's not me doing this to her. Ania is doing the best she can, for her people and her country. She does it knowing that it is dangerous. We all have to make sacrifices. We all have to do what we can, for the greater good. Ania knows that. At least we know the Germans are taking care of her and have seen that she receives treatment. I have a nurse inside the hospital who is one of my contacts. She is not a Jew, but she can be trusted; she wants to join the Freedom Army. She will get information to us by this evening, I am sure.'

Baruch's body shook as he spoke. Elka could see that he was distraught. She could stand it no longer. 'I'm going in. I'm going to find Ania.'

'No. You will put her, and yourself, in danger. You must not be captured. If news doesn't come in soon, I will go. I have done so before. I didn't make contact with Ania, but I stayed overnight and managed, in disguise, even to fool my contact. I took a chance and it worked. It was a kind of trial run, in case I was ever needed to go on an urgent mission. We have established safe houses along the route – the people there know me. And the final part of the journey is horrendous. The best thing you can do, Elka, is go home with the information that Ania has got out for us, and which I have given you. Tell your leaders about the wall that is planned, to fence our people into a ghetto. Tell them young Jewish men are going missing every day. Tell him that Poles are being taken for hard labour. Tell him everything your sister has risked her life to inform us about, then return to us and we will have Ania waiting for you.'

Looking into Baruch's bloodshot, impassioned eyes, Elka believed him. Her training had taught her that she must obey her instructions. She must return to Hungary, and from there go back to Britain. But she would beg to be allowed to come back, just as soon as they would allow her to. One day she would take Ania to England – to their mother, to their true home.

# 20

# *Edith*

## London, May 1940 – Eloise to the Rescue

Being in the arms of Eloise, her lovely cousin, soothed some of the pain that had taken root in every part of Edith.

'I can't tell you how good it is to have you here in London, Eloise. How long are you staying?'

'As long as it takes to get you sorted. The message from Laurent broke our hearts. Why didn't you tell me sooner? Douglas is very cross with you for not letting us know, too.'

'You have your own work to contend with and – well, your own heartache, with the girls leaving, and poor Douglas seeing Henry off to war and knowing that Thomas won't be far behind him. Besides, it is all so hush-hush – I don't know anything really. All Brendan said was that Elka was involved in something to do with communications, and that Jhona was doing something similar.'

'They're not together then?'

'No. Elka went first, for a little over two weeks, and Brendan went with her. He did tell me that much. Then soon afterwards, and before Elka returned, Jhona left. Elka was distraught when she returned, to find out that he'd gone on some kind of government mission. And then, within a short time, Elka left again. I had a postcard saying she was safe and well. But that was all. And I suspect it was written before she left. It came via the War Office. We all know how these things work. It wouldn't be so bad if they had joined up in the normal way. I'd be worried, but I would have some idea of what they are doing. But with Brendan recruiting them to carry out something that no one will tell me about, I . . . Oh, Eloise, I'm so afraid. I'm imagining all sorts of things.'

'That is to be expected, darling. You've been part of a war and have experienced it all first hand. But all we can do is hope, and carry on as best we can.'

'I know. Tell me, have you any news of Rose and Andria?' Edith found it frustrating not knowing what her own children were doing, and thought it was easier to switch the conversation to safer ground and talk about Eloise's girls. Hearing that they had volunteered for the Women's Land Army had sent her and Laurent into a fit of giggles. No two girls could be less suited for such a role. Their heads seemed full of nothing more than the latest fashions, partying and going on picnics. Picnics that entailed lots of other like-minded youngsters driving off noisily in open-topped cars, with champagne and cucumber sandwiches and a wind-up gramophone on board, heading for the riverside. But then, just as war had tamed and brought out the best in Eloise, who had been equally frivolous, with her late sister Andrina, perhaps it could do the same for Rose and Andria, judging by what Eloise was saying.

'Surprisingly, Rose and Andria seem to be in their element. Their letters are so funny. They talk of their uniform – dungarees and wellingtons – as if they are the height of fashion. Oh, and you know what a comedienne Andria is: she said she wears this attire with lovely accessories – bulging blisters!'

They both laughed, and the moment lightened for them. 'And they are really settling down on that farm in Kent?'

'So it seems. At least their letters are full of funny stories. They have names for each of the cows, which they have to milk at six o'clock in the morning. They never used to know there was such a time in the day! Rose wrote in her last letter – here, I have it in my bag.' Fumbling amongst the many items, Eloise brought out a bundle of what looked like well-read letters and selected one, reading it out aloud: '"Mama, I'm so cross. I milked Loopy-Lou – we call her Loopy-Lou because she is a little doolally. She doesn't fall in with the rest of the cows when they are called, and to get her into a milking stall is the Devil's own job – we push her one way and she goes the other! Anyway, I did exactly as I was taught, getting loads from her at the cost of aching arms and wrists, when she throws one of her silly fits, kicks out and knocks the whole blooming lot over! Farmer Whisky, as we call him, due to the copious amounts he swigs down, went berserk. It really wasn't my fault, Mama."'

'Oh no. Oh, poor Rose.' Edith could hardly talk for laughing. 'But it's so good, and so unexpected, to know they're all right. I'd love to see them in action.'

'I'd love to see them in those clothes! In fact, I would just love to see them – I miss them so much.' A silence fell. Eloise brought it to an end. 'Anyway, I'm here to discuss helping you. Laurent didn't only tell us in his letter about your sadness at Elka and Jhona having left to do war work, and you not having any news of Ania. He also told us how hard you're working to try and keep Jimmy's Hope House and your job going. What can I do to relieve you a little, darling?'

'I'm all right. You have your own charity.'

'Out of my hands in the main, now. The Salvation Army and the Red Cross have all the areas I was working in covered, and the British Legion, which is now well established. It takes care of all ex-servicemen. My job is chiefly fund-raising, and that doesn't take much of my time, as I have established sources of regular income and distribute it between the three organizations. Of course that isn't all of their income, as they each have their own sources of funding. I just contribute to it. But, Edith, I didn't realize that you have been coping on your own since – well, since dear Ada's passing. Oh, Edith, I miss her so much.'

Edith couldn't speak for a moment and had to swallow before she could answer. 'We all do. It is like a light has gone out for us. Brendan hasn't been the same man since.'

'I can imagine. Does his work keep him in this country?'

'Yes. He's still working in the War Office, but what he does is all top secret, of course. He rings now and then. I don't think he can cope with visiting much. He is a very confused and lost young man, at heart.'

'Maybe I'll get to see him while I'm here. I intend to stay until you're sorted. You and Ginny must be stretched to the limit. Now tell me, why haven't you employed another assistant to take Ada's place at the home?'

'It felt almost disloyal to do so. Ginny manages all the pregnant girls who live in, and oversees the baby unit. The nannies we have are excellent, and of course the mothers who still live in and those awaiting their confinement all have to work. They do cleaning and kitchen duties, that kind of thing. Leah is the exception to this, as she doesn't like to leave either my own or Ginny's side, especially now that Ada's no longer with us. You haven't met Leah, have you?'

'No. Who is Leah? Edith, you have been really very naughty about not keeping me up to date.'

Edith told Eloise about Leah, her background, and how she worked closely with Leah, teaching her to speak English and showing her how to do as many of the jobs as she could in the surgery. 'She is really grasping the language now. Which is a big help. And there's an investigation into the gang who put her to work on the streets, but they – and their organization – seem to have gone to ground. We've got several girls in the home who were mixed up with them. Some are ready to move on. We're looking into war work for them.'

'And what is Leah's long-term situation?'

'At the moment she doesn't have a set routine, like the other girls, but helps in the surgery or in the staff kitchen, looking after us and keeping things in order there. She is still so sad about all she has been through. It broke her heart – and mine and Ginny's – when Felicia died. I think Leah will stay. She has no family.'

After telling Eloise about how the bodies of Leah's parents had been washed up, and the outcome of Leah revisiting her rescuers, she was glad to hear Eloise say, 'Well, I'm sure we will rub along very well together, Leah and I. No, I'm not taking any objections. I'm going to take on the role Ada had. I know it inside out, don't forget. Jay will help me.'

Relief flooded through Edith. That Eloise's husband, Jay, Edith's half-uncle, was going to help too, made it easier for her to accept Eloise's offer. Eloise and Jay had run the home together with Ada's help, when Edith had returned to work in the Somme after discovering her twins were missing.

'Thank you, Eloise. And there's no time like the present. I have to leave for Jimmy's Hope House now – are you able to come along? I can introduce you to Leah.'

'Yes, I told Jay I would probably go along with you this morning. He has some legal stuff to see to. He keeps all things of that nature on hold as much as possible, until we come to London, then has to spend nearly a week going through it all with the solicitor.'

As they left the house they saw Jay leaving his own and Eloise's house, which was situated towards the bottom of Holland Park Road. He waved them down. 'Sorry, I haven't had time to come up and see you yet, Edith. How are you?'

'No time to talk now, Jay – sorry.' Somehow Edith had never been able to call him 'Uncle'. He'd been elevated so unexpectedly, and shockingly, to that position, after being just the gardener on Eloise's father's estate, that although she'd come to love him, she just couldn't see him in that light. 'Look, how about dinner tonight? Cook is queuing at the butcher's as we speak. She has taken my own and Laurent's ration books along with her, so she'll get what she can. And, knowing her, it will be plenty to feed us all.'

'Hasn't Eloise told you? We brought up the side of a pig from the farm estate for you, and some eggs and chicken. A sack of potatoes, veg . . . Oh, a host of stuff.'

'No – when were you going to give me that good news?'

Eloise laughed. 'We had too much to discuss to bother

talking about food. But dinner with whatever your cook manages to get will be fine. We'll have the goodies taken to your kitchen later.'

Saying their goodbyes to Jay, Edith drove off. Now was as good a time as any to unload one of her other worries. 'If you don't mind, I would rather the food that you have brought for me was taken to Jimmy's Hope House – we really need it there. To tell you the truth, I'm struggling for funds.'

'No! Edith, why didn't you say? How bad is it?'

'Bad enough for me to consider re-mortgaging my home. Quite a few of our sponsors have dried up. Some have given the excuse that they need to take more care, as the war could see them on their uppers.'

'Well, that is something I can help you with. Leave it to me. I have many contacts and a lot of them are in the milling industry, which is experiencing a boom. I'll shame them into giving some of their cash, made on the back of a war. I haven't had to tap into half of the folk I know for a long time, as the bigger organizations took on most of what I was doing.'

'That would be wonderful. I have been worried sick for months now.'

Eloise soon won Leah's heart, as she did with everyone who came into contact with her. Ginny already loved her, and had done from the moment they had met at Elka's wedding. Their way of working soon slotted in with one another. It seemed as if Eloise been helping them in Jimmy's Hope House for a lot longer than two weeks now.

It was a further relief to Edith to see her own role at the house diminishing once more, as this gave her more time for her work at the hospital. There were so many extra lectures to give and receive at Charing Cross Hospital – particularly lectures on safety procedures, as well as going over the best methods of fixing broken bodies. Edith was dreading learning all about this. War was taking on a deeper meaning than just food shortages and worrying about loved ones. They had already received their first wounded from the front, where the news wasn't good. Sometimes it didn't seem possible that they were still dealing with cases from the last war, and now here they were again.

Edith attended to the last patient of her free surgery for the poor of the East End, before quickly turning her attention to writing up her notes. The time had flown by, without her feeling that she was chasing her own tail. In fact, she'd really enjoyed the relaxed atmosphere of the surgery, whilst notes on each patient had been prepared for her or she had received old notes for those on a return visit. It was just like the old days, although, more than once since Ada's passing, she felt guilty at not realizing just how much Ada had done to make the place run smoothly.

With this thought came an idea. Just as it was forming, Brendan knocked on the door.

'Brendan! How lovely to see you. I was just thinking about your Aunt Ada. How are you, darling?' His look said everything. Huge blue eyes, rimmed with dark circles, stared at her. 'Look, don't answer that. Your Aunt Eloise is here – shall we call her and all have coffee together?'

Not indicating yes or no, he crossed over to her and held out his arms. A nerve of fear tingled in Edith's stomach as she went into his hug.

'What is it, Brendan. Is something wrong?' He held her to him in a grip that bruised her. The rough texture of his uniform jacket rubbed against her cheek. 'Brendan, you'll suffocate me.'

'I'm sorry. I have bad news. We've lost contact with Jhona.'

'What? But where is he? And Elka – does she know?'

'No. She doesn't know yet. We'll be bringing her home. She is at the end of her mission anyway.'

'Mission? What is it you have them doing? Brendan, I thought Elka was doing work in France that wouldn't put her in danger, and that Jhona was sent to do something similar elsewhere. What mission?'

'I'm sorry, Aunt Edith. I have permission to tell you very little. It is too dangerous for you to know. But they are both carrying out missions that will help our country in this war. Their work is vital to us, as things escalate. They are the bravest couple I know.'

The impact of this rocked her off-balance. All she could think to ask was, 'Is Jhona . . . is he likely to be alive?'

'We don't know. He was meant to make contact and he didn't. Enquiries have revealed nothing. Jhona has just disappeared. That is all I can tell you.'

Lowering herself into the chair she'd risen from, behind her desk, Edith looked up into Brendan's face. Part of her wanted to hold him and make all of his sorrows better, but there was a bigger part of her that wanted to hit him, and never stop hitting him, for his part in recruiting Elka and Jhona.

'I'm sorry. So very sorry. I only did what I thought was best for our country. Can you ever forgive me?'

Knowing that her feeling had shown in her face, Edith felt shame wash over her. 'No, it is for you to forgive me.' She could say no more and didn't have to, as Brendan once again opened his arms and she went into them. This time, as he held her, she could feel his strength, but it didn't stop her patting his back as if he were a child. The action bonded them once again.

Once Brendan had released her, he sat down heavily on the seat reserved for patients. 'Aunt Edith, my life doesn't seem worth living at times. I can't seem to rid myself of the memory of my mother and of Ada's final moments, no matter how I try. And I have caused so much pain to you—'

'No! You have caused nothing. It is this bloody war, and the actions of your mother, that have brought so much for you to bear. You are doing your best to play your role. No more can be asked of you. I'm shocked and saddened about Jhona, and terrified for Elka and for Ania, but none of that is your fault.' Edith's heart was ragged with pain, but she had to try and help Brendan, and get him to believe in himself and remain strong. Her experiences had taught her that, no matter what transpired – whether it was good or bad news – life went on. You just had to lift yourself up and carry on. That was never more apparent than in wartime.

'I'm wrestling with what I am asking of others every day. You know, Aunt Edith, recruiting and training can be worse than being out in the field. That carries a badge of heroism, whereas my job carries heavy guilt.'

Yes, she could see that. Recruiting, preparing and then sending young men and women on missions that might lead to their death was such a personal involvement. Especially when those you recruited were dear to you. Her earlier antagonism left her. All the love she had for this young man flooded through her. 'I wish I could protect you. But you have a job to do, and you have shown that you are willing to do it, no matter what. It is that kind of grit that will see us the victors in this war, as it did in the last. So hold your head up, Brendan, and be proud of what you do, not ashamed.'

A knock on the door interrupted them. Eloise entered the room. Leah followed her in, and then stood transfixed as Eloise ran towards Brendan and hugged him. Over Eloise's shoulder, Edith saw Brendan look towards Leah. Both held the other's gaze as if they would never look away. They didn't look as if they had never previously met. And yet Brendan had not mentioned that he knew Leah.

What Brendan had been saying now hit Edith in the gut. *If France is invaded, there are plans, he said. Plans for what? To send people on these dangerous missions that he'd spoken of? Does he mean Elka, as she can speak French? Or is he thinking of beautiful, fragile Leah, who is French and wouldn't have to pretend, or even try to blend in? No. He wouldn't. Would he?*

As Eloise chatted to Brendan, Edith kept her eye on Leah and Brendan, hoping that she would be proved wrong about the chemistry she'd seen flowing between them. But, far from it: Leah gave the impression of a little puppy waiting for a morsel, as she stood watching him, and when their eyes met again they held each other's gaze.

It was a mystery to Edith how they had met and nurtured such a deep feeling for each other without her suspecting anything.

But as small talk went on around her, it wasn't long before her thoughts turned to Elka and Jhona's plight. Brendan had said that Elka was being brought back home. Home to be told that Jhona was missing. *Dear God, how will Elka cope?* Edith trembled as if someone had walked over her grave.

Brendan felt like a man locked in a cage as he left Jimmy's Hope House. The moment hadn't presented itself when he could speak to Leah about his feelings for her. She'd slipped from the room whilst Eloise had him engaged in conversation. Leah closing the door behind her had given him a strange feeling of loss, and it was as if the light had gone from the room.

After going through the anguish of Jhona's disappearance once again with his Aunt Eloise, he'd changed the subject by asking what it was about his Aunt Ada that Aunt Edith had been thinking, when he'd first walked in. The answer wasn't a surprise. Aunt Edith had wanted to honour Aunt Ada in some way. Talking about this had provided a distraction for them, but didn't lighten the way he felt about the desperate plight Jhona might be in, or the anguish he held in him for the way Elka would take the news.

Several suggestions were made, but eventually they came up with the idea of building a special unit, which they would call Ada's Sanctuary. It would provide shelter and help for women who had been oppressed and battered by their husbands, as Ada had been in her first marriage. They planned to place a plaque on the exterior wall of the building. But it was a project for the future, as Aunt Edith had said she didn't have the funds to do anything at the moment, and didn't see any of the banks approving a loan for expansion, at a time when her income was drying up.

Funny how life went on. Ordinary life, like deciding on memorials, when deep inside themselves people were being churned up and hurt, and their lives torn apart. He marvelled, too, at how he could do this when his own life had been not only turned upside down, but gutted, leaving a void that he knew only one person could fill.

'Brendan, Monsieur Brendan.'

The accented voice calling his name stopped him in his tracks. A raindrop plopped onto his cheek as he turned round to face Leah. Another followed, and soon a deluge gushed from the sky. Running towards Leah, he grabbed her arm and pulled her towards the high wall that surrounded Jimmy's Hope House. There they ducked under the overhanging branches of a tree that stood on this side of the wall and spread its thick foliage in such a way that a secluded shelter was formed.

They didn't speak for a moment. Brendan's heart held the hope of his feelings being returned, as Leah gazed up at him. It swelled, too, as he took in how much better she looked. In French she said, 'You know nothing about me.'

'I don't need to. I – I love—'

'But I have had a baby. I have worked as a street girl. I do not know which of the men fathered my child. I . . .' Her tears of anguish mingled with the few drops of rain still dripping from her hair, and her eyes held the pain of the helpless. Brendan pulled her to him. These revelations hurt; not because he saw her as tainted, for he'd known most of it anyway, but because he could see her raw pain.

'None of it matters. I – I mean, none of it matters as far as we are concerned. Of course it matters that you have suffered, my beautiful Leah. I'll help you to recover from it. My love is strong enough to do that for you.'

A look of disbelief crossed over her face and her head shook in a sure way, as if she didn't think that possible. Pulling from him, she ran back towards the house.

Bewildered, Brendan leaned against the wall. His emotions were tangled. He wanted to run after her, but thought better of it. He would talk to his Aunt Edith. Tell her how he felt, and ask her how carefully he should tread with the fragile girl that was Leah. The girl he wanted to make his own, no matter what had gone before.

# 21

# *Ania*

**Krakow, Late May 1940 – Despairing of the Future**

Leaflets blew along the gutter as Ania made her way to the store. The bitter thought came to her that these pamphlets should have brought hope, but instead had become fodder for German reprisals. Yes, it had been good to know that the British were intending to help and were sending aid to the Freedom Army, but many people had been rounded up and searched. If they were found to have a leaflet on them, they were shot.

For Ania, seeing the leaflets brought the heartbreak of knowing that her sister had been over twice on missions and yet she hadn't seen her. The first time she had been in hospital, following the attack by Herr Guthridge Vandrick, an SS officer. After the fitful sleep she'd fallen into that day, she'd woken with a fever. Unable to get out of bed, she'd lain there until someone came. One of the office girls had been sent to find her. The next thing she knew, two ambulance men came and took her to hospital. She'd been found to have pneumonia, and had been lucky to come back from it. Only one nurse asked about her wounds and how she got them, telling Ania that she was one of Baruch's contacts and would let him know.

Ania had waited and waited, hoping that Baruch would now get her out, but her heart told her that although he would want to, she was too useful to them. So she resigned herself to continuing with her mission.

When the nurse had spoken to her again a few days later, Ania's heart had broken to hear that Elka had been over. The shock had been great, but had further intensified on hearing that Elka was working for the British Secret Service and had been forced to leave on schedule and was unable to wait and see her. Worse than that, Elka had been over to Poland again; but this time, even though she was well enough, Baruch hadn't let her know until after Elka had left. Ania didn't know what he'd told Elka, to stop her sister contacting her, as without doubt Elka would have wanted to do that.

Ania feared for Elka, knowing that she was a spy, just like herself. And knowing, too, the terrifying risks they both took. She'd been happy when she'd been able to think of Elka with their mother, safe from harm. Now she wouldn't have a moment's peace.

Besides this worry, something in her wondered if Baruch had changed: whether he still loved her, now that he knew of her defilement, or whether he just couldn't face seeing her. Thoughts like this brought her low. Even lower than the continued abuse from Herr Vandrick.

Herr Vandrick considered Ania to be his mistress. No, that wasn't the word. Mistresses commanded a certain respect, but Vandrick gave her none. He hadn't shown her any brutality since that first time, but – to Ania's disgust and extreme pain – had brought as many as three soldiers with him on occasions when he visited, and had watched as each man had raped her.

Each day she had to remind herself that she was a worthy human being. That no matter what they did to her, she had dignity inside her soul and would one day regain it outwardly, too. But the defiling of her in this way wasn't the only thing Vandrick did to her. He played mind-games with her too.

Thinking of this sent a tremble down her spine, making her feel fearful in a way she couldn't put her finger on. It was as if he wanted to control her and, in doing so, make her weak. Sometimes she thought Vandrick knew what she was up to, and this thought petrified her. But somehow she had to stay strong.

Reaching the store, she felt inside her pocket. The coded message for Stefan, in the guise of a shopping list, crackled under her grasp. Holding it in her hand, she wandered into the shop and, as if reading from it, ordered what she wanted from the shopkeeper. Most of the things the store hadn't got, but this didn't surprise her.

When the bell on the shop door rang, Ania turned around, expecting to see Stefan come through it. Her throat tightened when she saw it was Herr Vandrick. He nodded his head to her. Holding herself together, she acknowledged him in the same way, forgetting protocol and not moving out of his way.

Anger deepened the lines around his mouth.

'I beg your pardon, Herr Vandrick.' As Ania stepped back, she could see that speaking in German had surprised the woman behind the counter. The kindness the woman had shown her, since the day of the forced repatriation, drained from her expression. A look as cold as steel took its place.

Herr Vandrick stepped forward, shoving her as he did so. Over-balancing, Ania fell and landed on a sack of potatoes that was leaning against the wall. From the corner of his mouth, Herr Vandrick told her that he would deal with her later.

A sick feeling entered her as she pushed herself up, but not before stuffing the list into the sack. Her legs wobbled beneath her as she stood up. The doorbell rang again and hailed another shopper, taking away from her the attention of the shopkeeper and Herr Vandrick. Stefan had walked in. This time she remembered protocol. Stefan was classed as a German, and Ania knew she had to give precedence to him and give up her place in the queue. Why hadn't she remembered that when Herr Vandrick came in?

Stefan stepped in front of her. Herr Vandrick kept his eyes on him for a moment and then looked around the shop, using his cane to prod things. Taking a small knife from his belt, he began to cut through the linen sack of rice that stood next to the potatoes. The contents trickled out. Ania held her breath, releasing it when he bypassed the potatoes and sliced into a bag of flour, which was leaning against the other side of the sack of rice.

The shopkeeper stared in front of her, not protesting. Ania glanced towards Stefan. Tension weighted the air. Ania jumped as Herr Vandrick turned suddenly and asked, 'Do you know this man?'

The challenge was an accusation. Unsure what to do or say, Ania froze.

'I asked you a question, whore!'

Ania nodded. And, finding her voice, croaked out that

she had known Stefan as a passing acquaintance before the invasion, although they had never been on speaking terms.

'You, have you been with this whore, eh?'

Stefan stiffened at this question directed at him, but didn't display the fear that Ania had shown.

'It is as she has said: we have never spoken.' Stefan's learning of the language had him making errors in his speech. Herr Vandrick scrutinized him. Stefan held strong, not letting any fear that he might feel show.

'Would you like to fuck her? Look at her: she is scrawny. Women should have meat on their bones, to cushion us when we pound them, but she has none. Her joints crack and it is like mounting a skeleton. She gives no pleasure, only takes. Oh yes, she enjoys having a man – any man – stuck up her.'

Appalled, Ania kept her eyes facing ahead. *What is the meaning of this? What does Herr Vandrick hope to gain?*

Stefan laughed. 'There are meatier offerings in the brothel. You should give up on her and go there to find a juicy mistress.'

Herr Vandrick didn't laugh. Once more he scrutinized Stefan. If it had been possible, Ania would have said the tension in the store had increased. Her eyes caught those of the shopkeeper; in them she saw a bewilderment. Thank God she didn't understand what was going on. But then Ania understood the words being spoken and yet she still did not know the true meaning of what was taking place.

Without warning, Herr Vandrick's hand snaked out. His cane sliced her cheek. Her breath caught in her lungs at the stinging pain. Instinctively her hand went to the wound. The wet and sticky mess told her that he had ripped open her skin. But worse than that: the horror of realization hit her. *He suspects me!*

A protest and tears of anguish came from the shopkeeper, only to be rewarded by a similar blow, causing the woman to fall down behind the counter. Stefan stood still. Not a nerve of his body moved. His eyes stayed on Herr Vandrick.

'So, you're happy to see the whore hit, eh?'

'It is nothing to me.' Stefan shrugged.

'I believe it is.'

Stefan's expression still didn't alter. He and Herr Vandrick stood facing each other, like two bulls ready to fight. Ania held her breath. Herr Vandrick turned on his heel. 'I will find out. Somehow information is getting out. One of the girls who works in the office will be shot every hour on the hour, until the traitor confesses to me.'

The door slammed behind him.

The sobs of the woman behind the counter filled the space around them. Stefan turned to Ania. In Polish he asked, 'Is it you, whore?' Unable to answer him, she watched him bend and pick up some of the potatoes. 'I came in for some of these, but they are rotten. I will go to a better shop.' As he turned towards the door he looked at Ania. She couldn't read his expression. 'It could be you. You work in the headquarters of the Gestapo. You should save the lives of those innocent girls.' He left the store, taking with him the coded message.

Ania didn't move. *Why has Stefan taken the message? If Herr Vandrick is outside waiting for him, how will he explain it? And why did he say what he did, about me saving the girls?* Confused and dazed, she sat back down on the sack of potatoes, willing an answer to come to her. But none would, and neither would a solution. Should she confess to being the one getting information out of the Gestapo office? Is that what Stefan really wanted? *Oh, dear God, help me – help me.*

Getting up, she bent over the counter. 'Are you all right, madam? Do you want any help? Can I fetch someone?'

'No. Just get out of my shop and never return – you're not welcome here. GET OUT!'

Taking all her courage in both hands, Ania opened the door. The rush of warm air hit her. The shop was always cool. Stepping outside, she stood still for a moment, then looked to her left and right. The street was empty. Nothing other than the leaflets drifting about in the warm breeze gave any indication of the turmoil this beloved country of hers was in. The sun glinted on the many windows of the buildings. A hush settled everywhere. Ania felt that she was alone in a deserted world, until a scream penetrated the silence. A gunshot rang out, cutting off the scream. Ania leaned against the wall. Sobs racked her. '*No. No . . . Noooo!*'

Her legs buckled under her. She sank into a squatting position, feeling desperate and alone. At the sound of a door opening, she looked across the road and saw a hand beckoning to her. A trickle of hope seeped into her. Looking up and down the street and not seeing anybody, Ania fled across to the open door and flung herself inside. 'Stefan! Oh God, Stefan, what is happening?'

'I'm sorry for what I said, but I had to attempt to deflect suspicion from me. And then what I said afterwards in Polish was for the benefit of the old woman, so that she could not spread the rumour that we were friends. But now we have to get you out of Krakow and into hiding, with Baruch. How did Herr Vandrick come to suspect you so strongly, and why does he link you to me?'

'I don't know. He plays mind-games, and he tricks me into saying things. I try to be careful, but he terrifies me. He is insane. Look how he whipped me that first time, because he thought I still had the devil of Friedrich in me. Help me, Stefan, please help me.'

'That's what I intend to do. You are safe here while I work out a plan. This house belongs to Hadriel's family.'

Hadriel, whom she'd known since a child, stood just behind Stefan. His family had lived nearby and his grandmother had been a friend of Babcia's.

They greeted each other warmly. Ania had always liked Hadriel. Seeing him alive and unhurt, and not condemning her, brought some comfort to her almost-broken spirit.

'Ania, it is good to see you. Though I'm saddened to see what your work for our cause has cost you. You will be all right now. I have joined Baruch's Resistance movement. You can come with me; we will be safer there.'

Fighting the tears this evoked, Ania thanked him, before asking, 'How have you survived? Where is your family? Oh, Hadriel, how did all of this happen? We were all so happy.'

Hadriel swallowed and his prominent Adam's apple moved up and down. 'I've been working on the rebuilding of Warsaw. I was taken there on a truck.'

'But you're a doctor!'

'I'm a Jew – and that's all these Nazis see. I was working in the hospital, when they came and dragged me out. My German senior, a heart specialist, protested on my behalf and was hit with the butt of a gun. He turned to me and apologized for his fellow countrymen's behaviour, so they arrested him as a Jewish sympathizer. I don't know what happened to him. They dragged me out of the hospital and put me on a truck with many others. I escaped with the help of another Pole of German origin, who was working as a supervisor, but is really one of us, as Stefan is. He does all he can to save at least one of us a week. He knows of the Resistance movement, but not the details of where they are; he told me to seek out Stefan. I have been hiding in the cellar of this house ever since, while Stefan negotiated with Baruch to accept me.'

'But surely he didn't have any objections? How could he?' Once more Ania worried about Stefan and what his real motives were.

'Baruch has to be extremely careful – we all do. Old friends could be new enemies. No one knows what a man will do to save his own skin, or that of his family. How did Baruch know that I had not been got at, and was being planted as a spy? He wanted Stefan to be very sure of me before he accepted me. I have lived in fear of discovery for many weeks. But I have proved myself to Baruch now.'

Ania didn't ask how he'd had to prove himself, but understood Baruch's caution, now that Hadriel had explained, but she hated the idea of not trusting old friends, people they had grown up with. She didn't express these views; instead she changed the subject. 'And how are your parents, and your sister Ruth and your *babcia*?'

'My *babcia* has passed away. It was all too much for her. Her heart was weak and just gave out during the bombing. I don't know where my parents or Ruth are. They were taken away. I haven't heard anything from them.'

The silence that followed this wrapped them all in an atmosphere of desolation.

Stefan broke it. 'Hadriel has been acting as a go-between for the movement, taking messages a short way along the exit route, to be collected by another messenger and taken on further, and often bringing information back to me. There is a whole chain of people taking on the responsibility of relaying whatever information we can get. We use this operation to test new recruits. Often what looks like vital information, but is false, is sent along the chain to me. It could contain information that would lead to a collaborator's death, or something else as specific as that, so that we would know if there had been a leak.'

This appalled her. In their treatment of some collaborators, they had been wrong. To her, the Resistance was often as ruthless as the Nazis; the only mitigating circumstance was that it had right on its side. Unlike Hadriel, Stefan didn't acknowledge her part in getting information, nor had he ever expressed any sympathy for her plight. In his usual cold manner he told her now, 'The entrance door to the cellar of this house was bricked up and a new trapdoor was built into the floorboards.'

For the first time Ania took in her surroundings. The room she stood in had its carpet rolled back, from the sideboard on one wall to the shabby sofa that stood in the middle of the room. Behind the sofa, and against a window, stood a plain wooden table and four chairs. Everything was a shade of brown, from the lighter-brown carpet to the dark-brown sofa. The walls she imagined had once been cream, but had yellowed with neglect. A section of the floorboards about two feet long by two was lying beside a hole of the same size.

'That is your exit route. You must hurry. I need time to board it up again and to replace the carpet, and then somehow slip out without being seen. Hadriel has put everything down there that you will need.'

'But how long will we be down there? And what if you are caught and taken? And what of those secretaries . . . ? I think they have already shot one. Oh, Stefan, I can't bear it – I can't.'

'You mustn't give in now. The Germans will already be looking for you, as you haven't returned to work. That woman will have told people what happened in her shop. It is likely she will say that you are the informer. People will be outraged, especially the families of those girls. They will help to look for you. If you are caught, then you will face torture until you tell them what you know and then you will be killed. But long before that, you will be begging them to kill you. I can't let that happen. So many people will be in danger when you break – because you *will* break. You must both go into hiding now.'

Hadriel put his hand out to her. 'Come, I will be with you. Let's get ourselves into the cellar. There is a rope ladder; the steps that went to the cellar door are not within reach. But don't worry. I will go first, as I'm used to it, and will guide your footing.'

The dank atmosphere added to the sick dread lying like a stone in the bottom of Ania's stomach. As the last of the light disappeared as the boards were put back into position, a feeling of suffocation came over her.

'Will you light a candle, Hadriel? I can't penetrate this darkness.'

'No. It is better that it remains dark. Here, wrap yourself in this blanket. The Germans will search for you in the houses and gardens near the shop first. People who live around here know of you. You visit the store regularly. Many of them believe you to be a Jew. Even those I trust, and who know of my hiding place, could connect us both and provide information. When it comes to it, there are as many cowards as there are heroes. Now we must keep quiet.'

'But, Hadriel, everyone knows these houses have cellars. Oh, it's impossible – it's the first place they will look. And now I have gone missing, I have confirmed their suspicions of me and that may lead them to you. We should go now. What is the escape plan?'

Hadriel was quiet for a moment. Ania waited, giving him time to think.

'You're right. But we would be taking a big risk. There is an escape route leading through the wall between my cellar and the adjoining one. There are some loose bricks. We will work on getting them out and into next door's cellar, and then put everything back as it was. From there, we can get out and begin the journey on our route to Baruch. Even if they do get down into this cellar in their search for us, they may not find the exit route. Our original plan was to wait it out here, to give Stefan time to get a team of helpers in place, but after what I heard him say, I can't think why he wanted us to wait here. We will go at once.'

Ania didn't answer. A feeling of despair filled her. Every part of her body started moving in uncontrollable jerking movements. Fear had unleashed itself inside her and had taken her over. Hadriel, in such close proximity to her, was alarmed and sought to help her.

'Ania! Ania, no. Hold on, it will all work out. Snuggle up to me. Let me warm you.'

Ania allowed Hadriel's strong arms to pull her into his body. There she found comfort in his warmth and strength. Relaxing against him, she was conscious of his lips on her hair, pressing gently into her scalp. His sigh held her name. 'Ania, my little Ania . . . if only things were different.'

Shock registered within her as her heart lurched. *Hadriel loves me!* Then her head shook, as if denying this thought and the answering murmur within her. *No. I love Baruch, I do*. Pulling herself out of Hadriel's arms, she found words tumbling from her. 'Hadriel, I am married to Baruch. You must not—'

'Married. When? I – I . . . Oh, Ania, Ania. I knew that you and Baruch were in love, and that broke my heart – but married! It isn't possible.'

'We did it in private, before he left. We had one night together. That's all. I'm Baruch's wife, no matter what else has happened, and despite the number of violations my body has endured. I am his wife.'

'Forgive me. I would never have spoken, Ania – never. I just didn't know. As he hasn't got you out of here, I thought you were nothing to Baruch now, after those men . . .'

'I have thought the same. I don't know if I still mean something to him, and it is breaking my heart. He has denied me a chance of escape. My sister—'

'I know. None of us could understand Baruch's actions. Yes, you were in hospital the first time, but he forbade us to tell you, when we knew Elka was coming to Poland again. She is here now. I met the second messenger who was to take your information about the ghetto that is to be built, and he told me Elka is here. Baruch has told your sister that you insist on staying here in Poland. But Elka is saying that either Baruch forces you to come with her or she will come to Krakow to see you.'

'No! She mustn't. Why is Baruch doing this? The information I give him is important, but there is little in it that would help him, or the Freedom Army, make any difference. Sometimes I know of a train coming in, with troops or arms, but mostly it concerns arrangements for the Jews and who is on the various lists that are compiled. Why hasn't he saved me?'

A crashing sound, followed by footsteps above them, stopped Hadriel answering. Muffled, angry German voices filtered down to them.

'What are they saying, Ania?'

'I can't make it out. I think one said, "They must be here!"'

'They?'

'Shush – let me listen!'

After a moment Ania curled further into Hadriel's body. The trembling that had settled began again.

'What is it? Ania, what have you heard?'

'They said that the man with me had been seen coming out of here. They mean Stefan. They must mean him! But then they said that the man who lived here must be with me. Hush, they're talking again.'

Amidst the sound of falling furniture and of doors crashing, as if being kicked in, Ania heard an angry shout. 'The cellar! Where is the entrance to the cellar?' Then another one. 'We have checked, but there isn't one; it must have been bricked up.' Then Vandrick's voice. 'Lift the carpets – there has to be an entrance to the cellar.'

'Oh, Hadriel, they're coming down here.'

'Come on.' Rising, he moved away from her. 'Help me,

Ania. There's a heavy cupboard. It goes from the floor to within an inch of the ceiling, and we must shift it to come under the opening.'

The cupboard refused to budge. Ania had so little strength. Hadriel pushed and pushed, but only managed to get it to move by a little over an inch. They needed it to move four feet to get it into position.

'Take some of the stuff out of it, Hadriel. We can put it back after. Hurry!' Sweat soaked Ania's body. It ran in cold rivers down her spine as she worked away. It seemed to take an age to get some of the heavy toolboxes off the shelves, but at last they achieved this and renewed their efforts to push the cupboard. Now it moved when they shoved, making a fearful noise on the flagstone floor. But the sounds of furniture being moved above them must have drowned out the noise, as the Germans didn't halt for a moment what they were doing.

Having got the cupboard into place, they refilled it. It would buy them some time, as the top of the huge closet would be all the Germans would see when they prised up the floorboards that formed the trapdoor.

Flopping back down, Ania was overcome by exhaustion.

'We can't rest. Come on, Ania, we must work away at the loose bricks. Where are our packs? I am disorientated in this dim light, and it is worse with the cupboard not in its usual place.'

'They're over there, where we sat before. I'll get them.'

As she rejoined Hadriel and handed him his rucksack, he caught hold of her. 'Ania, I want you to know that I love you. I have always loved you. I will do all I can to protect you.'

A warm glow made her blush. She felt safe with Hadriel.

But the feeling didn't last long, because voices came to them saying, 'Roll back the carpet.'

Hadriel guided her to the wall and began frantically removing bricks. Dust clouded around her, making her fight against coughing.

'Here, take this wrench and help me. Help me, Ania!'

Hurtling through the hole they had forged, Hadriel grabbed her and pulled her through after him. As he did so, they heard the boards above give way. Curses rained down from above. 'Blast them, this must be the entrance. Get some tools – commandeer them from the neighbours. We have to break down whatever it is they have put there.'

'What if we set fire to it, Herr Vandrick?'

'No, you idiot, we want them alive.'

Ania quickly told Hadriel what was happening.

'Right, that will give us a head-start. We'll leave the bricks. Come on, follow me.'

Racing up the stone steps of the neighbour's cellar to the door above them, Hadriel opened it. It groaned its resistance, as if it hadn't been disturbed for a very long time. 'You might have oiled the hinges, Hadriel!'

Hadriel laughed and the sound made Ania feel better.

Before them was an overgrown tangle of bushes. The cellar door led directly to the back of the house. 'Keep as low down as you can. The occupant of this house is away. I think he was trying to make it to America with his family. He has no idea what we have done to his property to make it an escape route, or that we use his cellar to hold meetings in.'

Pulling some of the bushes aside as if they were a gate, Ania saw there was a door behind them. Once through, Hadriel leaned forward and pulled the brambles back in place. It was then that she saw the bushes were attached to a gated structure. She waited while Hadriel secured the gate. Looking around her, she saw they were inside a shed. Tools hung from the walls, and boxes were piled high in one corner. Taking her hand once more, Hadriel guided her to the pile of boxes. He moved them to one side, revealing a manhole, which he levered open. 'Get in there. Go on! Ania, there are steps – iron ones, like a ladder.'

As she did as he bade, a cold draught lifted her skirt.

'Be careful. Hang on to the sides, but go down as quickly as you can. I cannot get in until you have left room for me.'

Ania climbed down without questioning. A cloying darkness engulfed her with every foot of her descent. Now unable to see at all, she sensed that Hadriel was just above her. She heard him shift the manhole cover back in place, shutting out the small glimmer of light that the opening had afforded. It seemed to take him some time. 'It's all right. There is an ingenious device that allows me to pull the boxes back into place. The boxes are all stuck together. And there is a wire that comes up through a minute hole attached to them. It is set up so that everything is put back in place. They will not think there is an escape route from the shed. It is how members of the Resistance get in and out of the house.'

'Where are we? It is so cold, and the stench is awful!'

'We're in a sewer. The descent is steep and goes on for a long way. Just keep going. At the bottom there is a lamp, waterproof clothing and wellingtons. There is a route painted on the walls by means of red arrows that we have to follow to get out. It is long and gruelling and very unpleasant. It brings us to the outside of the city, and eventually to the Vistula river, where there are hidden stores in the banks. We will find more clothes and be able to wash in the river before we continue our journey.'

Ania was unable to ask further questions, as the disgusting odour made her retch. But it amazed her that such an escape route existed, and to hear that it was equipped with what they would need. She wondered how these things were replaced, but they were just details seen to by others, so that those who worked in the Resistance movement could function properly.

Through the tiredness that enveloped her, her mind teased her with unsettling thoughts. She tried to ignore them, but they persisted. Baruch could so easily have got her out this way, when he learned how badly she was being treated. *Why didn't he? Why?* It wasn't up to him to choose to sacrifice her for the greater cause. Sometimes it had to be admitted that the sacrifice was too great to fit the purpose, didn't it?

# 22

# Elka

## High in the Tatra Mountains, Early June 1940 – Seeing, but Unable to Touch

It had been three weeks since Elka had left England to visit Baruch's Resistance group – her third trip in eight weeks, as she had made a very quick visit in the closing weeks of April. This had been to collect intelligence on the exact location of the German training schools that were emerging in the area.

Her journey this time had been fraught with danger, and the right moment had to be chosen carefully. Snow now covered only the tips of the mountains, as if they were cakes dipped in icing sugar. Many forms of transport had to be used to get her here. Initially flown from Hungary and parachuted into Serbia, she had been taken by horse and trap along winding mountain passes. The pace was necessarily slow, and the possibility of coming across a German convoy was high. The journey had been done at night to avoid this, with long hours of daylight spent deep in darkened caves. The last thirty miles had to be done on foot, a gruelling climb that put all her skills to the test.

Helmut, the guide assigned to her, had been a pleasant

companion and was knowledgeable about what was happening in all parts of the world. This was useful to Elka. When she'd last returned to England she had discovered that Jhona had left England to go on a mysterious mission, and had struggled to pay attention to news of what was happening around her.

She'd absorbed the intelligence that she was to impart, such as where supplies would be dropped, new radio codes to use and how messages would be relayed over the BBC World Service, and the encouraging propaganda, which would need to be printed and distributed throughout Poland. Most of the latter was far from the truth.

The news wasn't as good as the leaflets said it was. It didn't tell of the Allied forces having been driven back. Nor could she add what she now knew: that in the last few days there had been a defeat and terrible loss of life, whilst a mass evacuation from the beaches of Dunkirk had taken place.

The news from Dunkirk renewed her fear that Germany would succeed in taking control of France, and that could only mean that Britain would be next. When she'd first heard the news of the defeat of the Allied troops, it had felt as if their efforts were falling into an abyss of hopelessness. But then yesterday they had managed to tune into the BBC and had listened to Churchill's rousing speech. He said that Britain would never surrender, and her spirits had lifted again, helping her to accept her own and Jhona's sacrifice.

One thing Elka was determined about was that she would see Ania on this trip. She would try and take her sister home with her, but if that wasn't possible – and she had to admit nothing was in place to make it so – then nothing short of seeing her would do. She had given Baruch an ultimatum: help her to see Ania or she would go into Poland on her own, and he'd have to kidnap her to stop her. She had decided she would begin the journey today.

She shivered as a chilly mountain wind blew around her. The camp was sparse in the extreme. They were housed in caves, because erecting any form of shelter would be too risky and would be seen from the air. Knowing that if she was to make the journey to Poland she would have to be prepared, she had packed extra items of clothing, as she couldn't travel in mountain gear. But dressed in them now – a twinset in pale blue, topping a navy skirt with a panel that fitted snuggly to hip length and then flowed into a flare that reached her calves – she found they were no match for the thin air at this altitude. Not even donning the jacket that had been a last-minute add-on helped to warm her. But then her worry was partly to blame for her coldness. *What will Ania look like? What has she suffered? Will my beloved Poland lie in ruins?* These and many other questions formed in her mind, making her feel an anxiety that almost undid her resolve.

The first part of her journey was to be by truck, travelling further down the precarious mountain pass. Then she was to take a track used mainly by shepherds, their herds and their beautiful, intelligent, white-as-snow Tatra sheepdogs. Once as far down as Zakopane, she would be able to relax and move around normally, as the risk of being questioned would be far less than if she was apprehended on the mountainside. From Zakopane she hoped to catch a train to Krakow. She expected the whole journey would take at least half a day.

'Are you decent, Elka?' Baruch's voice came to her from

behind the makeshift curtain created out of sacks, which they had erected for her privacy. Something in his tone spoke of trouble.

She pulled the sacking aside. 'Yes. Is everything all right?'

'No – well, yes and no. I have had a message delivered. Ania is on her way here.'

'Baruch, it won't work. I'm going, and no story about me not having to leave here, because she is coming to me, will stop me. Is there any sign of the truck?'

'I haven't made it up. Come to the entrance of the cave. We have a fire lit. The lookouts will signal to us if there are any aircraft about, which might be likely to see the smoke. There's a kettle on for coffee. I have quite a bit to tell you.'

She listened to Baruch's story about how Ania was under suspicion and was being brought out by Hadriel. The news both lifted Elka and concerned her. 'Will they be in any danger? How will they travel to here from the sewer exit?'

'There is a route we all take, with safe houses along the way. Mostly farms. Once they reach the first one, the people there will transport them to the next. It can take several days.'

'But can't we go and meet them? Surely we could take the route towards them and meet them somewhere along the way. We have to see that they are all right, and offer them extra help and protection.'

'I have already planned that. You see, there is something else. I – I have been informed that Stefan has been arrested.'

'Oh no! Can we trust him not to tell what he knows?' Baruch didn't answer. 'Baruch?'

'Look, Elka, you have to understand . . . Oh God!'

'Baruch! Understand what? Baruch, tell me.'

He looked like a broken man. His head was bowed, as if the weight of what he was about to tell her was too much for him. His shoulders were hunched over. When he looked up, his expression held intense grief. 'Stefan may consider Ania expendable now.'

'What! He can't. The bastard – I'll kill him if he betrays her. No, Baruch. I won't stand for that.'

'I couldn't live with myself, if he does. And I, too, would want revenge. But Stefan needs to give them something. Ania is compromised. The Germans need to capture her, to show an example, as much as to get information from her. I am worried that Stefan may think that, by betraying her, he could avoid having to tell them about us.'

'He can't do that – he can't. Don't you think Stefan will keep his mouth shut and go to his death, rather than betray Ania, and us?'

'I don't think he will betray us. But I do think he will try to save his own skin. His knowledge of what Ania has been doing, and where she is now, might be enough. He could cook up some story about remaining her friend, then being shocked to find out what she was doing; and that he had only helped Ania because he'd become afraid, when he'd come to realize the truth after the encounter in the shop.'

When she'd heard about the encounter in the shop, Elka had become extremely anxious about Ania's safety. But she couldn't imagine how Baruch could deduce that this was what Stefan would do. Had it been in their plans, ready if such an event occurred? She asked him this now. The answer made her despair.

'We did discuss how it would be better to rid the chain of communication of anyone who was becoming a liability, and it is why I think this is what Stefan might do. But never – never in my wildest thoughts – did I ever imagine Ania becoming that burden. Or that she would go through what she has. It's beyond human decency, and quite incomprehensible what has been done to her. How can any man treat a woman as Ania has been treated, or do the things they are doing to the Jews?'

Elka fell silent for a moment. If Baruch had known it was a possibility that Ania would be betrayed, then why didn't he get her out the moment he knew how badly she was being treated? Didn't he realize then that Ania could become a weak link in the chain of communication? And when it came to the way the Jews were being treated, she had come up against a barrier herself, when reporting back to HQ what she'd found out. It was as if no one wanted to believe it, or do anything about it if they did. Leaving both questions for the moment, she asked, 'What are your plans now, Baruch? How are we going to meet Ania, and when?'

'We leave immediately, but you will need to change your clothes. They aren't appropriate for the route we will be forced to take. We cannot go via Zakopane, for the German presence there makes it out of the question. We will still go by truck most of the distance, but it will be necessary for us to walk a good deal of the way, and there are some gruelling tracks over rough terrain to negotiate.'

'Do we have a chance of getting to the exit point of the sewer, before Ania does?'

'Yes, a chance. They only began their journey a few days ago. I imagine they are just over halfway there. It's not an easy trip, as you can imagine. At times they will have to wade waist-high through the human excrement of a city.

It is a slow process. And it will be especially so, if Ania is weak.'

By the evening of the next day Elka and Baruch and a contingent of four other armed Resistance members, code-named Eli, Filip, Karol and Gabriel, had reached the last safe house. Elka knew all four men from her childhood, as well as their families, so it was strange to her to call them by their cover names. They were all devastated that Ania and Hadriel had not yet made it to the house, but settled down to refreshments and to regroup.

'What now?' Elka asked.

Baruch considered for a moment as he blew the steam of the weak coffee away from him. 'We will have to make our way to the exit point. They should be out now, and we may meet them on the way. But we must approach with caution and will split up. Coming from different directions will give us a better chance if there is a German patrol in the area.'

'How far is it? Surely we would have seen some Germans by now, if they were going to waylay Ania and Hadriel?'

'No, if Stefan has given information, he might have betrayed Ania and Hadriel, but not us or the safe-house route. In that case, we would not see Germans this far up.'

Elka could understand this, and it made her heart heavy with despair. *Please God, don't let Stefan have betrayed Ania. And if he hasn't, then help him through the torture he must be enduring.*

'Right, Eli and Filip, you come with me. Karol and Gabriel, make your way around the edge of the woods and approach the river from that direction. Load your rifles now, and take care, everyone.'

Baruch's voice was charged with emotion. Elka couldn't speak. Falling in behind him, she followed him to the gate of the farm, where he stopped and loaded his rifle. She followed suit with hers, and so did Eli and Filip. These men had been out on so many missions before; they didn't have to ask questions. She had a dozen that she'd like to ask, but thought better of it. Baruch had ensured that she had been trained well and could handle herself in combat, should the need arise. She would prove his confidence in her and obey whatever he told her to do.

It was funny, but now she was actually involved in a real warfare mission, her fear had left her. As had all other emotions. A big part of her training had been about the ability to focus, no matter what the cost to herself. She was glad to find herself able to do that.

Within a short time, the four of them – herself, Baruch, Eli and Filip – were on their stomachs, crawling up a mound that would give them a viewpoint of the river below. Baruch motioned to them to keep their heads down. He lifted his own, then immediately flattened his body, turning at an angle to look at them. 'German soldiers! They're milling around the exit.'

Elka caught her breath.

'How many?' asked Eli.

'A dozen or so. Two trucks are parked nearby.'

Every nerve in Elka's body reacted to this. She waited, willing herself to keep calm; she had to put her trust in Baruch.

'We can take them by surprise. Karol and Gabriel should be in position. The moment we open fire, they will, too. The Germans won't stand a chance, as they won't know which way to defend themselves. On three, crawl up to my side.'

The ground chafed against her stomach, but within seconds Elka was level with Baruch, along with the others.

'Guns ready! Take a look over the top. And . . .'

Elka had seen what was happening at the same moment Baruch had, and she understood his hesitation. Her own heart dropped like a stone in water. Two bedraggled figures were emerging from the ground.

Squinting against the setting sun, Elka took in the scene some thirty yards ahead of them. Ania, her beloved twin, stood covered in filth, her hair stuck to her face, a gun pointing straight at her. Hadriel stood behind her; his body language showed his despair.

A shot rang out, making Elka jump. Hadriel slumped to the ground.

There was a movement next to her. Elka released the breath she'd drawn in with the shock of what she had witnessed. Biting her tongue to stop the scream that rose in her, she held her breath once more. Baruch aimed his gun and fired. The body of the soldier who'd shot Hadriel was flung backwards.

'Fire!'

A hail of bullets followed Baruch's command. Elka's shoulder ached with the kickback from her rifle. As she reloaded, she peered through the smoke and dust. *No!* Two soldiers had hold of Ania and were dragging her to one of the trucks.

'No! No, NO!' This time she shouted the words as she stood and aimed, firing shot after shot as fast as she could reload. But the truck pulled away, just as a force compelled her body to fall over backwards. When she hit the ground, the burning pain in her arm told her that she had been shot.

Rolling over caused her pain, but gave her a view of the scene once more. Guns firing and pain-filled screams and shouts filled the space around her. Below, bodies lay in hideous positions, but all Elka could do was stare at the retreating truck.

Before she could think about the implications of what had just happened, a massive explosion assaulted her eardrums. Parts of the truck soared into the air in every direction. Flames engulfed what was left.

Through her dry, cracked throat came a long howl of pain. 'Ania, no. Not my Ania. Please God, no, nooo! NOOO!'

Baruch fell to the ground beside her. His sobs joined hers. She couldn't comfort him; she had nothing left inside her. Ania – her darling twin sister Ania – was gone. She would never see her again.

A voice penetrated her anguish. 'We had to do it, we had to. We couldn't let her go through what the Germans would put her through. Ania didn't deserve that. She needed her friends to rescue her from that. This was the only way we could save her from torture.'

Reaching for her gun caused Elka a searing pain, but now that she had it, she pointed it at Gabriel. It had been his decision to throw the hand-grenades. He should die!

He stood straight, looking down the barrel. 'I stand by what I did. I did it for Ania. I don't blame you if you kill me, but my love for you and your sister drove me to do it. Always remember that.'

Elka lowered the gun and laid her head down.

Gabriel knelt beside Baruch and asked for his forgiveness.

'There is nothing to forgive. I only wish to thank you for saving my Ania from the clutches of those who would rip out her heart while she still lived. This way, she died instantly. I would want that for her.'

'Hadriel is dead too. I checked.'

Hearing this, Elka felt her world close in on her. All she wanted was to be with Jhona. *Jhona, my love, I need you. Come back to me. Please come back to me.*

## 23

# *Jhona*

### The Polish-Russian Border, June 1940 – A Terrible Choice

How could the sun shine, as if today was a normal, pleasant summer's day? How could he not feel pleasure in breathing in the air? But as Jhona asked himself these questions, he knew the answer. The sun was just a reminder of days that were never again to be, and the air had been fouled by the smell of death.

He was on the border of the Russian-held territory of Poland, outside the city of Krakow, and now in the German half of his beloved occupied country. It was funny how something as small as a stream – a stream he'd played in many times as a boy – could be the division between two countries.

His belly rumbled with hunger and he shivered with cold. But he couldn't attribute the cold to the weather, for it was betrayal that had chilled his blood. Vlady, his best friend of all time, had exposed him.

They had met up a week after his training had been completed. This had been arranged after Vlady had replied to the contact letter, which the service must have sent from

England within days of Jhona leaving. At first, all had gone to plan. Within a few days of being with each other, during which time Jhona and Vlady had renewed their friendship and caught up with each other's news, Vlady had taken him to a restaurant.

After the meal he'd excused himself and left the table. Something hadn't felt right, but Jhona had remained seated. When Vlady hadn't returned after a few moments, Jhona had turned and started to rise. As he did so, he saw a man of slight build leave Vlady's side and disappear through the door. Something about him was familiar.

Vlady had marched back to their table and fixed Jhona with a cold stare. 'You are a spy, Jhona. Did you think you could dupe me?' The words chilled Jhona. Vlady's whole demeanour had changed. Now he seemed like a stranger. 'Sit down, we have to talk,' Jhona commanded, in a clipped tone.

His friend was now his enemy, thought Jhona. His stomach had clenched and threatened to reject the meal he'd just eaten. The man Vlady had been talking to was Gevork Vartanian, a Russian agent who'd contacted the British wanting to become a double agent. He'd been on the same training course as Jhona. It didn't take a genius to work out that Vlady had arranged for Gevork to look at Jhona, to see if he recognized him.

Jhona had known in that moment just how ruthless Vlady really was, and his fear of him and of what would happen increased. Not only had he lost a friend, but he stood to lose everything life had given him. If Vlady didn't expose him, then Gevork would – and he would face certain death. A trickle of hope filtered into his mind. Maybe he could turn this into an advantageous opening, a means of becoming the double agent he'd been instructed to become.

'What do you have to say? Is this the way you use your friends?' Vlady had asked.

His words had hurt, but Jhona counter-attacked. 'What about you, Vlady? You have put me in great danger. What if I told you I am willing to become a double agent? I have allegiances to Britain, as they have promised to help my country, and to Russia, as I have a natural love of your country through its adoption of me when I was a child.'

Vlady's gaze had been unyielding. 'This is obviously the purpose of your mission. But it won't work, Jhona. Russian intelligence wouldn't work with a Jew. What were British intelligence thinking? They are obviously not well informed.'

There hadn't been anything Jhona could say to this. The words had stung. It was as if in the last few months his respectability had been stripped from him and he'd become a leper to all. Even Vlady had said the word 'Jew' with a sneer in his tone.

In the end, though, Vlady had shown that although his opinion of Jhona had lessened, he was still loyal to him. Overnight he had arranged to have Jhona whisked away by friends of his and brought to where he was now. Influences had been brought to bear, favours called in and threats made, all resulting in a journey across Russia and the Ukraine, and he was finally dropped not many miles from this border. For that, he found forgiveness in his heart. Vlady had taken a great risk and would have to convince his organization that Jhona had escaped, as there was no way that Gevork would not report his presence to his superiors.

It would have been easier and much safer for Vlady to

have detained Jhona until the authorities arrived, and not to have cared that he faced being shot or sent to his certain death by torture, starvation or sheer hard labour in a Siberian concentration camp.

Just before they'd parted, Vlady had said, 'Do one thing for me, Jhona. Keep Gevork's action a secret from the British authorities. They may think that by exposing one of their own he has shown his true allegiance to Russia.'

Jhona had nodded and shaken Vlady's hand, but had been puzzled by Vlady even thinking that the British would expect any less of Gevork. All he did was show Russian intelligence that he meant to carry out his duty to the letter, and that could only make him more valuable to the British, because he had already proved that he meant to do the same for them.

As he went over everything that had happened, Jhona began to feel a little less hurt by Vlady's actions. The business of spying was a cold-blooded one, and mistakes were punishable by death. He hoped and prayed that Vlady would be believed when he told how the British agent he'd had in his custody had escaped.

Jhona also hoped that he would meet Vlady again when war was a thing of the past, and that they could be friends once more, but he doubted it. Vlady would always be a spy. His action in helping Jhona was probably the last contact they would ever have.

For Jhona, there wasn't a lot of difference being in Poland from being in Russia. Here, even though it was his own country, he was the enemy, too. He was a Jew. Jews had no hiding place. Jews were interned, murdered and forgotten by the world.

His only hope was to try to get to the Tatra Mountains,

to Baruch and the Resistance. Hopefully Elka would be there and he could be lifted out with her. Or he could serve the purpose of war and liberation by joining the Freedom Army. But first he needed to see Elka. His heart thudded at the thought of his beautiful wife. *Where are you, my darling? How I long to be with you and to hold you in my arms.*

This thought weakened him. He sank down to the grass. From his vantage point he could see the beautiful city of Krakow looming in the distance.

In the days before his exposure, Vlady had told him about the Germans' treatment of the Jews and of their plans to pen them all in ghettos; and how the Jews were used as forced labour, and the weak disposed of. He said that he knew a lot about what went on in Poland, and none of it was good for the Jews. Jhona thought at the time that it wasn't only the Germans who persecuted the Jews, as he knew many had also been sent to labour camps by the Russians.

He found himself between two devils: behind him was the tyranny of the might of Russia, and in front of him was the tyranny of the German Reich. But he knew the geography of his own country well, was equipped with survival skills and had expert knowledge of many different aspects of clandestine operations. All of this would help him in his quest.

Feeling more confident, he made for the wooded area to his left. He needed to get out of sight. Patrols of either side could come along at any moment. Once shielded from view, deep in thick undergrowth in a ditch under a hedge, Jhona scraped away at the turf next to him, drawing a map so as to focus his attention on what he must avoid and which shortcuts would help to speed up his progress to Zakopane. It was a journey of only sixty miles or so, but one fraught with danger. He would need to keep away from the main roads and travel across fields, which would make the distance much longer, as he would have to skirt Krakow. But the good thing was that the land would yield plenty for him to live off. Water would be a problem until he reached higher ground, as the many mountain streams trickled along their way to meet up with the Vistula river.

Travel would have to be done at night, so that he would have the cover of darkness. It would be better too for breaking into buildings to steal items that he would need: a knife, a shaving kit and soap, a bottle for carrying water and a shoulder bag of sorts. He might even get lucky and be able to steal a gun and ammunition from a farm. Most farmers would have these for hunting purposes. Perhaps he could also steal a pair of binoculars, to enable him to keep watch and to check out the next part of his journey during daylight hours. They would also enable him to see patrols long before they were a danger to him, and to see in advance where checkpoints were situated so that he could avoid them.

Feeling much more positive, Jhona lay back. The damp of the turf beneath him seeped through his clothes, but he didn't care. He was free, and he had to concentrate on remaining that way. As his eyes closed, he hoped with all his heart that Elka had found his letter before she'd left for Poland again. Then she would know where he was and might feel confident that Vlady would keep him safe.

The news that he hadn't checked in with his contact might have set off alarm bells back at base by now. If it had, then he hoped the news hadn't reached Elka. Not yet. All he needed was time. A week at the most, and copious amounts of luck, and he could be by her side again. *Please God, make that possible!*

A sound woke him. He hadn't intended to fall asleep, and was surprised to find the light was fading when he opened his eyes. He sat upright, immediately alert.

As he peered around him, a movement to his left caught his attention. A figure darted from one tree to the next. Jhona swallowed. Apprehension prickled the hairs on his neck. He waited, not moving a sinew of his body. The figure moved closer to him, repeating his dash between the trees. Jhona wondered if the man had spotted him sleeping and was creeping up on him. Was he German, or a Russian soldier?

The figure moved again. This time Jhona saw that he held a rifle in front of him. A twig snapped beneath the man's feet and a squeal split the air. Jhona looked towards the sound and saw a wild boar running away. The man chased after it. Relief flooded Jhona, but he also realized that he was within yards of a gun. Yes, it was a hunting rifle, but any gun that he could get hold of would increase his chances of reaching Baruch.

Climbing out of the bush on the opposite side to the hunter, Jhona kept his head down and ran in the same direction as him, moving as fast as his bent position would allow him to.

The crack of a shot rang out. The echo of the explosion deafened him and sent flocks of birds soaring high in the sky, increasing the noise level with their squawks of fear.

Jhona fell to the ground and waited.

In the silence that descended, the smell of sulphur told

him he was near his quarry. Rising, he ran ahead once more. His tread was soft and soundless on the lush grass of the hedgerow. He spotted a hole big enough for him to crawl through. It was just what he needed. Nearby, he saw the back of the hunter as he bent over the dead pig. The knife that the man drew from his belt glinted in the weak rays of the sun that filtered through the trees. When the hunter slit and bled the pig, Jhona rushed forward and jumped him.

'What the . . . ?'

Jhona held the hunter in a lock from which he couldn't escape, before swiftly executing a move that rendered him unconscious.

Working at speed, he carved a leg off the beast, took off his belt, tied it around the leg and slung it over his shoulder. He felt satisfied that he had meat to eat tonight, but had left plenty for the hunter to take home to his family, or to sell on the black market. The knife would be useful to him. He smiled as he tucked it into his pocket. This chance encounter was proving a godsend.

It was then that he heard the rumble of wheels and a heavy engine. Fear once more made him alert. *It must be a patrol!* What if they'd heard the rifle shot?

The engine sound came nearer and then died. Jhona dropped the pig's leg to the ground. He didn't want to leave a trail of blood that could lead people to him. Grabbing the gun and rifling through the ammunition belt, he stuffed as many bullets into his other pocket as he could and ran. His body slammed against the side of the nearest tree that would put him out of sight. Voices came to him – Russian voices. Working as silently as he could, he loaded the gun, praying that the noise they were making would cover that of snapping the gun closed over the bullet he'd inserted. Trying to control his breathing, he listened.

'Come out, Mikhail, we know you are there. Show yourself. Share whatever it is that you have caught.'

The command wasn't aggressive. It was obvious as they came nearer that they were in a jovial mood. It seemed, from what they were saying, that the hunter often tried to elude them, so that he didn't have to give them some of his spoils.

Peeping around the tree, Jhona's heart sank. The men were Russian soldiers. One caught sight of Mikhail and stopped in his tracks, before shouting to the others. 'Get down. Get down, I tell you. Look, someone has attacked Mikhail!'

The three hit the ground. Jhona held his breath. If he moved, they would hear him; dry pieces of branch and dead foliage that would snap under his step were strewn all around him. Sweat beaded on his forehead and trickled down his face. A fly played around his bloodied jacket, and was quickly joined by another. Their buzz sounded to him like the engine of an aeroplane as more joined them, setting up a frenzy of activity that made him fear they would attract attention to him. He had no choice but to go on the offensive.

'Stay down or I'll shoot!' His command was obeyed, but Jhona felt sick at the thought that this is what he would have to do. He'd never killed a man in his life, and now he would have to kill three.

'Throw your guns away from you – now.' Jhona could see them from his vantage point behind the tree. One of the soldiers looked up and asked, 'Who are you? If you are Russian, why would you want to kill us?'

'Shut up and throw your gun away from you. Do it!' His internal conflict was agonizing. He prayed: *Please God, forgive me.*

The blast assaulted his ears, rendering him deaf. The head of the soldier who had questioned him splintered into a bloodied mess. The other two made as if to get up and run. Jhona reloaded and fired, and his accurate aim meant that the second soldier died in the same way as his comrade. Ready in seconds to take his third shot, Jhona looked down the sight of the rifle and no longer saw a soldier – his enemy – but a young boy of no more than sixteen years of age on his feet, begging, 'No, no, don't kill me.' His face held a terror the like of which Jhona had never seen before, and he knew as he squeezed the trigger that it would remain with him until his dying day.

Tears blinded him as he reloaded and stepped out from behind the tree. Stealthily he crept towards the prostrate body of the man he now knew was called Mikhail. He appeared still to be unconscious. If that was so, and as he hadn't seen Jhona and so couldn't describe him, he could be spared.

Jhona thrust the barrel of the gun into the man's ribs. It was not possible for Mikhail not to react, if he was faking. There was no reaction. With a cold calculation that he wouldn't have been capable of a couple of months ago, Jhona removed the bag Mikhail had slung over his shoulder, then searched him for anything that might be of use. He found a sling, more ammunition and a water bottle. Finally, picking up the pig's leg that was still attached to his belt, he left the scene.

Stumbling blindly through thicket, catching and tearing his skin on brambles and tripping on the protruding roots of trees, he tried to put as much distance as he could between himself and the carnage he'd caused. How was it that he – a gentle person, a man who loved people – could turn into a killer? Would he ever again be the same man he had been? At this moment he didn't feel fit to be the husband of his beautiful Elka. He'd killed, and for no other reason than to save his own skin.

When he thought he'd put enough distance between him and the scene, he sat down. Trying to get his thoughts into order, he went over the options he might have had, but none of them would have guaranteed that he would still be alive and free. Wasn't it his duty to remain so? Didn't he owe that much to Elka and his family? And yes, to his country? All those who could fight must try to remain alive to do so. Those soldiers would have killed him, or taken him prisoner, which would have meant that he'd have been sent to a concentration camp and his ultimate death.

These thoughts put strength back into him. Getting up, Jhona continued on his journey, knowing that he was now fully in the German-occupied territory of Poland. But he also knew that his fellow countrymen would not, or could not, offer him protection. He had to look to himself for this, and be prepared to tackle whatever was necessary to survive and to carry on to fight another day and, above all, to get back to his beloved Elka.

# 24
# *Brendan*

## London, July 1940 – A Strength to Admire

Seeing the dejected figure of Elka step from the plane caused Brendan's heart to flip. In the short time he'd known her, Brendan had become very fond of Elka and felt responsible for her. Now he had to face telling her that Jhona was missing.

Edith had asked to come with him to meet Elka, but Brendan hadn't been able to let her, as the plane was coming in to Biggin Hill and only authorized personnel could go there.

He stood on the grass verge outside one of the hangers. Around him air-force pilots sat in groups on the grass or on upturned oil drums, enjoying a respite from their rigorous training. None of them looked older than twenty years of age. All were seemingly relaxed, though all were fully kitted out and ready to go. Each, he could see, constantly looked to the skies. There had been intelligence that the Germans were planning to annihilate the airfield and destroy its fleet of aircraft, before invading Britain. It was a red-alert situation.

What these men faced, and the burden upon them, was

great. If they failed, then Britain wouldn't stand a chance. And yet Brendan didn't feel despair. Yes, the task would be enormous; and yes, it was known that the Luftwaffe had almost twice as much air power as the British did; but he felt confident that with the excellent radar system Britain had in place, and with the skill and courage of these men, Germany would not succeed.

As he waited, he looked back to see Elka walking towards him. He dreaded what he had to tell her, but her demeanour told him something else had hit her in the gut. She looked like a defeated woman. What had happened to cause this change in her? As he went forward to meet her, he held out his arms, not caring how it would look. When she came into them, a cheer went up, but he couldn't acknowledge the teasing joviality of the watching airmen. Something was very wrong. Elka slumped into him. Her body shook with sobs.

'Elka, what is it? What has happened? You're injured? How? Come on, let's get you through security. I have a car waiting to take you to London. We have to go straight to HQ, but then we can go to your mother. She can't wait to see you. I had the Devil's own job stopping her from coming to meet you.'

'I – I'm glad that you did. I have terrible news. I can't bear it, Brendan, I can't.'

The fear of what was weighing her down kept him from saying the one name he was certain was the cause. *Ania. Please God, no! Please don't let the news be that Ania has been caught.*

Leading Elka through the security checks, he was glad when they finally walked towards his car. He'd commandeered an official vehicle with a driver, so that he could sit in the back with Elka and gently break his news to her. Now he wished that he was anywhere but here, and had anything other than what he had to impart, as he could see that Elka was already struggling to cope.

As they settled into the deep red-leather seats, Elka eased herself painfully into a position where she could look at him. Her voice trembled. 'Ania is dead.' The breath she had sucked in came out on a moan. 'Ania, Ania – Ania.' Her head shook with each reciting of the name, and her face had the look of someone hearing, and attempting to absorb, terrible news.

Her eyes opened wide, giving her the appearance of having just witnessed a horrific act. 'They killed her! They dragged her through degradation – made her the dregs of the gutter. Then they killed her.' As she took another deep breath, her voice deepened into an angry growl, causing spittle to spray from her mouth and shattering Brendan's perception that she had been talking about the Germans. 'We have to kill them. Betray them to the Germans and let them die the slow death of torture. Help me to do that, Brendan. Help me.' Her body jerked violently. Spittle ran down her chin.

Alarmed and afraid for her, Brendan leaned forward and spoke to his driver. 'Take us straight to the nearest hospital, please.'

'That's about twenty miles away, sir, the Kent and Sussex.'

'Just do it, and as quickly as possible.' Leaning back, he held Elka to him, trying to soothe her without causing her more pain. As he stroked her hair she became calmer. Using his handkerchief, he wiped her face and eyes.

'I'm sorry, Brendan. I – I have so much pain knotted inside me.'

'Don't try to talk. Rest your head on my shoulder, that's right. Close your eyes for a little while, we're taking you to hospital.'

'No, don't do that. Get me back to my mother. She will take care of me.'

'But . . .'

'Please, Brendan. You know that Mother is a doctor – she is the best one to give me care. I need to be with her.'

'I'm sorry, but you have your debriefing to go through before you can go home. Even if we go to the hospital, guards will be placed around you until we can speak to you.'

As Elka slumped back in the seat, Brendan wanted so much to take her to her mother. They needed to be together, to share the grief that would be as devastating to Edith as it was to Elka. But he had to follow orders. 'If you feel up to it, we will go to HQ and speak to Colonel Wright, who is expecting us.'

Elka's trauma showed in her every gesture as she nodded her head and raised her hands in a despairing shrug. 'If that's what has to happen, then let's get it over with, so that I can go home.'

After instructing the driver, Brendan gently told Elka that if she needed to talk to him, she could. 'The driver is part of our team, he has signed the Official Secrets Act. You need have no fears about whatever you may say, but you need to be prepared to go through it all again at HQ. I'm sorry, my dear, I wish it could be different.'

Once she'd told him everything, Elka seemed calmer. But for Brendan the shock was immense. Had they been right to trust Baruch? What were his motives? How could he allow his wife to go through what she had, and then sanction her murder? As Elka had said, the two Resistance workers who were positioned ahead of the retreating truck could have shot at and killed the Germans driving the vehicle. They could have rescued Ania.

Colonel Wright greeted them, his manner that of a caring father towards Elka as she went through her story once more.

'Why do you think they went to the lengths they did? Are you sure they could have saved Ania?' he asked.

'I'm certain. We had the other soldiers engaged. They wouldn't have been a threat to Gabriel and Karol. They could have left their shelter and attacked the soldiers in the truck.'

'Did Baruch show genuine grief at Ania's passing?'

'Yes, he was like a broken man. I just can't understand it. I couldn't get near him to ask my questions. And anyway I was trying to cope with my injury and my own grief. But it seemed to me that the other members of his group shielded Baruch, telling me that he couldn't bear to face me. That he just needed time. The journey back to camp was horrendous, but I thought once we were there he would talk to me, but he wouldn't. Then, within hours of our return, the message came through that I was to be lifted out sooner than planned. Did he arrange that?'

The moment Brendan dreaded was upon him. But then, looking into Elka's distraught face, he knew it wasn't the time. He looked over at the colonel and shook his head, before saying, 'No, the plans were changed and we needed you back here.' It occurred to him then that Elka hadn't asked about Jhona. He was grateful for this.

'I can't go on another mission. Not yet. I'm not fit. And besides, what happened has changed me.'

'We know, and we won't ask that of you,' the colonel said. 'But, Elka, what we do ask is that you try and go over everything you know and heard and saw. There must be some reason for what happened to Ania. Does Baruch know that you feel her death was avoidable?'

'Yes. I screamed it at him, even though I couldn't see him. But his team closed ranks around him and I began to feel threatened.'

'It can't be because they thought Ania was a traitor. You said they thought Stefan was the one to betray the escape—'

'That's it, Brendan! Supposing it was a lie that Stefan was captured? Supposing they did suspect Ania of giving away their secrets, or of being on the brink of doing so?'

'It is an explanation, I agree. What do you think, Colonel?'

'Yes, if you think about it, the whole thing could have been an elaborate plan to make it look as though they were getting Ania out and it went wrong. You say that Stefan instigated her escape? And what of the chap who brought her out – could he have been involved?'

'I don't know. I did once know Hadriel, and wouldn't have said he was capable of doing anything to hurt Ania or me, but nothing is how it was . . .' After a moment Elka continued, 'But I don't think Hadriel was involved, as I got the feeling that he was used – a disposable person whose days were numbered. No one seemed to mourn his passing. One of them spoke of his bravery, but mostly they didn't make much of his death.'

'So, do you trust Stefan?'

'Again it is difficult. I have never met him. But from

what I heard of him, he always seemed to be in the right place at the right time. Take the incident in the shop that I told you about. How come that German officer turned up at that shop at the same time Stefan had arranged to meet Ania there? The officer's mission was clearly to terrify Ania into confessing. And I know that after she'd heard the shot that probably killed the first office girl, Ania would have admitted everything to save the rest of those girls. But Stefan was ready again. Just at that moment he lured her to the house across the road . . . Come to think of it, how did Baruch know every detail of what had happened concerning the shop incident, and so soon?'

'It all sounds very suspicious and too coincidental. It smacks of everything being arranged to dispose of Ania. But how? Though I guess the "how" is of little consequence now. We can't change anything. What we can do is cut all ties with Baruch's group, unless it cuts the ties with Stefan. I feel certain, from what you are saying, that Baruch was convinced of his wife's possible future betrayal of them, and that he agreed to her escape plan. Whether that included agreeing to her death, if anything went wrong with that escape plan, is debatable, but seems likely.'

'A plan, Colonel, that Stefan had put in place. Stefan is the key to all this. Maybe Ania had begun to suspect him and he needed her disposed of. I doubt that he has really been captured. I would even bet money on him reappearing and continuing to offer his services, with some plausible story of why they let him go free.'

The colonel nodded his agreement.

'How could Baruch have been taken in by Stefan?' Elka's plea held such pain.

'Didn't you say they were friends before the war?' asked

Brendan. 'Men capable of doing what we think Stefan is doing can be very plausible, and will court whoever they think could be useful to them. They are always charming and likeable. Stefan could have been in the pay of Germany, even back then, and could have made a point of befriending anyone who might be useful to him. Think about it, Elka. How did Baruch end up on Germany's "most wanted" list? How did they even know about him? He disappeared into the hills, once the invasion was under way. He didn't join the Freedom Army, as he thought that clandestine operations would be the only way to go. Why should his name be out there, unless somebody put it there?'

'Stefan – it must be. And it must be Stefan who made Baruch believe that Ania had betrayed him.'

'It's possible. Baruch sounds like one of those men who is passionate about his cause – and ruthless in the face of it. That shows in what he has allowed to happen to the woman he loved. And it shows in the grief you saw. His inability to face you was probably the result of guilt, but I would say that a good measure of it was genuine, inconsolable grief.'

'Yes, I can see that. You could be right, Brendan. Poor Baruch . . . But, what can we do to convince him? What if Stefan betrays him fully – not just by informing on him as a dissident, but by telling where he and his men are?'

'We will discuss this further with the whole team and will come up with a solution. Now, Elka.' The colonel softened his tone and glanced at Brendan.

Brendan turned to Elka. 'On another matter, Elka, I – I have to tell you—'

'Jhona! It's Jhona, isn't it? Y-you brought me back because . . . No, no, Brendan, not Jhona, please God, no.'

'My dear, I'm so sorry, but we have lost communication with Jhona. He didn't check in at the appointed time with his contact. He was supposed to report back, even if he had nothing to tell us.'

'Does that mean he . . . he is—'

'We don't know. We have recently acquired a double agent in Russia.'

'Russia!'

'Yes, Jhona was sent to Russia. Look, we now know that he was compromised.'

'No! No, Brendan – please tell me he's not dead.'

'I'm sorry, Elka. We will tell you all we know.'

After telling her what they knew from their informer, the double agent, Elka asked, 'But why didn't the agent tell a lie and say he didn't know Jhona?'

'He had no choice, as he had to show his loyalty to Russia. They would have found out if he'd lied, and then he would have been disposed of. These double agents are cold-blooded and dangerous; they constantly have to take actions that make each side believe in them.'

Elka didn't respond, but her demeanour showed her distress. Her glance at Brendan was accusatory. He wanted to shrivel away from it. At this moment he felt he was the guilty party, as he was partly responsible for Elka's suffering. He had to convince her that if they didn't know Jhona's fate, then there was still hope. There had to be hope. The colonel expressed this same sentiment.

'We are all hopeful at HQ. We think we would know if Jhona was dead or imprisoned. Our agent has told us only that Jhona is missing. He is worried because he cannot believe what he has been told: that Jhona has escaped and gone into hiding. Jhona was with another agent when he was identified, but we have hope, because that agent was a long-standing friend of Jhona's.'

'Vlady?'

'Yes.'

'Vlady is a spy! Though I don't know why I am surprised, because the whole world has turned upside down and has turned us into people we never imagined we'd become.'

'Vladislav Mihaylov has been a spy for a long time – since long before the war began.'

'Knowing that, you still trusted him with Jhona's life!'

The colonel looked shocked at this from Elka, but didn't react. He spoke in even tones. 'It may have been the best move we made, in the circumstances. We could have sent him out there as a cold spy, with no contacts on the other side. But whilst I agree we underestimated Vladislav, as it was he who ordered the double agent to identify Jhona, we also think there is a very remote possibility that once Vladislav knew Jhona's true reason for being in Russia, he helped him to escape, rather than accept him as a double agent – which was what we hoped he would do.'

Elka looked stunned. She sat stiffly and stared at the colonel. Brendan could almost hear her mind working and saw the moment when she came to a conclusion, as her facial expression changed to one of hardened determination. 'If Vlady helped Jhona, he would have taken him to the Krakow border. I have to go back there. Jhona will try to make his way to Baruch. I must be there to protect him.'

'You are not fit enough to go, Elka.'

'I will get fit. My arm is healing already, as nothing was broken – the bullet only glanced me. And yes, it has made a nasty surface wound, but with the care I received, there is no infection and it's already a lot better.'

'I actually think it is a good idea that you go back.'

Brendan couldn't believe the colonel had said this. Emotionally, physically and mentally, Elka wasn't ready. She had ulterior motives – she must have, after all that had occurred. Yes, she'd want to be there if there was a possibility that Jhona would make his way to Baruch, but she would also want to even the score and try to do something about Stefan.

'If you go back,' the colonel continued, 'you will make them think we still believe in them, despite what has happened. That will mean that if they do have a traitor amongst them, his guard will be down. The group is useful to us – very useful. Their activities help us, and the intelligence they have given has been of immense use to our future plans. We need them, but it is obvious something is wrong. We need you to find out what, or who, is the weak link. That is the greatest service you could do us, and Ania, Elka.'

Something about Elka had changed. Brendan saw a broken woman transform into a strong, determined agent once more.

'I will do it. I need to do it.'

This last sentiment worried Brendan, but he said nothing. He would wait and watch and make sure he detected no motive of revenge. If he did, then he would speak out. But if Elka's transformation had shocked him, what she said next shook him to the core. 'My mother is not to be told that Ania is dead. I will tell her that I have seen her from a distance and that she looks well. It is the only way I can cope with having a second devastation laid upon me. And I must cope. If Jhona is going to Baruch, then he is going blind, without the knowledge that we have. He will be in great danger. He will tell them what has happened to him and this will make him valuable to the Germans. The traitor will betray him. The Germans will not believe that Jhona doesn't know anything about the Russian plans. Added to that, he is a Jew.'

Brendan couldn't speak. It was as if Elka was a stranger to him. And yet he had to agree with her on everything she said about Jhona. 'Sir, I will go instead. My Polish is almost perfect now. I can communicate with the group. Besides, the journey won't have to be on skis at this time of year, so that won't be a problem. I will go. Elka can stay.'

'No. I'm sorry, O'Flynn, but only PMf can take on this mission. It will not be plausible to Baruch – or his men, and definitely not to the traitor – if it is anyone else.'

Hearing the colonel revert to using Elka's code-name, Brendan knew there was no arguing with him. But how was he going to face his Aunt Edith? *How can I carry on as normal with her, knowing as I do that one of her daughters is dead and the other is going back and will be in extreme danger?*

Elka didn't appear to have any such concerns. It seemed that she had focused solely on saving Jhona, and had put her grief for her sister to one side for now. What this cost her, Brendan couldn't imagine, but he knew he was witnessing extreme courage.

'I want my mother told that I will be home in a couple of days and that my debriefing will take that long. In the meantime I want to go somewhere I will have complete peace to come to terms with everything. Then I will be ready to leave in a week.'

Brendan went to protest, but the colonel spoke first.

'Of course, I know just the place. I have a cottage on the edge of Epping Forrest. It was left to me by my grandparents. My wife and I go there whenever we can. It is remote, and the area is as peaceful as it can be, given the times we are in.' He went on to tell Elka about the grazing pasture that had provided a haven of tranquillity, but was now a hive of activity, as farmers churned every available bit of land to cultivate it, in order to feed the nation. 'Elka, a new organization is now in force, and you have been seconded to it. You are now an agent of the Special Operations Executive. They mostly use the acronym "SOE".'

As the colonel explained to Elka about the new organization, Brendan felt excluded from the world they had both entered. A world where there was no pain of loss and the dangers of the near future didn't exist. At the same time he felt admiration for Elka, as he realized she had all the strength it took to be a spy – and now an SOE agent – and his colonel had the ability to turn a situation to its best advantage. He wondered at his own capabilities. Yes, he was strong, but his emotions ran high and he wore them on his sleeve, visible for all to see.

He thought of his Aunt Ada, and how she would hide her true feelings and act with courage and strength. He stood tall at the thought. He wouldn't let the side down. The colonel and Elka were right, and he would support them in their decision and not put forward any further objections.

# 25

# *Edith*

## London, Late July 1940 – Coping with Change

'I – I've come to tell you I'm leaving. Dr Edith, I want to do sommat as helps the war effort.'

'Oh, Ginny, no. I don't know what to say.'

Ginny's expression was one of determination, but it seemed to Edith that this was a mask she'd put on, in order to get through the ordeal of telling her she was leaving, and that it wasn't how she really felt.

As she stood up from her chair behind the desk, Edith felt more able to deal with the situation. Now she could be on a level with Ginny. 'I'll be so sorry to see you go. We will miss you. Won't you reconsider? Your work here is important, and we are contributing to the war effort by taking care of the people left at home.'

'I know that, but me skills could be put to better use helping the injured. Anyroad, I've joined the Queen Alexandra's Royal Navy Nursing Service, so there's naw turning back. I'm reet sorry, as I love me work here, and I know as I should've told you of me plans before, but I was afraid you'd persuade me not to go.'

Edith watched the emotions playing across Ginny's face.

She knew the reason behind them. Eloise had expressed her concerns about Ginny only a week ago. 'She's head over heels in love with Brendan, poor girl. But nothing can come of it, because it is a forbidden love.' Edith now knew Eloise was right and recognized that this would be Ginny's way of dealing with her feelings – distancing herself from Brendan and immersing herself in difficult and dangerous work.

Though her words came out on a heavy sigh, Edith meant every one of them. 'Go with my blessing and my prayers, Ginny. I'm proud of you. But worried, too, as I know what life in a field hospital in the midst of war is like. But on a moving ship? That will be far more dangerous.'

'I know, but I'm prepared for that. The recruitment office put me through some rigorous tests to see that I had the mettle that was needed. I passed with flying colours. I took the tests when I had a few days off, a while back. I lied to you about going back up north to see some mates. I – I shouldn't have.'

'It's all right. I know how it is. I had to do a lot in secret, for fear of others preventing me from going to the front. But, like you, I was determined and nothing would stop me, so I do understand.'

'Aye, Brendan told me some of what you went through, and it inspired me. And, well, I'm reet grateful for your blessing.'

'Oh, Ginny, what you are doing is a very brave thing, far more so than what I did. Your grandmother Ada would be so proud of you.'

'Eeh, I wish she were here.'

There was a knock on the door. Edith felt a sense of

relief. She thought Ginny was about to cry and didn't know how she would cope with that. It all left her with a sinking feeling, especially her worries about Elka. Her last visit home had been uncharacteristic – spending such a lot of time away, and then taking off again within days. She'd hardly discussed Jhona's disappearance and hadn't wanted to talk about Ania at all.

Fear wrapped around Edith's heart at the sight of her daughter, and yet there hadn't been anything physically wrong with her, except for an injury to her arm, which was bandaged. A burn, Elka had said. 'I fell and landed too near a fire.' But instinct had told Edith this hadn't been the truth.

The door opened. Of all the inopportune visitors at this very moment, Brendan popped his head round the door. 'May I come in? Oh, hello, Ginny. I haven't seen you for a while – how are you?'

Ginny burst into tears and ran from the room.

'What the . . . ?'

'No, don't go after her. Sit down, Brendan. That is, if you are not the bearer of bad news, for I couldn't bear any more at the moment.'

'Well, not bad news, but no news. At least not of the kind you are hoping for, and I know that is just as demoralizing. I have come to see Leah. Look, I need to tell you something. I know you won't approve, but I can't stop thinking about her. I think I am in love with Leah. There! I've said it.'

'Oh, is that all? Well, we guessed that a long time ago.'

'Really? And I've been agonizing about how you would take it – and how to handle someone so fragile – when all this time I could have spoken to you about it.'

'I'm glad you didn't, as there is another worry, where your affections are concerned. Lady Eloise and I think Ginny has feelings for you that she is finding difficult to cope with. Her reason for being in the office just now was to tell me that she is leaving to work on a hospital ship.'

'No! Oh, Aunt Edith, no – that is the last thing I wanted to happen. I did suspect her feelings, but we are related and I thought she was mixing up her feelings for me with how one would naturally feel for an uncle, or even a half-uncle, as I am to her. But our relationship is a lot more complicated, as we are cousins too; and then her grandfather is my father! God knows what that makes us. But I don't want Ginny hurt. What do you think I should do?'

'Nothing. And certainly don't broach the subject. Carry on acting as you are – ignoring the subject, and allowing Ginny the dignity of taking herself away from you, without the embarrassment of her thinking that you suspect.'

'But it's such a drastic action. She'll be in danger. I'll feel terrible if anything happens to her. I'm already weighed down with guilt over . . . Oh, damn it all!'

It seemed to Edith there was more on Brendan's mind than just Ginny going away, or his involvement in placing Elka and Jhona in a vulnerable position. '*Is* there news, Brendan? I know you've said not, but I *feel* something isn't right.'

Brendan hung his head.

As she looked at him, Edith's emotions swung as if on a pendulum, as they had done ever since he had first recruited Elka and Jhona. Part of her was very angry with him, but she fought this and allowed her love for Brendan to forgive him and recognize the difficult position he was in.

On her second huge sigh, she changed the subject. She

knew her gut feeling was right and that there was something she wasn't being told, but she didn't want to pursue it. 'About Leah – will you wait until Ginny has gone before you speak to her about how you feel? I think it would be the kindest thing to do.'

Brendan looked relieved, confirming that she had steered him away from whatever it was he and Elka were not telling her. She'd had this same uncomfortable feeling with her daughter.

'Yes, of course, but . . . there *is* something else. We need someone who can speak French and knows France.'

'You cannot mean you want to recruit Leah? No! Brendan, please don't even consider it. She's not strong enough. What do you need her for?'

'I can't tell you much, but Churchill has set up a new initiative. It is vital work. Specialist agents will be recruited to help Resistance movements and communicate intelligence back to us.'

'And very dangerous, no doubt. If you love Leah, you can't possibly consider her.'

Once again Brendan hung his head. When he looked up his expression was unreadable. 'We've found her brother.'

'What! How? I mean, were you looking for him?'

'No. Someone working for our department in France came across him. His name is Alfreed, and he is working with a Resistance group that has been set up under the direction of General de Gaulle. It appears that he was rescued from the water by a French trawler and taken back to France. He lost his memory. By the time he recovered and his amnesia had lifted, France was occupied.'

'That's wonderful. I mean, not that France is occupied

of course, but to find Leah's brother and hear that he is alive! I know Leah has referred to him as Alfreed. How on earth did you make the connection to her?'

'Alfreed made it himself. He asked our man if he'd heard of a boating accident off the coast of England, and if he knew what might have happened to his family. He believed they were all dead. Our man had heard of the accident, because of course it was reported, and told him that he thought his sister had survived, but not his parents. Alfreed then asked if our agent would try and find out something definite for him, when he made contact with England. When the message came through, we made the connection. You see, besides me knowing Leah, all foreign nationals are coming under our radar, and Leah is no exception to that. She was registered by the police; they did so when they were investigating the gang who had held her. They did the same with all of the girls they found in that brothel who didn't want to go home. The German girls are now living in a camp. They didn't have the choice to go home and, as you would expect, they have little freedom, but they are well looked after.'

'Well, I'm astonished. It never ceases to amaze me what goes on. But as regards Leah and her brother, I'm so happy. Shall I get Leah to come to the office so that we can tell her?'

'That's the rub. I can't tell Leah. I have to take her to HQ. They want to tell her themselves, and use the information to get her on board Churchill's new initiative. Look, I shouldn't be telling you this, but they have a particular interest in her. They think she will want to go to her brother and, if she does, they would like to talk to her about working for us. They need a messenger. A French girl would be ideal, because in the main the French can travel around their country without suspicion.'

'But you can't ask that of her, please, Brendan. It's so dangerous. Oh, this bloody war!'

'It isn't my decision. But before I take her to the War Office – and that is an order I can't refuse to carry out – I want to tell Leah that I love her. I want to offer her marriage. This wouldn't be as a way out, for she will still be asked to go to France and the decision will be entirely hers. But now that I am faced with the prospect of losing her, I want – more than anything in the world – to let her know how I feel and offer her another choice. I wouldn't be able to bear her going.'

The irony of this didn't escape Edith. An inner voice said, *Then you will know how I feel.* Feeling ashamed, she quietened it, and concentrated her thoughts on Leah. Leah pined for her brother. Not knowing what had happened to him had fuelled her hope that he was still alive. Of course she would want to go to him; but hopefully the possibility of being with Brendan would be a bigger pull on her emotions.

Brendan stood up. 'Look, I will have to take Leah back with me, but I can tell her how I feel at a later date. I do value – no, *need* – your advice, Aunt Edith.'

The way he said this tugged on Edith's heartstrings. Despite everything, he was still her Brendan, the little lad who had come into her life because of her friendship with his Aunt Ada. She must never forget that. *Oh, Ada, I do miss you. And I promise that, no matter how angry I am at Brendan, I love him and will take care of him.* The balance of her feelings swung towards her love for Brendan. Her anger was quelled. 'How about you come to dinner tonight, darling? We can talk everything through with Laurent. He has a clear, wise head about such things.'

'Thank you. I would love that.' He crossed the room towards her and hugged her. His body shook. 'I'm sorry, Aunt Edith, truly sorry for everything.'

Once more the feeling overcame her that there was something – *something* – that she still didn't know. She hugged him back, unable to face whatever it was. 'Don't be. None of this is your fault. As we were in our war, you are just a pawn. You happened to be where you are when it all broke out, just as I happened to be a doctor and needed at the front. We all have our part to play. None of it is easy. But you make me proud. Though your role is one of the most difficult, you have risen to it.'

'Thank you, Aunt Edith.' He stood away from her and looked down into her eyes. 'Always remember: the decisions I take are not because I want to, but because I have to.' He held her once more and in an anguished voice said, 'I know that what I ask of people is dangerous and could cost them their lives, but although that is difficult, I have to do it. And so do they.'

She felt guilty all of a sudden. She was sure Brendan knew about the pocket of anger that she held inside her, but she said nothing. As he released her, his voice and manner changed. 'Now, I think I should seek out Ginny. Don't worry, I'll handle her with kid gloves, but I can't just leave her like that.'

Ginny heard the door open behind her. She'd taken herself off to the laundry room and was busying herself with sorting the linen.

'What's this I hear about you travelling far away from me?'

His tone was too jovial, as if he was talking to a child. He obviously knew of her feelings. A blush spread over her cheeks, but she kept her voice steady as she answered him. 'Aye, I'm going. I need to feel that I'm doing sommat. Me skills can be put to better use than they are here.'

'But your work here is important. Can't you change your mind?'

'Naw, I'll not be doing that.' A glimmer of hope entered her.

'I'll miss you, and worry about you, but I have to say that I'm one proud uncle.'

That hope sank. He rarely referred to their relationship. Had he done so now deliberately?

'Eeh, you're too busy to think of the likes of me. Go away with you!' Turning the conversation into banter helped to put her emotions on a different level. She would cope – she had to.

'I'm never too busy to think of you, Ginny. You're very special to me. You're the only true relative I have, as I am yours. That makes for a bond that can't be broken. Thinking of you in danger will tear my heart out every day. Come here.'

Going into his arms was torture. Why couldn't she be normal and feel as he did – as a niece and uncle, or cousins or whatever, should feel for each other?

'Hey, you're squeezing the breath out of me. Ha, but it's nice to have this moment together. I'll think about it every day. You will write, won't you? And watch those soldiers: the married ones will be the worst. It will be hard for them to contain themselves around such a beautiful girl.'

Latching onto his joking manner, she came out of his arms and pretended to slap him. 'Eeh, give over. Anyone would think as you were jealous!'

The moment she'd said the words she regretted them. Brendan's reaction told her he'd taken them in a different way from the way she'd meant them. He looked into her eyes. 'Not jealous, but concerned. I meant it when I said you're special to me. You're my kin. You're a big part of Aunt Ada that remains with me. I don't want anything to happen to you. It would break my heart.'

Feeling hurt, but resigned, she managed a smile. 'And you're the world to me, Brendan. The bestest uncle a girl could wish for.' Tears stung her eyes as he held her to him once more. *If only, if only . . .*

'Well, I have to be going. When are you due to leave?'

'Next week, Wednesday. I'm to report to the naval base in Plymouth. I was told that as I'm fully qualified, I'd probably be deployed almost immediately. They gave me a rail pass to get there. I just need to look up the times of trains.'

'I'll try to get a day off and drive you there.'

'Naw. I – I mean, ta, but naw. I want to go under me own steam. I'd rather say goodbye here than down there.'

'Right. If you're sure?'

She didn't know how to break the awkwardness of the moment. Her heart was cross with her head; she should have said yes, then her time with Brendan would have been longer and she would have had him all to herself on the journey. But that was dangerous ground. She needed to distance herself from him, and to do so now.

'Look, I'll speak to Aunt Edith, see if she can arrange an evening before then and—'

'Don't do that. I don't want a fuss. It would be too much for me. Say goodbye now. I'll write, I promise, though I don't know what we'll be allowed to put in our letters. And I'll look for your letters to me. Let me know as everyone is alreet – that's important to me.'

Brendan looked as if he was going to say something, but changed his mind.

Ginny was so tuned into him that she detected something was terribly wrong. 'What is it, Brendan?'

'I – I cannot tell you. Orders. But when you do find out, please forgive me. Please know that withholding what I know from you all was not my choice.'

'Brendan?'

'I have to go. Take care of yourself, you're very precious to me.'

The door closed behind him.

Ginny stared at it as her mind worked along fearful paths. Was it Jhona? Or one of the twins? Oh, please God, don't let it be any of them.

Edith scurried away just as the door began to open. She'd decided to see that everything was all right and had heard them talking. Brendan's voice had carried to her. Her fears were confirmed. Taking a deep breath, she decided not to mention what she'd heard or question Brendan when he came to dinner. She would keep her own counsel, despite suffering all the uncertainty. If Brendan couldn't tell her, then she mustn't make him do so or put any more guilt on his shoulders.

Back in her office, she tried to stem the trembling that

had seized her limbs and made them like jelly. Going to the window, she looked down on the courtyard. Brendan and Leah were walking across towards the huge tree. If only this could be a lover's tryst in normal circumstances. If only Brendan wasn't so burdened, and didn't have such a difficult job to do. But he was, and the fact that it involved her family and loved ones had put a chasm between them that neither could acknowledge.

'Don't run away again, Leah. Please.' Catching hold of her thin arms, Brendan held her gently in front of him. 'Just listen to me.'

Her eyes were watery. As she blinked, tears plopped down her cheeks. They were silent tears, the worst kind. They told of far more pain than if she had sobbed her distress aloud.

'I'm not worthy.'

'You are. Oh, my darling, you are.' Brendan pulled her to him, cradling her, and in doing so felt all the splintered parts of him come together. Over Leah's shoulder he saw a shadow at Aunt Edith's window. What would she think? She'd cautioned him against taking this action, and he'd promised her he wouldn't speak to Leah of his feelings until a later date. Releasing Leah, he looked into her eyes once more. He spoke in French, so that she would understand everything he said, telling her of his love for her, and how her past didn't matter to him. 'None of it was your doing – you were forced. But, Leah, some good always comes from evil. Little Felicia was a beautiful happening, and she will always be in your heart. And don't forget it was the evil that brought you here, to find the love of Dr

Edith, Lady Eloise and Ginny. But, most of all, you have my love. I love you, Leah.'

'You can't, though. What about Ginny?'

'That is a love that cannot be. Ginny knows that. It's why she's going away. Ginny will be okay.'

She shook her head. More tears spilled over. Feeling helpless, Brendan let her go and turned his back to her.

'Let me talk to Ginny. I cannot hurt her. Please, don't be angry.'

Hope rose within him. Turning, he nodded. After a moment's hesitation he said, 'Forgive me. I should have waited. I shouldn't have put pressure on you, by declaring my love. My reason for coming here was a very different one. I have to take you to the War Office with me, Leah. I don't want you to be afraid – it's good news, but it has to be told to you by them, and they need to speak to you.'

She stared at him in shock. 'What is this? Why didn't you say? Am I in trouble? What good news?'

'I'm sorry – I've acted stupidly. Let's go to Dr Edith's office. She will reassure you. Leah, I meant what I said: I am in love with you.'

His Aunt Edith didn't conceal her anger at him, and her look told of her feelings. Shame washed over Brendan. He'd acted selfishly. What if Ginny had seen them? It would have been a cruel blow to her.

Once Leah had been reassured, and had left to get her cardigan, Aunt Edith spoke her mind. 'I saw what happened out there, and I'm more than disappointed in you, Brendan. However, I know what it is to be in love. Rash decisions are taken on the strength of it.'

'I know. And I think I should tell Ginny. It's the only way – she will have to know sometime. Better that time be now, instead of deceiving her and telling her about my feelings for Leah later, in a letter.'

To his surprise, Aunt Edith nodded. 'I'll be here to pick up the pieces.' Her tone was curt, but then she softened. 'Oh dear, what is happening to us all? I'm happy for you, my dear, really I am. Everyone deserves to love and be loved, and I would say that Leah returns your feelings. It is sad that Ginny will be hurt, but that isn't your fault. Break it to her gently.'

Ginny was sitting in the kitchen, blowing steam from a mug of tea and staring into space.

'Ginny?'

'Eeh, you made me jump. I thought you'd gone. We said our goodbyes.'

'I know, but there's something I have to tell you.' How could he do this without letting Ginny know that he knew how she felt about him? Or, more importantly, without hurting her even more? 'I wanted to tell you that had things been different – I mean, you and I . . . But I couldn't let that kind of love in.' Her eyes held hope. His next words crushed her. 'Something happened. I didn't mean it to. I – I'm really sorry Ginny, but I've fallen in love with Leah.'

Her gasp was audible, her pain visible. Brendan waited, unsure what to do and feeling like a cad.

The chair scraped along the floor as she rose. The sound grated on him. There had been no easy way, but had he chosen the worst way? He hadn't meant to raise Ginny's hopes, only to let her know that he could have loved her in that way, were they free to do so.

She rushed past him, her face awash with tears, and

slammed out of the room. *Oh, Ginny, Ginny. What have I done?*

Dinner was more than he expected, as full dishes of meat, vegetables and potatoes were put on the table. It seemed rationing hadn't fully restricted the Pevensy household. Brendan wondered how Edith and Laurent could reconcile being able to laden a table with so much food with their charity work at Jimmy's Hope House. But then he was cross with himself, as he realized they had probably used half of their weekly allocation of food, just to make him a welcome guest in the way they always did.

They had talked about Ginny, and how Edith had helped her come to an understanding, and how Lady Eloise had been a source of comfort to Ginny, too. This settled Brendan's heart a little, but nothing could totally soothe the ache there.

Edith was animated and was making jokes, after reassuring him that Ginny was all right. But for Brendan this compounded the horror of the secret he held about Ania – a secret that would definitely be revealed when Elka next came home. He wished he knew when that would be, but now that she was working for the Resistance movement as an SOE agent, he wasn't privy to all her movements.

'Is there any news on Jhona?'

'No, Laurent, I'm afraid not. Elka is fine and coping. She is one of the bravest people I have ever met. Look, I want to tell you something. Normally families who have someone working as an agent in the field don't know about it; they only know that their daughter or son is doing some kind of war work. And they receive cards on a regular basis. All of these have been written before the agents were deployed and are sent out by the War Office on a regular basis. But because you are who you are, and are so well respected and trusted by my seniors, I asked them not to do this with Elka. I think it is a deception that would insult you rather than help you. I am allowed to tell you that she contacts us regularly. But I'm afraid she isn't allowed to write to you, for it would be too dangerous for her.'

In the silence that followed, the sounds of their knives and forks were like cymbals being crashed together as they all made a play at eating. Red spots of anger tinged Aunt Edith's cheeks. Her voice didn't disguise this. 'And what has Leah decided to do?'

Even though he'd known this question would be raised, hearing her name twisted the knife-like pain inside his heavy chest. 'She has decided to go.'

'No! Oh, this is all unbearable.'

'As it was for our parents, Edith darling, and as it is for all parents today, and for Brendan, too. We must remain strong for our young, who have many difficulties still to come, and do all we can to help here at home.'

Edith nodded at Laurent. Her face was pale and pinched, her suffering visible in every line. But then her voice held a determined finality. 'Well, that has made a decision that I have been pondering over much easier. The Sisters of Mercy at St Bartholomew's Convent in Sussex contacted me recently. Sister Frances, who works as a midwife and is attached to the local Catholic Church, told them about us. They have asked if they can be involved in Jimmy's Hope House. They are looking for more outlets for their work. I'm going to hand it over to them. I will remain a trustee, as I know Lady Eloise will, but I can't sustain the place as it is, and losing my mainstays – in Ginny and Leah – has compounded that. Besides, I am needed more and more at the hospital. But I will make it clear that the proposed memorial to Ada has to go ahead, after all this is over.'

'That's a momentous decision, darling. I'm a bit cross that you haven't discussed it with me, but nevertheless I think it's a wonderful idea. Will you have any practical involvement at all?'

'No, except to raise funds. But Lady Eloise will do most of that, although I thought that if I did go through with this, I would try to persuade a team of doctors to give an hour a month to keep the free surgery open. So I would be one of those doctors.'

The conversation carried on for a few moments in this vein between Aunt Edith and Laurent, with most of it going over Brendan's head. All he could give his mind to was Leah: how she would cope with the training, and how soon she would be deployed. What was to come filled him with trepidation. But his one shining light in all this was that she had told him she loved him, too.

## 26

# *Elka*

### Krakow, Early August 1940 – A Mission Impossible

Elka finally arrived at the camp where she expected to find Jhona. He wasn't there, and there was no talk of him. Her heart hung like a lead weight in her chest; her grief was more than she thought it possible to cope with. Only the thought of being with Jhona had kept her going. It had taken all her strength to keep from breaking down and telling her mother everything, but if she had done so, she knew she couldn't have made this journey. Her mother's devastation would have compounded her own. As it was, being back here and with Baruch once again, and plagued with suspicions about everyone around her, was tearing her apart.

Looking across at Baruch, as he sat on the other side of the cave perched on a rock, she found it difficult to see signs of grief. Some of the dislike she'd felt for him in the past had come back to her, and once more she saw the callous, driven man she'd always thought him to be, although she kept this out of her voice when dealing with him. 'Baruch, it's time we discussed strategies. The exiled leaders of our country are to take charge of operations, but we will be supported by the team in London, who want to know what we need.'

Talking about clandestine operations was safe ground. Elka needed Baruch and his men to trust her, and hoped this would mean that their guard would drop and she would find out who the traitor amongst them was.

'We are waiting for the Freedom Army to contact us. We know about our leadership through them. Until they give us directions, we have to remain holed up and undiscovered.'

Baruch stared out at the view, like a statue with no feeling. The Tatra Mountains looked beautiful through the haze. They didn't tell of the horror they looked down upon, or of the Resistance movement hidden in their midst, but stood majestic and solid, promising a better time to come.

'Baruch, won't you talk to me about what happened? Have you any suspicions? Have you heard whether anything has happened to Stefan?'

There was a long silence before Baruch said, 'Walk with me.'

The path they took led further up the mountain. The dusty surface of the rough track had not been disturbed. 'Not many people come this way. The odd peasant or gypsy, hiding away from the Germans, may use it, but they are harmless. From a point up here we can watch German troops training. It's frustrating not to be able to take action against them, but we have to be cautious. If we do anything, we give ourselves away.'

'What are your plans then, Baruch? You haven't been active for a long time now. London wants the Resistance movements to get organized, but it is frustrated, too, by the Polish government-in-exile wanting to hold all of the reins.'

'Yes, I can imagine. It feels as if we have reached a stalemate, and yet there is so much to do. The Germans are building a camp at Auschwitz. They have taken forced labour from Krakow and Warsaw. One of our number deliberately went to Warsaw and into the streets there during a round-up and was captured. He was taken to Auschwitz, and his aim is to set up a Resistance movement within the camp. He managed to get out some intelligence about the building of the camp and the atrocities that go on there. Many inmates are beaten to death and . . . and there is extermination by shooting. Our people are being persecuted beyond endurance.'

'Oh God. We have to get this information to London. But, well . . . I don't know why, but nothing we have told them so far has been acted upon. What about Stefan? What happened to him?'

'Stefan is free. I – I put my trust in the wrong one. He is the traitor you seek. He betrayed our beautiful Ania. He now works for the Germans as a trustee – a security guard.' Baruch spat on the ground and his tone became bitter. 'That was his reward. Now he terrorizes his fellow Jews. The planning for the ghetto that Ania told us about is in its final stages.'

Elka walked with her head down, unable to absorb everything she was hearing. Her fight to remain strong took all the willpower she could muster.

'You're right, Elka, we have to do something! My heart burns with the desire to kill Stefan, but I can't formulate a plan as to how to do that.'

'I will do it. I will go to Krakow. You must help me

– provide me with a contact. A job, or something that will legitimize my presence.'

'But Stefan will recognize you. You will be in grave danger.'

'Is he still in touch with you?'

'Yes. We thought it better to keep him on our side, even though we all hate him. He's playing a double game, and for some reason it suits him to keep in with us and still try to get information out to us. We thought he would betray our group and where we are hiding out, but he hasn't. All that I have told you came from him. I don't think he suspects that we know what he's up to. He justifies everything, but others are informing on him.'

'That's good. He knows about my visits and my connections, so he will think he can use me, as he used Ania. The difference will be that I know what his game is, and Ania didn't. It is risky, but if Stefan is kept informed about me coming into Krakow to take over where Ania left off, then he will feel completely trusted by us. As for his plans and why he remains in contact with you, he obviously doesn't trust the Germans, so he is keeping you as a means of escape for himself, should things go wrong. If I'm right about this, then you are still safe, because betraying you would be the last thing he'd want to do.'

'I hope so. I'll set something up, so that you can go into Krakow.'

'Baruch, this may sound strange to you, but I don't want any of the others to know about this. I don't trust any of them since . . . Well, we have to take care. If one of them lets Stefan know the real reason I'm here, then we are doomed. They must believe that I am going in to take Ania's place, and nothing else.'

'I understand, and I was going to suggest that myself. Elka, you do trust me, don't you? You don't believe that I had anything to do with Ania's death?'

'I have had my doubts. But I have to trust you.' Suddenly she realized that she had regained her full trust in him, although she couldn't have said why. 'Yes, I do trust you, Baruch. I have been taught to trust no one, but I know of your patriotism, and how strong it is. I know that you will always work for the good of Poland.' As she said this, she knew that he had the capacity to betray the ones he loved, if it was for the greater good of Poland and the cause, for his country's freedom. So she left open the question of whether he had permitted Ania's death, once she was captured, and schooled herself in the knowledge that he would do the same to her, if she became a danger to his beloved country. Other than in those circumstances, she knew she could trust Baruch implicitly.

Four days passed before Baruch took her on another walk. He'd had word from his contact, a pharmacist called Adok Górski, whose shop, Orzeł Powyżej – meaning 'Eagle Above' – was on the corner of Sgoda Square. Adok was willing to give Elka a job as an assistant. She knew Adok well. He was a kindly man in his forties.

Adok, Baruch told her, had been helping the Jews from the moment of the invasion and the restrictions imposed on their people, even though he himself was not a Jew. False documents were provided, and escape was enabled from the back of his pharmacy. Medicines and food were distributed from there, and social interaction – a kind of 'men's club' – had grown up there in the evening, where men could discuss their fears and talk over world affairs.

The Germans seemed to trust Adok, and many of them dropped in for a chat or to buy medicines from him. 'Adok is the one who is sending information about Stefan, although Stefan knows nothing about Adok's clandestine work. Adok hasn't trusted Stefan from the beginning, and asked that his own involvement be kept secret from Stefan. I went along with his wishes, even though I didn't believe it. How I wished I did.'

'That is good. What Stefan doesn't know, he can't betray. When you tell Stefan that I'm coming in, tell him that I'm using Adok. Tell Stefan that, unbeknownst to you, I wrote to Adok, a family friend, and asked him to accept me into his home. Tell him that I have London's backing to take Ania's place and that I intend to do whatever it takes – even work in a brothel – if it means that I can get close enough to the Germans to get secrets out.'

'You will need to be disguised, Elka,' Baruch told her. 'You may come across the officer who abused Ania, or colleagues that she worked with. You must not be recognized. If you are, then Adok will be in danger.'

'I have a black wig with me; it is parted in the middle and cut to my neck, in a straight bob. It's made of real hair. And I have make-up that disguises my freckles. Also a pair of glasses that have plain glass in them. Even I don't know myself when I have these items on. Believe me, being recognized is the least of my worries. Stefan is a major worry. Are you certain that he believes you trust him?'

'Yes. He sent word saying that he was initially held under suspicion, when Ania went missing, but that the Germans decided to make him prove that he was loyal and then took him on as a security guard. He said he didn't tell them of the escape route, but admitted to betraying another of our couriers, a boy whom he suspected was a weak link. He said he told the Germans that he was always on the lookout for suspicious people; and that he was trusted enough to have secret conversations within his hearing, and that's how he knew of the activities this boy carried out. He swears he did this just to ingratiate himself with the Germans, and that he hadn't thought the boy would betray the escape route used by us. We know all this isn't true. Adok has sent word that Stefan had handed the boy in, after Ania was killed. Stefan *must* have betrayed her.'

'I have always felt mistrustful of him and despised his cruelty and callousness, which Ania told me about in her letters. Stefan's actions didn't feel right, no matter how he tried to justify them. Oh, I know you believed he had to act that way, so don't blame yourself. People like Stefan can make the Eskimos believe that the sun is going to shine in the middle of their dark season. But that is terrible news about the courier. What if he betrays you?'

'He doesn't know enough to do that. The poor boy only carried messages as far as the outskirts. He and his father were shepherds. Once they reached their first grazing stage at the bottom of the mountains, they were met by Karol.'

At the sound of Karol's name, Elka shivered. In her heart she hadn't forgiven him, and still questioned why he had gone along with Gabriel, when commanded to throw the hand-grenades. Karol must have agreed, and felt it necessary to kill Ania. But these questions might never be answered, and she had to work towards the future without dwelling on the past.

'Stefan included a private message for me in his last

communication,' Baruch was saying. 'It expressed his full sympathy and deep regret for what happened to Ania. He begged my forgiveness for misjudging the boy he'd handed in. He said he didn't think the boy knew of our secret route in and out of Krakow, and implored me to think about what can be achieved, with him in the position he now occupies: the Jews he can help to escape; how he can allocate them to factories, where they will work and therefore be spared; how he can ensure that they are secretly fed; and how he can get information to us.'

'He is despicable. I will kill him – have no doubt about that.'

'But what if he doesn't trust you and hands you in? Oh, Elka, this situation is hopeless. He holds all the cards.'

'I don't think he will hand me in,' said Elka. 'He is probably unsure whether you still trust him. If he betrays me, he will show his true colours to you. He wouldn't want to risk that. I think Stefan is all about saving his own skin and riding out this war in the most comfortable way he can. For that, he needs all the angles covered. As I said before, if the Germans turn on him, he needs you and the Freedom Army to help him. If the Germans continue to trust him, then he can live safely and in comfort until it is all over. Besides, when the war is over and we are the victors, he will not want to be seen as a traitor. Stefan is a very clever man.'

'I hope you are right. I wish you didn't have to do this, but I see no other way. Stefan knows we are all keeping a low profile. He also knows that we have no route in at the moment, and has promised to find us another one. So it is impossible for any of us to go into Krakow.'

'I will be all right. I have the benefit of my training. We will find another route in. I'll speak to Adok about it.'

'Well, if you are sure, then everything is ready. You will go to Krakow by train. Adok will meet you. He is already putting the news out that he has a new assistant coming to train with him. The story is that your family – old friends of his – were bombed out in Warsaw, and that you were away in college at the time and have been staying with a family in a mountain village. He has even bragged about you to the Germans and has joked with them, telling them that they will have him to contend with, if they try to assault you in any way. He is very funny in his communications. He says that they have all promised solemnly to respect you, but ask eager questions about what you look like.'

'Contact him, Baruch, and let him know about my disguise. It's good that he has this rapport with the Germans. He can make a further joke when I turn up and am a frump, rather than the beauty they are possibly imagining. I'll cut up my bedding to pad out my body, and dress in some of the dowdy clothes I have brought with me. With that, and the hair and glasses, it will look as though he was hoodwinking them, for the fun of it. All distractions are good, and this is a perfect one to stop them wondering why I am really coming to Krakow.'

Stefan came to seek out Elka within a day of her arrival. Two German officers were in Adok's pharmacy, having a laugh over her with Adok. 'So, is this the fair *Fräulein* you told us of? Ha, Adok – for a Pole, you have a good sense of humour.'

Pretending to blush, Elka kept her head down, but this

didn't stop her spotting a man who fitted the description Baruch had given her, sitting on a bench in the square, watching. Adok had seen him, too. He turned to her and said, 'Why don't you take those medicines over to the hospital? You remember where it is, from your visits here?'

'Yes, I do, in Skawinska Street.'

'Good girl. It is many years since you were here, so you remember well.'

She hadn't left the pharmacy long, when a voice beckoned her into an alley. Looking into the darkness, she saw the same man again. 'Stefan?'

'Yes. Are you Elka?'

For a moment she was annoyed, thinking that Baruch had used her real name, but then she realized that as Stefan had known Baruch and Ania before the war, he would also know of her. 'Yes, but you must call me Nina at all times.'

'Of course I will. Tell me, what are your plans?'

'Let's go further into the alley. I don't want to be seen with you.' A nerve tightened in her stomach. Her mind focused on the knife in her pocket.

'Yes, we will not be seen down here.'

She followed him into the dimness, made all the more so by leaving the bright sunshine as they walked between the tall buildings. The cobbles beneath her feet made her progress unsteady.

'Now, tell me quickly: how can I help you? Would you like a job at Gestapo headquarters, like your sister had? Your disguise is good – I wasn't sure it was you, as you look nothing like Ania.'

Her name on his lips uprooted the deep anger and hatred that were stored inside her. As if accidentally, she dropped the package she held. Stefan looked down at it. In one swift movement she kicked it away, extracted the knife and drove it into his neck, moving like lightning to avoid the blood that was spurting at her as he slumped to the ground.

Without stopping to think, Elka lifted the parcel and ran to the entrance of the alley. She loitered there for a while. One or two people passed by – hungry-looking people wearing purple badges with the letter P in the centre. None of them looked at her. Slipping into the street, Elka continued to walk towards the Vistula river. She would need to cross the bridge to get to the hospital. All around her lay signs of change to her beloved city. Swastikas hung from the majestic buildings, rubbish lay in heaps, rotting and stinking. A tram rumbled by.

Turning left, she walked along Podgorska, her destination about a mile away. Here, with the river on her left, she breathed in the fresh air that blew towards her from the water and walked purposefully forward.

'Halt!'

The shout from the German soldiers coming towards her made Elka jump.

'What have you there?' One of them poked at her parcel. She understood, but didn't want to let them know that, so she asked in Polish, 'Do you mean my parcel?'

'This – this.' One of the soldiers snatched the bag. As he did so, she saw the blood stain on its underside. Grabbing it back from him, she plunged her hand inside and lifted out the box of tablets. 'It is for the hospital. From the *Apteka*, Orzeł Powyżej.'

Flicking his hand across her face, the soldier took the box roughly from her and opened it. Elka prayed the thick glass bottle hadn't broken, and breathed a sigh of relief when she saw it hadn't, although the next second she exclaimed as the soldier threw it to the ground with such force that the glass splintered in all directions. Some of it cut her legs. Before he thought to snatch the bag, she bent down and wiped her leg with it. Fresh blood stains covered the ones she hoped he hadn't noticed.

'Clean that up. Do it!'

Some of the fear she'd seen on her fellow countrymen's faces, and had sensed in poor Ania's letters, entered Elka as she bent once more to do the soldier's bidding. A vicious kick sent her reeling. Pain made her catch her breath, as a jagged piece of the bottle dug into her cheek.

'That's where you belong, you fat, ugly sod!'

They walked on, leaving her lying on the hot flagstones of the pavement. The sun beat down on her despair. This is what Ania had put up with. *Oh, Ania, my Ania, I have avenged your death*. Elka stood up, as this thought breathed new life into her. She could see that some of the tablets had been trodden underfoot, but others remained intact. If she picked them out carefully, she could rescue most of them. Then she would brush the glass to one side with her feet. At the hospital they would see to her wounds, but most importantly she would have delivered what she could. Medication was scarce.

'It's done, Adok.'

'Already? My, you are a quick worker. But look at you – did he struggle?'

'He knew nothing. His death was swift.'

'Come on then, let's get you inside. I will get a message to Baruch, once you tell me what happened.'

Elka followed Adok through the pharmacy. The shop bell still rang in her ears. The sharp smell of medicines she'd taken as a child in this very room assailed her. Nothing about it had changed. The walls were still a dark moss-green. The dark-wood cabinets stood in a line in the middle with their glass doors, still displaying a mirage of coloured thick-glass bottles that caught the reflection of the sun through the window. The wall to her left was covered in a dark-wood cabinet of drawers with shiny brass handles, and to her right was a dark-wood counter.

A moment from her childhood came back to her again as she looked at this. In her mind's eye she could see herself and Ania trying to see the top of the counter. They had stood on tiptoes, until Adok had bent down and picked them up, sitting them both on the cold marble slab that topped it. Behind the counter were rows and rows of shelving, which held cream-coloured ceramic pots with brown necks and huge cork stoppers. On the counter top stood a set of scales, and behind it to the right on a shelf was something she didn't know the name of, but which looked like glass test tubes in a wooden structure, with rubber tubes and balloon-shaped glass containers entwined within it. It had always fascinated her, but that day it had seemed like something out of a witch's tale to her and Ania.

A tear traced a path down her cheek.

Adok said nothing. Walking back to the door, he closed it and turned his shop sign over to read, 'Back in five minutes', then he took her arm and steered her into the room beyond. His storeroom. From here, stairs led up to his living quarters.

Elka walked to the window and looked down on the square. More memories assailed her: two little girls running around with joy in their hearts, Mama and Babcia calling to them to be careful. *Oh, Ania, we were so happy and carefree.*

Her eyes traced the buildings that formed a small part of the Jewish quarter. Would the Germans really enclose it and force all the Jews to live in this one area? How would that work?

'Will you move, if the planned ghetto goes ahead, Adok?'

Her words faded against the sound of liquid tinkling against glass. As she turned, he offered her a beautiful cut glass, at the bottom of which some vodka swirled.

'No, I will stay put if I can, as this building has been in my family for generations. If I abandon it, I may never get it back. Now, do you take it neat or with water, my dear?'

'I think I need it neat right now, thank you.' She swallowed the liquid in one gulp and felt the effects of the warming alcohol. An involuntary cough made Adok laugh.

'That's better. I'll pour you another, but sip it this time.'

He smiled at her. As he did so, his dark eyes twinkled. He was a tall man who was still very handsome, with his black hair swept back and held in place with hair cream.

'We can't undo what has been done, but we can have the satisfaction of making someone pay for it. You're not to spoil what you've done, by feeling guilt. That man doesn't deserve a jot of guilt wasted on him. You have done a great service to the Jews of this quarter. Stefan was one of the worst kind, sucking up to the Germans and often doing their dirty work. People were afraid of him. Only last week I saw him take some soldiers to that apartment over there. A family were dragged out into the square – a mother, father and two children. They had hidden behind a wardrobe during the last round-up. The father had pulled it across the door of a small bedroom. The Germans shot them all.'

'No! Oh, Adok, no.'

'This kind of thing is happening all the time, my dear. I've seen countless atrocities, and I fear it will get worse.'

'Can I do anything? I will stay, if I can help in any way.'

'No. I didn't tell you immediately, as you were in a state, but while you were out I received an urgent message from Baruch. You have to go back.'

'But I have only just got here! I hoped to gather some intelligence. I thought that maybe you could secure me a job such as Ania had, by letting it slip that I speak many languages and that I was simply shy. Besides, we need to set up new routes in, for Baruch and the others. What is he thinking, sending for me to return so soon?'

'I don't know. He just sent a code-purple message. This means it is imperative it is carried out. He must know of some kind of danger that you are in. Besides, the longer you are here, the more likely it is that someone will recognize you. There are many Jews trading any information they can, to save their skins. For that reason I'm relieved you have to go. If your true identity is discovered, then I am compromised too, and I have much work to do here. I can gather a lot of information, just by being here and being trusted by everyone. A lot is discussed in my presence.'

Defeated by this and by her training, which had instilled in her always to follow orders, Elka didn't argue any more. 'If I must go, then I must, but how will you explain my sudden disappearance?'

'You have been taken ill. An ambulance will be here shortly. They will carry you out on a stretcher. Tomorrow you will be with Baruch, but I will be mourning your death. I will have a coffin buried tomorrow afternoon and a headstone with your name on it – at least the name you were given for this assignment, Nina Warszawski. There will even be a death certificate.'

He'd hardly finished speaking when the ambulance arrived. People milled around it. 'Now, my dear, time to be an actress; you need to look ill, in case any soldiers come and look. I want to take some blood from you and have it coming from your mouth. I will only have to say the word "typhus" and everyone will scatter. You must just tremble and mumble.'

'Ha! I hope those soldiers who attacked me make the connection between the woman they mistreated and the woman dying soon afterwards – I would love them to feel fear for a few weeks, as they search for symptoms of typhus, thinking they have caught it from me. But won't people avoid you, too?'

'No, they believe a pharmacist has magic powers. My assistant and I will be seen to scrub out the shop, and that will be that.' Chuckling, Adok said, 'Have a happy death! Look me up, when you are resurrected after the war.'

As the ambulance tore through the streets towards the hospital, Elka felt in awe of Adok – his endearing, sunny countenance in the face of all he witnessed, his resourcefulness and the wonderful work he did to help the Jews. He already had a new courier in position. He was a truly remarkable man.

Her thoughts turned to the reason why she had to return to camp so quickly. *Please let it be because my darling Jhona has turned up.*

*

Upon arriving back at camp, Elka scanned the faces looking at her. They all held pity.

'What is it? Baruch?'

'I'm sorry, Elka, but we have reports that Jhona has been caught. I didn't know he was even in this country! They have taken him to Auschwitz.'

## 27

# *Jhona*

### Auschwitz, September 1940 – *Arbeit Macht Frei* (Work Sets You Free)

The barbed wire tore at his skin as Jhona worked in a party of prisoners to remove the fencing from the wooden posts. Once a section was free, it was taken by another work party and fixed to new concrete posts standing just over three feet high. Attached to these posts was an electric fence that – rumour had it – would, once commissioned, project four hundred volts of electricity through anyone who touched it.

Up to today, he'd worked on the renovation of buildings that once housed the Polish Army. Some had been made ready by prisoners before he came, but others had been decaying and lice-ridden. Just like his own body.

Food for the five thousand or so prisoners was frugal: one bowl of watery soup a day. And sanitary conditions were almost non-existent, with a trickle of water being fought over for five seconds or so, and only two minutes each allowed on the long gutter-like toilet each day, alongside other prisoners.

For him and a few others, life was even worse than it

was for the Polish dissidents, because they were beaten more than the dissidents were, and were treated as if they were the dregs of society, to be spat at and given whatever was left over when others had eaten. This was because they were Jews.

Each day more prisoners arrived, and more and more of them were Jews. A sickening ritual took place after each intake. The older, weaker men and the very young boys were taken into hut eleven and never came out. Sounds of systematic gunfire – bang . . . bang . . . bang – could be heard, and then later in the evening a work party was put together to take the bodies from the enclosed yard for burning. Twice now he'd been one of the work party. Tired beyond endurance, his body had wept as he'd helped to load the naked bodies onto a truck and then fed them into the raging fire of the furnace.

When he'd first arrived, Jhona had thought that would be his own fate. Captured in the forest on his way up to Zakopane, with Russian firearms and ammunition on him, he'd stared down the barrel of a gun, aimed at executing him on the spot. But then one of the soldiers of the patrol who had come across him asleep, and had kicked him awake, cautioned that their superiors might want to question Jhona. Dread had settled in the pit of his stomach, as he'd known what that might entail. He'd tried to get to his cyanide pill, but they had grabbed and trussed him and then dragged him for miles until they reached Zakopane, an alpine town he'd once loved – it had been peopled by a jolly population, but was now teeming with Germans, and the locals walked around with their heads bowed.

Thinking about it, he knew he wouldn't have taken the pill. With life, there was hope, although many times in the days that followed his capture he'd not thought there was any, due to the agonizing torture he'd experienced – being burned with cigarettes, made to stand for days on end in a confined space and then, worst of all, having his hands tied behind his back and being hung backwards from the crossbar of a scaffold-like structure. Excruciating pain had racked him, as his shoulders had pulled against their sockets, and within minutes he'd passed out. Water hit him in the face and brought him back round, to experience the indescribable pain once more. He'd prayed he would die. But then Elka had come dancing into his mind, giggling in that beautiful way she had, teasing him and loving him, and he'd found an inner strength to survive.

Throughout, he'd stuck to his story. He wasn't Russian, he was from the Ukraine. He'd wanted to escape to the Tatra Mountains. No, not to join the Resistance or the Freedom Army, but just to live out the war. He'd been walking for weeks. He'd related the exact story of how he came to have Russian ammunition. The one thing that seemed to make them believe him was when he told them he was a Jew. Admitting to that must have made them realize that Jhona would not be able to work as a spy, or hold any other official position, in Russia.

That was when he thought he would be taken out into the yard and shot. But they must have thought that was too good for him, because they'd spat at him that he would die like a dog. He had been put into quarters that mostly housed Polish dissidents and young men who had been rounded up to work on getting Auschwitz camp ready for the purpose of being a concentration camp. Within a week he had been moved to another block, where he was housed with other Jews. There the mood was one of desolation.

They were forbidden to practise their religion, but in the depth of the night they huddled together and prayed.

With the fifteen-hour days of hard labour, hardly any food and being bitten by lice until he was red-raw, his body weight had dropped by many kilograms in the four weeks he'd been here. His head had been shaved, and blisters had formed on his feet and in the palms of his hands. Yes, he was dying like a dog.

Finding sleep difficult, Jhona watched the searchlight flicker once more through the window and illuminate each corner of the room. A shadow darted to the wall and just avoided the shaft of light as it swept past. Moving his aching limbs, he turned to watch Ephraim coming towards him. Ephraim's whisper was hardly audible. 'I have word out that you are here. Maybe London will do something now?'

Jhona couldn't speak. *Does Elka know that I am here? Please God, I pray she doesn't.*

'How did you manage that?'

'I have my ways, I told you. If you have things to bribe with, anything is possible. Here, I have a chunk of bread. It is stale, but eat it, there is still some goodness in it.'

'Shouldn't we share with the others?'

'No. We will be doing them all a greater service by keeping up our strength. I have plans.' For a moment Ephraim was silent as he looked around. He seemed to be waiting. Listening. 'It is all right – no one is awake. If they were, they would have begged for a piece of the bread. Eat it, Jhona, and listen to what I have to say. I am forming a Resistance group. I want you to join. We aim to cause disruption where we can without detection, and to aid escapes.'

Jhona's dry mouth struggled to chew the bread. Swallowing a lump of it down, he nodded. 'I will join. I have many skills that would be useful.'

'I know. Baruch has answered and told me of them.'

'How do you get messages in and out?'

'There are many local people who help us. Because I am an engineer, I'm often taken out to work on the munitions factory the Germans are building a few miles from here. I see these people then. They may be delivering materials or working in the fields around. They are good people. They take our messages and bring us food, and other things that we can use as a bribe.'

Jhona felt a flicker of hope in his heart. 'That's good. Just tell me what you need me to do.'

'They are bringing in more and more prisoners, and there is talk of expanding. That is what all that wood is for, to build more huts. One of the huts is to be a washroom, because dysentery is rife. And we saw a whole lot of stores on the way here. They are housed in that hut that was erected near the gate. We need you to break into it. We need more things to bribe with, and more food for the members of our group. We have to stay strong.'

'I can do that. It isn't a problem. But we can't get too strong, or it will be noticed. We have to be careful.'

'Yes. And it is good that you think as I do. Given that, and the training you must have had, we can succeed.'

Ephraim left his side and crept back to his own space. Jhona curled up on the floor once more, a dirty blanket his only cushion. His aches and pains were soothed by the hope that ran through his veins.

A noise beside him made him turn over. Had his neighbour heard? No one could be trusted. Jhona nudged the man. There was no response. He tried again, afraid of hurting him, as he'd been here longer than himself and was skin and bones. Still nothing. Putting his hand on the man's chest, he could feel it wasn't moving. The man was dead.

Tears fell down Jhona's cheeks. He didn't even know the man's name and yet he had drawn his last breath next to him. 'Go in peace, whoever you are. I will pray for your soul.'

With this, Jhona lay back down, knowing there was nothing he could do. In the morning there would be one – or, who knew, maybe many – fewer at roll call. A time they all dreaded.

The sun beat down on his head. Jhona stood as still as he could, knowing that movement could attract attention. German officers walked up and down, counting heads. Then they added the dead bodies to the number. Jhona had already seen that there were five naked skeletal bodies lying outside the lines of men. He had positioned himself as near to the centre as he could, realizing that if anyone was pulled out as an example for any reason, it was always those on the outside of the lines. This meant that the stronger men always had the best positions in roll call. It had to be that way, for the stronger could ultimately help the weaker.

Rage spat from Commandant Hoss's mouth. Understanding the language caused fear to pass through Jhona. He held his breath. The numbers were short.

Another count began. This would mean at least another hour standing in the heat. He prayed that no one would faint. Anyone who did was shot, as it was judged they were no longer strong enough to be of use. Jhona had hardly made the silent plea when a man slumped to the ground in the front row.

The sound of the gunshot sent the birds soaring into the sky. Another man dropped; possibly the shock had been too much. Another shot.

Seconds went by, as if each was an hour. The count went on. Then Hoss strode towards them once more and looked at the count result. His face bulged with anger. His order sickened Jhona: the count was down, and the conclusion was that one man had escaped. Three of them would hang, as a reprisal.

The soldiers came among them, looking into eyes, dragging screaming men out and shoving them towards the gallows, a permanent fixture that could accommodate up to seven men. Jhona counted. One, two . . . One of the soldiers had hesitated in front of him. *Oh God!*

A hand shot out. The man next to him was dragged towards the scaffold, his hollow screams turning into sobs. He begged, but there was no mercy. An order came for everyone to turn towards the gallows. Jhona saw that those chosen now had nooses around their necks. A silence descended. Even the victims were calm. In one movement the soldiers stood behind the gallows and kicked the boxes from under the men. An audible gasp wafted into the air above them. Two bodies dangled; one still kicked. Jhona closed his eyes. When he opened them, the third man was still.

The soldier who'd hesitated in front of Jhona ordered him and four others to cut the bodies down and take them, and those on the floor, to the crematorium. As they neared the bodies, Jhona quietly told the others to take their time.

'We have to be sure they're dead. It may not happen instantly; they could be unconscious, near to death, but not yet dead.'

One of the other men countermanded this. 'No, take no notice; if we dawdle they will kill us. We can make sure they are dead before we put them in the oven. I've done this before and had to finish one off. It is easy to do, and humane. If we revive them, they will be brain-damaged; and in any case, where could we hide them until they are well? Do as I say, if you want to live.'

Jhona obeyed. 'What is your name?' he asked the man.

'Rafal Rosak. I'm a Polish Jew. And you?'

Jhona introduced himself as they worked. This was a man that he would recommend joined the Resistance. His decisions were taken with his head, and not his heart, but they were sound and held compassion. He was a leader.

'*Strip the bodies!*' This order always sickened Jhona, but with his fellow workers he obeyed. '*And remove all gold teeth.*' At this command, each of the dead bodies had its mouth prised open, but thankfully no gold teeth were found. All had been previously extracted, or the men had never had any.

The heat and the smell made nausea wash over Jhona, but he swallowed hard. He had to remember that any sign of weakness would lead to death.

He and Rafal spoke to each other when they could. He learned that Rafal was a mechanic and worked in a building near Hoss's house that housed a garage. He kept the cars and trucks maintained and wasn't treated too badly.

When the task was finished, Jhona rejoined the group he'd been working with the day before. None of them spoke to him. He was glad of that. He needed to be alone with his thoughts, to bring to mind his beautiful Elka and spend the next hours working hard, but chatting to her in his head. *Oh, my darling Elka, will I ever see you again?*

# 28
# *Edith*

## Hastleford Hall, Late September 1940 – An Oasis of Peace on a Bed of Heartache

Nothing looked different here in the country, unlike London. Air raid after air raid had shattered and crumbled the area around the docks on the Thames. Hitler's warning that he would set London ablaze had seemed to come true, as fires raged, destroying houses, factories and warehouses in its wake.

Edith had worked day and night operating on the injured, and she was exhausted. Her work at Jimmy's Hope House continued, but thank goodness the Sisters of Mercy had sent along a group of six of their number to get the feel of running the place, and they had amazed Edith by how organized they were. As four of them were trained nurses, much of the work had been taken off her hands. And now, knowing how beneficial they were going to be for Jimmy's Hope House, and the area, she couldn't wait for them to take over completely in January. All that was left to do was make sure the legal papers were all in place.

The problem was that, with the bombing of London night after night and all the hospitals working flat out, she hadn't yet found more than two doctors who were able to give up an hour a week to help run her free surgery. Not that it had mattered too much, given everything else that was happening around them; the people of the East End were so absorbed in helping each other and trying to survive that they didn't worry about taking petty illnesses to a doctor. At the last surgery session she'd only had one patient, a woman with an ear infection. This lessening need for the surgery was also down to the nuns' innovation: they had immediately set up a district-nurse system, and clinics for pregnant women and mums with babies. The nuns had been to see the local GP and he had agreed to call-outs for half of his normal fee, which they would pay. Edith was full of admiration for the nuns, and had been surprised to find them such a jolly crowd to be around. She knew Ada would have loved them, and would approve of her letting go of the reins. So, all in all, it was for the best.

Waking up in her bedroom in Hastleford Hall in Leicestershire with the sun streaming through the open window, bringing with it the smells of the countryside, she'd lain quietly beside the sleeping Laurent, listening to his gentle snores and feeling her body relax. Her mind was a little bit more difficult to quieten.

As she had done so many times, she thought of her dear mother. Now she understood. Mother had been made of different stuff from herself. In the face of war, she'd wanted everything to remain the same and had continued her quest to find Edith a husband. Poor Mother; and yet, in a way, it was a nice outlook – the idea that life could be normal, despite everything. But it hadn't been one that she herself harboured. She'd taken up the challenge, and in the process had broken her mother's heart – a heart that held a weakness none of them had known about. Unable to take the strain of her missing daughter, and with her two sons fighting on the Somme, Mother had died. When Edith had said her goodbyes to her, as she left for France, she was still of an age when she thought of her mother as a silly, empty-headed socialite, not knowing that she would never see her again; and not knowing that one day she would know the exact pain that her mother had felt.

It was a pain bred of fearful uncertainty. The not knowing. Elka – her beloved daughter – was out there somewhere, and Edith felt sure she was in extreme danger. Ania was trapped in Poland, where the stories of atrocities towards the Jews, if they could be believed, were horrendous. Ania was of that faith, if not a born Jew.

What were they doing, each of them, and what were their lives like? *Oh dear God, it's unbearable.*

And Jhona – she hadn't even got to know him well, before he'd left. Now he was missing, and God knew where, or in which country. Elka was having to carry on with a broken heart, no doubt having to make life-threatening decisions while in a state of grief for her husband. It was cruel that she'd only just found her daughters as a second war broke out. Cruel beyond measure that it should snatch them away from her almost immediately.

She thought of Ginny and Leah, in an attempt to prevent herself from sinking into a sadness that she'd find it difficult to rise from. Their plight wasn't any less dangerous or worrying, but she'd had encouraging reports of Leah being so happy to be back with her brother, and doing work that was not too dangerous – that is, if she could believe Brendan. He'd said that Leah was billeted with some lovely people and was living as normal a life as was possible in occupied Paris, and her comings and goings on her bicycle were not noted, as far as they could tell. But that's all Edith knew. Knowing the way of things, it was probably a fraction of the truth.

Thinking of France, she at least had the comfort of knowing that Marianne was safe, although living under the traitorous Vichy government that was dictated to by Hitler couldn't be easy. However, Marianne's letters were uplifting and it seemed that little had changed for her small circle of friends, apart from one of their number dying and forcing Marianne to contemplate her own mortality. Edith had to smile at this. She was glad that war in all its horror hadn't touched the beautiful Marianne.

And the letter she'd received from Ginny had been heart-warming. Picking it up from her bedside table, Edith reread it. Ginny was loving her job, mainly getting the ship ready for use. Some wards were in operation and there were wounded aboard, but Ginny hadn't yet had much involvement in that. As a new girl, she had to do the 'scrubbing and stacking', as she called getting each ward and operating theatre ready.

As she continued to read the letter, Edith felt some peace, where the lovely Ginny was concerned:

*I've not suffered from seasickness at all, but many have. Not sure where it was that I got me sea legs from – maybe an ancestor was a sailor? Anyroad, because of this, I have to work twice as hard, but I don't mind.*

*Me mind's been turning over this a good while, and working flat out gives me little respite from its goings-on, but I have come to some conclusions. I'm getting used to the fact that I can never be with Brendan in the way that I wanted to, and am happy that he and Leah are in love.*

*Will you tell him for me, as I can't write to him – not just yet? Tell him I'm sorry for me reaction, and that I now know that I love him like a niece should an uncle, and had got meself confused over that feeling.*

*And you know, Dr Edith, I'm not just saying these things, but beginning to really feel them. I was a silly girl to ever think otherwise, I know that now.*

*We're not short of good-lookers on this ship, either, and I think I've caught the eye of one. He's a merchant seaman called Norman. We have a chat on deck sometimes, but we have to be careful, because if we're caught we could get into trouble. That makes it all the more exciting.*

Edith smiled. She remembered that order: 'No fraternizing!' And yes, it had made it all the more exciting when she'd snatched a moment or two with Albert. Her sigh held a great depth of memories, some of which she didn't want to visit, so she put her mind to the letter once more:

*A lot of the girls have formed friendships with the seamen. We have guessing games and look for clues as to which are the married ones. But most of it is just a bit of fun, a relief from the more serious work that fills our days.*

*I hope you don't mind me writing to you, for you feel like family to me. And I hope you can find time to write back. I'm really worried about reports of the bombing raids, and how Leah is doing, but I know you can't put a lot in a letter, if you do write.*

*Keep safe. And don't worry about me – we fly the*

*Red Cross flag and we have been told that, if called upon, we will treat all nations, so we reckon this will mean as we should be left alone and not torpedoed or anything.*

*Eeh, I'm going on a bit, have to close. Write soon.*

*Yours, Ginny xxx*

The smile that had played around Edith's lips widened. Reading Ginny's letter was just like having her here chatting. She must make sure she adopted the same style when she wrote back and didn't sound as stiff and formal as letter-writing often could. She would contact Brendan and tell him how Ginny was feeling. She was sure Ginny was being truthful about being able to define now how she truly felt. Distancing herself from Brendan had really helped her and had been the best thing Ginny could have done. She'd encourage Brendan to write a chatty letter to Ginny, too. Yes, that would be the thing. Keeping in touch would make for an easy reunion, when the time came.

Rolling over, Edith lifted her head onto her elbow and looked down on Laurent. One of his eyes opened. This made her giggle. His arm reached out behind her head, inviting her to nestle into the circle of it. She went willingly, snuggling up to him. She felt a stirring of need inside her. It felt almost wrong at such a time, but it was a battle she lost, as Laurent pulled her over him and sought her lips, cupping her breast in his hand.

For a while Edith lost herself, and all her disturbing thoughts, as she accepted her darling Laurent's love-making. As she reached a peak of ecstasy that wrapped her in a cocoon of blissfulness, her cares seemed to drop from her. If only this could be how life always was.

But normality prevailed, once they were up and sitting in the dining room to eat a breakfast that Edith was ravenous for.

Douglas and Thomas burst through the door of the dining room. 'Oh, you two are up! What time do you call this – there's harvesting to do, you know! We've been out there since the crack of dawn, and so have our girls.'

'Girls?'

'Our Land Army girls. Little crackers, they are.'

'Thomas, not at the table, please,' Janine said.

'Sorry, Mother.' Thomas gave a sly, amused glance in Edith's direction. She wanted to laugh out loud. He wasn't the joker his older brother Henry was, though he had a way about him that made you smile.

'Where are these Land Girls then?'

'Mother makes them eat in the kitchen. But they don't mind; they say they wouldn't feel comfortable eating in here with us.'

'There, you see – I was right.' Janine had a smug look on her face. Edith couldn't imagine how Douglas had ever come to marry her, let alone adore her as he did. No one was as snobbish as Janine.

'Yes, Mother, but why you don't allow Father and me to eat in the kitchen with them is beyond me. Don't you realize that to have to come in, get washed and don something clean, just to have breakfast, takes a lot more out of our day than we can afford?'

'That's enough, Thomas. Your mother is trying to keep some sort of civilized life going. It isn't her fault that you and I have to be hands-on at the farm.'

Changing the subject, Edith asked if they had heard from Henry.

'Yes, he's having a whale of a time in the Egyptian sun.'

Edith doubted this, but it would be the impression Henry would give, in his letters home.

'Archibald Wavell is his commanding officer. He's a decent chap, is Archie. We fought together at Ypres. Henry couldn't be in safer hands.'

Edith detected an over-joviality in Douglas's voice. Janine didn't speak, but Edith saw her body tremble. Whatever else she was, Janine was a mother.

'I know how you feel, Janine. But I'm sure Henry will be fine. He's a brave and sensible chap.'

'No, he isn't! He is foolhardy and sees everything as a joke. He won't take as much care as he should . . . I – I'm sorry. Oh, it's this war, it's fraying my nerves.'

'I understand. But, you know, those with Henry's disposition were the ones who had more wits about them than the serious ones in our war, weren't they, Douglas?'

'Yes, that's true. They seemed tuned in, when it was necessary to be.'

'I'm going soon, Aunt Edith – I can't wait.'

As Thomas finished saying this, Janine got up and ran out of the room. Douglas wiped his mouth with his napkin and, excusing himself, went after her.

'Thomas, that was inconsiderate at this moment.'

'Sorry, Aunt Edith, but it is a daily battle with Mother, and she just has to jolly well get used to it, like every other mother in the world is having to. She should be brave and encourage her sons, and she should be more welcoming to the Land Girls, who are away from their loved ones and doing a spiffing job. I'm very annoyed with her.'

Yesteryear came rushing at Edith. Hadn't she said much the same about her own mother, not knowing her pain and feeling frustrated by the obstacles that her mother tried to put in her way, to stop her doing her bit? Now she knew that pain, and at this moment she felt the only affinity she'd ever felt towards Janine. But it wouldn't be right to make Thomas see it that way. He needed to keep thinking as he was. He needed to be single-minded, for he was being forced to put his life on the line for his country. It was better that he did so without the burden of knowing his mother's feelings. In a lot of ways, he was right.

'Mothers have a part to play, as do fathers, but it isn't an easy one. Your mother will be all right; she has your father. Just make sure, when you do go, that despite being cross with her, you write to her often and speak of your love for her – and how it is her love for you that is sustaining you. Will you do that much for her?'

'Of course, Aunt Edith, I'm sorry. I . . . I'll go and apologize to Mother now.'

'Yes, do that. But keep your strength and your resolve. That is something you will need. Just channel it in a way that minimizes the hurt your mother feels.'

As she walked in the garden with Eloise later that day, Edith heard that Rose and Andria were coming home for a couple of days later in the week. 'I don't know how they've managed that, but they say their harvesting isn't beginning until next week and the farmer has given them time off before it starts. I thought we might arrange a picnic. Have some fun, for a change.'

'Really, Eloise, do you think we should? I mean, with what's happening in London and everything?'

'Even more reason to. Several of the boys in and around the village are approaching the age of conscription, including

Thomas. We should give them a happy memory of the life they are fighting to get back to. Fun isn't banned, you know.'

Edith laughed. Good old Eloise, she always lifted the moment. Looking back to see where the men were, she spotted Laurent and Jay deep in conversation.

'Whether we can persuade the men to relax for a while, though, is another matter.'

'We will. Come on, let's organize a game of croquet. I know it's out of fashion now, but I still love it. I'll go and ask Janine to come and join in.'

The afternoon passed pleasantly. Plans were discussed and everyone agreed that a barn dance would be a much better option than a picnic, which necessitated providing a lot of food. Though food was still plentiful in the countryside, no one felt it appropriate to organize a fun occasion at which eating was the main focus, when their fellow city-dwellers had to sacrifice so much.

'There's a lot of evacuee children in the surrounding area,' Eloise said as they finished their game of croquet as the victors over Janine and Jay. 'I'll make sure they all have a special treat that day, as we can't invite them to the dance.'

'What about lighting? I mean, we can't dance without light.'

'We'll make sure the barn is well blacked out. And we'll only use candles to light it. It's no good, Edith – you can't throw a spanner in this works, so stop trying. My girls only have a day and a night at home, and I aim to make sure they enjoy it.'

*

The jingly tune coming from the fiddles had them all up and dancing. Laughter reached to and above the rafters, as they all do-si-doed around the cleared barn. As Rose and Andria danced, their lovely faces glowed with fun and happiness. How was that possible, at such a time? But the sight made Edith realize that Eloise had been right. This is what was needed. For a brief moment in these terrible times everyone needed to forget. To let their hair down and enjoy life. To feel normal.

The moment didn't last long. An overriding noise drowned out the music, as an earth-shaking drone stopped everyone in their tracks.

'Blow out the candles, quick!' This was shouted by a dozen voices.

In darkness now, they opened the heavy doors. Outside afforded some light, as the dusk hadn't yet taken full hold. The pitch of the noise was unbearable, as was the sight of hundreds of planes heading in the direction of Coventry and Birmingham.

From nowhere, RAF fighter planes appeared. Stunned, they watched as a battle raged above them, until a German plane burst into flames, its debris spiralling down towards the ground. This alerted them all to the danger they were in. Murmurs of panic began to rise.

Douglas took charge. 'Right, everyone, we should head for safety. Hurry now. There's an underground shelter in the garden. And we have a cellar.' Walking among the crowd, Douglas stopped in the middle of them, his voice roaring out instructions. 'Those to my right, follow Thomas into the shelter; those to my left, follow me into the cellar.'

'Will we all get in?' Edith asked.

'Yes. It will be a squash, but by using the cellar as well,

everyone will be accommodated. Come on.' Douglas beckoned her with his arms.

As Edith brought up the rear with Laurent and Jay, not wanting to leave her husband as he struggled to put on his false leg, another plane spiralled down towards them. This time it was a British plane. 'Oh God!'

'He's safe,' Laurent shouted. 'Look – the pilot is parachuting down.'

Jay, Douglas and Thomas, along with three or four other men, ran in the direction in which the airman was coming down.

'Come in, Edith – come on, they will get him and bring him here.'

'But he may be hurt. I have to go too, Eloise. If they move him, they could endanger his life.'

Edith ran after the men. Skirting the barn, she kicked off her shoes, knowing that the heels would dig into the grassed meadow she had to cross. The darkness hampered her. The only light she could see was the faint glimmer of the men's torches, swishing backwards and forwards as they ran ahead.

Once across the first field, she stumbled in the ruts of the second field. Sharp stubble from the recently harvested wheat cut and scratched her legs, but didn't slow her. As she drew near enough to the men for them to hear her, over the horrendous noise above them, she took charge. 'Douglas, stop at once and go back. Fetch a door or something to carry him on. And bring something to use as a splint, in case he's broken something. Oh, and a blanket. You go with him, Thomas. And hurry!'

As they neared the pilot, Edith shouted to the others, 'Don't touch him. Let me assess him first. Everyone with torches, shine them onto him.' Kneeling beside him, she softened her tone. 'It's all right. I'm a doctor. You're safe now. What's your name?'

'Jack . . . Jack Lenton.' The answer came between gasps for air.

'I'm Edith.'

In the dim light afforded by the tiny torches that most country folk carried around with them these days, Edith looked into the face of a handsome young man. Taking his helmet off released a shock of curly fair hair. She ran her fingers over it in the way a mother would. She wanted to soothe him. 'Everything will be all right. I can't see you very well, but I will immobilize your body, so as not to cause you any further damage, and then get you to the house so that I can examine you.'

'Than . . . Th—'

'Don't try to talk.'

As Douglas and Thomas came back, Edith again took the lead. 'Help me to attach the splint. Be very careful.' They followed her every word. 'Try to lift him without bending his body in any way. Hold his head steady. That's right, let's get him to the house.'

Another explosion split the air. A fireball descended in the distance, but no pilot ejected this time. Feeling the sadness caused by the destruction of life above her, Edith concentrated on her patient, making sure the men who carried him took care not to jolt him too much.

Above her, the noise changed. Planes turned, and now the whine of ducking and diving transformed itself into a constant roar, as what was left of the German attackers headed for home. Hot on their heels, the RAF planes continued to shoot at them and to chase them away. The

Germans were no longer engaging; they were headed east, towards the coast and home. Their journey wasn't going to be an easy one, as the RAF remained on their tail. But soon the firing stopped and the drone disappeared into the distance. It was well known that the Luftwaffe planes had the edge on British ones, when it came to speed, although the British planes were much more manoeuvrable, and that gave them an advantage in a head-to-head fight.

'Ed . . . ith – it's too late . . . Tell my mo – mother—'

'No, Jack. Hold on. Please hold on!'

They were in the kitchen. The doors were closed and the blackout was in place, enabling them to have all the lights on. Edith could see that it *was* too late. A piece of metal protruded from Jack's chest. His breathing had stopped. There wasn't even the hint of a beat from his pulse.

'He's gone. Poor, brave chap. He's gone.'

The room fell silent. She looked at the men as they stood around a body of someone they'd never known, and saw tears running down more than one face. A loud blowing of noses broke the silence.

Edith couldn't cry. If she did, she would never stop. The ticking of the clock on the wall came into focus. She checked the time: nine o'clock. Jack was probably one of a thousand others in the world who had died at nine o'clock tonight, but he shouldn't have. He looked no more than twenty years of age and had been a healthy young man. *Why, oh why?*

'Aunt Edith?'

'It's all right, Thomas.' Taking the sobbing young man into her arms, she patted his back. 'It's all right.'

But it wasn't bloody all right! So many years of her life had been given to war. Now this young man in her arms had to give many of his years. And the young man lying on the table had given all of his. It wasn't all right, and she wondered if it ever would be.

# 29

# *Jhona & Elka*

## Poland, October 1940 – Achieving the Impossible

The window screeched as Jhona broke it away from one of the metal hinges securing it. Fear made him freeze. He waited, watching the searchlight swing round. Soon it would light this corner of the camp. He had to work fast. In one cat-like movement, he was through into the stores. He grabbed the swinging window and wedged it with the pieces of wood he had to hand, then ducked, just as the room lit up for a few seconds, as if night had been turned into day. Prayers tumbled from him. *Please, please, God, let the window hold.*

The floorboards creaked as he crawled across to the shelves that he knew housed the SS uniforms. Ephraim had gathered intelligence on this. Jhona hadn't asked how, but had memorized the drawing Ephraim had produced for him of the inside of the stores.

Now that his eyes were used to the dark once more, it was surprisingly easy to locate the clothes. His next task was to throw them through the window. Ephraim and Rafal would be waiting. Sweat dampened his body, but his fear had lessened and he felt a strength entering him.

Soon he was with the others behind the hut and changing into the uniforms. His uniform hung on him, but he managed to smarten it up with the belt.

'Now, Rafal. Go and fetch the car. And remember, walk like the SS do!'

Rafal had practised the walk until he was exhausted, marching up and down their hut into the small hours, and had now perfected a very good likeness to the SS movement – a purposeful, arrogant stride.

Nerves trembled inside Jhona, and he wondered how Ephraim felt. Ephraim hadn't had the benefit of his own training, so this mission placed a tremendous strain on him. All knew that if there was just one mistake, they would face certain death.

The sound of the car approaching made Jhona's anxiety deepen. This was it – they were really going to attempt to break out. Rehearsing a few German phrases, he knew he would need to keep from panicking, although he nearly passed out when he realized Rafal had stolen Commandant Hoss's own vehicle. 'We'll never get away with this, Rafal. Why didn't you bring one of the other cars?'

'This is the fastest vehicle they have. None of them could possibly catch us in any of the other cars. Jump in – and hurry.'

The gates loomed ahead. A light came on and shone at them, and a soldier took up a stance as if to stop them. Putting his head out of the window, Jhona shouted in German, 'Open the gates and let us pass!'

The soldier hesitated.

Jhona took a deep breath and screamed in the way he'd heard SS officers do so often: 'Open the gate at once, or I will have you shot.'

The soldier stood aside and opened the gate.

Rafal drove through. Once clear, he slammed his foot down hard on the accelerator. They were free!

Ephraim knew the area well. He guided them along forest roads towards the mountains. Somewhere along the route they would be met. But they would need to undertake several detours to make sure they weren't being followed.

Elka waited. Soon she would leave with Baruch and a party of Resistance workers. Karol was one of them, as was Gabriel. She now trusted them both. She hoped she was right in this, and she hoped and prayed that Stefan had been the only traitor amongst them. If she was wrong, then Jhona could be in even greater danger, if word of his intended escape was leaked to the Germans.

News had come to them a few days ago that an escape plan was in place. And then more details arrived, by means of a local from Auschwitz – the name they all used now for the village of Oświęcim, where the camp was. The network of people willing to help the Resistance was both heart-warming and a little frightening, as it was impossible to vet them all. Trust – until someone was proven untrustworthy – was the only yardstick they could apply.

'Elka, we go tonight. They are out of Auschwitz.'

Her heart flipped over. 'I need to contact London. I'm hoping they will put into place a plan to lift us out.'

'It's too dangerous. If the escape has been achieved, all German officers will be on high alert and they will be ordering intense searches and radio-frequency checks. We have to keep our heads down. Nothing must jeopardize this escape, and neither must the escape compromise the safety of the people in the Resistance movement.'

Yes, she could see the sense of this. Her desire to get Jhona out of the country had clouded her judgement. She must wait. Even though each day would be agonizing, she must wait.

With stealth, the party of five crossed the overgrown mountain pass, along a route that Elka had skied many times when she was on holiday in the uncomplicated past. How she wished for snow now, as the driving rain made their journey much more difficult than the snow would.

On reaching the first safe house, her disappointment threatened to weaken her, as no word had been received. *Oh, Jhona, my darling, where are you?*

'They should have got here. The road is passable. What could have happened?'

'They may have abandoned the car. It may be a giveaway to them. In which case they will take a lot longer, as they will be keeping off the main roads.'

Elka knew that Baruch was right, but nothing would stop her heart hurting until she was in Jhona's arms.

'We shall wait here for a couple of days.'

'No, I won't wait. I'll go down into Zakopane to see if I can pick up any word. Plus, I need to shop for dry clothing.'

'Elka, you are forgetting your training. Think! The actions you propose are driven by your love for Jhona, but you must channel your plans into protecting their safety, and ours. You are becoming a liability.'

Angry at this, she stormed out of the log cabin. It was still dark outside and the rain soaked through her jumper, but she didn't care. She needed some time to herself. To be herself. Not this machine that the Secret Service had created.

The tears flowed without warning. Hugging herself, she swallowed hard. It wasn't the time to give in completely. She still had to remain strong and wait, until she was in Jhona's loving arms. Then she could unleash her grief and her fears. *I have to go home. I have to tell mother about Ania.* Shame washed over her as she thought of her deceit. But in her heart she knew her mother would understand why.

'Come inside, Elka. There is news.'

As she re-entered the cabin, the hill farmer whose home it was closed a partition at the back of a cupboard and blocked out the sight of a wireless transmitter and receiver. Elka couldn't tell that the panel he drew across could even be moved, but she was annoyed and didn't dwell on this hiding place. 'I thought you said we shouldn't make radio contact?'

'I did, but here we are so remote that I allowed it. But don't get any ideas. That was a message coming in, and it was risky enough.'

'What was it?' Elka hardly dared ask.

'Not good. I'm sorry, Elka, but two of the escapees have been recaptured. One is still at large, but we don't know which one.'

'No! No . . . How did it happen?'

'We don't know. The message was very short. It was from a remote safe house. We didn't risk sending one back for more information.'

Elka found a chair and slumped into it. The room fell silent. Her thoughts raced. 'If Jhona is the one who has escaped, will he know his way here?'

'We can only assume they would have discussed the route. One of them was the member of our group that I told you about, who made sure he was caught in a round-up, in order to set up a Resistance movement within Auschwitz. We have received messages in the recent past that said he had to get out, as there had been rumblings that the Germans knew someone was organizing disruption. It would only have been a matter of time until they found out who. Their methods are cruel, according to the reports we have. Previous messages have informed us that the day after the escape they hanged fourteen men and stopped all rations for a day. I have asked the Freedom Army to help us storm the place, but they are not willing to. There's nothing we can do. Nobody seems to take our reports seriously.'

Elka wished she could take some concrete proof back to London and make them realize it was all true. But she had tried, and all they said was that it was German propaganda.

But she couldn't give her mind to that at the moment. Jhona might be dead, and she couldn't bear the thought of having lost him.

'Why not go and lie down, Elka – get out of those wet clothes. We will inform you the moment we hear anything. You're exhausted.' She was able to rise, with Baruch's help, though she was afraid of revealing too much weakness.

'I will go and change, but I would rather stay up for a while. Just in case.'

It had been four days now since they had left camp. The break in the rain heartened Elka. The light breeze and shifting rays of the sun battled with the clouds and showed signs of winning, as the mist lifted and the landscape gradually came into view. Soon it would clear the mountains. Elka feasted her eyes on the magnificence of it all, trying to let the promise of a nice day lift her spirits. It was difficult to do so, as no further news had come in and nerves were frayed. Tonight they would set off and return to camp. All hope would be lost. But for one more day she would keep it alive, for whoever was out there alone, trying to reach them.

The farmer came out, dressed in his milking frock. His poor goats had been almost milked dry in an effort to keep his guests sustained. But he'd done a sterling job and they had been filled at every meal with fresh bread and cheese, washed down with milk.

Elka looked away from him and across the terrain, her eyes seeking, her heart hoping. She thought she saw a shadow move. Not daring to call out, she waited. There it was again, so far in the distance there was no way of her knowing if it was friend or foe. Turning, she ran inside to alert Baruch.

Despite the change in the weather, the grass was very wet beneath her body as she lay next to the others, gun at the ready. Sweat prickled her skin and vied with the dampness of the ground. Hope held court in her heart. But there were no further sightings of the figure.

An hour passed. Whispers went back and forth, and all felt a nervous anxiety. 'What should we do?' 'Should one of us skirt around the back of where the sighting was?' 'What if it was a German scout and he's gone to alert the troops?'

But Elka had other worries. 'What if it is one of the escapees and they have collapsed down there?'

Baruch looked over towards her. 'Yes, that is a possibility. I will go.'

'No, Baruch, let me. I'm highly skilled in the techniques of moving around without being seen. I'll go.'

To her surprise, Baruch agreed. He'd seen Elka in action and knew her capabilities, and if he worried about the emotional impact upon her, he didn't show it.

'We will cover you at all times. If it is an ambush, we are ready.'

Elka nodded and crawled away from the group. Snake-like, she made it to the edge of the garden and into the longer grass. She could move more quickly from there. The figure had been about three hundred yards from here.

A silence unnerved her. There weren't even any birds tweeting. It was as if they sensed danger. What could be lurking out there, waiting for her? She prayed these fears would prove fruitless and that Jhona would be there – unhurt, but biding his time, wanting to approach the house under cover of darkness.

She whistled, remembering a bird-call signal they had learned together.

After a moment an answering call came.

*Jhona! My Jhona!*

She signalled once more, this time twice, to ask for confirmation that it was safe to approach, and listened once again for an answering call. It came, but it warned that it wasn't safe. Now she knew it was Jhona, but what danger was he in? She had to move nearer to find out.

She inched her way closer, with extreme care, her hand constantly touching her gun for reassurance. At last she came to a clearing not far from where she knew Jhona to be. Her heart thumped against her chest wall and her throat constricted. In the distance she could see a group of soldiers sitting in relaxed positions, as if taking a break. They were probably a party of trainees, for there were many in the mountains. Beating a retreat, she went back the way she'd come.

Baruch took the news as she expected. 'We will attack the soldiers. We can take advantage of the element of surprise.'

She had to agree. Despite the danger to Jhona, and to all of them, they had a war to win, and wiping out a group of soldiers could only help that cause. The soldiers were very close and any minute might see Jhona and kill him; or they might see signs of there being more people in this house than normal and come to investigate. These thoughts, and the practical consideration of the extra ammunition they could loot for their own store, helped Elka justify the attack to herself.

Once a strategy was in place, she advanced once more towards Jhona. When she was near enough, she gave the signal for an impending attack. His answer showed that he agreed. Her heart, mind and body longed just to run to him, but she stayed focused and returned to the house.

There were so few of them to launch an attack that getting as near as they could, as stealthily as they could, and then charging at the gang of soldiers was their only option. They couldn't spread out and attack from several fronts, as they would be too thin on the ground. Praying to every god out there, Elka loaded her rifle. Her hand-gun was already loaded.

Baruch gave out grenades. Ammunition was stored at each safe house. This one, being a hill farm and made of wood, was built on stilts to level it. The space under the house was boarded in, and this created a huge hidden area where supplies could be safely put out of sight, as well as a place where anyone who needed to be hidden could stay. If it happened that the farm was raided and searched, it was unlikely that the secret trapdoor entrance would be discovered. Hidden under a rambling tea plant and to the side of the chicken coop, it was well disguised. Around the back of the house were stables where the farmer kept his donkeys. Here the rafters were false and hid a secret attic space.

A smooth rock surface surrounded the house. This gave way to thick greenery that sloped down to a spot where a cluster of tall, majestic pine trees grew close together, on the next level of the mountain. Dark, ever-changing paths wove between the trees as they swayed as one in the breeze. It was here, in the undergrowth covering the tree roots, that Jhona was hiding.

When they were ready, Elka led the way, crawling once more on her stomach through the greenery. Baruch, Karol and Gabriel did the same. The farmer's herd of goats, his main source of income, roamed the slopes. Stubborn animals, they would protest loudly if disturbed, and often a goat had to be skirted as they made their way, inch by inch. The goats' excrement couldn't be avoided, and Elka wrinkled her nose as she wormed her way through clump after clump of it.

When they passed the position where Elka knew Jhona was, she didn't catch sight of him. She so wanted to, but wouldn't let herself even sneak a glance. She knew he would join the rear and that a gun would be handed to him. Her eyes remained on the group of soldiers. Their laughter and joking carried on the wind.

She ignored what they were saying. She had to. If she paid any attention to their light-hearted chat about their lives, it would undo her resolve. She had to think of these people as the vile enemy, who would kill in reprisal and starve people and burn them alive – atrocities that she knew the soldiers would carry out without a thought.

The group waited now, crouching in the long grass of the downward slope, watching the soldiers. The low whistle signalling the attack came from Baruch. Each person pulled the pin of a grenade and threw it. The resulting explosions deafened her. Bodies danced hideously in the air, then fell to the ground; limbs followed independently.

'Fire!'

Any soldiers who still moved were gunned down. Soon there was stillness. Before her lay a massacre. She counted ten bodies: ten young lives over.

A hand touched her shoulder. She turned and looked into a gaunt face with dry, sore lips. But embedded in that face were two beautiful dark eyes. 'Jhona, my Jhona.' His name came out on a sob.

'Come with me, Elka. Leave to the others whatever pillaging has to be done. Come with me, darling.'

She helped him all she could as they made their way to the house. The farmer was in a state of nerves. 'You will all have to leave, immediately. Leave everything as it was. I will be suspected. Who ordered this raid, without telling me?'

'Speak to Baruch when he comes back. Excuse us.'

This felt hard and rude, but it was all Elka could say to him at the moment. Yes, they had compromised the farmer, but they had had no choice. Baruch would have a plan for making him safe, which she knew would entail making him disappear. His way of life as he knew it would be over.

She helped Jhona to a chair. 'You must eat, my darling.'

'I can't, not yet. Maybe give me a drink, though? Just water. My stomach can't take anything else.'

Once in her room, her heart bled. It took a long time for both of them to reach a point of control, as they wept and told each other as much of what had happened to them as they could bear to relate. But mostly they just lay on the bed and held each other, gently so as not to cause pain to Jhona, with their love flowing from one to the other.

Jhona's strength amazed Elka. He managed to get back to the camp. Each day he ate a little more and was getting stronger.

The farmer and his wife had been helped to escape to their son's house, deeper in the Tatra Mountains, where he ran an outpost for skiers. They would be safe there. They had never previously been brought to the attention of the Germans, so there was no damaging profile on them. Their house was ransacked and partly destroyed, to make it look as though it had stood empty for a long time. Some of the farmer's goats and all of his chickens were killed and shared between them and the farmer himself, who took some on his journey to his son. The remaining goats were driven onto the mountain, where it was hoped they would fend for themselves.

One night Jhona felt able to tell the story of the capture of Ephraim and Rafal.

'We had already abandoned the car, because we knew it was well known and very distinctive. As we walked through a forest near Krakow, we came across a group of soldiers, much the same as the ones we just attacked. But these soldiers were alerted by our tread on the dead bracken beneath our feet and were ready for us. I spotted them just as they were going to attack. There was nothing to do but run – it was every man for himself. We had no defence, no weapons.' His head flopped into his hands. 'I – I suppose my superior training saved me. I was able to tap into my knowledge of escape and survival skills. I'd used many as we journeyed and I tried to teach Ephraim and Rafal, but they didn't stand a chance. They were gunned down before they could get away. I was hunted for days, but I managed to keep one step ahead, setting traps that delayed them, stealing food, drinking from streams. All the time the deaths of those very brave men weighed on me, as I couldn't have escaped without them.'

Five days after returning to camp, a communication came in and at last Elka and Jhona were on their way back to Britain, the only place they could now call home.

The journey was often harrowing. Both of them were physically and mentally weak, yet on arrival they had to go for a debriefing. All Elka wanted to do was spit in the faces of these superior beings who sat behind their desks and ordered others into the field.

It was to a different London that they returned – one that was battered and broken. But that was only the buildings, not the spirit of the people. People talked to them as they walked out of the War Office. Strangers shook them by the hand, not because they had an inkling of who they were, but just because they were glad to be alive and in all likelihood could see the suffering etched on Elka's and Jhona's faces.

Elka tried to latch onto that spirit and let it enter her as Brendan drove them home, where another ordeal awaited her. Brendan had broken the news of Ania's death to Edith.

Elka thought how beautiful her mother looked. Courage shone from her as she stood on the doorstep. Laurent was beside her, sitting in his wheelchair. Brendan must have called them to say they were on their way.

Her mother's face held a quiet pride. Her arms were outstretched and Elka ran into them. She felt her hair being stroked and heard gentle words. 'My darling, you are my Ania and my Elka – I haven't lost her.'

Elka couldn't find any words, but a peace came to her. She would make sure her mother knew Ania as well as she herself had known her. And with this came the resolve to stop addressing her as 'Mother'. From now on, she would be 'Mama'. Because that was who she was.

# EPILOGUE

## 1946

## Lest We Forget

# 30
# *Edith & Elka*

## St Barnabas Church, London, 1946 – A Final Goodbye and a New Beginning

Edith stood in a cocoon of grief. Grief for the child she only had memories of lying swaddled in a blanket, passive and calm against her twin sister's demanding wail. She had known then that the girls were very different characters and, as Edith listened to Elka as she stood in the pulpit and spoke of Ania, it seemed that this had continued. Though identical to look at, their characters had developed in different ways.

Yet both had taken traits of hers: Elka strong-willed and determined to do things her way; Ania steady and studious.

'We were always like one,' Elka had told her. 'Or rather, two halves of a whole. The differences in us bound us together just as much as the similarities.'

Edith knew this was true. They were two halves of her.

Light poured through the stained-glass windows of St Barnabas Church, throwing a kaleidoscope of colour onto the congregation. Edith looked around, from her stand at the pulpit. She was there as a support to Elka, whose voice shook as she gave a eulogy to her sister. But Edith's mind wandered, unable to give her full attention to the words it would be painful for her to hear.

A Jewish memorial service had already been held. This service was for so many of their loved ones – Ania being the main one. Edith had wanted to have a service to help Ania lay the ghosts of her life to rest, and to help herself find a peaceful place in her heart for them, something she couldn't do while war raged and her pain cut so deeply. But she found, as she stood here, that although almost five years had gone by since Ania's death, the hurt was still raw and ground into her. There was some respite, of course; and as Ada had once said to her, 'It comes and goes in waves.' It certainly did. But this service had opened up a tsunami.

Her eyes rested on the dark strip on the chancel roof, testament to the brush with war that this church had suffered when an incendiary bomb hit it. Luckily it had failed to burn the church down – unlike Edith's usual church, All Saints, which had been extensively damaged and remained closed, though plans for its restoration were afoot.

In front of her stood what was left of her beloved family – a family whose heart had been ripped out by two world wars. Douglas sat clutching the hand of his wife Janine, with their son Thomas on his other side. They had a haunted look about them, as they were surely thinking of Henry, their beloved elder son and the joker of the family, who had been killed in France on D-Day two years ago. Her heart went out to them. As Henry's lovely, smiling face came to her, Edith had to swallow hard. She mustn't let go.

Focusing again, she listened as Elka read from one of

her letters from Ania: 'My darling sister, I hope you have found our mama and are with her. Give her a hug from me and tell her that one day we will meet.'

*But we didn't – oh, Ania, we didn't!*

Edith looked over at Brendan, trying to shut herself off from the painful words. He smiled a 'you can do this' kind of smile. His had been a difficult job during the war, but he had done it with courage and dignity, although she knew that guilt had scarred him.

Next to him sat Leah, looking so well and recovered from the trauma that she'd seen and been a big part of, during the liberation of her own country. And next to her sat Ginny and, on her left, her Norman. They, too, had been through a period of recuperation after escaping the torpedoing of their ship in 1943, when more than forty colleagues and patients had died.

Next week would be a happy occasion in this very church, because these four brave young people would be sharing their vows in a double wedding.

How proud Ada would have been of her son, Edith thought – for that is what Brendan was, even though he was not birthed by her. Dear Ada. Happy memories came to her of their friendship, and of the wonderful Jimmy's Hope House that had emerged from it. There was now Ada's Sanctuary, which housed and sheltered battered wives. Its aim was to give them strength and hope, and to try and make them realize they didn't have to put up with being beaten, and that there was a safe place to go. Just as Ada had given Edith herself hope, when she was at her lowest and had come home from war, having lost her children.

Laurent had supported her, too. There he was, as strong

as ever, despite his disabilities. Her rock, her husband, her lover.

Next to him sat Jay and Eloise with their daughters, Rose and Andria. Two beautiful young women who had missed out on a youth of dancing, doing the rounds of their coming-out year and, sadly, of finding a husband. But there was plenty of time. Life was coming back again, very slowly, and occasions of the kind at which the young met were once again being arranged by hopeful mothers.

It did her heart good to see that Jay and Eloise's love and compassion shone also from their girls. They had turned out well. Looking at Andria, she thought of how Eloise had been torn between calling her after dear Andrina – her late sister, whom she still missed so much – and Ada, whom she had come to love. They hadn't wanted to use Andrina's name in its entirety as it was too painful. Nor could they call her Ada. So they had come up with a compromise. It was funny that 'Ada' wasn't an acceptable name for the child of an aristocratic family, and yet it had been the name of someone who was more deserving of being elevated in life than any of them were. *Oh, Ada, how I miss you.*

On Eloise's right sat her parents, Edith's dear uncle and aunt; and then Marianne, still very lively and a rock upon whom everyone could lean.

Behind them was Christian's devoted nurse. There was no one better to represent her late brother than this lovely woman. Of all the deaths the family had suffered, Christian's had been the least painful. It had come as a relief when a sudden stroke took him from the agony of what was really a non-existence and, she hoped, towards a blessed happiness in heaven. Yes, she missed him, but time had tempered the grief, as missing Christian had begun years ago when the whole of *him* hadn't come back from what she and Douglas always called *their war*.

And there, at the back of the church, sat others – dear friends who'd served with her in the First World War, and who'd done their bit in this second generation's war: Connie, matron of a military hospital in Kent; Nancy, who'd worked in the munitions factory close to her, and who was now happily married and a grandmother; and Jennifer and Mark, who had spent the war years working in the same hospital as Connie, but who were now setting up a general practice in a small village. Proud parents, they had remained relatively unscathed by the war. Though was that possible? No – no one remained free from the pain of it. No one.

Surely this would be the end of war for them all. Truly the end? They had lived their youth and middle years under a cloud of terror and grief. Enough was enough. Would the peace they'd won now really mean peace forever? Oh God, she hoped so.

The hand in hers tightened, bringing her back to Elka's words: 'My wish for my sister is that she is safe and happy in the arms of her beloved Baruch. He was one of the bravest men I ever knew, who died in the Warsaw Uprising two years ago . . .'

Edith's conscience pricked her at this. Did *she* wish that? Could she forgive this man? Hadn't Baruch been the channel for her darling daughter's suffering? But then Ania had loved him. And, as she herself had done with Albert, Ania had gone to the farthest point that her man had asked her to travel.

Asking so much of the women they loved was in the nature of men driven by the circumstances of their time – time spent in a war-torn world, where different decisions were needed. Yes, Edith concluded, she would, eventually, try to forgive Baruch.

The eulogy came to a close. One day she would read it through and take in all the parts she had blocked out.

A strong hand grasped her waist. She turned to see Jhona, who had stood behind them throughout, ready to help them if they needed it. But they had faced the ordeal of the memorial service with courage – a courage that now shone through the glistening tears in her darling Elka's eyes, as she turned towards Edith. 'I am here, Mama, and as I promised you once before, I will be your Elka and your Ania.'

Pride filled Edith and a peace came into her. 'You are, my darling, you are.'

War bound people through courage. That courage, she knew, would bind her and Elka, and all of those gathered around her today, as they rebuilt their lives. She must be a source of strength in the centre of those lives. Ada would want that of her.

Elka took the hand Jhona offered her. His eyes showed concern as they looked deep into hers. Still emotionally and physically drained, she held on to the comfort she found in his touch. Theirs had been a long, harrowing war, with most of it spent apart as they had undertaken missions to Poland and France. They had come through alive, but scathed.

In the year since their last mission they had allowed each other time to recover. To talk. To cleanse. And then to rekindle the passion they had found in the early days before their marriage and just afterwards, and which they had rarely revisited when they had come together for a few days between assignments. Now she had the best news of all to tell him. She was expecting a child.

Their child – their future. She hoped this would finally lay to rest Jhona's ghosts and allow him to embrace whatever was to come, knowing that he was doing all that was asked of him. Although he didn't need to recompense for the lives for which he felt responsible – Ephraim, Rafal and the men hanged in reprisal for his escape – she hoped he would at last realize that he had done so, in the part he'd played in bringing about world peace. The dangerous missions he'd accomplished, and the times he'd put his own life on the line, had done that. It was time for Jhona to come to terms with what had happened and shed the guilt of blame.

Squeezing his hand, Elka gave him an 'I'm all right' smile. His answering one, she could see, came from his heart. Feeling joy surge through her, she turned to see that her mother was already seated and was beckoning them to their places next to her.

Together they walked towards Edith. As they did so, Brendan began to clap. Within seconds the whole congregation had joined in. Brendan stood and his applause became more fervent, whilst others took up his lead. It was as if Britain was saying 'Thank you' to Elka and Jhona – two Polish people who had taken up the challenge and done all they could for both countries.

Tears filled Elka's eyes. They were a mixture of pride at this humble recognition, joy for the secret she held of the new life inside her, and sadness that her own country wasn't really free. The communist regime had taken over Poland.

She didn't know whether she would ever go back there. For now, and for the foreseeable future, Britain would be their home. Once their child was born, they would keep their promise to visit America to see their family there. Thank God they had got out and hadn't suffered the fate of the six million Jews of Europe who had perished in the Holocaust or had their lives torn apart.

As the applause died down, the couple took their seats. Her mother clasped Elka's hand in her own. Looking into the beloved face of the woman who had given so much of herself in the First World War, Elka felt proud that she and Ania had followed in their mother's footsteps and had done their duty in the second one.

# *Acknowledgements*

For a writer to create a novel, many things have to come into play. Long hours spent in solitude, supported by family, friends and readers, is one, and I am blessed in having the most amazing family. My beloved husband, Roy, my children, Christine, Julie, Rachel and James, their husbands and partners, my grandchildren and great grandchildren, sisters, brothers, nieces and nephews, and cousins. And my wonderful 'in-law' family, the Woods of Sharnford. And friends, and readers who have become friends (too numerous to mention), but all valued. Thank you, I love you all. Without you, I couldn't climb my mountain.

A special mention here to my daughter, Christine Martin, and son, James Wood, for the many editions they painstakingly read and advise me on. How you do it, I do not know, but I couldn't get to the end of the journey without you. Thank you. And to my nephew, Chris Olley, for advice and guidance on historical matters and German phrases. Thank you, you make my journey easier.

Next there is the team who work at my publishers, the award-winning Pan Macmillan, whom I am proud to be associated with and thank very much for the opportunity you have given me, and the people you have put in place to take care of me: my brilliant editors, Louise Buckley and Victoria Hughes-Williams, and Laura Carr and her team. When you work your magic, you all bring clarity and something special to my raw manuscripts. Thank you, I wish every author had you all behind them. No team is complete without a publicist, and mine is Kate Green. Kate, I appreciate everything you do for me. Thank you. All of you work so hard on my behalf. Your support and encouragement means the world to me.

And not least, my agent, Judith Murdoch. Judith has a reputation for standing like a rock beside her authors, and she has done this for me. Picking me up when I am faltering, and there in my corner at all times. Thank you, Judith, onwards and upwards as you always say.

# *Research and Inspiration*

A thank-you to, and in remembrance of, the woman who inspired this book: Christine Granville. Christine skied over the Tatra mountains, no matter how cold it was, to take messages of hope and encouragement from our government to the Polish people, and then went on to carry out many more dangerous missions to further the Allies' cause in the Second World War, before being cruelly murdered by a thwarted love. I honour you, Christine, and thank you. May you rest in peace.

I would also like to thank the lovely guides I had in Krakow, Poland. You all went the extra mile to help me experience the many places that are soaked in the blood of the horrific Holocaust, and the suffering of the Polish people. My experience at Auschwitz brought me to my knees. The beauty of Zakopane in the Tatra mountains took my breath away. And the poignancy of the chairs standing in the square that was once the Jewish Ghetto made me cry.

# *Reading Matter*

Piotr M. A. Cywinski, Jacek Lachendro and Piotr Setkiewicz, *Auschwitz A–Z*
Anna Pioro, *Magistar Tadeusz Pankiewcz: A Biography*
Tadeusz Pankiewcz, *The Krakow Ghetto Pharmacy*